GODBORN

Gods of Bronze
Book 1

Herkuhlos and
Leuhon of Nemiyeh

DAN DAVIS

Godborn

Copyright © 2020 by Dan Davis

For information contact:
dandaviswrites@outlook.com

ISBN: 9798652628482

First Edition: June 2020

1

The Koryos

DARKNESS WOULD SOON fall and in the night they would raid the clan. It was bitterly cold and the wind howled across the plain behind them.

Holkis followed his spear-brothers to the crest of the ridge, remembering to keep his spear low so the warriors of the clan in the valley beyond would not see it. Their cattle would be fat and if they could separate one or two and drive them away they would see his brothers through to the winter rite. Some of them claimed they would take women in the raid also but he doubted they would have such courage. Taking cattle from their grazing was dangerous enough, let alone attacking tents, killing men grown and taking their wives and daughters. One day they would do so but they were not yet men themselves.

"Holkis," his brother Belolukos said, turning to whisper from in front. "Hurry."

Bowing his head, he trotted faster in a crouch and dropped to his belly and crawled through his crouching spear-brothers to Belolukos' side.

They were twelve in all. Boys on the cusp of manhood. Surviving half the year ranging beyond the homeland of their clan was their final test and they had almost completed it. After running across the plains and raiding and hunting to survive they had just one more moon and they would return to take their place as men in their clan.

"I think they will have mead," Holkis said, his voice low. "There is a woodland beside their camp, is there not, Dhomyos?"

Dhomyos turned his big head and nodded once. "There is."

Holkis grinned. "They will have mead brewing for the midwinter rite."

"Do not go near them, Holkis, just count the cattle and return," Belolukos said, nodding his head at the top of the ridge. The grass there was short and the soil thin, stripped by the winds coming up the valley. "And remain unseen."

I shall creep in close and search one of the tents if I can, Holkis thought. "I will, *koryonos,*" he replied, suppressing a smile.

With his spear pushed before him, he crawled on his belly through the grasses and sedge to the top of the ridge. Before the peak he slowed to a stop, turning to look over his shoulder at his spear-brothers behind him. His *koryos.* All twelve wore wolf skins over their woollen tunics and trousers, their faces looking out of the open jaws of the wolf. Each brother of the *koryos* was sworn to serve the wolf god Kolnos and to obey their leader, the *koryonos.* Belolukos was his true brother, born on the same day to the same mother.

Obey your brother in all things, their mother had said to him

2

before they were sworn in the rite. *He will need you if he is to be clan chief when you are grown.*

"Go!" Belolukos hissed.

Holkis turned and crawled to the brow of the hill where the icy wind cut into his face and made his eyes water. The clan they were to raid was known to them. The *koryos* was returning to their home range and was in familiar territory. The clan wintering in the valley beyond was a strong one with at least a hundred cattle and thrice as many sheep. If they could not get a cow then driving away a few sheep would see them to midwinter. Failure would mean, at best, days of hunger as they ran for the winter pasture of the next clan up the valley or across the plain and into another valley many days away. At worst, one or more of them might be caught, wounded, or killed. The clan in the valley had more than thirty warriors, at least twice as many boys and women, and they would defend their people, their cattle, and their horses with all their strength.

On Holkis crawled through the undergrowth, pushing aside the cold, damp, long grasses until he could see down into the valley. The river frothed and bubbled from the east and flowed west. The vale was wide with pasture on both sides with plenty of trees. A good land for a clan to winter in, just as his own was doing further downstream.

Something is wrong.

The feeling came first and it was a moment before he understood it. There was no woodsmoke on the wind and instead there was a whiff of blood and death. The stockades were broken here and there, the ground churned up everywhere. Dead animals lay with stiff legs. Cattle, sheep, dogs eviscerated. A naked human body, or part of one, lay trampled in the mud by the distant riverbank. Shadows cast by the low sun stretched from the woodland across to the shattered tents of the broken camp. The only movement was the thrashing of yellow grasses and clattering of bare branches.

The clan was destroyed.

He slipped back on his belly and hurried down to the *koryos*. They were busy blacking their faces with oiled ashes in preparation for their raid.

"What is it?" Belolukos asked, scowling, his face smeared with ashes. "Did they see you? I told you to stay hidden, Holkis."

Holkis stared. "They are raided."

All of them muttered until his brother silenced them with a look.

"How many cattle remain?"

"None."

This time they crawled to the ridge together and they looked down as one.

"By Kolnos," Belolukos muttered. "What has happened here?"

"We should flee," Wedhris said. "Strong clan did this. Might find us."

None of them disagreed but there was no sign of anyone along the valley or on the other side of the river.

"This is old work," Kasos said. "No life. No fire. They burned the god's house. See? The timbers are blackened on this side. Yet no smoke rises. Old work."

"No," Dhomyos said, furrowing his brow. "We scouted four days past. All was well."

"It happened three days ago, then," Kasos said. "There is no clan here now."

"And no wolves," Holkis said. "And where are the crows?"

That silenced them. They each made the signs to ward against evil.

"We go, then," Belolukos said. "East. To the next clan."

"I cannot go many days longer without food, *koryonos*," Dhomyos said, scowling. He was the broadest of them all and lived in perpetual hunger.

Kasos agreed, glancing at the sky. He was small for a warrior and had delicate features but there was little that his pale eyes missed. "Snow coming."

Wedhris elbowed Kasos. "We do as the *koryonos* commands."

"Of course," Kasos said. "But the truth is the truth."

"Let us go down here, Bel," Holkis said to his brother. "They left so many animals dead. They may have left more."

Belolukos frowned, looking left and right. "

"Evil was done here," Sentos said. "We should not approach."

"Not even for meat?" Holkis asked.

Kasos made the sign against evil again. "Wolves should not eat carrion if they mean to become men."

Holkis turned to him. "Wolves should do anything to survive. We will be men when we return home."

"You will bring the curse onto us by eating rotten flesh," Kasos said. "We must raid and hunt only. That is the lore."

"Our oath was to survive," Holkis said. "And so we will do whatever is necessary to see it done."

"Let us flee, *koryonos*," Sentos said. He was tall and broad-shouldered and everyone knew that he would become a fine warrior for their clan.

They all looked to the *koryonos*. Belolukos turned his face from them and nodded at the ruined camp. "You go first, Holkis. If anyone can avoid a curse, it is you."

The eyes of his spear-brothers met his own for a long moment before Holkis climbed to his feet, the wind cutting into him even through his woollen clothes and wolf skin, and descended the long hill into the wide river valley. Upriver the woodland, black shadow beneath the pine trees, took his attention. How many warriors might hide in those shadow? Fifty? A hundred?

The ground all around the tents and the god's house had been churned to mud before freezing again and he stepped carefully around deep puddles crusted with ice. A cow lay on its side with its legs out straight, the belly cut open and the guts pulled out. Its head was severed, lying nearby with its tongue and eyes gone.

The crows have been, then, he thought. But where did they go?

Closer to the trampled tents and huts, he found three dogs that had been cut to pieces. What kind of men would tear dogs to shreds rather than skin them?

Holkis slowed to a stop at the sight of a body lying frozen in the churned mud ahead of him. It was the upper part of an elder in a torn and blood-stained tunic, the grey hair of his chest and beard visible, though his face had been caved in. The legs were nowhere to be seen and the rent across his abdomen trailed shredded guts, frozen hard. It was a terrible sight but the horror of it was not what made him halt, nor what made his heart pound.

There was a sprig of fresh meadowwort on the dead man's beard.

He looked left and right but there was no sound in the ruined camp other than the gusting wind.

Holding his spear tightly, Holkis advanced into the settlement.

Structures still stood, though all were damaged. Tents were broken and crushed. Leather and felt folded and trampled, poles and beams snapped like twigs. It was as though there had been a terrible winter storm, and a stampede of cows, and a raid, one after the other.

He bent and looked closer at the ground. It was hard to discern tracks when the earth was such a mess but he fancied he could see something, perhaps, leading away. Looking up, he saw the chief's house ahead. Built in wood with a reed thatch roof it was the largest house and the only permanent one in the settlement and was occupied always, even when the herds were taken onto the plains for summer grazing. Holkis had been raised in just such a house until the age of seven when he and Belolukos had taken their first steps toward manhood.

The chief's house before him was intact but one wall had been burned black and the thatch above singed by the fire. But it was otherwise sound and the sturdy door was closed against the wind.

Glancing left and right at the ruined tents all around he crossed to the door and held his breath to listen. The wind was too loud and all he could hear other than that was his blood beating in his ears. The shadows had lengthened since he had crossed to the camp.

Shortening his grip on his spear, he yanked open the door. It creaked and banged back against the wall, bouncing into stillness.

It was black within.

A human stench came out of the darkness, one of urine and blood and rotting food. After a moment, he could see shapes inside. A central hearth with no flame. Benches.

His mouth dry, Holkis swallowed. "Come out," he said in a

hoarse cry. Clearing his throat he raised his voice. "Come out of there!"

The wind rustled the thatch over the doorway.

He stepped inside, his spear held before him.

A cry of anger at his side and a figure rushed from the shadow, thrusting at his guts. Flinching, he knocked the knife aside with his spear shaft and swung the butt of it into the face of the attacker.

She fell, clutching her face and scrambled back.

"Do not move," Holkis said, flipping over his spear and holding the flint point before her face.

She glared at him, spat a curse and threw herself across the floor for the knife she had dropped. Snatching it up, she came at him again in animal fury while he backed away deeper into the darkness with his spear shaft across his body ready to block another attack.

Movement in the doorway and Belolukos was there, grabbing the woman while she tried to twist from his grasp to slash at him. He thrust her away, hard, and she tripped over the hearth backwards and cracked her head loudly on the floor and lay still.

"I saved you from a woman," Belolukos said and Holkis could hear his smile even if he could not see it. "A woman! Perhaps you are not so special after all, Holkis."

"You killed her," Holkis said, taking two steps toward her before she moaned and moved her head. Her furs had fallen open to reveal a dirty white robe, the skirts ridden up to the top of her thighs from her fall.

"It was the right choice to come down here after all," Belolukos said, also moving closer to her and looking down. "She is young."

"Do not," Holkis said, kneeling beside her. "She wears white, brother. I think she is a seeress."

"Stand aside," Belolukos commanded, his ash-coated face grim. "You may have found her but I am *koryonos*. Besides, I defeated her in battle." He smirked at his jest.

"Look at her. She is no older than us. She wears white. And look where she is."

"So?"

"She is a seeress, I am sure of it. The keeper of the hearth fire for her clan," Holkis said, looking up at his brother. "To defile her is to bring destruction upon yourself."

His brother scoffed. "Raiders have taken her. She is already defiled. Even if she was the keeper of the hearth she has no power now she has been made a woman."

"That does not take away her power," Holkis replied. "She is sacred. While she keeps the hearth and before she is married she is to remain untouched. The gods and the ancestors of her clan will curse you if you take her."

"Nonsense," his brother replied, though without conviction. "That law is only for girls in our own clan not those we raid."

Holkis shook his head. "Ordinary girls, perhaps. But look at her robe, it is white. She is a seeress and if you touch her the gods will curse your manhood."

His brother halted unfastening his two leather belts. "I never heard that."

"Do it, then," Holkis said, gesturing at the dazed girl. "But when you father no children or your manhood shrivels and rots off, remember this moment, and remember that I warned you. I am only trying to help you, brother."

Belolukos spat as he pulled his furs around him and fastened both belts tightly. "You have her, then. What is a curse to the likes of you?" At that, his brother stamped out and called to the rest of the *koryos* to search the camp. Their voices answered from the dusk outside as they spread out through the tents and animals.

Sighing, Holkis pulled the girl's skirts down, covering her bare legs. When he looked up at her face he found that she was staring at him, unmoving and wary.

"I will not do you harm," he said, speaking softly as if to a frightened whelp and spreading his hands.

Keeping her eyes on him, she sat up and pulled her legs under her. Her face was dirty and wisps of curling dark hair had escaped her long braids. For all that he could tell she had a good face with high cheeks and a wide mouth.

She sniffed. "You are a *koryos*."

"Yes."

She frowned, looking him up and down. "Where is your mask?"

A *koryos* was never supposed to be seen by anyone. They had passed beyond the ordinary world and were outside of order and control. They wore the skins of wolves and blackened their faces in all raids so that their faces could not be seen. Holkis' face was not covered.

He shrugged. "Your clan was destroyed and I thought none would be alive to see me. It does not matter now."

She held herself still. "You mean to take me?"

"*Take* you?" Holkis looked at the open door and back to her. "Tell me, are you the keeper of the hearth?"

"My mother..." she trailed off, her eyes looking through him before focusing once more. "I am."

Holkis glanced around the gloomy interior of the building. "Is this your house?" In answer she nodded and he continued. "So your father is the chief?"

"Yes."

"What is his name?"

Her eyes narrowed. "You think to test me, raider?"

"You could be anyone. You could say anything."

"This is my home. How could I lie? You are the outsider. Raider. Lies are your way, not mine."

"Tell me your father's name."

"Hartkos. We are Udros."

Holkis nodded for he had suspected as much. "Udros Clan. My chief Gendryon is guest friends with Hartkos, your father."

She looked down, nodding. "You are Kweitos Clan."

"What happened here?" He spoke softly. "Where are the rest of your people?"

She turned away and struggled to her feet. He stood with her. She was tall, almost as tall as his brother, but still Holkis was a head taller. She looked up at him, squinting in the darkness. Her eyes shone as if fired from within.

"You are bigger than the other boy, and you outwitted him with ease," she said, her voice low and steady. "Why are you not *koryonos*?"

He started, shocked that she could see into his heart. See the question that lay within him. But he could not answer her question and so he ignored it. "What happened to your clan?"

She turned away and crossed to the cold hearth, staring down. "They came from the east, up the valley. They were so swift. So many."

"What clan was it? Did you know them?"

"Clan?" She scoffed. "It was no clan."

Holkis shook his head, confused. "What else is there?"

"Some were warriors. Some were captives, driven like cattle. But the leaders. The ones who killed us." She shivered. "They were... not men."

A nameless fear tugged at Holkis' spirit. "What were they?"

She turned, her eyes shining with tears. "They were demons."

2

Demon Clan

"DEMONS?" HOLKIS STARED at her, his heart racing as if he had been running all through the night. "You would not lie."

She scoffed and spat at the floor between them. "I know what I saw. They could be nothing else."

"But how did you see them?"

She crossed to one wall and pulled aside the edge of the sheet of felt there. A gap in the planks let in the dying light of the evening, softly illuminating her face and a line of swirling dust. "I watched them come. They came fast. So much noise. Great demons on two legs, taller than the tallest man. But they acted more like beasts than men... they were like nothing that lives on the plains or the valleys or the woods or the mountains. I watched as one of them alone killed all our dogs with a club and a spear, as if..." She stopped, letting the felt fall back into place.

"How many demons were there?"

She shook her head. "Ten? And hundreds of warriors with them. Hundreds of captives. Animals, also."

"Hundreds?" Holkis could scarcely believe it. "What of your men? The women and the children?"

"Gone. All gone. My father and his brothers fell before the demons reached the camp, I have seen their bodies down by the marsh. My mother, my sisters, the women, the girls. They were taken. The demons came at a run, driving men and women in bonds and herds of cattle and sheep and horses before them and amongst them."

"Why were you not taken?"

She stepped over the benches to the back of the house and looked at him until he went to her. Bending down, she lifted a pile of furs and heaved up a broad plank to expose a black square below.

"Food store?" he asked.

"I hid amongst the meat. Warriors came in. I heard them throwing everything down and trying to set fire to the wall. Their leaders called for them and they left." She gestured, wrinkling her nose. "After pissing on the sacred flame."

Holkis looked around. "You hid? You were not found?" He looked at the evening light beyond the door and lowered his voice. "You were not defiled?"

She stared at him with her chin up. Whether she shook from fear or from the cold, she did not flinch from his gaze. "And you will ensure I remain so."

Holkis shook his head. "Say nothing to any of them about this. Let them believe what they already believe."

"I will not lie. And you will protect me. You are strong."

He lowered his voice and grasped her arm. "You understand

14

nothing, girl. I must obey my *koryonos*. If he wishes to take you, to kill you, to do anything, I will not stop him."

The seeress shook off his grasp and he let her go. "You are the stronger. I see it. Throw off your oaths, become the *koryonos*. Be a true wolf."

He looked down at her. "I thought you had wisdom. Now I see you know nothing. You are merely a girl." He walked away.

She stayed where she was. "You will give me to him, then?"

Holkis turned back. "I swore an oath to Kolnos the wolf god to be loyal to my *koryonos*."

"What about the law?"

He shook his head. "The *koryos* has no law but the word of our *koryonos*. Now, we cannot stay here. We must go on and you will accept whatever fate comes to you." He pointed to her hiding place. "Bring that food."

Outside, the sun was low in the sky and the wind was growing in strength. "Brother!" he called.

"Did you take her?" Belolukos said, thrusting his spear in the direction of the girl who trailed behind Holkis.

"I would not risk a curse."

Belolukos waved his spear at Holkis' face and sneered. "Perhaps you are warded against curses. What if I commanded you to test yourself?"

Holkis shook his head, scowling. "How could I be warded against curses, Bel? How could anyone?" He lowered his voice and stepped closer, pushing the spear aside. "We should go."

Belolukos frowned. "There is much here that the raiders left. Such wealth as you would not believe. The tents contain skins, furs, even weapons. And we shall butcher the dead cattle and sheep and preserve the meat." He waved a hand at the trees upriver. "We should make a camp there tonight and feast. And this is a good place. We will clear the dead and spend the winter here." He smiled. "The gods have favoured us at last."

The wind gusted hard, rattling the branches in the woodland and whistling between the tangle of poles and slashed skins of the broken tents. A long tether thrashed in the air, the frayed ends whipping up and down and lashing the earth.

Holkis almost argued that living on the scraps of a raided camp was nothing for a *koryos* to be proud of. No songs would be sung of their deeds when they returned to their own clan. But if the girl was to be believed that was the least of their concerns.

"Bel," Holkis said. "Evil was done here."

Belolukos turned and spat downwind, making the sign against evil. "A raid is not *evil*."

"Depends on who the raiders were, no?"

"Who were they?"

"What if they were not men?"

Belolukos scowled. "What do you mean? What else could they be?" His eyes darted to the figure of the girl over Holkis' shoulder as she bent to the body of an old man lying twisted in the mud. "What lies has she spoken?"

"She says this was done by demons. Great demons, twice the size of a man, leading hundreds of warriors."

His brother's eyes widened and his mouth hung open. "Demons?" He laughed. "She is mad and you are mad for believing her."

"I did not say I believed her."

"So why repeat the lies?"

"I do not believe she is lying."

Belolukos scowled. "Why do you always speak nonsense, Holkis?" He glanced around at the figures moving through the shadows. "Say nothing of this madness to the others."

"I am speaking to you alone, Bel. But believe her or not, think on this. Whoever raided this camp, destroyed it, has acted strangely, have they not? Why slaughter so many beasts and leave them rotting on the earth? Why leave all these skins, furs, weapons lying here? If it was a raid then perhaps they were driven off by others or chased after some who were fleeing. They could return at any moment. Or other raiders could be following on their trail. We should be gone from here. For now at least. We can get beyond the horizon and keep watch from afar."

"And lose what is here to others who might come?" Belolukos scoffed. "Anyone would think the mighty Holkis was afraid. But that cannot be so, can it?" He looked up at the darkening sky. "The gods sent us here, this is ours. But we will watch from the shelter of the woodland tonight, if that will help your knees to cease their quaking. You will stand guard while the rest of us warm ourselves." As he said this, he looked at the girl, smiling.

Holkis clenched his teeth and nodded. "As you wish, *koryonos*."

A sudden call from the other side of the camp sent them running through the wrecked tents and dead bodies toward their spear-brother Kasos. He was crouched by a dead cow at the edge of the long, dying grass by the river. The water frothed over the shingle and rocks close to the bank as half of the others ran up to join them and peer through the gloom at Kasos.

Belolukos almost growled in annoyance. "I thought there was danger with you shouting like that. What is it?"

"Something is wrong, here," Kasos said. He pointed with his spear at the tattered skin around the neck and belly of the cow. "What did this?"

Belolukos stared in bafflement at the question. "Dogs?"

Kasos shook his head. "No dog, no wolf, could do this. Look at the holes in the neck. Nothing has teeth that big."

"Spears, then," Holkis said. He noted that the girl had kept close behind him.

Kasos nodded slowly. "But they would have to be big spears. Bigger than would make sense. As big around as your wrist."

"That is what they are, then," Belolukos said, rolling his eyes.

"Perhaps," Kasos said. "But look at how many wounds there are. Look at the size of the cuts. No man could wield a spearhead of that size. And you see how some of them have been ripped through the flesh?"

"I see nothing," Belolukos said. "Who cares how a cow died, Kasos? Cattle die. You are almost as strange as Holkis. Enough of this."

"It is not this cow alone. The cattle, the dogs, the men. I never saw anything like this. It is as though the gods themselves came down from the Sacred Mountain and exterminated this clan."

The girl spoke up. "It was not the gods."

Belolukos' head snapped up and he glared at her. "Keep her quiet, Holkis, or she will regret it."

He looked at her and she glared at Belolukos for a moment before catching Holkis' eye. She lowered her head but he knew her anger had not subsided.

"All I mean," Kasos said, standing and looking at all of his spear-brothers gathered around him, "is this all seems... wrong, doesn't

18

it?"

Holkis looked again at the girl behind him. She stood watching them through her eyebrows while the strands of hair loosed from her braids whipped her face in the wind. He exchanged a look with his brother.

"That is not all," Dhomyos said, stepping forward from his place behind the rest of them. "Come and look at these tracks."

They walked to him and looked down at the churned ground. It was as deeply pitted as the edge of a river where a herd of cattle drinks daily through the autumn rains.

Belolukos waved his spear at the ground. "I may not have your talent for reading the earth, Dhomyos but even I can see a hundred men and beasts walked here, with a dozen or more wagons. What of it?"

Dhomyos lowered his spear point and jabbed it. "Look closer. Here, you see these? Look at the size of these prints. Like a man's but far larger."

"So a big man walked here," Belolukos said. "What of it?"

Dhomyos shook his head. He had never been wise or quick-witted but he was no fool either. "Holkis? Your feet are huge. Step into this print, will you?"

Holkis pushed through the others and did as he was bid. His foot was lost inside the massive footprint. "Half as long again," he said, looking at Belolukos. "And twice as wide."

Nodding, Dhomyos pointed at a dozen places all around them with his spear. "Once you start looking, you see them everywhere. You see? Here. And here. You see, *koryonos?*"

"He is right," Kasos said.

Holkis looked at his brother. They all did.

"All I see is footprints," Belolukos said. "Horses there, oxen there, lines of wagon tracks. A great clan moved through here and one of them was even bigger than Holkis. That is all."

They stared at him and many glanced at Holkis.

"Very well, *koryonos*," Holkis said. "That is all."

His brother nodded slowly and then pointed at the black shadows of the woodland upstream. "Night is upon us, brothers. We will spend it there."

They made a camp deep inside amongst the old oaks, building a fire so they would be comfortable through the night while the wind howled above them. As the flames grew to a stuttering roar and the meat roasted above the coals, Holkis thought about what the seeress had said about the demons. He believed her, especially after seeing the tracks in the mud. The others knew something strange had happened but none understood it as he did. At every strange sound in the woodland he sat up with a jolt and reached for his spear. He wondered if the demons and the warriors they led were out there in the darkness, waiting to fall on them.

When the meat was cut up and passed around, his *koryos* brothers stared at the girl who sat hunched beside Holkis. No longer did she wear the white robes of a seeress but had dressed much like they were in woollen trousers and a belted tunic with a fine cloak of fox fur that the raiders had missed. She had stayed close enough to touch him since changing and leaving her home but had said nothing.

"You know you cannot keep her," his brother said, his mouth full.

Holkis chewed his piece of undercooked meat. The outside was burned and the centre was cold and bloody but it was the best thing he had eaten since the new moon. Of late, exposed out on the plains, they had eaten their dried meat cold.

The girl kept her head lowered but stared up at them through her wild hair.

Holkis swallowed. "I know."

His brother kept his voice low, looking between them. "What are you doing with her, then?"

Attempting to be relaxed, Holkis shrugged. "We cannot touch her. Cannot harm her without being cursed."

"Says you," Belolukos replied.

"It's not me that says it." Holkis looked across the flames. "Kasos? What does the lore say about this?"

Kasos yawned and shifted closer to the fire. "If it's as she says and she's the chief's daughter and he was Gendryon's guest friend, that's clear enough in itself. Shouldn't harm her. But that would dishonour Gendryon, not the gods necessarily. Although to transgress is to anger the gods, so perhaps. But if she was the keeper of hearth, she carries her ancestors within her." Kasos waved his piece of meat around at the *koryos* around the fire, all listening to his words. "Just as we do."

"We must not harm her," Holkis said. "So we must let her go free."

"If we do that," Belolukos said. "We might as well kill her now."

Holkis took another bite and chewed while he thought about what to say. He knew what his brother meant. No one could survive the winter alone without a herd, not even in a sheltered valley.

"Killing is different to leaving to die," Holkis said.

"Is it?"

"You know it is," Holkis said and regretted it immediately.

His brother frowned. "You will go to the edge of the trees and keep watch until dawn."

Holkis stood, took both his spears and the fur he had been sitting on and turned away from the warmth of the fire. The girl got to her feet also.

"Not you," his brother said to her. "You can stay beside the fire. Better yet, sit beside me." He patted the ground beside him.

"I go with him," she said, jerking her head.

Belolukos frowned. "I did not give you permission."

"I serve the gods, not you," she replied and came to Holkis' side.

His spear-brothers looked between them all from under their eyebrows, waiting to see what their *koryonos* would do. After a moment, Belolukos scoffed and waved a hand. "At least we'll discover if you are warded against the curse when your manhood rots off."

They laughed and yet they were uneasy. The authority of their *koryonos* had been challenged and he had not reasserted it. Holkis knew it was his fault and he knew it would be best for his brother if he, Holkis, told the girl to stay. Better yet if he struck her, knocking her down. Best of all would be to cut her throat there and then, taking the resulting curse upon himself to rid his *koryonos* of the problem of the girl.

Instead, he turned into the darkness and made his way back toward the edge of the woodland closest to the camp, the girl hurrying to keep up with him.

"How do you see in the dark?" she muttered at his back.

"I do not," he replied, holding his spears before him and lifting his feet high with each step. After months in the wild, living only on what they could hunt or steal, he had learnt much about stealth and moving in darkness.

Before long, they could see by faint moonlight the edge of the wood and the open camp beyond, with the glint of the river beside. He found a dry patch of fallen leaves beneath a stand of young oaks and sat on one fur, pulling another around his shoulders. The girl stood beside him, shivering.

"May I sit by you?"

"Of course."

Still, she hesitated. "Only to sit, I mean. Nothing more."

He shifted sideways on the fur and she placed herself upon it with her knees to her chest and her arms wrapped around them. She flinched when he draped his fur around her shoulders.

"I knew you would protect me," she said, her voice low and steady.

"Be silent."

They sat while the wind whipped through the trees above and the river rushed ceaseless in the distance. Fast clouds passed in front of the moon and he frowned at the shadows flickering. Were they out there now? Would they return? And if they did, could he and his *koryos* hope to stand against them?

"My people are gone," she muttered.

"You will be silent or you will go back."

"There is no one here."

Holkis sighed, shaking his head. "How can anyone be so disobedient?"

"And who are you that I should obey you?"

"Obey me by choice or you will find yourself compelled into obedience by my *koryonos*."

That silenced her for a long while and he thought she was

falling asleep when she spoke again. "Why should you be warded against a curse?"

"I am not."

"But why would your *koryonos* say you were?"

Holkis considered telling her but he could not bring himself to do it. It was good to be with someone who did not know about him. He had never before spoken to someone who did not know what he was.

"I am on watch while my spear-brothers sleep. Their lives are in my hands. We must be silent."

"There is no one here."

"Why can you not hold your tongue?"

She turned to glare at him. "Because my people are gone. Those who are not dead are taken by those demons and that is worse than death. In the morning, or soon after, your *koryonos* will rape me and my worth will be nothing. You are a *koryos* and none of you can take wives or followers and so I will be killed or abandoned. So with the life I have left, I will not be silent, not even for you, who has protected me."

Holkis did not know what to say but found himself repeating something Gendryon always said. "We must all accept our fate."

"So says a boy whose fate is to live to see spring."

"What can I do? There is nothing I can do."

"Take me to another clan."

He turned to look at her then. "You are mad."

"Why? You must raid to survive and so you will prey on another clan soon, somewhere. Take me with you until then and leave me with them."

"We may stay here for the rest of winter."

"You do not wish to."

"My *koryonos* does."

"But you can control him. I have seen it. You will change his will to yours."

Holkis shook his head. "Even if we did run from here you could not keep up with us. We run for days."

"I can run."

"And no clan will take in a stranger." It was dishonest to say it because he knew no clan would reject a healthy girl on the verge of womanhood.

"I know all the clans. My father was strong and knew many chiefs." Her voice broke as she said the words. "There are others who would shelter me. Even your clan. Your father would give me sanctuary. When you return to your people, take me with you."

"That is not for another moon from now. How can I protect you for so long?"

"Your father would be pleased by it."

"I should not even be speaking with you. We are a *koryos*. None should see my face or hear my voice until I return to the clan."

"You could take me near to your winter camp and send me in alone. That would be allowed, would it not? It is not far from here, I know. East, downriver to where our river meets yours. It is a three or four day ride."

Holkis began to put an arm around her shoulders before he caught himself. "Tell me the truth now," he said softly. "You did not see demons, did you?"

She looked up, her eyes glinting from the shadow of her face. "They came through so swiftly up the valley out of the mists at dawn, like a nightmare come into the world. But I know what I saw.

Yes, they were demons." She shivered again.

"They came from the east," Holkis repeated, a chill taking him also and his heart began to race. "From downriver. Your river runs into the Kweitos River. And you said they were driving captives and herds when they came?"

She nodded, watching him closely. "Hundreds of them."

Holkis stood, staring into the darkness to the east while the wind howled. "My clan."

3

Outsider

AS THE RIM OF THE SUN came up above the horizon, all twelve
boys of the *koryos* stood at the edge of the woodland and looked to
Belolukos, their *koryonos*. Holkis had explained to them what the
girl had said, demons and all.

Although they were not entirely convinced, even Bel looked
worried. "These raiders could have come into this valley from
anywhere," he argued.

"True enough," Holkis agreed. "But what if they came from our
vale? We must follow the tracks back along the route and find out
if they attacked our people."

"We cannot return to the clan before the Great Sacrifice,"
Belolukos said.

Holkis felt the eyes of the others turn to him, expecting him to
argue or at least to disagree. It was his place to accept the word of
the *koryonos* but Holkis could not hold his tongue.

"It is as you say. And yet they may have suffered a raid as severe as this one." He waved a spear at the camp. "The *koryos* must survive but they must also protect the clan."

"From outside of it. If we return now we will have failed. You want to live the rest of your life as a wolf, Holkis?"

"No."

"Do any of you?"

They looked back in silence.

Dhomyos scuffed a foot against the earth and shrugged his broad shoulders. "Let us look from afar, Bel? Without returning to the clan."

"We will be seen," Belolukos said.

"We are wolves," Holkis replied. "We are the dead. The ancestors are within us. None of the living shall see."

Belolukos jabbed his spear toward the distant girl. "What about her?"

"She is not of our clan. She means nothing."

Belolukos wiped a hand across his mouth. "If she means nothing, I shall take her."

Sighing, Holkis looked up at the lightening sky. "She is a seeress, Bel. To defile her would be an affront to the gods."

Bel snorted. "You would know." He looked out over the camp and at the wide trail of strange tracks beside the river. "We cannot go home before the time. It has never been done."

Holkis knew that his brother was thinking of his future as the chief of the clan. Gendryon was the chief and Bel would take his place in time, as long as he did everything he was supposed to do. He had to learn the lore, the stories of the clan, and he had to follow and perform and maintain the rites precisely as he had learnt them. More than this, he would have to win wealth through raiding. If he did all this, he might become leader. It was the way of things.

There was little that could stand in his way, other than the disfavour of the gods and if another man was better, more suitable. In their generation, there was only Holkis who might conceivably do so. But he was not an ordinary youth and the clan had always been unsure about what he meant for them. He could be a great leader or he could lead them to destruction. And if he did not lead, what would his role be? Could Belolukos rule as chief while another man was stronger?

"A *koryos* returning before its time has never been done," Holkis said. "But neither has there been a raid such as this in the land."

Belolukos scowled. "This story of demons is a lie. She is a liar and so she is no seer. This was a raid by a strong clan."

"What about the tracks?" Kasos asked.

"We don't know what they are. No, we go on as we were. We must find cattle or sheep to see us through the next moon but we can winter here until it is time to return for the Great Sacrifice."

"What of the raiders?" Dhomyos asked. "They might find us."

Belolukos scowled. "We are wolves. We know no fear."

"We should bury the bodies of the slain," Kasos said. "We cannot live here while they pollute the earth. It must be cleansed."

"The ground is too hard to bury them," Dhomyos said. "Let's throw them in the river."

"But that would pollute our clan downstream," Holkis replied.

"That is so far away," Kasos said, waving his hand. "Days away from here."

"And we shall not waste our strength and our days in burying strangers," Bel said. "We will put the dead into the waters and the river will carry them off. Then we shall cut all the good meat that remains and dry it and smoke it. We have much to do today so let it be done."

A few eyes glanced at Holkis but he did not challenge his brother. He had sworn an oath to Kolnos the wolf god, to the ancestors, and to their mother to obey Belolukos. Breaking it would not only anger the gods but would shame him before his ancestors and risk his place in his clan. Holkis looked at the girl across the camp.

"I know your concern is for mother," Belolukos said as the others moved away. "But you need not worry. Gendryon is there and he will protect her and the clan. He always has."

"Yes," Holkis said. "What of the seeress?"

"She will stay in her house, alone. She may relight the fire and tend the hearth all the while that we are here. If she has not been defiled as she claims, the goddess will keep her safe. Besides, it is not for us to protect anyone but each other, is it, Holkis?"

"No, *koryonos*. I will speak to her and we shall clear the bodies of the slain."

Belolukos nodded. "Do it swiftly, brother. Do not tarry overlong with the girl. I see how you look at her."

"I don't know what you mean," Holkis said and Belolukos laughed as he turned away.

Holkis found the seeress standing in the dying grass by the river. She crouched by the body of a man. A wreath of woven stalks lay upon his chest but it could not hide the great wound that had been punched through him. A hole as large as a man's hand spread wide. Worse still was the man's head, or what was left of it. It had been cleaved in two and crushed. The smell of decay was strong.

"Who was he?"

"My father."

Holkis looked at the man's clothing and his broad shoulders and the scars on his hands and well-muscled forearms. He should have known that this was Hartkos because the swirling designs of his tattoos showed he was a leader and a priest.

"He died defending his clan," Holkis said. "It is time to send him on his way."

She looked up. "We will bury him there, on the high ground above the flood plain."

Holkis shook his head. "There is no time. We must preserve what we can today or we will starve before midwinter. Your father cannot lie here so he must go into the waters."

She stared. "We must not. He was the chief of this clan, he was not some old herder you can throw away."

"And yet we must."

"I will not allow it."

"We will return to this place after our raid and it must not be polluted."

"His ancestors will be angry. They will haunt this place, they will haunt you."

"My ancestors protect me. His have no one now. His line is ended."

"They have me. They will fill me with their wrath."

Holkis shook his head. "You are a woman. A girl. Their wrath cannot live through you."

"I feel them in me even now."

He looked at the dead man at his feet. "We shall dig a grave at the edge of the camp where the ground is soft. Will that assuage your ancestors?"

She looked at her father's ruined body. "As long as we treat him well," she said.

When he stooped to pick up the body, he turned his face away and still the stench of death almost overcame him. Chunks of rotting flesh fell from the man's wounds and his brains slid out in pieces as he walked through the mud to the outskirts of the camp beyond the last of the tents. The mud under foot was crusted with ice and the long grasses crunched as he walked. He laid the body down and they hacked at the ground with spades that the girl brought until they had a shallow grave with brown water in the bottom. Picking up the remains, he lowered them into the damp earth and climbed out, his legs caked in sticky mud.

"You wish to speak the words?" he asked her as they looked down at the ruined body.

She nodded. "I will do so alone and cover him. First I must find a spear and an axe for him."

Relieved, he took up his spear. "I will help my brothers be rid of the rest of your people now."

"What about your own people?" She said without looking at him. "You know where the demons came from and you will abandon your clan when they might need you?"

"It is none of your concern."

"You are my concern," she replied. "You will protect me."

"No."

"You have protected me. You protect me still."

He grew angry. "What do you expect me to do for you? I cannot claim you, I am on a *koryos*. I cannot marry you, I am not a man and you are not a woman. You must stay here and tend the hearth. Cut wood by day and keep the fire burning."

"And if your *koryonos* decides not to take me home with you when you go, what happens to me then? I will starve to death."

"Perhaps. If you wish, I could kill you before we go. It would be swift, at least."

She shivered and looked at his spear. "How many people have you killed before?"

"None."

"How many women have you lain with?"

"None."

She nodded. "You have not been raiding long, then?"

"Half the year since the spring rites. We have hunted, taken cattle and sheep, taken weapons and tools and clothes from other clans in the night. Next year, we will join all the unmarried men of the clan and go on a great war raid, likely to the west. Then it will be time for me to kill my first man, take my own cattle, and return to be welcomed as a man of my clan. Then I will take a wife."

"You must become chief."

He looked at her closely. She had been a seeress for her people, reading the signs in the entrails of sacrifices and in the flight of birds and the ever-changing skies. Not all seers were equal, however, and she was young. "You said so before. Have you seen this?"

"I see it now. You have the strength to be chief. The other does not."

"My brother will be a fine chief."

"If you share the same blood then why should it not be you?"

He shook his head. "We share the same mother. We were born from the same womb, on the same day. But we do not share the same father."

"I do not understand," she said. "Which father is the chief?"

Holkis almost smiled. "Neither. The man we have always called pater is the father of neither of us. My mother is Alkmene, daughter of Elektryon, son of Perseyus."

"Perseyus? The godborn?" She frowned. "If Perseyus is truly your ancestor, how is it then that you are merely Kweitos Clan?"

Holkis shook his head. "My mother, when she was first married—"

A cry of fear from upriver. A shout of anger followed and the clashing of spear shafts.

He looked up to see his brothers running from different directions in the camp toward a single point by the edge of the woodland.

An attack.

Without a thought, he ran toward the sound. As he ran, he saw beyond the camp a commotion in the shadow of the trees. A fight, he was sure of it, spears being wielded and cries of warning and terror and anger.

Ahead of him, Dhomyos ran as fast as he could along the churned-up tracks. Holkis overtook him and as he passed the last of the tents he saw all the way to the edge of the wood.

There, a strange man fought his spear-brothers.

Just one man fighting five of the *koryos*.

One of them was down, lying still in the mud, possibly dead.

Belolukos fought furiously with his spear but the strange man was big and he was faster and stronger than any of them, knocking their weapons aside as he danced around them, defending himself.

When he came into range, Holkis considered throwing his

34

spear at a distance but did not wish to hit one of his own. He overtook the running Kasos so swiftly it was as though the smaller youth was standing still.

Just ahead of him, the strange man ripped Belolukos' spear from his hand, smacked the *koryonos* in the side of the face with his spear shaft and stepped forward to drive his spear into his chest.

Holkis dropped his own spear to the ground within Belolukos' reach and tackled the big man to the ground. He was running at such speed that the impact was terrible, jarring his shoulder and sending them both flying before they smacked into the earth. Holkis rammed his elbow into the man's face and then wrapped his arms around him, pinning his arms to his side. The man roared and struggled but Holkis held tight.

"Yes, hold him!" Belolukos shouted as he aimed a spear point and readied a thrust into his chest.

"No!" Holkis said, twisting and heaving the man aside and away from the blow before it fell.

"What are you doing?" Bel said, raising his spear again. "He tried to kill us."

Holkis' heart throbbed in his chest and his breath was gone. More than that, his legs felt weak and his head felt light enough to float away on the wind. Sucking down mouthfuls of air, he shook his head while the man struggled. "Kill him after." He gritted his teeth as he sucked in more cold air, burning his chest. "Find out who he is first."

Bel was filled with rage and he would have done it anyway but Kasos rushed to his side and put a hand on his arm.

"He dies after," Belolukos said, stepping closer and stamping his heel down on the man's head.

It did not render him unconscious but it knocked the fight out of him. Holkis felt the fire going out, as if the spirit had slipped out of his body.

"I'll let you go," Holkis said into his ear. "But if you fight, I'll kill you."

The man shook his head, which Holkis took for ascent. He pushed him away as he stood, and the man fell over to lie panting in the mud beneath the trees. For all his size, he was thin and underfed. The man had a big skull, and big hands and heavy bones but the flesh on them was all but gone so the muscles of his legs and arms stood out like twisted cordage. His tunic was almost black with filth and the bearskin cloak over it was caked in mud. His hair was long and unkempt, as was his beard. From his appearance along with the man's skill with his spear, Holkis understood at once what he was.

In every clan, in every generation, there were some men who never left the *koryos*. Just like the youths, they never cut or combed their hair and stayed devoted to Kolnos the wolf god for their entire lives. Or until such time as they decided to finally give it up and become a member of their clan. Some men might remain as a wolf because they never won enough cattle to do so but such men were never respected. Most said that they felt the wolf god was not ready to let them go. Kasos said they simply liked raiding too much to ever settle for the clan life of managing their herds, raising children, performing the rites and only raiding on some years and only during the time permitted for it. And so they lived like wolves, usually leading the *koryos* during the great raids of the young men and teaching them all they needed to learn, year after year. Such men were necessary for the *koryos*, and so for the clan as a whole, but they were not fully part of the clan. If anything, they were feared for the violence and wildness that was inherent to them as wolves. Holkis had always believed that was what his clan expected of him when his time came. They wanted him outside the clan, that much was obvious, and Bel wanted it most of all.

"What clan are you from?" Belolukos shouted at the fallen man. "Where did you come from?"

"Let me go," he said without looking up, his voice deep and commanding. "Just let me go, boy."

Belolukos stood up straight and brandished his spear. "I am the *koryonos*. You will show me respect."

That seemed to amuse the man and he looked up through his tangle of hair. "I beat you. I beat all of you."

"Not me," Holkis said, looking down.

The man pulled the hair aside from one eye and peered up at him. "No, not you. Why are you so strong?"

"Do not speak to him," Belolukos snapped. "I am the *koryonos*. Now, tell me who you are. Why did you attack my men?"

The man sighed, rolled over and got to his feet. He moved stiffly, straightening until he stood before them while they levelled their spears at him. He watched closely while Kasos helped their fallen brother to his feet. Blood soaked the side of his head and his nose was broken.

"I could have spitted that one when I tripped him," the man said, pointing. "But I did not."

"Why did you attack us?" Belolukos shouted.

The man winced as he took a step forward. "Ask him," he said and pointed.

"He surprised me!"

The man shook his wild locks. "I called out a greeting and came in peace, you fool," he said. "You attacked me. You all did."

Belolukos glared at his follower. "Is this true?"

Holding his bloody head, the youth looked down. "He surprised me. Came out of nowhere."

Belolukos stared for a moment and lowered his spear. "You should know better than to approach a *koryos*."

"Is this not your clan?" the man asked, looking between them. "I saw you placing the dead into the river?"

"We came here to raid," Holkis said. "And found it like this. We will stay until it is time for the Great Sacrifice and then return to our own clan."

Belolukos scowled. "You should not have told him."

The man shook his head. "I care nothing for you. I follow the *yotunan*."

They froze, staring at the man. Most of the *koryos* frowned, confused by the word, but some of them understood. Kasos and Dhomyos exchanged a look.

"You saw them?" Holkis asked.

His eyes seemed to shine. "Saw them? Yes, I saw them. Once, I got close, tried to slay the one who had taken my people. But I failed and they left me for dead. I have followed them ever since but they are ever ahead of me. You saw them, then?"

They were silent, some shook their heads, but then a voice spoke behind them.

"I did," the girl said.

The man nodded. "So this was your clan," he said. It was not a question. "They did the same to mine. And to many others."

"You call them *yotunan*," Holkis said. "She called them

demons."

The stranger shrugged. "*Yotunan*, demons, *dura*, giants. Different people call them different things. But we all know what they are. What they want. Where they come from."

Kasos cleared his throat. "Where do they come from?"

"They have come from the underworld to destroy all clans."

"All clans?" Belolukos said, shaking his head. "How can this be? We would have heard of it."

"When they find a clan, they destroy it. Any that survive flee from them."

"You do not," Holkis said.

He took a deep breath and looked at the sky for a long moment before answering. "My clan are gone. I took my *koryos* against the *yotunan*, seeking vengeance and death. They did not even slow. One of them alone turned and killed all my *koryos*. Fifty of us. When I woke, I thought I was dead. Perhaps I am. I have followed them since but they are too fast. It is as though they never tire. I tried to come up on them from the south but they changed direction to come into these valleys where they meet the great river in the east. I was well past here when I heard wood being cut and I came back to ask you how long ago they came through here. And to ask if you would join me. We can die together. Perhaps we can kill one of them before we die."

They looked at Belolukos and at Holkis and back to the stranger.

The seeress spoke first. "When these demons attack a clan, not all are killed or taken?"

The stranger brushed the hair from his face. "You saw them yourself. And you live. They are giants and kill with ease and pluck women and girls for the wagons but they slow for nothing. Herders tending the flocks have survived. Boys cutting wood in the forest hiding under leaves. But the men fight and the men die."

Holkis held up a hand. "And they came through the Vale of the Kweitos River, to the northeast?"

The stranger turned and looked downriver. "I don't know what you call it but they came up a wide valley a few days that way and from there into this one. They are so many it is like a dozen clans all moving together. Thousands of people and animals. The tracks are as wide as the valley itself."

The seeress looked at Holkis. "Then it is as you feared. They came through your homeland, Holkis. Your clan was attacked. But it is possible that some of your people, your mother perhaps, may still be alive."

They stared at her in horror while the stranger nodded slowly.

"Our people?" Dhomyos said, his eyes wide. "You mean these demons destroyed our people?"

No one could bring themselves to answer him.

Holkis stepped forward. "Belolukos, my brother, my *koryonos*. What is your command?"

Shaking his head in wonder, Belolukos cast his gaze downstream for a long moment.

"Yes. We shall return to our people."

4

Homeland

"YOU KNOW THAT I CANNOT come with you," the stranger said as the wolves packed meat into leather bags and rolled up furs in preparation around them. "I have sworn to Kolnos to slay the *yotunan* or die in the attempt. My path lies opposite to yours."

"I understand," Holkis replied, thinking on the man's words. "You are a superb warrior. My spear-brothers are not weak but you defeated them with ease."

The man snorted a laugh. "I have been fighting longer than any of you. My name is Makros," he said, offering his hand.

Holkis took it. "Meghaholkis," he replied. "My people call me Holkis."

"Meghaholkis?" Makros smiled and looked him up and down. "Your name means *great elk*. I can see why your father gave you that name. I was the tallest in my clan yet you are taller than me and you are not even a man yet. How old are you?"

"I have sixteen years."

Makros shook his head in wonder. "Who is your father?"

Holkis looked across at Belolukos before answering. "Our mother was wed to Gendryon the chief of the Kweitos Clan. We have always called him pater. He is a good man."

"Very well," Makros said, speaking slowly. "But how is it that you are so strong? And so fast. I saw you coming across the camp and a few heartbeats later you were on me like a bear. How is it so? I have initiated more than a hundred boys and never felt the like of it."

Holkis glanced at Belolukos before he answered. "I have always been strong. And fast."

"Do boys practice running in your clan?" Makros asked. "And wrestling?"

Holkis shrugged, unwilling to speak the truth about his blood. "Of course. I do what every boy does. Riding, wrestling, hunting, the spear dance..." He looked at Belolukos again. "The same as my spear-brothers."

"Then they must breed you well in the south," Makros said, shaking his head. "For I never saw the like anywhere else and that's the truth."

The girl stepped forward, looking up at the three of them. "He is descended from one who was godborn," she said.

Makros' eyebrows shot up.

Belolukos scowled. "You told her?"

"She asked about mother."

Makros frowned at that. "Your mother is descended from a godborn, is she? Who was the godborn ancestor?"

"Did you ever hear of a man named Perseyus?"

42

Makros gaped. "He was Chief of Chiefs in my grandfather's time and I have heard his glory sung many times. As a boy, I liked to hear about his slaying of the death serpent in the mountains between the seas but as I grew older I preferred to hear how he subdued clan after clan. You are truly one of his descendants?"

"Yes."

Makros looked between Belolukos and Holkis. "But if that was your mother's ancestor and you are brothers, why is it only you who has this strength?"

Belolukos scowled. "Enough talk! You, Makros, be on your way. We have delayed enough and now we must go home. You, girl, stay here until we return."

"No," she said. "Whatever you find, you will not return. And I will not die alone here."

Belolukos pinched his nose. "You cannot keep up with a *koryos*."

"I will."

"It is not permitted." Belolukos sighed. "Why am I wasting my breath on you, girl?"

"If she can keep up," Holkis said, "what is the harm?"

"She should not be with us at all," Belolukos said. "But if she falls behind, we leave her, do you understand?"

With that he walked away, shouting to the others to hurry up and finish their preparations.

"I will not fall behind," the girl said to Holkis.

"See that you do not."

She looked at Makros, who regarded them both in turn. "You should join this *koryos*," she said.

Makros shook his head. "My oath takes me after the *yotunan*, not away from them. I am already far behind."

She pursed her lips and glanced at Holkis. "What will you do if you find your clan is destroyed as mine is?"

"They may not be."

"What will you do, though? Will you not go after your people? The ones that survive, I mean."

"Go after them?"

"Your women might have passed through here already, Holkis. Along with the women from Makros' clan. Together they are being driven across the plains. Will you not go after them and seek to bring them back or die in the attempt?"

"That is not my decision. I follow my *koryonos*." He looked at Makros then back at her. "But yes. If my people have been taken I must pursue them."

"So," she said, turning to Makros. "Would it not be better for you to come with us to the Vale of the Kweitos River? And if his clan is gone these boys will go after the demons. Surely together you are stronger than if you are apart?"

Makros laughed quickly. "Sometimes I think I miss women but then I am reminded of how much they scheme and plot. But it is well, dear girl, it is well. If the *koryonos* will allow it, I will run with you for a time." Makros looked her up and down. The hunger in his eyes aroused a spark of jealousy in Holkis. "You have strong legs. If you can keep up with me, you may run at my side."

She shook her head. "I stay beside Meghaholkis."

Belolukos rubbed his eyes. "She is as stubborn as you, Holkis. Keep her, then. But we do not slow for her. If she cannot match our pace, she will be left behind."

He turned and called out to the wolves, gathering them to him.

Together they ran northeast down the valley with the river beside them. Ever since their seventh year, they had spent months every season in the forest and on the plains, hunting and running wild before returning to the clan. Sometimes they went alone with an older man who taught them how to make traps, how to camp, how to make fire. Other times they went in threes or nines. Every year they had ranged farther and for longer until that year when they had made their oaths to Kolnos as twelve brothers together, not cutting their hair or shaving their beards—if they had them—until the end of the year when they would return to their clan in time for the feast of the Great Sacrifice. In the days before, they would be bathed three times in the river. They would be washed and their hair cut and their faces shaved and they would be dressed in new clothes before undergoing the rite to welcome them back into the clan. If the signs were well, that spring they would join the others in a great raid deep into the west to find the people of the long halls. They could be gone for up to seven years before returning to become men of the clan. Sometimes, Holkis knew, men never returned but stayed to found their own clans in the territory taken from the people they raided, taking foreign women for wives and using foreign men as herders. That was always how new clans had been founded.

But if his clan was gone, none of that would happen. All he could hope for was to find his mother and his sisters somewhere and even that seemed a faint hope.

Their years in the wild had made them all as strong and as fast as wolves. Indeed, they had outrun wolf packs more than once. But the young seeress was not a wolf. She had spent her childhood sitting in wagons or riding on horse's backs and could not keep up with the others, even on the first day.

Holkis dropped back as far as he dared so that he could see her behind him and his brothers ahead. By the end of the day, he slowed until she caught him and they ran in silence together. She was breathing hard and wincing with each breath. Holkis knew then that he had made a mistake in allowing her to come. It would be worse for her the next day, he knew, and Bel would not slow for her. If anything, he seemed to be setting a faster pace than normal.

Though she fought for every step, she did not stop and she did not fall. It was full dark when they found the camp in a copse of alder by the river. The wind howled through the trees and the bare branches and narrow trunks did little to slow it. She dropped by the fire and curled up into a ball, still breathing heavily. His brothers laughed at her and at him but he ignored them and wrapped her in furs, gave her a piece of meat to chew on and brought her water from the river before she fell asleep. The others made lewd noises but he lay beside her and wrapped his arms around her until she stopped shivering. Holkis soon fell asleep himself.

It was dark when he woke but morning was coming and he found his arms still around her, both of them covered in the furs he had taken from her camp. Even though he could not see her face, he knew that she was awake. She stirred and whispered.

"Your name is Meghaholkis."

In reply, he made a low sound in his throat.

She shifted her body closer to his. "I am Helhena."

It meant *deer-eyed*. He knew she had told him because it seemed fateful, in some indefinable way. He was *great elk*, and she was named after the eyes of the red deer. It was too dark yet to see but he recalled her large brown eyes and their long black lashes and knew why her mother had given her that name. He squeezed her slightly and she nestled against him further still. Holkis wondered if she would allow him to do something more with her body but she seemed content and, tired as he was, he soon fell asleep again.

When he woke it was light. Helhena was gone and he jumped up in panic before seeing her crouching to make water a few paces away. The sun was touching the horizon and he blinked and looked around.

"It is late," Makros said from where he stood across the camp beside Bel. The others sat or stood here and there, chewing on dried meat.

Belolukos snorted. "Always, he sleeps long."

"And he snores like an aurochs," Dhomyos said, grinning. The others laughed.

"Be quiet," Belolukos snapped and turned back to Holkis. "Go for your morning piss, grab the girl and let us be off."

"And a good day to you also, my brothers," Holkis said, laughing, his breath glowing in the light of dawn. He yawned and stretched, making a show of it and sauntered away a few steps to urinate. Helhena passed him as she returned to the group and he called out to her. "Cut me some of that meat, will you, Helhena?"

"I do not serve you," she said but she did it all the same, handing over a piece with a glare in her eyes when he came back.

He wiped his hands on his clothes before taking it and shoving it into his mouth. "Your legs must hurt this morning."

"I can run," she said quickly.

"Of course you can," he replied. "The pain will ease after half a day but tomorrow it will be worse."

Her expression wavered. "I will not be left behind."

Holkis nodded. "Then you will have to keep up."

They ran for three days. All the while they ran along through the tracks left by more than a thousand feet. Men and horses, cattle and sheep, and wagons drawn by oxen had ruined the earth from the riverbank to the high ground. Detritus left by their passing littered the sacred ground. Torn shoes and strips of cloth. Broken pottery and holed leather bags. Frayed cordage and broken poles. Trampled dung everywhere. The remains of campfires showed where they had rested overnight and every bush and small tree had been cut down. Copses were stripped bare and branches of trees ripped off.

Every now and then they came across the rotting corpse of an animal or a human discarded on the march.

On the second day they found a dozen old women lying together. Their skulls had been smashed in.

"Why take them if they were just going to kill them?" Kasos asked, shaking his head as they looked down at the bodies.

"To make room on the wagons for something more valuable," Makros said, bending to look at the faces. He used his thumb to wipe mud off the cheek of one. "I do not know these women. Do you?"

"No," Belolukos said. "We must go on."

On the evening of the third day they came into the lands of the clan. The river had joined with the Kweitos River at a boiling confluence that marked the boundary of their home territory. As boys they had been warned never to stray further upriver than that point and so they had delighted in daring one another to do that very thing. Holkis remembered when they were six and still living in their mother's tent when the older boys fell back, afraid, and only he and Belolukos had dared to go on into the next valley. Only when darkness had threatened did they decide to turn back. When they returned, cold, hungry, and filthy, their mother had beaten them bloody with the whipping stick. But that night in their bed they had held their hands over their mouths as they laughed in joy at their bravery and their victory over the other boys.

The valley was narrow where it met the other but widened soon into a wide pasture with woodland along the river and in pockets here and there. The land rose gently to the plains beyond that stretched for days with no water or trees. They were never the strongest or the largest clan but it was a good homeland and had to be defended against raiders who would take it if they could. The water was sweet and the trees provided them with fuel for the bitter winters and poles for their tools, homes, and weapons. They also harvested herbs and mushrooms and hunted deer and fished.

It was a good home and to see it again after so many months away brought on a powerful feeling in Holkis. What that feeling was he could not place precisely but it was a mixture of relief and dread.

The tents that they lived in for winter were always erected on a spit of rocky land that stayed dry even when the surrounding pasture was sodden by the fall rains and spring thaw. The largest woodland was close by and it was at the edge of this woodland at sundown on the third day that they smelt smoke on the air.

They slowed their run and peered through the shadows along the tracks of the woodland. Holkis loped along at the rear with Helhena breathing heavily beside him. The tears she had shed from the pain of the run had long since dried in the bitter wind, though she ran with her face twisted into a grimace. They came up to where Belolukos and the others clustered beneath the bare branches.

"You smell that?" Dhomyos said, grinning. "Smoke on the wind, Holkis. Our people are well."

Kasos frowned. "If they are well, we must not enter the camp."

"It cannot be your clan," Makros said, frowning. "We followed the trail of the *yotunan* all the way here. You can see the tracks even now." He stabbed his spear at the broken ground stretching away into the shadows before them. "They came right through this woodland. Your people lived beyond? Then I am sorry to say they are slain."

"We know nothing, yet," Belolukos snapped. "Holkis, you will go forward alone and see what has happened. See who it is that makes fire."

"Do not be seen!" Kasos said. "Perhaps you should put on your mask. Perhaps we all should?"

Holkis shook his head. "Fear not, brothers. I shall discover the truth of this and come back to you."

As he started through the trees, Helhena made to go with him and Holkis stopped her.

"I will come with you," she said.

He was about to command her to stay but he looked back at his brothers and Makros behind him and then nodded. "You will stay well behind me and you will be silent."

"I will."

He raised a finger. "Silent."

She scoffed. "I am not a child. Go on, now. Night will fall soon."

Holding his spear in both hands he went forward through the

trunks and the undergrowth, looking down at the mass of tracks in the churned earth and up at the broken branches overhead. Surely some giant had snapped the twigs at a remarkable height as it had travelled the woodland. How could his clan have survived the assault of such terrible creatures?

As the trees thinned, he slowed and advanced at a crouch. Helhena did the same and she was as silent as a hunter.

Though the sun had set there was light enough out in the open and he looked upon his home. When he had last seen it there had been more than fifty tents between the river and the ridge. Each tent belonging to a warrior of the *tauta* where his wife, his young children, and servants lived. Other tents were home to the herders and their families. As their chief, Gendryon had three tents and his wife Alkmene had one of her own. As older boys they had lived a life somewhat outside all of it, whether learning to hunt in the woods or learning to ride on the plains or learning the spear dance far from the eyes of the women and children. But until leaving with the *koryos* it had been the only home he had ever known.

The camp had been wrecked.

It reminded him at once of what had befallen Helhena's clan. Tents were thrown over and trampled. Bodies of animals and people littered the land.

But voices drifted across the open ground all the way to the woodland, along with the smell of the cooking fires. Men's voices, calling out to one another.

"There are people there," he said. "Beyond the tents." He saw shapes moving between the shadows. A horse walked out from behind a tent, scraping the earth with a hoof. Its stiff mane stood up from its neck and there was a riding blanket over its back.

"It is too dark," she said. "I cannot see them clearly."

"I see their horses." He smiled and sighed.

"How could there be survivors?" Helhena asked. "How do you know it is your people?"

Holkis chewed his lip. "It is not full winter yet. A few warriors are sometimes away for long stretches to visit the other clans. Trading. Arranging marriages."

She nodded beside him. It was the same for her people.

"Or it could be herders," he said. "Bringing in the last of the herds from the plains and finding this. I will go to them. Wait here."

She came with him, hurrying to keep up as he strode across the meadow. The grass had been trampled everywhere and the ground was soft but he meant to reach the survivors before full darkness fell for if they could not see him they might believe he was an enemy.

A figure moved into view and Holkis raised his spear over his head and called out a greeting.

The man jumped and froze, staring at him. Holkis and Helhena were hard to see with the shadows of the woodland behind them.

"I am Holkis," he said. "Returning home."

When the man turned and shouted, Holkis felt sick and his heart raced.

"We have to run," he said.

"What do you mean?" she asked, as a dozen warriors came into view from behind the tents with their horses in tow. They began mounting as they shouted hunting cries.

"They are not my people." Holkis looked at Helhena. "Run!"

Their feet slapped against the cold ground as they raced hard for the trees. Helhena ran as fast as she could while Holkis looked back over his shoulder at the mounted warriors catching them up. Fleeing back through the wood, Holkis shouted a warning.

When the others appeared through the trees, he waved. "Enemy! Riders!"

"How many?" Belolukos shouted.

Holkis glanced over his shoulder and made a guess. "Twenty!"

To stand and face so many would likely be death and Belolukos made the sensible decision. "Into the trees. Come on, we will go deeper."

Makros approved and he directed the younger men toward a dense stand of coppiced trees and undergrowth away from the main track. Already it was almost black as charcoal beneath the bare branches.

Still, Holkis did not wish to run or to hide. Hooves pounded behind him and the shouts of the riders grew louder as they pushed into the wood.

"Go on," Holkis said to Helhena. "Go with Bel."

She pulled up and turned back.

"No!" she said and her eyes focused behind him. The riders had slowed, riding no more than two abreast as they came along the track.

"Go on," he said and she turned and ran after the others deeper into the trees.

"Holkis!" Belolukos shouted as she passed him. "Come!"

Hesitating, Holkis looked at the approaching riders. They were cheering and shaking their javelins. Even as he looked, an arrow crashed into the undergrowth a few paces away and he saw the bowman readying for another shot.

He knew he could not stand against so many. And yet he wanted to fight. The riders had destroyed his clan, desecrated the homes and land of his people, and he would fight like the cornered wolf he was rather than flee like a startled deer.

Unbidden he recalled the words of Gendryon, spoken to him years before when they were first to accompany a raid across the plain. Both Holkis and Belolukos had been afraid though they tried hard not to show it. Gendryon had knelt before them, placing a hand on their shoulders.

"You fear death, boys," Gendryon had said. "You will not fight in this raid but you fear failure and death. You fear to see me fall and the other men of the *tauta*." They had both nodded slightly despite their shame in the admission. "You are right to fear. All men fear. But war is a test. The greatest test. War separates the strong from the weak, the courageous from the cowards. Some men fall, others assert themselves. You can never be a man if you are not tested by war." He had lightly slapped their faces, smiling. "Come. Let us be tested."

Now, clutching his spear tight Holkis prepared himself to face the raiders thundering toward him. He would fight and he would win or he would die.

"Holkis!" Makros shouted, the older man running to his side, his feet kicking up the leaf litter as he skidded to a stop. "Do as your *koryonos* commands."

"Fight with me," Holkis cried. "We will die with honour."

Makros grabbed his arm. "We *will* fight but not like this. There is a better way. Come on. Come!"

Hesitating but a moment, Holkis growled as he turned and ran with Makros deeper into the woodland, pushing through the tangle of bushes and sapling to the sound of snapping branches and the cries of the warriors behind them. Another arrow struck a trunk nearby and broke in two, the shaft clattering. Holkis ducked and ran on after the others.

"They do not follow," Makros said as they darted between the trees. "We must stop. We must hide."

It was full night when they huddled together deep in the woodland. A fine rain fell, spattering against the branches and the leaflitter.

"We should be fighting," Holkis muttered, shamed by his flight. "Not cowering like sheep."

"Are you calling me a sheep?" Makros whispered, anger in his voice. "Wolves lie in wait for the deer, do they not?"

"So let us attack," Holkis said. "Bel? We can go forward again now. Catch them."

"We will," Belolukos said. "Let them tire themselves out looking first."

Holkis sighed. The riders crashed around up and down the tracks, some calling out honeyed promises of friendship if only they would show themselves. Others jeered and shouted insults, calling them cowards, fools, and frightened boys. This last had a significant effect on them and many of them took up their spears and stepped away into the darkness.

"Wait!" Belolukos hissed, driving them back.

"They mean to anger you," Makros said. "We will attack them when we are ready."

"Why not now?" Dhomyos asked.

"We will attack when it grows light enough to see," their *koryonos* said. "Rest now. I will stand watch."

But none of them could sleep while the enemy warriors circled the woodland.

"You are safe for now," Holkis muttered into the ear of Helhena.

"I am not a fool," she replied softly and shivered. Standing behind her, he wrapped his arms around her shoulders and pulled her close. She leaned against him and soon her shivering stopped, though it was a cold and tiring night.

Before the grey dawn came, they whispered a plan for attacking the riders.

"If they wish to stop us escaping then they will have men on all sides of the woodland," Makros said, his voice low and raspy from tiredness.

"We don't want to escape," Holkis said. "We want to kill them."

"That's right and we will. They will be spread out but we will not be. If there are five of them together we can fall them and slay them swiftly, do you see? And when the others come for us we will have reduced their numbers. It will be a more even fight especially if we stay close to the trees. And remember, boys, we must stay together."

They all nodded.

"Even you, Holkis," Makros said.

Holkis frowned. "Why do you single me out?"

A few snorted laughs silenced him.

"Even if your numbers are made even can you kill warriors grown?" Helhena asked.

Holkis nodded. "We shall destroy them with ease." But his words were stiffly spoken through a tight jaw.

Makros grunted. "I'm a warrior grown, girl, and I'll break a few skulls. Listen, we do not need to slay every one of them. When enough have fallen they will ride away." He addressed Helhena. "When we attack, you should stay in the wood until it is over. If we all fall then you will be alone. It may be another day or more before they ride off and the cold may kill you but you must stay still and hope none of them saw a woman was with us. If the gods are with you, the warriors will leave you be."

Helhena gripped Holkis' arm. "I will not lay waiting for them to find me. I shall watch your battle and if you fall, I shall slay myself."

Holkis held her tighter. It was the men who died and the women who were taken. Helhena could expect to be taken as a prize and in time would be married to one of the men of the enemy clan. She would become one of those people, her children would be full members of that clan, and no one would expect anything else. Men died, women were taken, that had always been the way and always would be. But Helhena was unlike other women and girls and although Holkis was disturbed by it, he did not waste strength arguing with her. Especially as he knew it would be futile. The only way he could protect her was by defeating the enemy riders and that was almost impossible. He wished he could have lain with her, spoken to her, looked at her but even those thoughts were small and distant, pushed down by the cold, hunger, fear, and exhaustion.

All he could do was hold her tighter until Makros tapped him on the shoulder.

When he looked into her eyes to say farewell, it was too dark to see clearly so he touched her cold cheek with his frozen hand and crept out with his spear where the trees thinned and came out upon the track. The ground was soft where the hooves had churned the rain with the earth and Holkis found each sliding step being sucked down and released with a faint sucking pop. There was no chance of running through such ground. He looked at his spear-brothers emerging from the shadows to either side of him. They splashed forward, listening for the sound of hooves or the breathing of horses or men. There was nothing but the wind and the sound of the fine rain falling.

Together, the *koryos* and Makros fanned out through the trees to the edge of the wood. By the time they reached the open meadow, the sky had lightened enough to see all the way to the river, and to the broken tents, and to the ridge beyond.

Belolukos turned to Holkis and shrugged.

"They are gone."

Holkis was almost disappointed. "Why would they leave us?"

Makros shrugged. "Why would any man fight when he did not need to? They have taken their booty and gone back to the plains. Back to their clan, ready for winter. Thanks be to Kolnos, eh?"

Helhena emerged and stood with them as they inspected the tracks and squinted into the gloom for signs of trickery. But the enemy were truly gone.

Dhomyos scratched his dirty face. "Now what?"

Holkis looked at the shapes of the ruined camp ahead. One of those tents had belonged to his mother who had lived there with his sister.

"Now we see what is left."

Taking a deep breath, Holkis walked out into the open as the sun rose on the horizon.

5

Kinsmen Die

IN SUMMER HIS CLAN HAD LED their herds and flocks across the plains to the north to graze the endless expanse of grass. It was a time for raiding, marriages, trade, rites, and feasting and sometimes the men would ride away to attack some other clan leaving the women and children, and the herders and their families, to fend for themselves. One summer when he was five or six years old there had been three raids one after the other while Gendryon and the men had been off raiding elsewhere and he recalled his mother hiding him and Bel in a wagon before taking up her spears and her bow to defend the clan.

Winter, though, was different. They came south to the river valley and hobbled the horses and erected the tents and cut mountains of firewood. When the snows came the shaggy, stocky horses would scrape their hooves through the snow and ice to expose the grass beneath so that they could feed. The cattle and sheep followed the horses, grazing on the exposed grass. Cattle by themselves never scraped the snow away and would stand and starve in a snowfield with ample grass below the surface but with horses clearing the way, their herds would eat in the day and crowd together at night against the relentless winds.

Even in the tents with the fires burning and furs around them, it was always cold in winter. But the hot broth from the stews of horse meat made life worth living. As did the stories told in the lamplight during the long nights with the wind howling outside. Holkis remembered being very small, leaning against his mother's warm flank while Bel sat on her other side, their mother's arms around them both and furs covering them. That was how he first heard the songs of his clan sung. The songs of the deeds of the gods and of the great men that had come before. When he grew older and moved from his mother's side and from her tent to that of the men, the tales grew bloodier and he learnt the ways that a man may be slain.

Holkis walked through the ruined camp, examining the mutilated bodies of the men and women of his clan. Most of the herders had been killed, even the women and children.

The men of the clan, the *tauta*, had likewise been struck down. Old Kelh who had taught him the spear dance, Wordos who had shown him the bow, and Pyek who fought only with a war club and who had mastered it like no other mortal before him. Their strength and skill and prowess had awed Holkis from the day he had left the women's tents to the day he had joined his *koryos*. All dead and cold and their limbs stiff. Just like with Helhena's clan, many had been broken and mutilated so terribly that it was difficult to know who they had been in life, though there were limbs and pieces of hewn flesh recognisable by their tattoos alone.

The horror of it was more than Holkis could comprehend. All he had known was gone. It no longer existed but for the cold, pale remains lying scattered like discarded meat. There were stories of clans being destroyed by others but even in the songs the destruction was never so total. Even when one clan defeated another the survivors were brought into the victorious clan. The cattle were added to make larger, stronger herds, not slaughtered and left to rot. Tents were taken on wagons, not broken and torn and discarded.

"It is all so wrong," Holkis said.

Helhena nodded as she stared at the destruction.

"I cannot find mother or Laonome," Belolukos said, stepping over the broken poles and sodden felt of a tent as he approached.

"Me either," Holkis replied. "There are not so many of the women dead here. Hardly any young women."

"Most of the boys are dead," Belolukos said. "All Dhomyos' brothers. Sentos found his all together in their tent and his mother with Welut slain outside."

Holkis rubbed his face. They looked around at their brothers of the *koryos* mourning over their dead fathers and uncles and mothers and brothers and sisters. Sentos sat on his knees weeping outside the ruin of his father's tent.

"How many do you think were taken?" Belolukos asked. His eyes were red and he stared through Holkis, as if looking at a distant horizon.

"Half the women and some of the girls," Holkis guessed.

"I cannot believe mother would allow herself to be taken."

"And yet it is likely she and Laonome yet live. We will find them and we will free them." Holkis stepped forward. "Bel, we must go after them."

Belolukos looked at him and seemed about to argue when there was a shout from the other side of the camp.

"It is Gendryon!" Kasos called.

Holkis followed Belolukos across the camp to where Kasos waited, his head hanging. The others gathered and they stood together looking down at the broken body of their chief. In his right hand he held the broken shaft of his stone axe and in the left was his spear. Both weapons were stained with blood.

"Are you sure it is him?" Dhomyos said, coming up beside them. "The head is..."

"It is him." Holkis said and clapped a hand on his brother's back as Belolukos nodded.

"He was your chief," Makros said. "And he was your father?"

"No," Belolukos said, his voice a growl.

Holkis nodded. "Our mother Alkmene's husband. We have known no other father. All our lives, we called him pater."

"And now he is dead," Belolukos said. "And our clan is destroyed."

"What do we do now?" Dhomyos asked.

"We go after our women and their daughters," Holkis said and then looked to Belolukos. "And we must hurry. Already we are so far behind. We should have followed them back there at her clan and not come home at all. We have wasted days that we will have to make up."

Belolukos scowled. "What is done is done. Our people are no more. Our bonds are broken."

Holkis turned on his brother. "Those monsters have taken our mother. And think of Laonome. We must follow. We must do it."

"I am the *koryonos*. I will decide what we must do."

Holkis stepped closer. "Our people are no more, you said. The bonds are broken. If that is true then what of our bonds to the *koryos*?"

"You swore your oaths to me. To me! And I am still here and I will be obeyed."

"Then command us to free our mother and our sister. Our brothers of the *koryos* have their own mothers and sisters to follow," Holkis turned to them. "Do you not, brothers? We all want to find what is left of our people."

"And then what?" Belolukos asked.

"Find them and perhaps we may free them."

"We twelve?" Belolukos said, laughing. "We twelve and a girl and an old man cannot hope to fight a vast clan of demons."

Makros grunted. "I am not so old, boy. And I will kill as many of them as I can before I fall."

"That's right," Holkis said.

"It is madness," Belolukos said.

"What else can we do?" Holkis asked.

Belolukos shook his head. "We must bury Gendryon before anything else. He was our chief. We will not allow the crows and wolves to feed on his corpse. It must be done."

"And my father," Dhomyos said, his big face twisted in grief. "My brothers."

"And mine," Kasos said, his voice flat but his eyes wet with tears.

All had people that had to be buried. That was something they could all agree on. After finding spades and digging sticks from the wreckage and choosing favourable places, they began hacking out graves beyond the limits of the camp.

Holkis and Belolukos together dug out a grave for Gendryon and placed him inside with his broken weapons. Holkis looked down at his remains for a long moment. One of his first memories was of his horse dying. She was an old mare with a round belly and a knotted coat that could hardly manage much more than a walk but Holkis remembered being very small and loving the swaybacked nag with all his heart. Most horses needed to be controlled with a bridle, reins, and a bone bit in their mouth or at least a noseband but she was docile enough for him to hold on to her stiff mane and control her with his thighs and feet, and with whistles and clicks. One day, when the herders were rounding up the herd, she fell and broke her leg. The herders cut her throat and began butchering her before she was cold. Holkis saw the butchery from afar and ran off before he shamed himself in front of the other boys. Somehow, Gendryon had found Holkis crying by the river.

"Why do you cry, boy?" he had said. He was huge and towering, his face always serious and terrifying.

Holkis had not been able to give voice to his pain and expected to receive a hard thump for his failure to answer. Instead, Gendryon had crouched at his side, his massive, calloused hands hanging close to Holkis' face. He must have stared at those strong hands, for he could not remember Gendryon's face as he spoke in his steady, rumbling voice.

"Holkis, you weep for a horse. Horses die. Cattle die. One day, you will find that your kinsmen die. All things die." He paused. "Holkis, do you know the one thing that never dies?"

He had looked up then, desperate to know this secret, grasping at it from the depths of his grief. "What?"

Gendryon's green eyes were filled with an inner light like the glow of hot coals at night. "Only glory never dies, son. The deeds of a man's life win him glory so that his name goes on in the songs of the kin he leaves behind. And the undying glory that he has won carries his spirit to the afterlife on swift horses. There he will be judged and if he is worthy his spirit will live forever in the halls of the gods beside the mightiest of his ancestors."

"Oh," Holkis said, awed and yet also disappointed that it was not something easier.

Gendryon had smiled and ruffled his hair. "One day, son, you will be a man. But today you are a boy and boys may weep a river of tears for beloved horses."

Looking down on his body, Holkis felt the tears brimming again and fought them down. He was a boy no longer. Gendryon had been a good man but had he won the undying glory that all men sought?

They threw earth down upon him until the ground was filled and there was a slight raised area of fresh mud piled atop it.

"He deserves better than this," Holkis said, gesturing at the grave. "He should be buried on the plain. A mound raised over him."

"If we had not returned here he would lie unburied," Belolukos said. "Perhaps that would have been for the best, now that I think of it."

Holkis was shocked. "How can you say that?"

"Chiefs protect their people. We always knew Gendryon was not a great man and should not have expected too much from him but he failed at this his first duty."

"This was not some ordinary raid," Holkis said, determined to defend Gendryon from the unfair accusation. "He protected us from the other clans all his life but no one can stand against this."

"Exactly, brother. And yet you would have us—"

A cry from the ridge caused them to run to where Kasos crouched in the grass. Thinking their enemies were approaching, they ran to him with their spears in their hands. Kasos waved an arm low, side to side at his waist, to show that there was no danger and they slowed, calming themselves.

From the ridge they could see across the grasslands where they opened up to the south, west, and east. The wind was bitterly cold and gusted about their ears. Grasses whipped in waves all the way to the distant horizon.

Holkis turned to see Helhena hurrying after him up the slope. She was never far from him. He could understand her fear but he had never decided to be her protector. She had simply attached herself to him and he was not sure how he felt about it. He wanted her. But he had no idea how he was going to protect her when he did not know how he was going to protect himself. When she caught up with him he nodded and turned away.

"Why are you screeching like an old woman, Kasos?" Belolukos said as they came up to him. "We are lying our people to rest. What are you even doing up here?"

"Makros said one of us should keep watch and sent me up here."

Belolukos scowled. "That old man is not your *koryonos*."

"No, Bel, he is not but it was a good idea. Besides, I wanted to get away from the..." he waved down at the camp behind them. "And when I came up here I found these tracks."

"What tracks?"

"The tracks of the riders," Kasos said. "They met here before riding south across the plain. You see where the grass is thin here their tracks show well? Thirty riders and spare horses."

"Thirty?" Holkis said. "More than we saw last night. Are you sure?"

"I am."

They accepted that. Kasos was the best tracker amongst them. Almost as good as his father and uncles had been.

"So they had spare horses," Belolukos said, turning to spit downwind. "What of it?"

"Look here," Kasos said, pointing out the tracks with his flint spearpoint. "Hoof prints where they gathered up here before they set off. Some deeper than others which makes me think some were unladen. But not many." Kasos said, pointing out the tracks. "And here, you see?" He pointed to a footprint. And his finger moved to another. Just the edge and very faint but overlying those of the hooves. "There are more, here and there. All smaller than those of a man."

"What does it mean?" Helhena asked.

"Those riders led prisoners away from here on foot," Holkis replied as Kasos nodded in confirmation. "And small tracks mean they were women and children."

"Survivors," Helhena said, her eyes widening. "Those that the demons left alive."

"Our people, Bel," Holkis said, nodding south across the plain. "They went that way."

Together they went down to the camp and called in the others from their burials. Belolukos explained what they had found.

"You mean some of our people survived the attack by the

demons?" Dhomyos asked. "But were captured by mortal raiders?"

"That must be it," Holkis said. "Perhaps they hid in the trees while the demons passed. Perhaps our fathers gave them time to get away. Whatever happened, some survived and came back to the camp perhaps a day or two after the demon clan had passed. And then those raiders from last night caught them. And led them away."

"We were so close!" Wedhris said.

"We were a day too late to save them," Belolukos said, shaking his head. "But we will go after them now. We will follow across the plain and get our people back."

Makros laid his spear shaft on his shoulder and smiled. "I am glad for you, boys. But if you will not pursue the *yotunan* then I will say farewell, for I cannot delay my pursuit any longer."

"You wasted four days to come with us and four days to go back to where you were," Holkis said. "I am sorry for that."

"What is done is done. I am glad I met you all." He looked at Helhena. "Girl, you run well. You can come with me if you like. We will go after your people and mine. And together we will die."

She nodded. "You are a good man, Makros. But I must stay with Holkis."

He pursed his lips and shrugged. "Probably a good choice, girl." Makros held out a hand and Holkis grasped it. Instead of letting go, Makros pulled Holkis away from the others and they walked off out of earshot.

"You have something to say?" Holkis asked.

"You have a hard road ahead. It is not only the monsters out there that you must fear. Your people will need the strongest leader they can find and your brother may not be it."

"He is our *koryonos*."

Makros squeezed his arm. "Don't you understand, son? Your *koryos* is over. Your clan has likely been destroyed. You must take charge of them, gather other survivors to you and take all the cattle you can and find somewhere to see out the winter. If you can make it to spring, you might have a chance but you will have to fight every *koryos* and every clan who comes for you."

"I am just a boy," Holkis said.

Makros snorted and released his arm. "You have no clan left to make you a man. But this is the way of things. Kinsmen die. So stay a boy forever or make yourself a man. And marry that girl, quickly, or take her at least. If you don't, someone else will. Even then, you'll have to fight for her until you're the chief and you don't want to let one like her get away. Believe me, I know." Makros pulled out a knife. The flint was chipped at the binding frayed. "Give me your hand." He sliced into the ball of Holkis' thumb and did the same to his own. They grasped hands so their blood mixed. "In the name of Kolnos the wolf god, I release you from your oaths." Makros let go and slapped Holkis on the shoulder. "I wish you were coming with me. I could do with the descendant of Perseyus at my side." He held up his blood palm. "But perhaps some of the *yotunan* slaying powers of the godborn will go into me, eh?"

"You are a good man, Makros," Holkis said. "Die well."

6

The Raid

THE STEADY RHYTHM of their feet upon the hard, thin earth was the only sound other than the relentless howling of the bitter wind. They breathed hard as they ran, their packs banging against their backs and hips, the wolf furs bouncing on their shoulders and over their heads.

It had taken them two days to catch up with the riders. Running from before sunrise and collapsing onto the plain after dark. Holkis had wanted to run through the night but the others were too tired. Helhena suffered the most but Dhomyos and Wedhris were hardly any better and so Holkis had relented. Yet still he was the first to wake in the purple-tinged grey of morning and the last to stop running after dark.

"Give us a chance to rest," Sentos groaned on the first morning.

"No," Holkis said before kicking his feet. "Get up."

All he could think of was his mother and his half-sister. They could be captives of the riders ahead. If the *koryos* could catch up and ambush the riders then Holkis might have a chance of freeing his kin. But if the riders reached their own clan first then there was no chance of saving them. A *koryos* of twelve boys and a girl could not hope for victory against a clan.

"We could bargain for our people," Wedhris suggested in the darkness as they huddled together against the wind. He was the shortest of them all and had always seemed to be far younger than the rest of them despite being almost the same age. "Bargain instead of fighting."

Those that were still awake groaned. They had no fuel for a fire and would not have lit one if they had for the light may have been seen by those they pursued.

"Do not be a fool, Wedhris," Belolukos muttered. "They would only take us, too."

"They might not," Wedhris replied. "Might they not welcome us as guests? We are wanderers, now, are we not? They must offer us feed, drink, shelter."

"We are twelve boys dressed in wolf skins, you witless clod," Belolukos said. "They would spear us on sight. Stop trying to think, it is beyond you. Now go to sleep."

Late on the second day they smelled something on the wind. A faint animal taste. There and gone again.

"Horses," Holkis said, crouching beside Kasos.

Kasos nodded. "Dung, also. Lots of it."

"You think so?" Belolukos asked, sniffing the air. "Cattle?"

"Must be a lot of it to smell it from so far away," Kasos muttered. "Big herd."

Holkis shook his head. "There is nothing upwind but the open plain. It is the wrong season for a herd to be out here."

Kasos looked at him. "It is a big herd, Holkis. The warriors rode toward it. That means a clan is there." He pointed. "Probably just over the horizon. Why don't you tell their chief it's the wrong season to be on the plain?"

Belolukos rubbed his face. "That is it, then. We failed."

Holkis stared. "I am not giving up the chase. Bel? We are not giving up the chase."

Sighing, Belolukos looked at the sky. "If we go on now, we should be on them by nightfall." He looked at Kasos. "If they are where you say they are."

Kasos took a deep breath in through his nose and nodded as he breathed it out. "How can you not smell that?"

Smiling, Holkis nudged him. "All we can smell is you."

They approached in a single file, following Kasos. All of them hunched as low as they could as they ran forward, keeping their spears low and flat to the ground. They were ready to throw themselves into the grass at the first hint of danger. The smells of the clan grew stronger as they approached. Dung, animal sweat, leather. Then they ran across the tracks of wagon wheels and past piles of spore left by the clan's dogs. By sunset they jogged through grass cut short by the grazing of cattle, horses, and sheep. As night began to fall they heard dogs barking and herders shouting.

They came to a stop behind a slight rise in the ground and gathered, crouching, around Belolukos.

"What is it?" Helhena whispered to Holkis.

"We must wait until full dark before going closer," Holkis said, looking at the sky. "If we are seen we have nowhere to hide and nowhere to flee to."

"*Koryonos*," Wedhris said. "What do we do?"

"Find our people," Holkis said.

"He asked me," Belolukos snapped. "And I am thinking."

"But what is there to think of?" Holkis said. "Our people are in there. We must get them out. Now."

"Can you not control yourself for a moment?" Belolukos said, his voice low.

Dhomyos grunted. "Of course he cannot. He is Holkis."

There was a little laughter but all of them were nervous.

"There will be half a moon tonight," Kasos said. "Not much cloud."

"That's good," Holkis said. "We will be able to see our people."

"Dangerous," Wedhris said. "We will be seen."

"All we need to do," Holkis said, "is find our way past the boys and dogs on watch and find where the captives are."

Wedhris almost sobbed. "You say that as if it is easy."

"Not easy," Holkis said. "But it is simple. That is what Kelwas the Lame said on the cattle raid of Henseh, is it not, Kasos?"

Kasos sighed. "That's what he said."

Belolukos reached out a hand and grabbed Holkis by the shoulder. "Well you're not Kelwas the Lame, are you. You're Holkis the boy."

Holkis pushed his arm away. "What else is there, brother?"

"It is a large clan," Belolukos said. "Larger than ours. We may not even find our people."

"We have raided clans before."

"For food, for cordage and water skins, for sheep." Belolukos looked at the darkening sky. It was entirely black in the east. "Nothing like this. How do we get our people away from an entire clan?"

"We just do it."

Belolukos shook his head. "Always, you wish to rush in without thinking. When will you learn to use your wits? We cannot get away without horses."

"We will take their horses," Holkis replied, looking around the group as he spoke. "We will free all our mothers and sisters and we will steal the horses of the enemy and we will ride them home again. Our clan is not lost to us. They are there, brothers. Just there."

Belolukos scoffed. "You think we can steal a hundred horses without being caught?"

"What else can we do?"

The boys of the *koryos* looked at one another and looked between Belolukos and Holkis.

Belolukos shook his head. "It was madness to believe we could do this."

"We cannot give up now, not when the last of the clan are just there, Bel. It is almost dark, we must go now."

"I do not want to lead my *koryos* into death," Belolukos admitted. "Not when we could have life."

"How can any of us live knowing we could have acted and yet did not?" Holkis looked around the circle of faces. "Kasos? Dhomyos? Sentos? Wedhris? Any of you?"

They shook their heads.

"We could cross the plain to the west?" Kasos said. "There are people there. Fat people that live in wooden houses all year. We can go there, take their wealth and find a warm valley to live in."

Dhomyos nodded. "We can take their daughters, make them wives, raise children. We could have our own clan and Bel will be our chief."

The others muttered agreement with this plan.

Belolukos growled his assent. "We will have a chance for wealth in the west. The people are weak, so they say."

"You will be brave enough to raid clans in the west but you fear this one here?" Holkis snorted. "You are running away, you mean. What use is such a life? I will die tonight rather than live like that." He looked at Belolukos. "Mother may be right there, Bel. Laonome, too. I am going to free them or die trying."

"You cannot disobey me," Belolukos said, his voice low. "You swore an oath."

"Without a clan, brother, we are freed of our oaths."

Belolukos stared. "A man cannot throw off oaths as if they are nothing, you fool. We are bound until the rites at the Great Sacrifice."

"There will be no rite, Bel. All the men are dead." He looked at Helhena. He could barely see her in the darkness. "Go with Belolukos, he will keep you safe."

"I will not," she said. "I can help you."

"It will mean your death," Holkis said. "Or worse."

"All things die." Her voice did not waver.

He looked into her eyes and saw that she meant it. She had lost her people. Even more thoroughly than he had. She was of an age with him but something in her eyes made her appear older.

"Then you can come with me," Holkis said. "While the others go into the west and seek a better life."

"Stop," Belolukos said, scowling. "Why is everything always so difficult with you, Holkis? We will go together. You hear me? We will save our people. All of us. Let us free our women."

They breathed deeply. Kasos muttered a prayer to Kolnos.

"Can you speak to the gods for us?" Holkis asked Helhena.

"The gods of the hearth and the dawn have no sway here," she replied, her voice flat.

They approached the clan as the darkness obscured the land before the moon rose. A cold rain fell, blown sideways by the wind. When they came close to the outermost cattle they stopped and crouched, peering at the shadows before them.

The clan was large. The domes of the tents could just be discerned stretching away into the darkness. Between the *koryos* and the clan was a great mixed herd of cattle and sheep and horses, some settling down for the night and others shuffling around. The wagons creaked and groaned and shouts filled the air. Tents were still being erected and boys ran from horse to horse to hobble or tether them. Dogs barked from within the camp.

Holkis' heart raced. It suddenly seemed madness to attempt to raid such a clan. He had the urge to grab Belolukos and tell him to call off the raid.

But then he thought of the captives. Imagined Laonome at the mercy of some stinking warrior. Anger rose inside him and he gripped his spear tighter.

"Some horses are not tethered," Kasos whispered. "Already they spread out. We shall have to catch each one and cut the hobbles before we can flee with them."

"There must be a better way of doing this," Wedhris muttered.

"Some trick, some deceit, like in the songs," Holkis agreed. Eyes turned to him and he shook his head. "I cannot think of anything."

They crouched in the darkness and watched. Eventually the moon rose and by its faint light they could see boys wrapped in furs sat on wagons to watch the flocks and herds. Deeper within the campfires were lit and the smell of cooking filled the air.

"Horsemeat stew," Dhomyos muttered. "By Kolnos, I am hungry."

Holkis wiped the corners of his mouth. He was not hungry. He could not have eaten for anything. He knew that their lives were balanced on a spear point. If the gods were not with them they would be dead before nightfall.

"We should have made a sacrifice," Holkis said.

Kasos agreed. "Perhaps we should do so now? Even leaving a little of the dried horse meat here may help."

"Sacrifice your own meat," Belolukos said. "Be silent."

They crouched, shivering, waiting for the cooking fires to die down and for the warriors and their women and servants to go to sleep.

"We should circle the clan," Holkis said softly. "Find where our people are being held."

"In the centre," Belolukos said. "They will be in the centre so what difference does it make?"

The rain eased off but they were all wet and cold and shivering on the sodden grass.

"I'm so hungry," Dhomyos said.

He was ignored.

"Where do you think they are going?" Kasos whispered to Holkis. "This clan, I mean. Why are they here and not somewhere sheltered?"

Belolukos pulled his furs tighter around him. "Who cares?"

Holkis had been thinking about it. "The clan of demons goes southwest and these men look to be heading south. Perhaps they will meet with the demons somewhere in the south."

"Or perhaps they are also fleeing from the demons' path," Helhena said, her teeth chattering. "Going to some wintering ground in the south. This is a strong clan, is it not?"

Holkis clench his jaw. "It is."

"Once we find your people," Helhena said. "What then?"

"We must get our people free in silence. If we kill none while we do it, so much the better. They might give up the chase if all we take is our people back and a few horses. If we kill them..." Holkis shook his head. "We find them, free them, steal some horses. Flee to the Kweitos River."

"Simple," Kasos said. "But not easy."

Belolukos scoffed. "Enough talk. Let us do it."

They crept after Belolukos, keeping close to him. Cattle lifted their heads as they crept amongst them, one lowing as they passed. A dog began barking and they froze but it was on the other side of the camp. Holkis had trouble hearing anything over the pounding of his heartbeat in his ears. A horse trod slowly toward them, perhaps in hope of food or just attention. Holkis crouched at its forelegs and reached down. It was hobbled, a length of rope tied between the legs so that it could walk freely but not run. He clicked his tongue and stroked its nose when it bent its head down. Behind it, another mare approached them, snorting and sniffing.

Holkis grabbed Helhena, pulled her to him and put his mouth against her ear.

"These mares shall be ours," he said, whispering. "Helhena, wait here and hold these horses. I will find my people and free them. I will come to you here and when I do you must cut the hobbles and we shall flee on these horses. Together."

She shook and held him. "I do not want to wait."

He peeled her hands from his arm. "You will guard these horses, Helhena. You must. So that we may flee together."

She spat on the ground and pushed him. "Go, then."

He did not wish to leave her but Holkis moved away with the others behind him. Belolukos was ahead and he turned as Holkis came up.

"Wagon," he whispered, nodding.

Before them, the shape of a parked wagon loomed.

Belolukos signalled that he would continue deeper into the camp but he wanted Holkis to go the other way around the wagon.

"Why?" Holkis hissed.

Belolukos jabbed a finger at the wagon and then at his own eyes. Then he dragged his finger across his throat.

Watcher on the wagon. Kill him.

Holkis nodded and Belolukos and the others crept away through the horses and cattle while he edged around the parked wagon. There were other wagons beyond it, parked at the edge of the camp and providing something of a wind break for the tents within. More than that the wagons with their covers provided an elevated position for guards to keep watch over the animals through the night. Usually the sons of herders did the job but often the sons of warriors stood watch. Woe betide any boy who failed in his duty by falling asleep or failing to stop a wolf from making off with a sheep or calf. Herders would be armed with a sling and a stout stick but the sons of warriors might have a bow and a spear.

However they were armed, any watcher who raised the alarm would be killing him and his spear-brothers. Even a woman with her eyes open would mean his death.

Checking his flint knife was still in his belt he gripped his spear and crept closer to the wagon, keeping his eyes on the seat at the front. The hooped poles over the top of the wagon were covered in reed mats. The finest wagons were covered with leather to keep them dry and some were even lined inside with felt, like tents. Whatever the one before him was made from, he could not see inside. The open front was as black as the blackest night. Keeping his eyes fixed upon it he crept closer. If he was quick he could stand, jump into the driver's bench at the front and spear whoever was inside.

But he would have to be quick. If he hesitated or missed his strike then the entire clan could be alerted and then not only would the rescue fail he would be fortunate to escape with his life.

A boy, no older than seven years, stepped around the side of the wagon.

He looked right at Holkis.

By his threadbare clothing and the narrowness of his shoulders, Holkis knew he was the son of a herder. The lad frowned at the big stranger for a moment before recovering his wits, taking a breath to cry out a warning. But Holkis lunged forward, grabbed him and pulled him down into the shadows with a hand clamped over his mouth. Dropping his spear, Holkis drew his knife and held the sharp flint to the boy's neck. The boy stopped struggling.

"Where are the captives being held?"

The boy stared at him, eyes wild.

"The captives, you fool, what tent are they in?"

"Captives?" the boy said.

"Keep your voice down. The people who your warriors took from a camp two days ago. They would have just come in today.

From a camp that had been destroyed by the demons."

The boy shook. "Are you one of them demons?"

"What?" Holkis frowned. "Of course not. Now, where are they?"

"Think they went to the chief's tent." The boy trembled. "Chief's tent and his wife's tent and his other wife, probably."

"The chief's tent?" Holkis pushed the flint blade harder against the boy's throat. "Why would they take captives there? You are lying."

"I ain't lying!"

"Quiet!" Holkis sighed, looking around. The wind blew. In the distance, two dogs barked at each other. "Where's the chief's tent?"

"I don't know how to say it." The boy licked his lips, his eyes darting left and right. "I can point to it?"

Holkis shoved the boy upright and held him by the shoulder with one hand. "Show me, then. Quickly, now."

The boy raised a hand, pointing into the darkness and the dancing shadows. "Well, now, you see... his tent is right..." the lad whipped a hand around and slapped Holkis across the cheek.

A moment later the boy charged off into the darkness.

"Help!" the boy cried. "Raiders! Raiders!"

Recovering his wits, Holkis jumped to his feet, snatched his spear and in a few strides caught the shouting boy and dragged him close. Clamping a hand over the boy's mouth, he hoped that the wind had taken his words away.

Someone shouted from the next wagon.

Another cry came from deeper within the camp and then another. Dogs began barking everywhere.

The warning cries had begun.

He had failed.

The lad squirmed in his hands, striking his forearms and trying to kick him. Holkis knew Belolukos would say to kill the boy and he raised his knife. The lad went still, his eyes wide as he stared at the knife catching the moonlight.

Holkis held the boy in his grasp and turned him around to look down at his eyes. "You did well, boy. Especially for a herder. You have the courage of a warrior."

The boy tried to spit on him but Holkis shoved him away and he let the boy go.

"Go on, you little goat turd," Holkis said. "I give you your life, though you have taken mine."

With a last fearful glance at the knife, the boy flitted away into the darkness.

The shouting came closer and Holkis ducked low, holding his spear ready. His heart sank. There was no way he could free his people now. He could fight and die or he could try to escape. His inclination was to die. His clan was destroyed. His brothers would likely be caught also. If he ran, he would probably be run down and shot with arrows or javelins. That would be an ignominious death. If he went forward, deeper into the enemy camp, he could face his death as if he really was a man.

But Helhena was behind him. He had told her to wait with the horses and if he died she would be alone. She would be taken and made into a servant or a wife. Not a bad fate for a young woman but he had said he would return for her. And because he had said it, he had to do it.

He hunched low and backed away from the wagon.

His enemies were behind him.

"You!" a voice cried. "Who are you?"

Holkis turned with his knife in hand to see two men with spears approaching out of the dark.

He froze.

More voices approached and the men around him cried out and called others to them. They were armed with spears and stone axes and some held torches aloft, casting flickering orange light all around.

Holkis knew he was finished. A dozen thoughts flashed through his mind. He thought of Bel, his mother, sister, Helhena, his spear-brothers. He wished he could have lived longer, become a man, taken a wife, won glory.

Instead of waiting for his fate, he rushed them. Charging at the two men closest to him.

His sudden attack caught them by surprise and he got inside the spearpoint of the first man and drove his knife into the man's throat, bearing him to the ground. Hot blood gushed forth as he drew the knife out. The second man thrust his spear at Holkis' chest but he twisted away and came upon him from the flank, knocking aside the warrior's spear shaft before aiming his flint blade at the warrior's neck beneath. The man twisted, trying to wrest the spear from Holkis and his knife stabbed into the warrior's cheek, glancing off the bone. The warrior howled in pain and dropped his spear, backing away and shouting with a hand on his face and blood pouring through his fingers.

Holkis turned as more warriors rushed him with shouts of anger, their torches roaring in the wind.

The first spear thrust came straight at his face and he darted aside. Another spear came at him from the flank and he swatted it aside with his own and swung further to crack a man over the ear with his spearhead, sending him sprawling. More came and he backed away, knocking their weapons aside.

A voice roared over his shoulder and he turned to find a huge warrior rushing in with his axe held aloft ready to crush Holkis' skull. Without thinking, he stepped closer and jammed his knife into the man's eye. The eye burst and the flint shattered when the edges stabbed into the bone of the eye socket. Holkis' blow drove the blade into the attacker's brain. The impact jarred his arm but the warrior jerked back and fell, pulling the knife from Holkis' hand. The warrior dropped his stone axe as he fell and Holkis meant to grab it but the others were coming for him again and he turned, swinging his spear in an arc. They jumped back, seemingly afraid of him.

Holkis laughed at them.

"Come and die!" he shouted. "I am Holkis! This is my spear! Come and die!"

Two shouted something back at him and came at him with quick thrusts from two sides. Using his spear with both hands he knocked aside the shaft of the man on his left and stepped closer. With a quick thrust he stabbed at the man's belly, meaning to open his guts. The man jumped back and the spear only cut the man at his hip. By then the other was on him from behind and he danced away from the attack, swatting away the spear with a great clack and began his own attack. With a look of surprise and fear the warrior backed away at full speed and then turned to run in full flight.

Holkis laughed again as he turned to look at the circle of warriors around him.

I am mightier than all these men together, he thought. *I am a great warrior. I shall win glory.*

"I am Holkis!" he said again. "Who else wishes to die?"

One of the men behind him stepped forward and hurled a war club with both hands, sending the heavy wooden head spinning in the air. The knotted club head cracked Holkis on the skull behind his ear and he staggered forward and fell to his knees.

He did not know what had hit him. He looked at the spear in his hands and thought that he should use it but he could not lift it. Could not stand.

Holkis watched through blurred vision as the warriors rushed in and swung their weapons down.

7

Captive

PAIN WOKE HIM. Pain in his chest and most of all in his head. A throbbing, terrible pain behind his eyes and a sharp pain in his lungs. It hurt to breathe. It hurt to open his eyes but he did so.

He found he was lashed to a wagon, his arms spread wide and he was hanging from his bound wrists. That was why it hurt to breathe. His ankles were bound also but he got his feet under him and stood so that he could take a breath.

It was night but dawn was coming. The world was grey and growing lighter.

There were people around him. Men's voices and women's too, moving around in the shadows cast by flickering torchlight. He was unregarded. No one nearby.

Where was Belolukos and his brothers of the *koryos*? Where was Helhena? Escaped? Dead? Captive?

"Water." His mouth was dry and he licked his lips. "Anyone

there? I want water." he said. He spoke softly and even that hurt his head.

From the rear of the wagon an old woman limped over to him and peered into his face. She had milky eyes and deep lines around her mouth with red veins across her cheeks. "You can die thirsty, murderer."

Holkis tried to swallow so he could ask the old woman if his mother was alive but he did not have the spit to do it. He shook his head and the old woman scoffed and limped away, raising her voice to call to unseen others that he was awake.

He looked at the clan around him. Women wailed in the distance, calling to the gods and crying out. It was the cry of mourning. Women mourning the men he had slain.

There was no doubt that he would be killed but he wondered why they had not done it already. Perhaps they wished to punish him before they killed him. He recalled the fight with the warriors, remembered stabbing one in the eye, another in the throat. Holkis smiled to himself. At least he had fought one good fight in his life. One good fight was better than none.

He shivered at the thought of the torture that was coming to him. There were stories of captive raiders being given to the women. Women who would cut pieces off a man until he died. He listened to the wailing in the distance and shivered again. How could he die well if he was to be subjected to such punishment? But that was the purpose of it, of course.

The rope around his left wrist was not as tight as the other and he pulled at it, wriggling his hand. It felt as if he might be able to ease his hand out of it if he pulled at it for long enough. He worked his wrist against the rope, trying to stretch it and fray it without tightening the knots. The rough cords chafed his skin raw but he thought that was good. If he could scrape away his skin, the blood would lubricate the rope. Someone looked his way and he stopped, feigning a disoriented, despairing writhe to mask his movements. When they passed he began scraping at his bonds again, scratching his skin. The sensation burned and then he felt sharp pain. Good. That meant he was cut. He twisted and pulled again, trying to open the cuts up and get some blood flowing. The danger was that he would heal quickly before he got the blood flowing properly.

Soon, a commotion ahead brought his attention. Women and herders moved away from something coming through from the tents deeper within the camp.

A great chief approached.

He walked ahead of six warriors of his *tauta*. The chief was a powerfully built man in the prime of his life. Almost as tall as Holkis but his arms and chest were far thicker. He wore a copper dagger and a copper war-axe in his belt. A bronze pin held his bearskin cloak closed. The chief's wide jaw clenched as he came to a stop and looked at his captive.

"You killed my men," he said. "What madness possessed you to raid my clan, boy?"

Holkis licked his lips and rasped an attempted reply but he coughed and gagged.

The chief nodded to one of his men. "Water."

A bowl was lifted to his lips and Holkis slurped at it gratefully. The water was stale and yet each drop was wonderful. "I am Holkis of the Kweitos Clan. You took my people. I came to free them."

The chief shook his head and sighed. "So your brothers tell me."

"You have them? Do they live?"

He tilted his head. "They live. Unlike the men you killed. You must be punished."

Holkis stared at the chief. "I know. But tell me about my *koryos*. About my clan. Who did you take? My mother Alkmene, is she with you? And Laonome, my sister. A girl of eleven."

The chief took a deep breath and looked at his men who stared back impassively. "You are Holkis, son of Alkmene. You are a descendent of Perseyus, Holkis." He shrugged. "And so am I. Perhaps you do not remember it but we met before. You have grown since then. I am Orysthos. Your mother is a cousin of mine."

"Orysthos?" Holkis hung his head. "But why are you here? Your lands are in the north. The banks of the Rasga."

"The world has changed."

"Do you have my mother? Do you have Alkmene? And my sister Laonome?"

Orysthos shook his head. "No, son. We have followed the demon clan for months, always at a distance. They move relentlessly and we dare not come too close. I tried to reach the Kweitos River before they got there but we were too late." He raised a finger. "You and your brother got there a day after us. We found a few of your clan, they came out of hiding and we brought them back here to join us. Your mother was not one of them, nor your sister. The demon clan has them now. Or they are dead."

Holkis closed his eyes for a moment. "Then I made the wrong choice. I should have followed them right away. I might have freed them instead of ending up in bondage here."

Orysthos snorted, half glanced at his men behind him before speaking. "You would have failed to free her even if you had tried.

Have you seen the demons?"

Holkis shook his head.

"If you had, you would not speak so easily of freeing your mother from their grasp."

Holkis looked at the warriors and the tents and the people standing at a distance. "Surely you could do it, Orysthos? You have the largest clan I have ever seen. It must be the strongest there is."

The chief stared at Holkis as if he were an utter fool. "My men could not hope to defeat them. No one can. At least they are heading away from our lands and soon enough they will be gone. And then everything will be as it was before."

"But not for my mother and sister."

"You should count yourself fortunate that you yet live, as does your brother. With your blood, you could be powerful men."

"What about my punishment?"

Orysthos nodded. "As an outsider, even as a cousin, you must die for your transgressions. But if you were to swear an oath to serve me, I will punish you less severely and you may live."

"Serve you?" Holkis frowned. "If I served you, Orysthos, would you let me try to free my mother?"

"Were you always slow witted, boy, or did my men break your skull? Your mother is dead or beyond your reach forever."

"But I could find her. Catch up the demon clan and free her. You could let me try, at least."

Orysthos stared. "I will not let you go. If you serve me and flee then you will be an oath breaker." He gestured over his shoulder. "My men will catch you and then you will wish you were dead."

"But then I cannot serve you," Holkis said. "I cannot abandon my mother. My sister."

The chief ran a big hand over his face. "And I cannot let you go without joining me. Your brother has already taken the oath. As have all the others of your *koryos*."

"I do not believe you."

He seemed truly shocked. "You call me a liar?"

"I do not. It is simply hard to believe Bel would give up on mother. And he adores our sister."

"He understands that you really have no choice."

"Choosing to serve you will be giving them up to death."

Orysthos barked a laugh and shook his head in disbelief. "How will your own death serve her? You are so young, everything appears to be simple when you are a boy, I know. I remember it and I have sons of my own, not much younger than you. Holkis, I do not want to kill you but if you do not swear an oath to me, I will have to do it." He lowered his head. "Even if you are godborn, I will have to."

"I do not want to die. I want to save my kin."

"Take the oath."

"I cannot."

Orysthos sighed. "You are as stubborn as your mother but you do not have her wit, I see. Well then, Holkis, son of Alkmene, you will die today. I shall see you fed well and I will end your portion of life by my own hand." He patted the bronze dagger at his belt. "You killed four of my warriors and so I will pierce your chest four times and then I shall cut your throat. We will leave you on the plain, unburied. You will be carrion and you will be forgotten."

It was almost like a dream, hearing those words. He never imagined ending his days in such a manner.

"It is a shame," Orysthos said, smiling ruefully. "My clan would have been made stronger by you. Four warriors you killed and you are not even a man. Do you not wish to change your mind?"

Holkis was tempted. It was madness to choose death instead of life. And yet somehow it felt wrong. It was wrong. Choosing to live for the sake of saving one's own life. It was choosing the body over the spirit. The choice that a woman or a herder would make.

He shook his head. "All men must do as the gods command. And the gods command us to do what is right even if it means death."

Orysthos was growing angry. "You are not a man but a boy. And because of your bullishness, you will never be one." He pursed his lips and tilted his head. "You never asked about her, so perhaps you do not care or perhaps you hope she escaped. But of course we have your girl."

Holkis jerked his head up. "Where is she?"

Orysthos smiled as he shook his head. "We caught her trying to free you. She says she is bonded to you but she is yet a child and cannot swear such a thing. I like her. She is beautiful and her legs are strong. She will come of age this summer." He pointed a long finger at Holkis' face. "If you had become my man, she might have been your wife. But now I will take her for myself." He sneered. "So much for the godborn."

He strode away, his warriors following him.

Holkis had a sickening feeling in his guts. Anger filled him and he felt suddenly as though he had made a mistake. Why had he chosen death when he could have asked for life? There was no dishonour in submitting to a chief, especially one so mighty. He had an urge to call out and beg for his life and yet he could not do it. Something stopped the cry in his throat before it was given voice.

Was it not madness to die when his brothers had chosen life?

He wondered where Bel and the others were. Would they witness his death? Would they stand and watch while his chest was pierced and his throat cut? If they served Orysthos then they would have to. Even Bel.

And Helhena would stand and watch, too. Women were taken by raiders, by conquerors, and they became a part of the new tribe. She would be unhappy to see him killed, he knew that much, but he knew also that she would lie with Orysthos and bear him children and if the gods were with her she would love them and raise them into men and women. Helhena would do well, he knew.

Holkis sighed and squeezed his eyes tight. His eyes burned and tears wet his lashes. Four cuts to the chest and then my throat will be cut, he thought. That is not so bad.

The people around him became suddenly agitated and then a hush came upon them. Men and women halted what they were doing and stared with open mouthed astonishment at something across the camp behind him.

Holkis craned his head to the left and right but his view was blocked by the wagon.

The people of the clan kneeled and bowed their heads. Holkis twisted as far as he could and ducked his head into his shoulder to peer between a gap in the side planking. The gap let him see through to the open rear of the wagon and get a glimpse of the camp beyond.

A gigantic figure dressed in grey wolf fur strode through the camp, followed by two men of ordinary size similarly dressed. The enormous man was at least a head taller than anyone else. He had a long grey beard blowing in the wind.

The giant figure glanced around from under his fur as he

walked and seemed to look directly at Holkis.

He had only one eye.

All he got was a glance before the figures passed out of view. The people of the clan got to their feet and drifted away in the direction of the visitor until Holkis found himself alone.

It was getting lighter all the time. It was not long now until dawn.

He writhed and twisted his wrist in its bond, pulling and wringing until the skin burned once more and then came the sharp pain as the fibres cut his skin. Pulling and pulling, he was sure that he could slip his hand out but it did not come, it would not come.

He heaved against the loop so that the plank he was tied to creaked and the joints of his shoulder and wrist and elbow seemed about to pop but still he could not free himself.

In desperation, he yanked on the rope, jerking it harder and harder.

The plank cracked and splintered and his hand broke free, the rope still wrapped around his bloody wrist. He looked around. No one cried out or came running. He reached across to pull at the knot tying his other wrist, ripping out a nail in his anxiety and making him whimper. But he pulled the knot loose and freed his hand. He pulled apart the bonds at his ankles and then he was free.

He was free.

Crouching in the shadow of the wagon he peered underneath it at the people crowding across the camp.

Staying low, he hurried in the opposite direction.

Had his brothers truly sworn an oath to Orysthos? If he could find them would he be able to free them? And what about Helhena? She would be better off as a member of the clan rather than riding for freedom across the wide grasslands. Taking her with him was selfish and unrealistic. But he somehow knew she would not see it like that.

Before he found any of them though he would need to prepare horses and so he crept away from the tents and the wagons toward the herd. It was still grey but he saw a group of nine horses standing tethered near to one another and made his way towards them, starting to mutter soft words under his breath to let them know he was coming and that he meant no harm.

Light footsteps sounded behind him and Holkis froze.

He turned and saw a young boy running toward him.

The boy drew to a sudden stop. "I been watching you," he said.

Suddenly, Holkis recognised him as the herder boy he had grabbed in the raid. The one who had slapped him and fled, raising the alarm. The boy who had ruined everything.

Holkis nodded slowly and stood, spreading his arms wide. He knew he would have to silence the boy properly this time. The lad was small enough that a blow to the head should do it. Failing that, he would have to strangle him.

"Truly, you are vigilance itself," he said, stepping closer and smiling.

"Take me with you!" the boy blurted.

Holkis stopped. "What did you say?"

"I been watching you, I saw what you done. You're godborn. I heard them talking and they said you was godborn. A real godborn. You broke that wagon. You killed them warriors." The boy cuffed his nose. "You said I had the courage of a warrior."

"Did I?"

The boy nodded. "Take me with you when you run. I want to

be a warrior, like you!"

"You cannot," Holkis said, frowning. "I should not have said that. You are a herder. Your fathers were herders. All you can be is a herder. You must strive all your life to be the best herder you can be. The gods demand it and so you must do it."

The boy stared, his mouth hanging open as if he had been slapped across the face. Holkis was ready to jump on him to silence his cries but the boy simply hung his head, turned, and slouched away. He knew he should crack the boy's skull. He should at the least tie him up. But his heart would not allow him to do it. Cursing himself for his weakness, Holkis watched the boy wandering away with his head down, kicking at the turf.

Holkis bent to the horses muttering soothing sounds and untied the hobble of the biggest mare. They were not harnessed and there were no riding blankets on them but they would have to do. He tied the length of hobble rope around the mare's neck and began to lead her around the edge of the wagons and tents. Inside the camp, the people seemed to be massing somewhere between the tents and holding torches aloft as if they were holding a rite.

He hoped the gods would continue to favour him. If only they would keep busy for a little while longer he could perhaps creep back and look for his spear-brothers.

If they had truly sworn themselves to Orysthos, would they come with him? He had to find out even if it was a terrible risk. The fact that he had freed himself suggested that the gods wished him to escape and so he meant to make the most of his good fortune. There would only be so many tents he could search before full daybreak and before his escape was discovered. But he had to try.

A cry came from behind him. He ducked behind the mare and

peered beneath her round belly and through the wandering animals. The commotion came from the direction of the wagon that he had escaped from.

They had discovered his escape.

There was nothing more he could do for his brothers. If he could return for them and for Helhena one day, he would.

But first he had to live and to live he had to escape.

He led the horse further into the grey of the predawn, stroking her nose and whispering to her as they made their way through the hundreds of milling horses and cattle toward the plain.

"You must be swift," he whispered to his mare. "You must run like an antelope. You must fly like the falcon. Come now. Carry me, we will be free together." He slid onto her back and urged her forward.

As she picked up speed he chanced a look over his shoulder.

The sun was coming up and he knew that soon they would be coming after him.

8

Alkmene

ALKMENE JERKED AWAKE. The wagon had bounced into a hole and the impact shook her from her dream. It was daylight. She looked around at the other women and children packed into the small wagon and closed her eyes to it. Waking from one nightmare into another.

"You were dreaming," Old Henu said softly from the other side of the wagon.

"I know," Alkmene said.

There were fourteen women and girls crammed into the narrow space. She looked up at the wagon cover arcing above them and then at the back of the driver sat on the bench managing the team of oxen pulling them across the plain. Out of the rear she looked at the masses of people and animals trudging along all around them. Herds of cattle and sheep spread in all directions and were scattered to every horizon.

How many days now had it been since the *yotunan* had come?

She looked down at Laonome. Her daughter's sleeping head lay on Alkmene's lap. Idly, she stroked her hair for a moment and then eased her up into a sitting position, leaning her back against the side boards of the wagon. Laonome muttered in her sleep and licked her cracked lips.

"Do not wake her," Henu whispered. "When we sleep, we forget our hunger."

Alkmene did not respond but got to her knees to look past the driver. The sea of walking and riding people stretched away into the distance and through them all she thought she caught a flash of light on the horizon. She smelled the air. There was nothing but the stink of the herds of beasts and men. She ducked to peer out of the side of the wagon through gaps between the boards. The earth was pitted and churned by thousands of feet and hooves, as it always was, and yet the wounds in the ground were deeper, softer than they had been on the dry plain. Some men twirled slings and shot at birds flocking ahead of them.

"We are approaching a great river," Alkmene muttered. "It must be the Don."

"Sit down before they see you!" Old Henu hissed, tugging Alkmene's fur cloak with a gnarled hand.

Alkmene slapped the old woman's hand aside. "I care not if they see me," she said, loudly.

"They will punish you!" Henu snapped. "They will punish all of us."

Alkmene recalled the cries of warning when the *yotunan* had poured into the valley and overrun the camp. It had all happened so fast. The warriors had run to defend them and Gendryon had taken up his weapons and shouted at Alkmene to take their daughter and flee for the horses. Alkmene had wanted to find her spear and her bow. Wanted to face the raiders who came upon them without warning. But she had done as her husband had wished, running from the tent and calling for Laonome. Her daughter was with the other girls by the river near the woods looking for mushrooms. When Laonome had turned at the cries and saw what was coming for them she had screamed. Alkmene saw the girls drop their baskets and stare in horror. When Alkmene had looked over her shoulder and seen the *yotunan*, she had frozen in terror. Recalling it brought her shame. Ever since her dreams had been haunted by that moment. She found herself stuck to the earth and unable to flee, unable to fight, unable to do anything but scream like a young girl. No matter what came now, she swore to the gods that she would not hesitate again.

"Get down," Henu said again.

Alkmene craned her neck to see further. "I must know what is happening around us if I am ever to free us."

Henu scoffed. "Stop it with that talk. You have seen what the *yotunan* do to those who try to escape."

"I would rather die than live as a prisoner to these demons," Alkmene said.

"And what of Laonome?" Henu lowered her voice to a whisper. "Would you leave her without a mother? Would you have her punished because of your disobedience?"

"I will not be a slave to evil. None of us should be, including Laonome."

Henu shook her head. "I do not doubt the strength of your spirit, Alkmene, but your pride will be the death of you. And of your child."

Ignoring the bitter old woman, Alkmene watched a cluster of the *yotunan* in the distance. They had gathered together to speak, she thought. They were giants, taller than the tallest mortal man, and each of them was monstrously strong. Most were twisted in their bodies or deformed in their features. And all were evil. She had seen them kill prisoners at will, sometimes tearing them apart with their hands to feast upon the warm flesh, collecting the blood in bowls and cups and drinking it. She shuddered to think that such a death might befall Laonome. She could not allow that to happen.

The great procession slowed around them. Soon their wagon halted and their driver shouted a question, asking what was happening. Alkmene strained to listen for a reply but there were too many voices calling to make out what was being said. Someone asked if they were stopping for the day already. It seemed no one knew.

"Is it *them*?" Henu hissed. "Are they coming?"

"Those at the front must have reached the river," Alkmene said, reaching for the nearest hooped pole arcing overhead. "And so we are all stopped."

Ahead, the group of *yotunan* were arguing. The one that wore a cloak of bearskins shouted something and stormed away back to his own clan. Each *yotunan* was something like a chief unto himself, with his own mortal warriors that served him and corralled and guarded their prisoners and wagons and herded their flocks. These warriors also attacked each new settlement that they came across, descending on it like vultures to rip it apart for the spoils to be shared amongst the *yotunan*. Alkmene counted twelve *yotunan* in all and all were revolting great monstrous things.

Alkmene's clan had been taken by a *yotunan* named Leuhon.

Leuhon was built like an oversized warrior with enormously broad shoulders and long arms and a great head with big teeth and a flat nose. His long curling hair might once have been fair but it was filthy and hung in greasy strands down to his massive shoulders. A great beard framed his head, long enough to be matted like half-made felt. Upon his head he often wore the pelt of an enormous lion, his ugly face glaring out from beneath its jaws, and the huge mane of the beast hanging over his shoulders. Alkmene had seen a lion once from afar and the men she rode with had wanted to hunt the beast so they chased it into the hills before losing track of it. Gendryon had owned a lion pelt that was worn and moth eaten, the beast slain by his grandfather, but the fur was still magnificent. Though that one was from a fine beast, Leuhon's pelt must have been from the biggest lion that ever walked upon the earth.

In the distance, the remaining *yotunan* argued. Leuhon was not the largest of them but he surely had the loudest voice. He bellowed at the others while jabbing his finger in their hideous faces.

"They are arguing again," Alkmene said to the others in the back of the wagon.

"Good," Henu replied. "If the gods are kind these demons will kill one another and we can all go home."

"The gods have abandoned us," Alkmene said.

"How can you say such a thing?" Henu said, scowling. "You will bring their curses down on us with such words."

"Their curses are already upon us or else why would we be here?" Alkmene said.

"At least keep your voice down. You are upsetting the others."

Alkmene snorted, looking at the hungry, thirsty, miserable women and girls sitting and lying around her. "I hardly think my words will make things worse."

"But if Laonome hears she will be upset."

"She should be upset. She should be terrified. We all should be. We face only misery, servitude, and a terrible death if we stay here."

Henu clicked her tongue. "You do not know what is in store. Remain calm. Be obedient and we shall survive."

"What use is survival without a people?"

Henu reached across and grasped Alkmene's wrist. "We are alive. Your daughter is alive."

Alkmene shook her off. "This is not life."

"Your sons, then. Their *koryos* is back there, out on the plain, free and alive. Let that ease your pain."

"Nothing shall ease my pain but the deaths of my enemies."

Henu scoffed. "Your enemies? They are our lords now. We do not like it but we must accept it."

"How can you live with yourself? It is pathetic. Your brother was a chief, as was your nephew. And now look at you."

Henu spread her arms. "Yes, look at me. Alive, carrying their memories inside me." She brushed her mouth with her fingertips. "The songs of my people will be on my lips again one day when all is settled."

Alkmene pointed at the distant *yotunan*. "They will eat us one by one until we are all dead. If you think there will be any other end to this then you are mad."

Henu scowled. "Run, then, mighty one. You think yourself above us because you were once violated by a god? See how far your blessed womb carries you into freedom. Go on, go now. Why do you not?"

"I shall," Alkmene said, sitting down beside her daughter. "When the time is right."

The great mass of wagons and walking prisoners had completely ground to a halt. Ahead the *yotunan* stood at the edge of the river, still arguing. Alkmene looked at her sleeping daughter and wondered yet again how she could get her to safety. Crossing a great river was no easy feat for an ordinary clan and the bloated procession was many times the size of a single clan. The mass of people reminded her in some ways of her first wedding when her clan and her husband's had come together with all the lesser clans to celebrate the union with days of feasts and rites and hundreds of lesser weddings planned to follow her own. As far as the eye could see in all directions and beyond, the clans had camped in their river valley. Hundreds of horses and cattle were slaughtered for the feasts and young men from this clan or that raced horses in the open spaces between the clans and fought battles with their fists, coming home bloody and laughing, filled with the tales of their struggles. Those days leading up to her wedding were the happiest of her life. Everything was right in the world, everyone was full of joy. Her husband was as wonderful as a man could be. They were cousins, both descended from the great chief Perseyus who had defeated the death serpent in the mountains to the south a hundred years ago and their union was destined to bring unity once more between the clans.

Instead, the Sky Father had come.

On her wedding night, lying entwined in the arms of her new husband as he stroked her hair, the god arrived. Defending

Alkmene, her husband had fought the god and he had died swiftly. So many had died that night as they sought to defend against the intruder but the god had left her with a child in her womb, to grow beside the child planted by her husband.

She thought then of Meghaholkis and Belolukos, off with their *koryos* somewhere. She knew they had likely gone west, seeking cattle and the more settled of the peoples to prey upon. But they would have been sensible enough to have avoided this great procession of evil.

Let them win glory and fame, she thought. She had nothing with which to sacrifice to the mother and so she bit through a piece of skin on the back of her thumb, quietly spitting out the little ball of skin before squeezing a few drops of blood over the side of the wagon to the earth. She had to lift the edge of the cover to do so and leaned out to watch her blood drip onto the track formed by the wagon wheels.

"It is not much," she whispered. "But it is all I have."

"You!" a man snapped as he rode closer. "What are you doing?"

He was one of the followers of Leuhon. One of the assorted men from countless clans who had submitted to the *yotunan* in exchange for their lives. Some were herders and others were warriors but all were cowards who deserved nothing but her contempt.

"It is none of your concern," Alkmene replied and spat at the hooves of his horse.

He stared for a moment, either at her gesture of defiance or at her beauty, faded though it was. Then he sneered. "My concern is whatever I say it is. Get back in your wagon, woman." He looked her up and down, staring at her chest as though he could see through her tunic. "You'll get what's coming to you soon enough."

As he turned his horse with his knees, Alkmene began to utter a retort but strong hands pulled her back. "Mother," Laonome said softly. "Do not."

Letting the man go without another word, Alkmene shook off her daughter's grasp. "Do not restrain me, child," she said. "I am your mother, you are not mine."

Laonome bowed her head. "Yes, mother."

Glaring at the back of the rider, she muttered a curse. "He is nothing but a herder and yet he has power over me, Alkmene of the Kweitos Clan. We have entered a place of evil. It is *wrong*. We must be gone from here, Laonome."

Though there was fear in her eyes, Laonome nodded her head once. "As you say, mother."

She lowered her voice to a whisper. "We must flee before we cross the river. From here, we can ride back to the Don and find a crossing point and be home in just a few days."

"Home?" Laonome said, a catch in her voice.

Alkmene again recalled the battle as the men fought the raiders when Leuhon himself came striding through them with his spear and war club. Ever since she was a girl, Alkmene had been afraid of little in the world. But she was frozen in terror at her first sight of the *yotunan* Leuhon killing her friends, her cousins, and finally her husband. Eventually, she tore herself away from the sight and ran for her daughter. But by then it was too late. Laonome had been in her arms as the raiders gathered them up and threw them into the wagon along with other women. She had been sure she would be violated then and had resolved to die before letting them hurt her or her daughter. Laonome was too young for marriage but that would not stop evil men from abusing her.

The first day, she had expected the young raiders to climb into the wagon to choose their women but they had not come. That first night, already so far from home, she expected them to drag women out to hold down beside the campfires but still they had not come. She imagined then that the women were being kept for the *yotunan* himself, Leuhon and she shook in fear at the thought of it.

"They want to start their own clan," Henu had whispered a night or two later.

"Why do you believe this?" Alkmene had replied in the dark.

"Every demon we have seen has his men, and the men have taken wagons, and herds, and women. What else would they be for?"

To eat, Alkmene had almost replied but she had stopped herself first. *Yotunan* meant devourer. And devour they did. The *yotunan* ate people and drank their blood and even fed people to their closest followers.

They are herding us, she realised that night. They are herding us as we herd beasts. That is all we are to them.

"If we can get away when they cross the river we can get back to our people," Alkmene explained to Laonome in a low voice. "There are other clans who I have not seen here with us or with the other *yotunan*. My cousin Orysthos would take us in. We must reach him."

"I understand," Laonome whispered. "But how?"

Alkmene had been thinking about little else. They would need at least one horse in order to get away fast enough. More would be preferable but taking even one would be a great risk. Many of the horses around her were ridden daily by the servants of the *yotunan* but they were tethered together or hobbled or tethered to sticks driven into the ground overnight. If she could slip through the crowds during the night and avoid the servants, she could, perhaps, get away with Laonome before anyone knew they were gone. If the gods were with them then no one would even notice they were missing.

Best of all would be to take a horse already laden with water and food that the servants led behind them.

"It will take days to get across this river," Alkmene said. "It has been a long time since I have seen it but if we are where I think we are then I do not believe it can be easily crossed just here. To the south the land falls away toward the sea and the river becomes a raging torrent of white water between great rocks and many tributaries fall into it. To cross they will have to go north to where this river meets another and first cross the smaller at an easy ford and then go west along the bank to a place where there are many islands and shallows between them."

"That is why the demons are angry," Henu said, listening closely. "Their guides have failed them. They will devour those men tonight."

"Do you think they misled the *yotunan* purposely?" Laonome whispered, admiration in her voice.

"If they did then they shall die as heroes. Would that we knew their names."

Henu snorted. "Much good it does them or us."

"Yet the clans on the west of the river may be warned enough to flee and escape this onslaught," Laonome said, keen to cling to some sense of heroism.

"Not our people, are they," Henu said. "The men of the west

talk as we do but they are not *us*. They hide behind their stone walls and tend their cattle and know little of the wildness of the plains. Whether those men fall or flee will not bring back my husband or your father, girl." The old woman stopped to sniff before carrying on. "If anything we should wish them to stay in their *woikos* so that our master Leuhon will stop this endless flight and begin to make a new clan in a new place. When that happens we will have to fight for power against the other women but you are strong, Alkmene. You can beat any woman here with your strength and the power of your name and you are young enough yet to be a prize for a good man. You could bear three or four more children if the gods are with you."

Alkmene leaned over and grasped Henu's upper arm, squeezing tightly. "My husband and all our men lie unburied, being eaten even now as carrion and you are planning your next hearth! Be silent, old woman."

Henu pulled back but could not free herself from Alkmene's grasp. "I am merely being practical," she protested. "Someone has to be. And you are acting like some foolish girl. Or worse, like a man!"

"Keep your voice down," Alkmene said and released her. "Your wisdom might have worth if we had been taken by a stronger clan. What else could we do but submit and make the best we could of it? But that is not what this is, Henu. We have been overcome by *evil*. And you know the lore as much as anyone. The gods tell us to reject evil. This is evil."

"The lore says also to know that you are mortal, Alkmene! Do not think yourself godborn because you are descended from one and have given birth to one. You were a renowned woman. Wife to

110

a good man and a fair chief. The gods also tell us to be content with what we have. Cattle die. Kinsmen die. But we must go on."

Alkmene was too angry to speak and so she sat watching the chaos through the gaps in the wagon cover. She would not live as a slave, she could not. No matter what Henu said, or the gods for that matter.

She swore to the Great Mother that before the *yotunan* brought their herds of humans and beasts across the river she would flee.

Or she would die trying.

9

Wolves of Kolnos

THE DAWN FOUND HOLKIS alone on the endless plain, riding hard for the river valley that was once his home. If he could make it there, he might be able to escape any pursuer in the trees of the woodlands or in the rocks and undulations of the shallow slopes. If it came to it, he could cross the freezing river and flee further north across the plains there.

And yet his horse was already tired.

She would be hungry and thirsty, just as he was, and there would come a time when she could run no further and soon after she would not walk either.

The same was true for him.

He could run, he could hide, but then what could he do? There were dead cattle and sheep and pigs on the trail left by the demon clan and though he had already taken and eaten some, they would continue to become corrupted until they were poison to any man that tried them, fit only for beasts and worms. How could he find enough food for the days to come? If he stopped to hunt it could take days to find and kill prey.

Face one problem at a time, boys, Gendryon had told them often enough. Before he worried about what might happen in days to come, he had to first live to see them.

He saw the riders by midday.

Just a glimpse as he crested a rise in the land and looked behind him. Through the shimmering distance, two dark shapes wavered on the horizon before disappearing.

At least two riders pursued him. Two that he had seen but there were likely more. He had killed the warriors of Orysthos and that could not go unpunished if the clan was to retain its honour. He leaned forward and patted the neck of his tired horse and urged her on, promising food and water if she got him to safety.

By the end of the day, he doubted that he would make it. His mare plodded on with her head down and he led her to a hollow on the plain. Cold collected there but at least it was out of the wind and he eased her to the ground and together they lay shivering in the dark, listening to the wind.

The mare woke him in the night, lifting her head and snorting before scrambling to her feet. Holkis jumped up with her but it was too late.

They had found him.

The moon was obscured by cloud. A fine, cold rain fell, whipped along by the wind. He could see nothing but vague shapes. And yet he smelled them and he heard them out there in the night.

Men. Horses. Very close.

Without a spear or even a knife he would have to fight with his bare hands. Wrestling was his favourite form of combat because he was always the biggest and the strongest. But this was no game and the warriors coming for him were not playing. If they caught him they would run him through with their spears before he could grapple with them.

Holkis made to run but they cried out, one in front of him and one behind.

"Stop!" one said, his voice deep.

"We will not harm you," said the other.

"Liars," Holkis shouted, crouching low and ready to pounce. After he spoke he edged away from both voices with one hand on the bridle of his skittish horse. She tossed her head as she walked away and he went with her.

If he tried to fight them in the dark, he would lose. He had no idea how many there were and he could not see them. He meant to leap onto his horse's back and urge her into a blind dash through the night. But would she do it? She was in such a high state she might kick and throw him or she might not run at all. He had no choice.

Jumping up, he threw himself across her back, leaned forward and found himself being pulled right off again. Strong hands gripped his arms and shoulders to hold him down against the cold earth. It was so dark that he could hardly see the face of the man who held him and then another figure arrived and grabbed his legs, leaning his weight down.

Holkis writhed and growled but they were stronger than any man he had ever wrestled before and he could hardly do anything against their power.

"We are not," the man over his face grunted, "your enemies."

Holkis continued to struggle and got an arm free to strike up at the man. Though he was on his back there was enough strength in the blow to hurt the man and to drive him away. Holkis dragged his feet away from the other man and jumped up to scramble away. Before taking two full strides he was brought down again and their fingers dug into his flesh as they gripped tightly. How could they even see him, he wondered?

"We are sworn to Kolnos," one said through gritted teeth. "He bids us bring you to him."

Holkis thought of the enormous figure dressed in wolf skins back at the clan. The figure who had looked at him with a single piercing blue eye. He had had two men with him.

We are sworn to Kolnos. All boys in a *koryos* were sworn to Kolnos. Something told him that was not what these men meant.

His strength already fading, he slowed his struggle and allowed himself to be held down. All three of them breathed hard.

"Let me go," Holkis said.

They did not move, seemingly unsure if they could trust him.

"I swear I shall not flee," he said.

"You have spoken the words," the voice said. "And so you are bound by them."

With that they let him up and he squinted into the darkness.

"You say you are bound to Kolnos," Holkis said, still breathing heavily. "What do you mean?"

"The wolf god is our master," one of them said. "You are not to be harmed, he told us. But you are to return so that the god Kolnos might speak with you."

Holkis rubbed his face. "How can I believe what you say? I do not know you. You could be anyone."

"We could have killed you," the other one said. "By arrow, axe, or blade. But we did not."

Holkis nodded. "My mare has fled."

One of the shadow men rustled. "She is just there by our horses. I will retrieve her." Footsteps led away.

Holkis peered into the darkness. "You can see? How is it that you can see anything?"

The remaining man grunted. "We are given a taste of the power of Kolnos."

Holkis did not understand and said nothing about that. "What happens now?"

"Kolnos wishes to speak with you. He waits with the clan of Orysthos. It will be dawn soon enough and then we will ride to him. That is what will happen."

He appeared to be waiting for Holkis to speak. "Kolnos himself wishes to speak to me. But Orysthos said he would kill me today. If I go, won't I be killed?"

"Orysthos is a chief."

Holkis waited for the man to say more. When he did not, Holkis nodded. "That's right."

"Kolnos is a god."

"Then you had better take me back to Kolnos."

"As you say, godborn," the man said and seemed to bow his head.

Holkis paused. "Do you have anything to eat?"

"I have food and water, godborn. Why do you not sit, eat, drink, and rest. My brother and I will watch over you until morning."

"Well, I don't need..." Holkis began but the man pressed a few strips of horse meat into his hand and gave him a water skin. Holkis sat on the ground and ate and drank, chewing and drinking furiously. This might be the last meal I ever eat, he thought as he chewed. I wish I had some mead.

When he was finished he looked at the sky. It was still full dark and the moon was faint behind the drifting cloud. "Are you sure I can sleep?"

"Rest, godborn. Tomorrow we will ride hard."

Slowly, Holkis lay on the cold earth and wrapped his furs around him.

It seemed he had hardly closed his eyes but when he opened them again the dawn was approaching. The men stood before him, looking down. Holkis jumped up, rubbing sleep from his eyes. It was light enough to see them properly and he was surprised to see how similar they looked. They were both tall and broad shouldered but lean. Their dark hair was long and their beards were thick and unshorn. Around their shoulders the wolf skins were thick and beautiful. The beasts must have been enormous before they were slain and skinned. The three horses stood ready behind them.

"You awaken, godborn," one man said, smiling.

He did not like the way they kept calling him that. "My name is Holkis."

"I am Gera and this is my brother Prek."

He looked between them. "Are you true brothers?"

Gera laughed. "Brothers of the blood, godborn."

Prek stared and did not speak or smile.

Holkis stretched his back and eyed the horses. "You wish to depart?"

With a scoff Prek mounted his horse and began riding away.

Gera smiled. "You slept late, godborn. Make yourself ready for a swift ride. The god awaits."

When he mounted his horse, Holkis was tempted to ride away once more. Take his chances at escape. But the horses of the servants of Kolnos were stronger than his stolen mare and he knew it would be futile. Besides, they served Kolnos himself. And Kolnos wanted Holkis. With a glance at the brightening sky, he rode after Gera.

They rode hard. The brothers were magnificent riders. As good as any he had ever seen and their horses were well suited to the speed as both animals had long legs and they seemed able to run forever without slowing or tiring. All that held them back was Holkis' mare. And Holkis' backside and thighs ached and chafed from his ride the day before. He had been a wolf so long it was like his body had forgotten how to ride.

It was about high sun when Gera slowed, dropped back and rode beside him. Prek stayed far ahead but always in sight.

"How do you fare, godborn?" Gera asked, smiling. "Do you need a rest?"

Holkis shook his head. "I am well."

Gera laughed. "You do not look well. You ride as if you wish to keep your buttocks from the horse's back. You ride like a man who has fouled himself!"

Although Gera seemed to find this highly amusing, Holkis scowled. "I am unused to riding such poor horses."

"Ah!" Gera said, nodding sagely. "And tell me, godborn, have you ever heard the wisdom that a bad rider always blames his horse?"

"I am out of practice, that is all," Holkis said. "I do not need a rest."

"Good!" Gera smiled, looking Holkis up and down. "Tell me, godborn, do you heal faster than mortal men?"

Holkis looked over at him. "I do."

This seemed to please Gera. "That is good. Very good."

"Why do you ask?"

Shrugging, Gera gestured with a hand as if to indicate the entirety of the plain before and around them. "Only my own curiosity. Some godborn have more power than others. I wonder how much you were blessed with."

"You know other godborn?"

"*Know* them? No, I would not say so. The godborn are rare indeed. Which is why it is such an honour to ride with you."

Holkis did not know what to say to that. His own clan had treated him always with a wariness bordering on distrust and he had always longed to be like Belolukos or one of the others.

"Do you know what happened to my brother?"

Gera glanced sharply at him. "Your brother?"

"My half-brother, Bel. Belolukos. Chief Orysthos captured him and the rest of my *koryos*. Or so he said. Did you see them when you came into the clan?"

Gera shook his head. "I know nothing of that. We had hardly arrived when your escape was discovered." He laughed. "That chief was angry, godborn. Truly, you have something of the god in you. Untameable, yes?"

"I don't know about that."

Snorting, Gera peered at him. "You are certain you do not need a rest?"

"I do not."

"Then let us ride. Kolnos awaits!"

It was late in the day when they reached the clan which was encamped in the same place. The herders were bringing the cattle back from further out so they could be guarded through the night. Boys whipped the cows with their long thin sticks and dogs ran this way and that. Older herders rode at the rear, overseeing the roundup and talking together in groups. As Holkis and the two wolves of Kolnos came amongst them they turned and watched their passage.

When they approached the tents, warriors came out to meet them. A dozen riders with spears in hand. Holkis thought that he would be grabbed and bound once more and yet they simply formed up around him and the wolves of Kolnos as they came in amongst the tents. The people of the clan stopped to watch as he made his way through them, falling silent and staring grimly.

Holkis looked down at them and called out to one as he passed. "Where is my brother? The boys of my *koryos?*"

The faces stared at him.

"Are they alive?"

None replied.

He called out to a herder scraping at a skin in a frame but the man simply gawped and said nothing as Holkis rode by. On they rode with the dozen warriors of Orysthos' *tauta*, deeper into the camp and between the maze of tents.

"What is going to happen?" Holkis asked Gera.

"The well-born of the clans do honour to Kolnos when he is amongst them." He raised a hand and pointed at the chief's tent, taller and wider than the others in the middle of the camp. "The god will be at the centre. Come."

When they came close the warriors stopped and dismounted.

They stepped back with their horses on both sides, leaving a path toward the tent. The wolves of Kolnos dismounted and looked at Holkis. His throat was dry. Swallowing his nerves, he slid off his mare's back and stretched his sore muscles. When he walked to Gera and Prek they turned and escorted him through the warriors toward the entrance to the chief's tent. Behind the warriors, children and women craned their necks to see. He heard their whispered voices. *Godborn*, they said. And *Kolnos*. Holkis, his thighs chafed terribly from the riding, tried his best to walk with dignity.

"You will wait," Gera said and ducked inside while Holkis stood outside beside the silent Prek with the people watching them warily.

"Where are my friends?" Holkis asked the nearest warrior. "Do you know? Are they alive?"

All he got was a stare back but someone else answered, unseen behind the warriors and their horses. "They live, son. They are well."

"Where are they?" he asked.

He saw a hand pointing. "They are there, on the eastern edge of the camp by the herders."

"And the girl?" he asked, taking a step forward so he could see the speaker. He was a grey haired elder. Once a warrior. "The girl called Helhena, where is she?"

The man shrugged. "Probably someone claimed her by now. Don't know. Not me."

Holkis nodded his thanks just as the tent flap was thrown back and Geru gestured him inside. He stepped carefully across the raised threshold and was blinded by the sudden darkness. As he stepped further inside, Geru and Prek stayed behind him, taking up positions either side of the entrance.

The fire in the centre burned low. It was a luxurious tent, as befitted a great chief. The walls were thick felt and the ground was covered with hides, furs, and woven woollen fabrics layered two or three deep around the fire where the chief would sit with his household.

Orysthos was there. But Holkis barely registered the chief who had sentenced him to death.

For opposite the door in the place of honour sat a vast figure.

The wolf god, lord of wisdom and song.

Kolnos.

1 0

The Wolf God

ALTHOUGH HE WAS A HUGE figure, Kolnos was surprisingly slim, with long arms and legs, and his hood and cloak were wolf fur, like those worn by a *koryos*, and his tunic and trousers beneath were a pale grey wool. Kolnos had grey hair and a long grey beard that reached almost to his belly but the skin beneath hardly bore a wrinkle and it was unblemished. Indeed, it almost glowed with good health and youthful vigour. The only fault to be found was his missing eye.

The god sat on the chief's low stool while Orysthos sat on the furs to his right, in the guest-place in his own tent. But that was fitting for all men served Kolnos, even chiefs.

Kolnos was chewing on a roasted leg of mutton. The juices ran from his mouth down his beard and he cuffed his lips, burped, sighed, and took another huge bite before chewing slowly and looking at Holkis with his single bright eye.

It was astonishing to Holkis that the immortal Kolnos was so very much like a man. He ate and breathed, he reeked of sweat and of horses.

Some said that when they descended the mountains to come to the forests and plains of earth the gods took on mortal form as a man might wear a cloak and was otherwise a being of shining spirit. But others claimed the gods were mighty giants who could either see beyond every horizon at once and climb with ease above the sky or shrink themselves to the height of a man as they needed. Whatever was the right of it, Holkis found it difficult to imagine the stinking, belching figure before him transforming into a shining spirit of the night and of the wolf and filling the hearts of men as they sang the songs of their ancestors.

But he supposed it had to be true.

The god picked at a piece of flesh in his teeth, rolled it between his fingers and flicked it into the fire. His hands were huge and strong and looked capable of crushing a man's skull. The god narrowed his eye and when he spoke it was a low rumble.

"This boy is the one who killed your warriors?" Kolnos said, gesturing with the mutton.

"Yes, lord," Orysthos said, glaring at Holkis. "Four of them."

Kolnos grunted. "He is no more than a sapling."

Holkis stared between them. "I am almost a man," he said, irritated suddenly by their scrutiny, by their dismissal of his prowess in battle.

Orysthos jerked upright and scowled. "How dare you speak before the god has given you leave to do so! My deepest apologies, lord. He is a boy and knows no better."

Kolnos sat watching Holkis without moving for a long moment

before slowly stroking his long grey beard. "Leave us," he said, finally and slowly turned to fix Orysthos with his eye.

"Lord?" the chief said before getting to his feet and bowing to the seated god. As he strode out of his tent, he glared at Holkis.

"Sit," Kolnos said, holding out a hand to the place vacated by Orysthos.

Feeling weak at the presence of the god, he crossed the tent on shaking legs to sit beside him. Holkis had grown taller than the tallest man of his clan in the previous year and had not felt small since he was a boy. But Kolnos made him feel small.

"You ran from me," Kolnos said at last, tossing the leg of mutton onto a wooden platter beside the hearth.

"No, lord," he replied, causing the god's eyebrows to fall into a scowl and so he went swiftly on. "I do not mean to disagree with you, lord, only that I did not run from you so much as run from Orysthos."

"From his punishment, you mean."

Holkis' heart sank. "Yes, lord. But also I had to go to find my mother."

"Find her? You have lost her?"

"Taken, lord. She was taken by the... by the demons."

Kolnos stroked his beard as he regarded Holkis. "Do you believe your impending punishment to be unjust?"

Fighting a rising panic, he searched for what to say. What was the proper answer? He found himself suddenly unable to remember the lore on such matters but he thought it was probably that justice should be served and not avoided.

"If what I did was wrong, I will admit that I did wrong before men. But the men that attacked me were trying to kill me and I merely defended my own life. As for the punishment, perhaps that is just but it does not feel so to me. And I would avoid death, at least for now. I cannot allow myself to die until I have saved my mother and her daughter, my half-sister Laonome."

The corners of Kolnos' eyes wrinkled as he looked at him. "Orysthos thinks you are a fool."

Anger flared up in Holkis but he fought it down. "He does not know me."

Kolnos lifted his chin a little, still regarding him with that bright eye. "I heard you fought like a great warrior."

"Who told you that, lord?"

Kolnos smiled. "Your insolence is remarkable. Are you not afraid of me, boy?"

"I suppose I am. But I suppose also that I am to be killed now for my crime. What is the use in fear, now?"

Kolnos' smile widened. "You think death is the worst thing?"

"No," Holkis admitted. "My clan is dead. Only my brother and my *koryos* live, so I am told, at least. My mother and sister suffer terribly now. To think of their suffering is to suffer myself and to know that I have failed to protect them is the worst of it all."

"Orysthos was wrong about you, I think. You speak well. Like a man beyond your years. Who taught you to think? To speak thus?"

"My father. The men of the clan. More than that, I cannot say."

"You are angry. Deeply angry. There is a rage in you, boy. A fire." Kolnos lifted a long arm and pointed a massive finger at Holkis' chest. "A great fire, here. The fire of the gods, perhaps." Kolnos tilted his head. "You think to hide it but you can hide nothing from me."

"No, lord."

"Do you know why I am here?"

"No, lord."

Kolnos seemed amused. "Guess."

"The demons, lord?"

"They are not demons but *yotunan*. You know what the *yotunan* are?"

"Monsters, lord. Great beasts who warred against the gods long ago. Defeated and banished to the Vale of Tartaros, beyond the Sacred Mountain."

"You learned the lore well enough, I see. But they are not beasts, though they might be mistaken for them." Kolnos took a deep breath. "They are abominations, Holkis. Twisted, hideous things who seek only to destroy. They are devourers. They drink the blood and eat the flesh of men. For years beyond counting they have been held in Tartaros where they could not wreak their disorder against the gods and men. But these twelve contrived to escape their bonds and together they have carved a great gash into the heart of the earth, slaughtering clan after clan in their desperate rush for freedom."

"Twelve of them, lord? Who are they?"

Sighing, Kolnos looked at the smouldering fire. "The twelve worst *yotunan* that ever lived. There is nothing in their hearts but hatred. Vile creatures, every one of them. They are ancient and they are evil."

"If they are so evil, why were they not killed?"

The god grunted. "They should have been. Long ago. But they were not and now they are free they mean to unmake the world. It is time that they died."

"I am glad, lord."

Kolnos raised his eyebrows. "And do you know to where they go?"

"South and west, lord."

"Destroying all in their path, they stop for almost nothing. Soon, if they carry on this path, they will reach the sea."

"What will happen then?" Holkis asked, imagining the great mass of monsters and their captives charging right on into the depths.

Kolnos shrugged. "I do not know."

"How do you not know? You are a god."

Kolnos frowned and he leaned forward. "I might have killed any other mortal for speaking to me as you just did." He sat up. "It is true that I know a great deal. I know all that happens on the plains. My eye sees far and wide." Holkis nodded, for everyone knew that. "But my eye does not see what has not yet come to pass."

"Seers do," Holkis said. "Seers and seeresses."

"It astonishes me that you could have learnt so much about fighting in your short life and yet have never learned to control your tongue."

He bowed his head. "I beg your forgiveness, lord."

"You are godborn." The god shrugged. "If you were not, I would not be speaking to you at all and your wild tongue would not be unleashed. Seers do not see the future, boy, no matter what they tell you. They read the signs and these signs tell them what may or may not happen." Kolnos waved a massive hand. "Any fool can do this. But even I cannot see into what will be and see for certain what will come to pass. But we may consider it, may we not? Ponder what is to occur, as you might think before you raid another clan for its pork and its mead. Do you understand?"

130

"I think so."

"Then I will tell you what might happen. The *yotunan* will fight one another."

"Why would they do that? They are raiding together."

"Not raiding. Fleeing. They are not a clan and not a raiding band. They fled together for safety and have stayed together right across the plains and across the vales and the rivers. But when they realise that they are free, they will not stay together much longer."

Holkis did not understand. "When they realise they are free? They do not know it now?"

"They fear your father and the other gods. Fear us catching them before they get away." Kolnos watched him closely. "The speed of their flight shows this." He breathed in, deeply. "I can smell their fear in it. And yet surely some of them will already start to feel as though they have travelled beyond the realms of the gods."

"But all the earth is the realm of the gods."

Kolnos snorted. "Of one god or another, perhaps. Some mightier than others."

"But you are pursuing them, are you not? You mean to stop them. To return them to Tartaros."

Kolnos took a slow breath and picked at something in his teeth with a massive finger. "In time, perhaps."

Holkis was confused. "In time?"

"They are even now passing beyond my lands and my people, into the lands of other gods and other peoples. One might say my duty is complete. And yet, I cannot abide such evil being free in the world. Which is why I would send you."

Holkis blinked. "Send me?"

"We create order. We are the enemies of chaos."

"We?"

"The gods."

"Then I do not understand what you mean when you say you will send me?"

"You are half a god, are you not?"

"I am mortal."

"You are godborn. Half a man. Half a god."

Holkis shook his head. "I am not even a man yet, lord. My *koryos*... we have not completed the rite."

"Ah, yes. The rite." Kolnos stroked his long beard. "Your *koryos* acted always with honour. And alone you defeated warriors of this clan with your spear. You have won your maturity, Holkis. I proclaim it."

Holkis shook his head. None of it was how it was supposed to be. He had expected, all his life he had *known*, he would be welcomed into the clan by the men all together, the *tauta* surrounding him and his brothers of the *koryos*. There would be sacrifices and feasting and wrestling and the racing of horses for prizes, all in the name of Kolnos, the wolf god.

"I am a man, lord?"

"Have I not said so?"

"You have, lord. But a man has a clan. What is my clan?"

Kolnos sighed and raised his eye to the roof of the tent. "One cannot be a man without a people, that is true." He looked at Holkis. "But you are godborn. You shall be a clan unto yourself and raise your clan around you." He clapped his enormous hands. "But as a man, you must have a man's name."

Kolnos stood, his head bowed beneath the roof of the tent. "Come with me."

132

One stride carried the god across the hearth and another to the entrance. Gera threw back the flap and Kolnos went outside. Perk glared at Holkis and jabbed a finger at the opening. Quickly, Holkis followed the god out of the tent to find Orysthos and the warriors of the tribe gathered. It was dusk now. The conversations and movement amongst them stopped when they turned to see Kolnos standing before them.

The wolf god drew Holkis before him with a massive hand upon his shoulder until they stood face to face at arm's length. Kolnos was more than a head taller than Holkis. Never had he seen someone so tall, so powerful.

Kolnos fixed Holkis in place with the hand on his shoulder and with the look in his eye. When he spoke, he raised his deep voice, projecting it so that the gathered lords of the clan could hear it clearly. "Here stands Holkis, son of the Sky Father and the mortal Alkmene. You served your clan with honour. You learned the lore of your people, carried out your duties and never transgressed. Your *koryos* travelled the plains, raided, and strengthened your clan. You obeyed your *koryonos*. The ancestors of your clan filled you and your spear-brothers. But now your *koryos* is over. And I have heard how you fought the men of this clan with the strength beyond your years, beyond the thickness of your arms, beyond the will of a mortal. You are a boy no longer. You are Holkis no longer. From this day on you shall be a man. You are *he whose spear strikes with mighty strength*. And so you shall be known as Herkuhlos."

Holkis nodded, fighting back tears. Herkuhlos. He was Herkuhlos. The name meant *strong spear*.

"Give me your hand, Herkuhlos" Kolnos said.

Holkis, now Herkuhlos, raised a shaking arm that Kolnos grasped. Drawing from his belt a great bronze dagger, he drew it across the open palm of Herkuhlos and watched the blood pour forth. The god gripped the mortal's hand tight as the blood flowed, wiping it away with a swipe of the thumb and pursing his lips.

The watching men muttered amongst themselves until Orysthos silenced them with a look.

"What are you doing?" Herkuhlos said softly.

Kolnos said nothing as he wiped the blood away once more. The wound was already healing. The blood had stopped flowing and the cut beginning to knit together. Before nightfall it would be completely healed.

"You truly are godborn," Kolnos said softly with a quick smile. He turned to the watching men and raised the bloody fist in his own. "I show you this man who is called Herkuhlos."

The men knew the proper response and as one they called out in turn, raising their own fists, their spears, their war axes. "We see this man, Herkuhlos!"

"I tell you his name, which is Herkuhlos."

The *tauta* cried out. "We hear his name, Herkuhlos!"

Kolnos nodded and spoke. "May his deeds bring to his name undying glory."

Even Orysthos roared with the others. "Strive for undying glory, Herkuhlos!"

All eyes turned to him and he swallowed before raising his own voice. At first he spoke softly, his voice shaking but as he spoke his voice grew to a shout. "See me and hear my name. By my deeds I shall win undying glory. I am Herkuhlos."

They chanted his name three times and Kolnos clapped him on

the shoulder, as any mortal uncle might, although there was such weight behind it that Herkuhlos staggered a half step to the side. "You are now a man. Tonight, you will eat and drink and rest. Tomorrow, you will go after the *yotunan*."

"With your permission, lord, I will take my brothers of the *koryos* with me."

Kolnos stared. "You do not have my permission. They will certainly die if they accompany you."

Herkuhlos began to argue but Orysthos approached, bowed his head to Kolnos and smiled. "My cousin is now a man. A glorious day. Lord... is he now a man of my clan?"

Kolnos laughed a deep laugh. "No, Orysthos! He is godborn and you are mortal. He will not serve you."

The chief's face fell. "I am descended from the great Perseyus, lord."

Kolnos raised his eyebrows. "So are half the chiefs of the plains, Orysthos. Do not mistake my meaning. Herkuhlos would do well to make such a strong clan as this. But his path lies elsewhere. Have your best horses prepared."

"My best?" Orysthos said, swallowing.

"Your best ten, shall we say. No, twenty. Can you handle twenty horses alone, Herkuhlos?" Kolnos looked at him strangely, as if there was more to what he was saying.

"If there is a lead mare for the others to follow."

"Twenty it is, then. And your fiercest young stallion for Herkuhlos to ride when he reaches the *yotunan*. You will need a mount that does not balk at the stench of blood. See them well provisioned, Orysthos. Each horse must carry skins of water and also food enough so that all together Herkuhlos might ride for half a year."

"Half a year!" Orysthos exclaimed.

Kolnos frowned. "You have such provisions, surely? Then see it done and see it done immediately. Your godborn cousin will leave before dawn graces us with her light."

Bowing once, Orysthos turned and strode away after throwing a glare at Herkuhlos.

"Lord, I still do not understand what you wish me to do."

"You will swear an oath to me."

"An oath, lord?"

"An oath to destroy the *yotunan*."

"How am I meant to do that, lord?"

"Follow the *yotunan* but do not fight them yet. If you attempt to free your mother and your sister they will catch you and they will kill you. Even the least of them would best you with ease."

"So how am I to destroy them, lord?"

"You are young, Herkuhlos. You will grow in strength as the years pass. There is no rush to fulfil your oath. I am certain that the *yotunan* will separate from one another. It is that or they will destroy each other, fulfilling your oath for you." Kolnos smiled. "Why not spend a few years as a lone wanderer? You can watch the *yotunan* from afar, learning to which land each of them goes. One day, you can return to the plains and find me. Perhaps then we shall destroy them together."

Herkuhlos was confused. "Spend years as a lone wanderer? How many years?"

"However many it takes. One year or ten years." Kolnos shrugged. "Or a hundred."

"A hundred?"

136

"If you are not slain in battle you will live a hundred years at least, perhaps a thousand. You are godborn, Herkuhlos."

Herkuhlos shook his head. "And I must go alone?"

"Would you disobey a god, son?" Kolnos looked closely at Herkuhlos with his shining blue eye, as if trying to see through his flesh and into the depths of his spirit.

Herkuhlos looked away. "No, lord."

"Then speak your oath, Herkuhlos."

"Why me?" Herkuhlos looked around. "Why can you not send Geru and Prek?"

Kolnos' eye narrowed. "My wolves are not godborn, Herkuhlos. You have a strength beyond that of mortal men."

"What about the gods, then? Why do you not pursue them yourself?"

"I told you. They will pass beyond the plains. Beyond my realm."

"What of my father, then? His realm is all the world, is it not? Why does he not return them to their captivity? Why does he not destroy them?"

Kolnos sighed. "Your father created you, Herkuhlos. Why do you think he took your mother? Put you in her belly?"

"I don't know."

"To serve him, Herkuhlos. To serve the gods. To bring order to the earth. Why does your father not destroy them? He destroys them through you."

Herkuhlos stared at Kolnos, a knot forming in his guts. "That is why? That is my purpose?"

"Of course." Kolnos frowned. "Your mother is descended from Perseyus. Do you know his song?"

Herkuhlos nodded. "He was the Chief of Chiefs for fifty years. He defeated a hundred clans and died in battle. I have seen his burial mound with my own eyes."

"Before all that. You know the tale of the serpent demon, no?"

"I do. He travelled south to the mountains between the seas and there slew the serpent demon."

"She was a *yotunan*, Herkuhlos. A *yotunan* escaped from Tartaros who fled beyond our realm and beyond our reach. Or so she thought. But I sent your ancestor the godborn Perseyus, son of the Sky Father, to slay her. He took the oath. And you will take it also."

"He had to slay one *yotunan*. You would have me slay a dozen."

"Yes."

"You think I can do it?"

"You will do it," Kolnos said, "or die trying. You seek undying glory, Herkuhlos? This is your path. Now you must walk it."

"What then is my oath?"

"You know your oath."

Herkuhlos swallowed. "I, Herkuhlos, swear before Kolnos and in sight of my father the daylight sky that I will slay the *yotunan* escaped from Tartaros. And I will save my mother Alkmene and my sister Laonome."

Kolnos grunted and smiled at this last addition to the oath. "Good. Very good. Glory awaits, Herkuhlos but go fill your belly, now. Your new life begins at dawn."

Herkuhlos bowed his head and made his way through the camp. He felt a powerful exhilaration mixed with a terrible fear. He sensed that Kolnos had manipulated him into swearing an impossible oath and yet he was thrilled that the god had thought him worthy of it.

If he succeeded in slaying just one *yotunan* then his glory would be like that of the famed Perseyus. For the first time in his life he felt like he had a clear purpose. A path.

Kolnos had said he would have to walk that path alone. To travel with his spear-brothers would mean their deaths and so he was not to take them with him when he went after the *yotunan*.

But he knew that he could not leave without speaking to them. He had to find Belolukos and the others.

And he would ask them to disobey a god.

11

Defiance

HERKUHLOS WATCHED FROM the shadows as a servant carried a basket of dried meat and fresh cheese into the tent before emerging empty handed a short while later. As she walked away he bent low and walked swiftly across the space between the tents and ducked inside the tent. He cast his eye over the seated figures lounging around the hearth.

"My brothers," he said, smiling.

Belolukos jumped to his feet, a strip of dried horse meat in his fist. "Holkis!"

The others stood, smiling and crowding him to pat his back and grasp his hands. "I tried to find you earlier, brothers, but I could not."

Nodding, Belolukos looked him up and down. "Orysthos told me that he freed you."

Herkuhlos snorted. "Kolnos freed me."

Kasos gasped. "You saw him? We heard he was here and Dhomyos said he saw him but..."

"I did see him," Dhomyos said. "He was even taller than you, Holkis."

"My name is Herkuhlos now."

Belolukos stared. "You were *named?*"

"It was not the proper rite. Not even close. It was rushed and nothing like it should have been. But Kolnos himself performed it." He shrugged.

Belolukos, scowling, took a step back. "If you are mighty enough to converse with Kolnos, why have you lowered yourself to speak with us?"

Herkuhlos looked over his shoulder and lowered his voice. "Kolnos sends me after the *yotunan*." He met the eyes of each of them in turn. "The demons."

Stepping closer once more, Belolukos grasped his arm. "You go to free mother?"

"Kolnos says I should not try but I will."

"You go against the will of the god?"

"The gods are to be obeyed but we are not their slaves," Herkuhlos said. "He said I might attempt it but if even one of the *yotunan* catches me I would be killed."

Belolukos scoffed. "And yet you think to do it anyway."

"We cannot leave mother and Laonome to the *yotunan*."

"They may already be dead," Belolukos said.

The others hissed and muttered, some making signs to ward against evil.

"Perhaps. But if they are not, we shall have a better chance of finding them if we go together."

Belolukos stared. "Kolnos sends me also?"

Herkuhlos hesitated. "The god said I am to go alone."

Belolukos relaxed. "So you go and we stay. Then you came to say farewell. I understand."

"I would have you come." Herkuhlos looked around. "All of you, I would have you all at my side. We remain sworn to one another. My rite alone has not changed that."

"They are all sworn to *me*," Belolukos said, approaching. "As are you, brother."

"I am sworn to Kolnos now, not to you, Bel. I do not understand any of this, you know. None of this is as it should be. All I know is, our mother and our sister need us. We agreed before to go after them and nothing has changed."

Some of them nodded their heads in agreement but not all. And Belolukos was the least convinced of all.

"Orysthos has offered us a place in his clan. I have accepted."

Herkuhlos had heard that very thing from the chief and yet it still surprised him to hear his brother say it. "You cannot accept. You would be forever in his debt. Bel, you would have been chief of our clan and now you will be almost as low as a herder."

"No." Belolukos frowned. "No, I shall prove my worth. Besides, he is my cousin on mother's side. And my father's."

"And by accepting him as your lord he keeps you where he can control you."

"What do you mean?"

"Bel, my brother, if these monsters had not destroyed our people, you would have become our chief. In ten years you might have brought our clan against this one, you might have challenged Orysthos for power."

"I still can. I will do so. I will prove my worth by my deeds and then I shall challenge him."

Herkuhlos could see it, even if his brother could not. "He will never allow you to become powerful. He will kill you long before then."

"Not if I am loyal."

"Even then. You know how it is done, Bel! We have all heard sung the tales of our ancestors and their struggles with their rivals. What would you do, if you were chief and a strong young man fell into your hands? A cousin with the same mighty ancestors as you, the same glorious blood. You know what you would do."

Belolukos fell silent. The others looked down, embarrassed.

"But I have already accepted," Belolukos said quietly.

"You swore an oath?" Herkuhlos asked. "Sworn in blood?"

"No but I spoke it. I said I would gladly join his clan. As would all of my *koryos*."

Herkuhlos shook his head. "It was not sworn in blood, it means nothing. Throw it off and come with me! Kolnos has commanded our cousin to prepare twenty of his finest horses. Twenty! If I know our cousin they will not be his finest. He thinks nothing of defying the god, I can see it in his eyes. But they should serve. One for each of us with a few spare. Orysthos' people are preparing food enough for me alone and so we must provision properly."

"When?"

"Now! Tonight, this very moment. They expect us to rise with dawn and so we must be gone before then. Brothers, we must steal all we can find. Food, water, furs, blankets, baskets, skins, and weapons. Spears, javelins, bows, arrows, axes, maces, and daggers of copper and bronze if you can."

144

They stared at him.

"We shall be caught," Wedhris said.

Sentos nodded. "They will kill us."

Herkuhlos spread his arms and lowered his voice. "Have we not done this very thing for months? We have crept by packs of dogs and dozing boys to take these very things from a dozen clans this last year. By Kolnos, have we not done it every summer for seven or eight years before this one? Kasos, your uncle took you on a raid when you had but seven years and you stole a bag of bridles and bits from the lap of a sleeping girl, did you not?"

Kasos smiled. "The gods gave me many talents."

"We shall do this because we must. Kasos, you will find where the horses are being prepared. Choose two others to help you and be sure they are loaded with the supplies before we take them. Dhomyos, you and three others find all the food you can. Dried horse meat is best. Sentos, see if you and Wedhris can find blankets and furs and extra clothing. Bel and I will find weapons. We meet back here before dawn. Kasos, send someone back here to lead us to the horses." He looked at them all. "Now, we will not find everything that we need. That is well. All that matters is we get away together, leaving not one of us behind. Come then. Let it be done."

They crept out in groups of two or three and spread out through the tents in the darkness. The wind whipped the ropes and skins of the tents and the noises hid the sounds that the young men made.

"Are they not looking for you?" Belolukos whispered in Herkuhlos' ear as they crouched outside the tents of the chief and his men. Three women stood talking about another woman who was not there and it seemed as though they would be standing there all night.

"I told the men following me I was going to eat in the tent of Orysthos' wife. The men outside her tent I asked for directions to the pissing trench. On the way to you some others challenged me and I said I was following the commands of Kolnos and they bowed and let me on my way. Everyone will think me somewhere else."

Belolukos shook his head. "Let us hope our cousin and his men are even more dull-witted than you are, brother."

Herkuhlos smiled. "Let us not hope for too much." As the three women moved off, still criticising another, he elbowed his brother. "Come on."

They slipped inside the tent to find a fire burning low and the rest of it in shadow. They blew the embers into flame and suddenly there was light enough to see by. The lord had two good spears and one bad one and an old bow with six arrows lying beside it.

"A few more empty tents and we shall be the best armed *koryos* there ever was," Herkuhlos said, grinning.

"And a single occupied tent and we shall be dead," Belolukos replied.

"The one north of this one is quiet," one of their brothers whispered and they ducked out, slipping through the shadows like spirits with their stolen weapons in hand.

They came close to being seen a dozen times. A herder stood and listened, frowning in the starlight, not two paces from where they lay shivering face down in the shadow of a tent.

"One more," Herkuhlos whispered, nodding at a large and fine tent. It was beside the tent of Orysthos and so was that of a powerful man. Herkuhlos knew there would be bronze weapons within and he wanted them. But there were so many lords and women and herders coming and going from the chief's tent that it would be a great risk to go so close.

"No!" Belolukos hissed. "We have enough."

"It would be so easy," Herkuhlos muttered.

"You are mad. Listen to your own advice. We have weapons aplenty now. Come, you fool. Come!"

Herkuhlos punched a fist into the hard earth. But he agreed.

When they returned to their tents, they found a few sacks and baskets of food and skins of water and milk but only Sentos, Wedhris, and Dhomyos were there. Dhomyos stepped forward, his head down and clutching at his hands.

"Where are the others?" Herkuhlos asked, fearing the worst.

"They would not stay," Dhomyos muttered. "I tried but they would not."

"Where have they gone?" Herkuhlos asked.

"They wish to stay with Orysthos," Sentos said.

"The sons of pigs!" Belolukos snapped. "I will kill them all."

"It is well, brother," Herkuhlos said.

"They have betrayed me," Belolukos said. "Betrayed us."

"It is done, now," Herkuhlos said. "At least they gathered this for us first."

"They are even now going to Orysthos, I know it," Belolukos said. "We will be caught, now. It is too late."

"No!" Dhomyos said. "They would never. They are hiding until we are gone, that's all. They would never tell. It is simply... they said our clan was destroyed. A new clan was right here, offering us all a place amongst them. But they took most of the food to the horses before they went."

"Where are they now?" Belolukos said. "I will find them and beat the loyalty back into them."

"I don't know," Dhomyos said.

"They did not say where they would hide," Sentos said, spreading his hands wide.

"It matters not," Herkuhlos said. "We must get to the horses."

"Someone comes!" Wedhris hissed from the tent flap.

"Arm yourselves," Herkuhlos said and they backed away from the entrance into the shadows with their spears and daggers levelled. The flap was pushed back and a figure crouched there.

"Are you in here?" a female voice whispered. "Holkis? Bel?"

"Helhena?" Herkuhlos said and went forward to her.

She ducked inside, holding a bow and a quiver of arrows. "You are here, thank Kolnos."

Belolukos scowled. "What is she doing here?"

Herkuhlos waved at him to be quiet. "Helhena, why are you here? How did you find me?"

"I had to find you," she said, breathlessly. "Those two huge men who serve the god are looking for you."

Geru and Prek.

"The wolves of Kolnos? Where are they?"

"I said I had not seen you but they also asked where your brothers were. I said I did not know where they were either but if they ask someone else they could find their way here any moment. They would not say what they wanted with you. That made me afraid for you. And so I came."

"We must go. Thank you. I wish..."

"You are leaving," she said. "To find your mother."

"How do you know?"

"They said I was now a servant of Orysthos' wife." She scoffed. "But I heard the women talking about the food they were preparing for your horses. For your journey." She raised her voice. "Take me with you."

Herkuhlos was surprised. "You cannot come. It is dangerous."

Belolukos stepped forward. "We do not have time for this, girl. We must go!"

"You go," Herkuhlos said. "All of you, go to the horses. I will meet you there soon."

His brother looked at Helhena and then back at him. "Leave her and join us quickly." He turned to Dhomyos and the others. "You know the way to these horses?"

"The westernmost part of the camp," Dhomyos said, pointing.

With a final glare, Belolukos ducked outside and the others went after him, laden with the weapons, food, waterskin, and furs.

"Helhena," Herkuhlos said. "Please understand. I do not want to leave you here but I must. The plains are no place for a girl."

"I have this bow," she replied, holding it up. "And these arrows. Almost twenty of them."

"That is not... you cannot come. We might all die. We probably will, Helhena. Do you want to die?"

She stared at him. "I will not live here with these people. Not while my own might yet live. Is that not why you go? To find your people?"

"But I am a man. You have a place here. You should not die."

Helhena poked him with her bow. "My mother went raiding at my age. She taught me the bow and I am strong enough to use it."

"Our mother also went on raids before she married. But this is no raid."

"What is it then?"

Herkuhlos sighed because he had no name for it. "I have sworn an oath. I am bound by it. You are not and so you should stay where you are safe."

She stared at him. "I heard them calling you godborn. It is true, is it not?" She stepped closer, looking up at him. "I knew you were special. I knew you would keep me safe."

He shook his head. "I cannot keep you safe out there, Helhena."

"Will you stop me from riding with you?" She lifted her chin and held his gaze. "Will you tie me up and leave me behind? Unless you do that, I will come."

I must be out of my wits, he thought. "We cannot stand here arguing. If you are determined to die, you may come with me. Come then."

In response, she nodded once, as if confirming to him that he had made the correct decision.

They ducked outside. It was growing quieter but there were still people going from place to place throughout the camp.

"This way," Herkuhlos said and rushed from the tent into the shadows of another. She followed, keeping low and together they ducked into the darkness just as two large men marched down the path. The moon was bright enough to see who it was.

The wolves of Kolnos had come.

"Herkuhlos!" Geru said, throwing back the flap and stepping into the dark tent. When Prek went inside, Herkuhlos pushed Helhena and they ran lightly toward the horses.

Most of the people had retired to their tents and as they passed them they could hear laughter, music, conversation and one noisy bout of lovemaking. Soon, most people would be sleeping and only those on watch would be awake. They went west until they passed the last of the tents and then wove their way beyond the parked wagons. In the moonlight he saw his spear-brothers and the horses and ran toward them.

With grins they greeted each other. Out of all the *koryos*, only his brother, Kasos, Dhomyos, Sentos, and Wedhris had come. It was disappointing but there was nothing to be done now.

"You brought her," Belolukos said, staring at Helhena.

Herkuhlos looked at her. "Well, she insisted."

Belolukos shook his head. "Weak, brother. Weak."

"Perhaps you should stay, Bel," Helhena said. "If you do not wish to ride with me."

He pointed at her. "You should know your place."

"The horses look ready," Herkuhlos said quickly while stepping between them. "Bridles, bits, reins, blankets. Strapped with packs, bags, baskets. All twenty of them."

Belolukos nodded. "This is a strong clan, Holkis. This was nothing for them. And our boys have done well. We have plenty now."

Kasos whistled a warning and jerked his head.

Two herders strolled over with a boy. Herkuhlos eyed them warily and Belolukos pulled a war axe from its straps on his horse and started towards the herders. Hurrying forward, Herkuhlos placed a hand on Belolukos' shoulder and pushed by him, raising an empty hand to the men.

The elder of the men nodded his head. "You ready to ride now, lord?" he asked. "Making ready for an early start, then, is it?"

"That's it," Herkuhlos confirmed, smiling. "We have a long way to go and mean to get to it well before dawn."

"A good decision, lord. Can we help you?"

Herkuhlos smiled. "Generous of you to offer but no, I think I am ready now. My friends here have helped me to prepare the horses."

"Right you are, lord. We go to keep watch from the rise in the north there," the herder nodded and gestured into the darkness. "May the gods ride with you, lord."

"Good fortune to you," Herkuhlos said and waved them away.

"Always poking their fat noses up our horses' backsides," Belolukos muttered. "Poxed herders."

"We should go, now," Herkuhlos said. "Before the wolves of Kolnos find us."

Helhena had chosen a horse and was already mounted. From the way she turned her mare this way and that he knew she rode well and Herkuhlos was as relieved as he was pleased. He knew she was not a liar but some people were mistaken about their own abilities. With a nod to him, she urged her horse away past the others.

"What are you waiting for?" Herkuhlos said to the others. "Get after her!"

Together, they rode and led the laden horses away. When dawn's light touched them they were away to the west and the camp was lost over the horizon.

Herkuhlos found himself thinking of his mother and sister. Would they see the same sunrise that day, he wondered? Or had they already seen their last? He wondered also how much they suffered at the hands of the *yotunan* and the anger inside him grew into a rage. He found himself thinking of the *yotunan* and all those who served them and he pictured his fists bashing their faces in, imagined his spear piercing their throats, and he could almost feel his axe splitting their skulls.

By Kolnos and by my father the god of the sky I swear I shall kill every one of them.

1 2

The Lion

ALKMENE THOUGHT OF little but escape. She had lost count of the days since they had crossed the great river and since then they had crossed the plain heading always west and often edging south. There had been one day when the great mass of warriors, captives, and beasts had ground to a halt and the word was that the *yotunan* were arguing again amongst themselves. One of the demons broke off from the others and went south, taking warriors and a few wagons with them and then the rest carried on across the grassland.

"Told you," Henu crowed when the rumour reached their wagon.

"What did you tell me?" Alkmene replied.

"The *yotunan* wish only to create clans. We should count ourselves fortunate."

"Absurd. The demons war amongst themselves. That hardly

brings us any fortune."

"Count yourself fortunate for the gift of travelling inside a wagon, then."

Alkmene could agree to that, at least. It was bitterly cold. None should be travelling the plains in winter. There was hardly any water and no rain fell. Only tiny flakes of ice driven almost horizontally by the winds. The warriors and herders hunched on the backs of their horses. Those that walked suffered most. Captives not deemed worthy of a place on the wagons like fertile women and girls on the edge of womanhood.

"You are the most fortunate of all," Alkmene said to Henu. "To find yourself in here with us."

"They recognised a woman of importance when they saw me," Henu said, lifting her chin. "The men of my blood were chiefs and warriors of renown."

Alkmene almost smiled. "More likely they did not notice the lines on your face when they threw your big backside in with the rest of us."

Henu crossed her arms across her bosom and turned away, her mouth pressed closed. That was one way to silence her, Alkmene thought.

The wind buffeted the cover above them and the driver crouched lower in his furs. If only I was driving this wagon, she thought, I would turn it around and drive us east. She snorted at her fancy, imagining the oxen lumbering away a few paces before the warriors caught her. That was no way to escape.

Escape.

How could it be done?

At night. It was the only chance she would have of getting away unseen. Imagining herself riding hard through hundreds of warriors made her shudder. She longed for her spear or even her javelins or her bow. But they were weapons for fighting and she could not hope for victory and freedom by fighting. No, she needed something smaller. Something to slit a sleeping man's throat without him stirring or his spear-brothers waking.

She looked through the open rear of the wagon at the herders riding behind her. Even they would have a flint knife. Perhaps she could lure one close and snatch it from him. He would have to be close indeed, however. Alkmene knew well enough that her looks could drive men to idiocy. But taking that path could lead her somewhere she did not wish to go. Ever since their capture she had been afraid of the men taking her, taking Laonome. That they had not was strange. That they had been put into covered wagons rather than forced along on foot was strange. Henu was convinced they were intended as wives in some new demon-led clan but that seemed ludicrous to Alkmene.

The herder riding behind them looked miserable. His eyes were screwed almost shut and he held his furs closed about his throat with one hand as he rode. It was growing dark already and they would stop soon. Water would be passed to them and they would share a few cold mouthfuls each before the skin was dry. If they were lucky there would be strips of dried horsemeat that they would have to chew on laboriously before they fell into a sleep, all huddled together like children in a winter tent. Alkmene longed for the chance to stand, to run, to ride. She longed for warm milk fresh from the cow, for soft white cheese, for roasted meat dripping fat from the fire. For the warmth of a fire and the shelter of her own tent.

Stop it, she told herself. Stop thinking like a child wanting only to satisfy the needs of her body. Freedom was all that mattered. Victory over her captors.

Escape, she thought as she fell into a fitful sleep that night. Great Mother grant me the strength to escape and I shall honour you daily for the remainder of my portion of life.

Escape.

Halfway through the next day, the gods sent her a chance.

Ahead the great procession ground to a halt. Perhaps they had come across some barrier like hills or a river or a dry gorge. Or, more likely, the *yotunan* were warring again.

Whatever the cause, the great masses of men and animals were driven against one another and shouting erupted all around as men roared at those behind them to back away, and those men complained that they could not and turned to shout at those behind, all the way back. A large group of the cattle were bunched up ahead of the wagons and the herders kept them close so that they did not impede the shuffling riders all around them, flicking their whips at the rear and flanks of the cattle that were pressed belly to belly.

"They grow skittish," Alkmene said, watching from her knees through the front opening of the wagon cover. "The herders are driving them out of their wits."

Henu sighed, uninterested. "Herders know herding. You do not."

Alkmene ground her teeth and held her tongue.

Unseen at the head of the herd, something frightened them. Though the herders shouted and pushed up their horses, the cows backed up and backed up until they turned and ran. The ground shook and the wagon wobbled as the herd charged past. The driver jumped from his seat and yanked hard on the harnesses of the pair of oxen to keep them from joining the fleeing herd.

A spear-throw away from their wagon, a brave herder pushed his horse into the path of the panicking animals, shouting and holding out his arms while expertly controlling his horse with his legs. For a moment, it seemed as though he was succeeding and Alkmene was impressed by his courage and his skill.

But then a large cow jumped up and pushed him over. He fell from his horse and his horse likewise fell under the weight of the animals. Soon, they were all gone and the herders chased after them to bring them back.

Alkmene took a deep breath. She knew that the Great Mother had granted her this chance.

"Wait here," Alkmene said to her daughter and slipped out of the rear of the wagon to rush across the churned ground to where the herder had fallen. Her legs, so long unused, almost buckled beneath her but she ground her teeth and forced herself on until she fell to her knees beside the herder.

His horse was dying, its ribs crushed and its skull broken by the hooves of the cattle, and its breathing was laboured. The herder's legs were pinned beneath the fallen animal.

"Help me!" the herder croaked when he saw her approach.

"You were very brave," she said, searching his clothing. At his belt she found a copper dagger and took it from him, sliding it inside her tunic. "The likes of you should not have this."

"What are you doing?" he asked, wheezing as he pushed uselessly at the horse on his legs. "Help me."

She looked around at the men riding after the cattle and at the faces of those nearby, all turned to the chaos.

"All things die," she said to the herder.

Leaning over him she wrapped her hands around his throat and squeezed. He gasped and grabbed her wrists, pulling at her. As a girl she had learnt all the ways to kill and knew that choking a man's throat was not an easy way to do it. Although she was from a line of great warriors, and she had strength enough to shoot a strong bow, she was yet a woman and the injured herder was able to ease her hands up and away from his throat.

Angry, she snatched her hands away, yanked the dagger from inside her tunic and shoved the blade up under his chin. She saw the glint of the blade inside his mouth as she pulled it out. Blood welled from the wound and the herder clutched at his throat, trying to keep the blood in as it gushed over his fingers. He coughed, spraying blood from his mouth and she flinched away as he struggled, coughing once more before the blood filled his throat and his eyes rolled back into his head. Quickly, she wiped the knife on his furs and hid it once more before rushing back to her wagon.

Her heart raced when she sat beside her daughter and the sound of it throbbed in her ears so loudly she was sure all the women in the wagon could hear it. Most turned away from her but Henu glared.

"You better beg the gods that no man saw you," Henu said.

"What will you do with it, mother?" Laonome whispered, her eyes wide. She came to lean against her mother, her fingers brushing the front of her tunic.

Alkmene shook her head and wrapped an arm around her. After a moment she noticed Laonome was picking at the tiny spots of blood the herder had coughed out and she slapped her hand away.

"Never you mind what I will do with it," she said.

Later, when darkness had fallen, she sat stroking Laonome's hair as she looked out through the gaps in the planks.

"I know what you plan," Henu said softly.

"I doubt that," Alkmene replied in a low voice.

"You mean to end your own life," Henu said. "And that of your daughter. Such an act would be evil."

"And submitting her to life with these demons is not?" Alkmene hissed, causing her daughter to stir. She lowered her voice. "Better the knife than as the wife of a herder, under a *yotunan* chief."

Henu folded her arms. "Do what you will to yourself but do not harm your daughter."

"She is my daughter. Mine. Not yours."

"The girl is my relative also."

Alkmene ignored her and turned back to the gap in the planks.

"Wake up," Alkmene whispered in her daughter's ear.

Laonome began to mutter a question as she sat upright until Alkmene hissed gently and put a finger against her daughter's lips. Leading her by the arm, Alkmene shifted to the rear of the wagon and looked out.

The camp was settled in for the night and was as quiet as it ever was though it would be dawn soon and so she had to act swiftly. There was the noise of hundreds of sleeping men and women nearby and the stirring of the animals, the snorting of pigs and stamping of horses' hooves. Muttered conversations drifted on the wind.

Alkmene aimed for a group of horses left unattended nearby. The *yotunan's* servants had strutted away from their little fire when it went out, heading for a larger blaze closer to the river where a noisy group appeared to be intoxicated and the smell of burning *kanab* drifted across the sleeping people and animals. It was a disgrace that the servants of evil burned the sacred flowers and seeds for such mundane purposes.

"Quickly now," she whispered and rushed forward with her daughter behind her. She raced to the horses who started in surprise, tossing their heads and snorting.

Alkmene and Laonome at once made soothing sounds in their throats as they stroked and patted the horses' necks and flanks.

"Here, you lead this one," Alkmene whispered while taking the bridle of another. Both had stinking old blankets over their backs and the panniers over their hind quarters had not been removed in so long that the straps had worn long sores into the beasts' skin. The stiff manes were likewise matted with filth and the lower legs caked in mud. So neglected had they been that they would suffer dearly on the long ride back to the Don river, assuming that they even made it so far. But it was too late to change her mind and so she went on.

"Walk as though these horses are our own," she said. "Do not mount until we are clear."

Leading her horse with a firm, close grip on the bridle she set off at a careful stroll, peering into the darkness and hoping she did not step on anyone. The stars and the scattered fires gave off just enough light to pick a route through the parked wagons, their sleeping oxen, and the hundreds of servants and prisoners between her and the herds beyond. If only they could get by the people, she would have Laonome mount and together they would ride to freedom. With any luck, they might not be missed for a long time

162

and if the gods were truly with them they might never be missed at all. If they made it back home she would find her husband's body and see him properly buried. And the others if she could. But first she would find Orysthos' clan, for they would look after Laonome while she waited at the camp for her sons to come home. All her children might be together again in a few months.

A commotion to her left woke her from her reverie and a loud voice intruded.

"Who's that there? Where are you going?"

Raising a languid hand into the air in the direction of the speaker, Alkmene spoke to her daughter. "Mount, my daughter, and ride east. Stop for nothing."

Her only girl slid swiftly into the saddle but her voice was thick with terror. "Mother!"

The man raised his voice further as he came closer, other servants rising to join him. "Who are you?"

"Ride!" she said and leapt atop her own horse. Servants leapt up from their camp to grasp weapons as they shouted warnings. Beneath her, the horse quivered in fear at the voices all around them. "On, on!" she shouted and leaned forward as her horse broke into a skittish run.

A deep voice roared a command that chilled her heart.

"Kill them!"

Almost at once a bowstring hissed and an arrow cut the air by her head. Men ran in front of her horse with their hands spread and the mare tossed her head and tried to pull up but Alkmene kicked back her heels and shouted at her to run on. The men leapt aside and she found herself with nothing but the shadowy grassland ahead and the sleepy herds milling about here and there. They would be after her but if she kept ahead of them she might have a chance.

A scream behind her turned her head.

It was Laonome.

Her mare had an arrow shaft in her neck that she shook off, leaving the arrowhead and foreshaft in the animal's flesh. Laonome clung on as the mare bucked and tossed her head.

Behind, the servants of the *yotunan* ran close with their weapons in hand.

There was hardly a thought in her head but Alkmene knew it had to be death. She yanked on the horse's mane and leaned hard, turning the beast about and racing back for Laonome.

An arrow struck her horse just below the ear, driving the shaft deep. It stumbled and on the next stride its legs collapsed and Alkmene was thrown forward, jolting on the horse's back before tumbling to the earth. Men roared all around, coming close and shouting.

"Laonome!" Alkmene shouted as she struggled to her feet.

"Mother!" came a distant cry.

Torches flamed around her and spears were levelled.

Batting one aside, she charged toward her daughter. A scowling man with a long beard grabbed her, seizing her shoulders with his hands. She drove them up with a shove from her palms and stepped forward to jam her fingers into his eyes. She felt her nails push into the wet softness and heard herself snarling as she did so. The man fell back screaming with his hands over his face and she shouldered him aside.

"Mother!" Laonome cried just ahead.

She caught a glimpse of her blonde hair amongst a group of

laughing men.

Someone shoved a spear shaft into Alkmene's legs and tripped her before she could reach them and a dozen hands were on her, grabbing her by the shoulders and ankles and arms while she struggled and thrashed face down in the churned earth.

A strange hush fell upon the crowd.

All at once, the hands upon her loosened their grip and Alkmene jumped up, shaking off the last of them and rushed for her sobbing child an arm's reach away.

The *yotunan*.

A man and a half tall, Leuhon scowled down at her. The deformed features twisted in malice and contempt, he looked between Alkmene and Laonome. All around, the men kneeled and bowed their heads, those with them holding their flickering rushlights aloft.

Alkmene shook and breathed heavily while Laonome seemed frozen in terror.

"They almost escaped, lord," said the enormous warrior at the *yotunan*'s side. "Shall I slay them now? Or do you wish them punished?"

Some of the men smirked as they glanced up at her and her daughter and the mighty *yotunan* stared.

While Alkmene's heart raced she reached slowly for the blade inside her tunic. She would not allow them to violate her daughter. She would kill her first and then herself but she would only get one chance before they stopped her.

Keeping her eyes on the *yotunan*, she edged closer to Laonome until she was almost within striking distance. Her blade would have to be drawn and she would need to thrust between the arms of the two men holding Laonome and drive her blade into her neck. If the gods were with her, she would have time to fall onto the blade before they reached her. If not, she knew her punishment would be terrible.

Sensing her mother's approach, Laonome dragged her eyes from the towering *yotunan* and looked at her.

As their eyes met, Alkmene knew she could not do it. Slaying herself would be nothing but she lacked the courage to save her daughter with the knife. She would not leave her little girl and so they would suffer the same fate together. Alkmene prayed only that their suffering would not last too long.

And she would try to kill and maim as many of the demon slaves as she could before they stopped her.

As her fingers brushed the hilt of the dagger, the *yotunan* struck.

He was faster than she would have believed. Faster than a striking falcon, he reached down and grasped her in both of his enormous hands.

Before she could take out her blade she found her arms pinned at her sides and he lifted her off the ground as easily as a man lifts a young child. Holding her at arm's length his eyes ranged over her face and body, searching hungrily. He licked his fat lips and they glistened in the firelight. Making a low growling sound, he brought her closer and sniffed at her, breathing in her hair from the top of her head. Though she struggled, he was twice her size and held her with ease. His skull was enormous. His lips spread wider and his pupils glinted, reflecting the light of the fires around them. Holding her tighter still with one arm so that she could barely take a breath, with the other he felt her body, grasping her backside and ran his fingers down to brutally rub between her legs for a moment. Then he touched her golden hair and peered at it as if transfixed.

It was like when the god had visited her. On her first wedding night, after she had lain blissfully with her husband. The god had destroyed her life, killing her husband and the others who resisted him before forcing himself on her. And the repulsive *yotunan* meant to do the same and even worse to her.

The *yotunan* dragged his eyes from her and looked down at Laonome.

"Daughter?" Leuhon said. His voice was so deep and rasping it took her a moment to realise he was speaking her language.

With a great hunching of her shoulder, she wrenched her arm over his grip, snatched out her hidden dagger and drove it toward his eye with a roar of hatred and despair.

The *yotunan* was faster than she.

He threw a protective arm across his face and flinched away so that she drove the blade into the thick muscles of his forearm.

His grip on her tightened, crushing her so that she could not take a breath while he peered curiously at the weapon, twisting his elbow this way and that while he frowned.

When he looked at her, he tilted his head. If she had not known better, she would have thought him amused.

He dropped her and she fell in a heap, breathing again and dreading what was about to come.

The *yotunan* looked at the warrior beside him and spoke.

"Good blood," Leuhon said, his voice a rumble. He gestured at Alkmene and Laonome and then yanked the weapon out of his flesh as if it were no more than a splinter.

"You wish to drink them, lord?" the big warrior said, eyeing Alkmene.

Drink them. Horror gripped Alkmene and she gathered herself to leap to her daughter's defence.

"No." Leuhon idly scratched his face with a massive hand. "You keep them safe."

The big warrior's eyes shone in the torchlight as he regarded Alkmene. "They are for me, lord?"

"No, Kreuhesh. They are mine. No hand touches them."

"Yes, lord," the warrior named Kreuhesh said, bowing his head. Alkmene saw the hunger and the disappointment on his face before he did so.

Leuhon grunted. Without another look, he turned and strode away into the darkness while his servants and followers bowed and shuffled aside. The servants stared in surprise until Kreuhesh began snapping orders at them and quickly they moved away.

"Throw them back in their wagon and be sure someone watches the mother," the big warrior said to another, catching Alkmene's eye as he spoke.

"Aye, Kreuhesh," the man answered and

Kreuhesh snorted in disgust but gestured at the men near him.

Jumping to her feet, Alkmene shoved aside the men holding her daughter and wrapped Laonome in her arms.

"My daughter," she said into her ear. "My little one."

"Thought I lost you," Laonome sobbed. "Thought you were gone!"

Alkmene held her. "Never. I will never leave you, never. I am here. I am here."

13

Dog Warriors

FOR THE FIRST FEW days, Herkuhlos looked back often, expecting pursuit by the warriors of Orysthos or the wolves of Kolnos. The spear-brothers that had chosen to accompany him rather than stay with Orysthos were likewise concerned that they would be brought back.

But no one came for them.

First, they headed for the Valley of the Kweitos River and from there they followed the trail of the *yotunan* clan. Two days later they came to the remains of Helhena's clan. She poured a libation of mare's milk on her father's grave and slept beside it all through the night to commune with his spirit. Herkuhlos left her alone and she did not speak all the next day or the day after.

Day after day they rode through the devastation wrought upon the earth by the passage of the *yotunan*. Soon the trail passed from the valleys and out onto the plain in a straight line heading relentlessly west. At first, the gods were kind and the weather, though cold, was dry and the wind was from the south. Then the weather turned and a bitter wind came whipping down from the north so that they rode hunched in their furs and spoke hardly at all. At night they gathered close and ate cold meat and warm milk from the mares.

The tracks of the demon clan were impossible to avoid. There seemed to be a hundred wagons and carts and a thousand horses and countless feet. It was as though all the clans of the east had been driven into a great herd and Herkuhlos imagined the world behind them had been emptied of life. There was dung everywhere. Some had already been so dried by the wind that it could be burned in their campfires. Ahead, flocks of birds hopped through the churned ground and feasted on the carrion left lying in the dirt. Guts, offal, shredded skins, skulls and sometimes whole animals were found rotting along the route and at night they often heard wolves but only rarely saw them in the day.

"They want to be hunting," Kasos said one night as they listened to the howling on the wind. "Only the weak and the outcasts will follow such an evil herd."

Belolukos grunted. "What does that make us?"

"We are hunters," Herkuhlos replied. "Go to sleep."

Once in a while they found the remains of a man, woman, or child lying discarded amongst the refuse. They examined every one, fearful as they did so that it would be one of their own people. They rode far behind the *yotunan* and by the time they reached them the remains were always well eaten by animals and corrupted by rot but they were as sure as they could be that each body was that of a stranger.

Once, Helhena burst into angry tears at the sight of what had once been a young girl. She had thrown herself off her horse and fallen to her knees beside the body before striding away.

Herkuhlos dismounted and embraced her, his heart sinking. "It is not... it is not one of your sisters?"

"No," Helhena said, pushing herself away from him and dragging her arm roughly across her eyes. "No but it might have been."

Herkuhlos nodded, understanding. "We will find them eventually. They will have to stop somewhere and then we will catch them and free our people."

Helhena looked at him with scorn. "There is no hope for our people, Herkuhlos. Do not lie to me."

"I am not lying. I believe it."

"Then you are a fool."

Before he could reply she had run after her horse, remounted, and rode away through the debris and death.

Every day they rode as their fathers had taught them. Most of the riders and spare horses rode together but a trusted man was always sent far ahead to scout for dangers. Likewise one always rode on either flank and one took up the rear. These were lonely and trying tasks. The need to be ever alert wore down the wits of the outriders and so they took turns at it. At first, Helhena had wordlessly insisted on accompanying Herkuhlos in his duty, still wary indeed to be alone with his spear-brothers. Soon, though, she found that they became almost disinterested in her. The novelty of her presence wore away into familiarity and their jokes, leers, and insults declined into nothing but grudging acceptance.

Every night, Helhena curled up beside Herkuhlos and

sometimes they shared their furs and kept each other warm. But no more than that. For the first few nights, Herkuhlos was sure she intended to lay with him but every time she fell asleep immediately and snored as loudly as Dhomyos. In a way, he was relieved that she did not. Everyone knew that when the gods got a woman with child it was likely that both the mother and infant would die before or during the birth because the god's seed was too strong. They also said that the godborn did not often father children of their own and his mother's ancestor Perseyus was unusual for making so many children with his wife. Herkuhlos had often wondered about his own seed and whether he would ever be able to father a child. And even if his seed did take then he might harm that woman by getting a child on her. Helhena was strong but perhaps it was for the best if they did not lie together.

"She given it up to you yet?" Belolukos asked one day as they rode together at the front of the central group. "Or are you still afraid of a curse?"

Herkuhlos glanced over his shoulder to see that Helhena was ten horse lengths behind them riding beside Kasos as he talked away at her about some old story.

"She was a seeress and is the daughter of a chief," Herkuhlos replied. "Curse or not she should not give herself up outside of marriage."

Belolukos scoffed. "Daughter of a dead chief."

"Dead or alive, blood is blood," Herkuhlos said, realising as he spoke that what he was speaking was the truth. "And she would make herself worthless by lying with me or anyone else who was not her husband."

"She is worthless now. She has no people."

172

"Neither do we."

"We are our people," Bel replied. "We will make a new clan. All we need is women and herders."

"And cattle," Herkuhlos said.

Belolukos grinned. "And some servants would be nice."

"Tents to live in. Wagons to transport them." Herkuhlos waved a hand at the plain. "And territory of our own. Summer pastures and a wintering ground. Fifty more horses."

"Yes, yes," Belolukos said, laughing. "All easily come by, brother. Do you remember when we were boys..." His face fell as he looked ahead into the distance. "Something is wrong."

Herkuhlos followed his gaze and saw Sentos riding back to them. He was riding far ahead, almost to the horizon.

"Wait here," Herkuhlos said to the others behind him and he and Belolukos rode on ahead to meet Sentos.

"What is it?" Belolukos shouted when they came close. "Danger?"

Sentos, breathing hard, waved a hand. "Nothing comes. No danger. Not like that."

"Then what is it?" Herkuhlos asked.

"There is," Sentos said, "something ahead."

Belolukos raised his voice. "Well spit the words from your lips, you fool. You are a greater tease than his woman." He jerked a thumb at Herkuhlos.

Sentos glanced at Herkuhlos, who remained silent, and then addressed them both. "I don't know what it is. But I smelt it. Death. And smoke."

"How lies the land ahead?" Herkuhlos asked.

"It rises. You can almost see it from here, see?" He pointed. "But it falls away beyond. I did not ride there. Once I smelled the smoke."

Herkuhlos turned his horse around and waved the others forward. They took little time in riding up, leading the spare horses behind them.

"Danger?" Kasos called as they closed.

"Smoke," Sentos said.

"And death," Belolukos said. "Is that not so?"

Sentos nodded, brushing his horse's neck. "

"A *woikos*?" Helhena asked, meaning the cluster of tents and houses that a clan made in their home range for wintering in. "A *woikos* burned by the demons?"

"No *woikos* on the plain, girl," Belolukos snapped.

She scowled. "They do things differently in the west. Clans live in a *woikos* year-round."

"We are not that far west yet," Herkuhlos said. "Are we?"

"Could be a destroyed camp," Kasos suggested.

"Do you think we could have caught up to the *yotunan*?" Wedhris asked, his eyes wide.

"Don't be stupid," Belolukos snapped. "Of course not, we have barely begun."

Wedhris' head dropped. "Yes, you're right."

"How far ahead?" Kasos asked Sentos.

"Not far. There is a sort of ridge there and I did not go beyond."

"Perhaps it's men cooking a stew," Dhomyos pondered, speaking almost to himself. He was ignored.

"We will not find out staying here to talk about it," Herkuhlos said. "Let us go on."

"Yes!" Belolukos said, reaching to pat the head of his weapon.

174

"We ride on!"

As they approached the ridge that Sentos had seen from afar, the smell of woodsmoke drifted to them on the wind. There was the faint taste of meat on it.

Herkuhlos slowed to a stop and the others rode to him. "It could be anything ahead. Stay with the horses, I will go to lay my eyes upon it."

"A *koryonos* sends others to do his scouting," Belolukos observed. "Send Kasos."

Kasos stared in surprise. "There is no lore that says so. In truth, there are many songs telling how a chief—"

"Enough," Herkuhlos said, dismounting. "Wait here until I return."

Taking his good spear he ran forward ahead of the group to the brow of the low hill. The earth was churned up here and there from the passage of horses and cattle but most of the tracks led down to his left to the lower ground. Whoever had passed through had done so recently. Perhaps some of the attackers were waiting behind.

He lay in the trampled damp grass and eased himself forward, feeling the cold soak into his chest and belly.

A noise behind him made him pause.

Belolukos came crawling quickly behind him, nodding once when they caught each other's eye.

"I said to wait," Herkuhlos whispered.

"Never mind that," Belolukos hissed. "Come on."

He slithered forward ahead of Herkuhlos to the top of the hill. Herkuhlos followed him and together they looked through the grass. A long shallow slope led down onto soft ground around a stream that flowed toward a river crossing the horizon. By the stream was indeed the remains of a camp that had been destroyed. Little was left of the tents and buildings. Timbers had been burnt and their blackened remains jutted up from the earth. The *yotunan* had smashed right through it.

But the camp was not devoid of life.

A band of young men picked through the remains while others crouched by a fire. What was more, they had dogs with them. A pack of half a dozen dogs paced through the site or sat gnawing on bones. Some of the young men wore dog skins over their shoulders and over their heads.

Silently, Herkuhlos and Belolukos eased back out of sight.

"A *koryos*," Herkuhlos said.

"Dog warriors," Belolukos replied, his eyes dark. "Youths from the west."

Herkuhlos nodded. "Well, we cannot fight them. We must go around."

Belolukos stared at him. "What do you mean we cannot fight them? Why not?"

"I counted nine boys and six dogs. There may have been more we could not see but even at nine warriors and the dogs, we are outnumbered."

"Not by much. And if we wait until dark, we can come up on them and slaughter half their number before they awake."

Herkuhlos considered it. "We risk so much. We cannot afford to lose men. We have so few as it is."

"Men die. That is what they are for."

"Not for this. It is nothing compared to what we must do. And even if we lost no men, we would lose time waiting for dark."

"But by going around them we must go far out of our way and

this will cause us to lose more time."

"It is the better path," Herkuhlos said. He grasped Belolukos' shoulder. "There will be plenty of chances for glory to come, brother. Come, let us return to the others."

He led his band around the high ground, going north for a while rather than southwest. As he rode he glanced repeatedly to his left to watch the low ridge there for sign of anyone following or watching their passage. If they did see him he hoped that they would not attack either. Indeed, they would be fools to do so, for they were eight riders and seen from a distance surely they would not see that one of their number was but a girl. If somehow they discerned she was not male, they might also see the bow she carried and would know she was dangerous. And though they might not have dogs, they did have horses which gave them an advantage.

Herkuhlos was not afraid of a *koryos* from some tribe but he did fear losing spear-brothers that he would need when he met the *yotunan*. But when he thought of that he had no notion of how he might defeat such mighty enemies and the sick feeling in his guts turned his thoughts aside to other matters.

"You did the right thing," Helhena said, riding up close beside him.

"In avoiding battle? Yes."

"They were boys?"

Herkuhlos kept his eyes on the brow of the long hill. "I suppose so. They wore dog skins."

"You are wolves and need not fear dogs."

Herkuhlos scoffed at her ignorance. "Dogs can kill wolves."

"Not these ones."

He glanced at her. "You have *seen* it?"

She turned to face ahead. "There is seeing and there is seeing. To truly see, I have to perform the rites. But I know you. And you cannot be defeated."

He had a strong feeling but did not know what it was. Something like shame, he thought. "All men can be defeated."

"But you are godborn."

Godborn can die, he thought.

But Herkuhlos said nothing, glancing at the hills. The ridge was already lower and would slope away to nothing well before they reached the big river ahead. But night was coming soon and by the time they made camp they would be out of sight, sound, and smell of the *koryos* in the little valley. The ground was different here, away from the plain proper and closer to the river. The earth was softer, wetter, and the soil thicker so that the grasses were long and thick. Clumps of sedge sprouted thickly to waist height and there were spindly bushes here and there. It was the first time in days they had travelled through ground that had not been scarred and trampled.

Wedhris was out ahead of them all, scouting the way. If they were lucky they would make the trees and thicker bushes by the river before nightfall going at a steady pace. If they were spotted by the dog soldiers behind the ridge to their left then he would have them ride hard for the shelter of those trees. If the gods were with them they would outpace the other *koryos*, dogs and all. If they made it to the trees by the river first then perhaps they could ambush the dog warriors, if they were foolish enough to pursue them.

Was that the right choice, he wondered. What else could he do to protect his men, his horses.

Out ahead of them Wedhris pulled his horse to a stop. He was looking ahead. Peering at something.

Herkuhlos slowed and looked around. "Sentos? Go up and see what worries him."

Belolukos, hearing, turned and snorted. "What does *not* worry Wedhris? You should not have chosen him to lead, brother."

Ignoring the rebuke, Herkuhlos watched Sentos ride by them all the way up to Wedhris who still had not moved. Herkuhlos laid his spear across his hips and spat into his hands, rubbing them together before taking his spear in his grasp again.

Seeing him, Helhena frowned. "Should I string my bow?"

He smiled. "Should I not be asking you, seeress?"

Silently, she took her cord from the bag on her belt and slid from her horse. While she was yet reaching for her bow, Sentos and Wedhris turned their horses and rode back towards them.

"What is this?" Belolukos said. "What are they doing?"

Sentos waved his javelin over his head as he rode. "Flee!" he shouted. "Enemies!"

As he was speaking, hidden warriors rose from the long grass and scrub ahead and on their right flank. They were armed and coming at them with their weapons up, lifting their knees to run through the long grass.

"Mount your horse," Herkuhlos snarled at Helhena, anger and fear rising in him.

He turned about to shout to Kasos and Dhomyos to get the spare horses away quickly, for they carried much of the supplies, only to see more warriors approaching from behind them. A group of three men, all with javelins, burst from cover to rush the horses. Herkuhlos looked around for a route to escape from. A handful were in front, on their flank, and behind. All that left was the ridge to the left, beyond which lay the camp and the *koryos* of dog warriors. He turned his horse to the slope and froze.

From the brow of the hill, more men ran at them with their weapons in hand.

Panic rose. Herkuhlos breathed hard, blood pounding in his ears as the attackers began to scream and howl their battle cries.

Their horses flinched and tossed their heads in fear as hounds, running beside the men from the hills, began barking. There were nine men descending the hill and six hounds bounded down with them. He quickly counted the others. Another half a dozen warriors ahead had been waiting for them in ambush.

Herkuhlos understood at once that he had failed.

The dog warriors had seen their approach and had followed them closely ever since, waiting to spring the trap.

Belolukos was shouting in fury and the others were crowding close to him as their horses turned this way and that. They were almost surrounded but they could ride free if all of them made for the gap at once. But there was no chance that they would hold on to all the pack horses as well and without them their success in pursuing the yotunan would be unlikely.

Without waiting for the commands from his leader, Wedhris rode hard for the gap in the approaching men.

"Wait!" Herkuhlos shouted. "We do not flee!"

There were three men directly ahead and three on their right flank. His only hope was that he and his brothers could defeat them first before turning to face the baying hounds and the dog warriors coming after them.

"Kill them!" Herkuhlos shouted, pointing his spear and kicking his frightened horse forward.

Kasos and Dhomyos tried to drag the pack horses away from

the approaching enemies behind and coming from the left flank on the hill but without riders on their backs they were uncontrollable in the face of such noise and fury.

"Leave them," Herkuhlos shouted. "Leave the horses, come on!"

Belolukos was already racing ahead with Sentos and Wedhris beside him. Helhena was back on her horse, her bow now strung and in her hands. The only way she could fight, he knew, was if she could stand at the rear to shoot her bow. Shooting from horseback was difficult even for the most skilful riders and archers, for the bow was so long it could only be shot from one side and for that the horse had to stay still. But Helhena could not stay back from the danger of the spears to shoot as the *koryos* and their dogs would have her.

"With me," Herkuhlos shouted to her. "Helhena, you stay with me."

Her eyes wild with terror, she nodded and together they rode after Belolukos, Wedhris and Sentos.

Belolukos charged his horse toward the three figures ahead so Herkuhlos turned to ride at the three on his right flank, hoping that Kasos, Dhomyos, and Helhena would follow him.

When they saw him approaching they turned and ran from him through the long grass, lifting their legs high and hitching their spears and javelins up. But they did not flee in a blind panic. They also ran together and soon turned, their weapons ready with their backs together, ready to fight.

Herkuhlos slowed and looked for Belolukos up ahead. He was fighting them from the back of his horse, thrusting awkwardly with his spear as the horse turned this way and that. Sentos rushed forward to help while Wedhris fumbled with his javelins behind.

Fighting from the back of a horse was so difficult that few warriors ever mastered it and Herkuhlos knew his chances were better on foot. But he feared dismounting, for then he might lose his horse and his chance of escaping.

"Let us ride around!" Kasos cried, coming up. "Between this group and Bel's. See, they cannot stop us."

Herkuhlos turned to look at the dog warriors. The foremost of them were already grasping their pack horses and whooping in victory. They knew the contents of the leather bags and baskets would feed them for weeks or more and the horses alone were a mighty prize.

A rage stirred in him. Rage at the enemy and rage at himself for his foolishness in not seeing it coming. At not distributing the pack horses evenly amongst his people.

But he fought the rage down.

The supplies and horses could be found again but the lives of his men could not be replaced.

Turning to Kasos, Herkuhlos nodded. "We go through them and on to the river. Leave the horses and the supplies."

"Our food!" Dhomyos wailed.

Helhena shouted in horror, pointing at Belolukos.

His brother's horse was hit in the chest with a javelin, throwing Belolukos to the ground. The warriors whooped and rushed for him. Sentos rode his horse in amongst them and threw himself from its back and fell atop the three enemies before they could finish Belolukos. Sentos thrust at one with his spear but was stabbed in the neck by another and the third smashed his head in with his axe, splitting his skull open and ripping out shards of bone and brains.

The death of his friend and the sight of the blood stirred something deep within Herkuhlos.

It rose up inside him like a beast clawing its way up from the centre of the earth to take control of his limbs. It was like a fire sparking to life inside his heart and then roaring into flame throughout his body until he shone with heat and light.

He forced his frightened horse to run toward the blood and the men roaring in victory until it tossed its head and would approach no further, veering away. Sliding easily from its back he pulled a javelin from its loops, hefted it and launched it at the warrior approaching Belolukos who was by then backing away from the three men.

His throw was good and it struck his man high in the chest and penetrated deeply. He coughed a mouthful of blood as he fell, twisting to the ground with confusion on his face.

Herkuhlos was already running with his strongest spear in hand. His enemies saw him and circled away from each other, thinking that they would save themselves.

Belolukos saw his chance and rushed one, ducking beneath the thrusting spear to drive his axe into the man's neck at a run before shouldering him to the ground, yanking his axe free and chopping it into the man's face, caving it inward. Too late, the last man turned to run and Herkuhlos' spear took him in the spine, shattering the bones and bursting through his abdomen. Herkuhlos ripped the spearhead free before the man fell. It was a cheap death, a coward's death, and Herkuhlos' rage was not satiated but whetted further.

He turned, looking for more men to cut down.

Dogs.

A pack of dogs came bounding for him and his brothers, barking and growling as they ran with their teeth bared and their eyes wild. Six of them running at full speed to maul him and his spear-brothers. He recalled an antelope hunt from when he was a boy and seeing his clan's pack bringing down the stag with such savage fury that he had turned from the sight of it. His legs shook and he flinched, half turning.

Gendryon's words, spoken many years before, came to him suddenly. *Never run from dogs, boys! Never run!*

"I will not run," he muttered.

Roaring a wordless cry he stepped forward and thrust his spear into the chest of the first one to come within reach, the impact jarring his arm and almost ripping the spear from his hand. Its dying yelp cut short as he ripped his spear free, stepped back and thrust it at the chest of the next one just as it threw itself at him. Instead of impaling the chest the spearpoint ripped through the dog's throat in a shower of blood.

Nearby, Belolukos and Wedhris stood back to back as they fought the dogs that reached them, swinging their weapons to fend off the snarling dogs.

Herkuhlos had no time to help.

Two more dogs came for him. These were not young dogs rushing wildly in but older females, wily and scarred from their past battles and they snarled as they slowed, their teeth barred, crouching and circling him, looking to strike. Some part of him wondered if the dogs he had already killed might have been their pups and the blood was driving them into a frenzy as they circled him.

Behind, the warriors of the enemy *koryos* came on at a run and they were the prey Herkuhlos truly wanted.

He turned his back to one dog and thrust at the other to keep it away, before turning to drive the spear into the one he had baited. The second was faster than he would have believed and it sank its teeth into his knee before he could withdraw his weapon.

Herkuhlos roared in agony and fear. He had seen a dog bite turn bad and kill one of the strongest men in his tribe and so knew how terrible they could be. The pain of its teeth grinding into his bones caused him to drop his spear, still in the chest of the other dog.

On instinct alone he punched the bitch in the head once, twice, and then grasped its muzzle and jaw, pulling it from his knee. The jaw was locked powerfully on him and the teeth were sharp but the enemy were coming closer with every moment and so he growled and roared as he forced the teeth apart. The bitch's jaw snapped and it yanked its head back, the jaw dislocated so thoroughly it hung loose beneath the whining dog's head. Tearing his spear free from the dog, he kicked the wounded one over, stamped a foot on its head to hold it still, and destroyed its chest with a blow.

Someone was shouting his name. He looked up to see four of the enemy converging on him warily with their axes and hammers in hand.

Herkuhlos almost laughed with joy, for he knew suddenly that he would kill them. They were so slow, so clumsy, and before he did it he knew what would happen.

The first had his axe raised overhead, his face twisted in rage, and Herkuhlos stepped forward and thrust his spear into his chest beneath his raised arm. The blade caught on the ribs but Herkuhlos ripped it out, spraying blood into the air. Before the second man came within range of his axe, Herkuhlos changed direction and thrust his spear low, taking the man in the belly just over his hip. When he drew the blade out he opened up his belly all the way to the navel and the man screamed as he fell. This time the spearhead was caught on the enemy's clothes and he had to stand over the wailing, dying man to yank it free of his tunic. As he did so, a javelin flew at him.

From the corner of his eye, he saw it coming and twisted aside so that it passed no further than a hand's breadth from his head. He ran straight at the thrower, who turned and ran in fear without even throwing either of his remaining javelins. Herkuhlos chased him down in just a few strides and speared him in the back of the leg, bringing his screams to a stop by jamming his spear butt into the boy's face. For he saw how young the boy was before he split his nose in two with the blow.

The youths from the *koryos* were leading the pack horses away. Herkuhlos' fury grew to see the cowards attempting to flee rather than to fight and he snatched up the dropped javelins, ran forward and threw one at the nearest one. The shaft was not true and its wobbling flight took it away from its target to embed into the soil. He ran forward and threw the next one. It arced up and swooped down to pierce the dog warrior low on his flank.

Herkuhlos roared in victory and rushed at the others, ready to kill every one of them.

They let go of the pack horses and fled in panic from him, some even throwing aside their axes so that they might run faster. They ran in a state of terror and he knew with certainty that they would never return.

Upon reaching the frightened horses, Herkuhlos felt his rage subsiding. He spat on the ground at the fleeing figures but his mouth was so dry little came out. Wiping his mouth he turned to the sound of whimpering.

The boy with the spear in his side sobbed.

Herkuhlos approached.

"Help me," the boy said, his face grey and tears streaming down his face. He clutched his ruined leg. "Help me."

"You do not deserve it," Herkuhlos said, looking at the body of Sentos. "But I will help you. In the name of Kolnos, I release your spirit."

Standing over him, he swung his axe into the boy's skull. He looked down at the body and felt his anger diminishing further. What remained was focused on himself and his own foolish decisions. There was supposed to be glory in battle and joy in victory but he felt little of that.

They rounded up the panicked horses and calmed them, drawing them together once more and leading them upwind of the blood. The bodies of the slain enemies were searched. They had little of value. Even their weapons were poor.

All the while, his friends glanced repeatedly at Herkuhlos with a mix of wonder and fear. Even Belolukos was hesitant when he approached.

"I would have killed them without your help," Belolukos said. Herkuhlos said nothing. "But I thank you for it all the same," Belolukos added quickly.

"We are brothers," Herkuhlos said.

"And we did well, did we not?" Belolukos said, forcing a smile onto his pale face. "They were so many and they had us, ahead and behind, and yet here we all stand with bloodied weapons while their spirits go to their ancestors or they flee in terror."

"We all but one," Herkuhlos said.

Belolukos nodded, looking across the bloody ground at the body of Sentos. "He died to protect me."

"I saw. He did not hesitate. There is glory in that, at least."

"He was always loyal," Belolukos said.

"And now we must honour him."

They made a camp in the lee of the low hill and dug a grave for Sentos on the top of it, in view of the distant river. His weapons were laid beside him. There was not the time for the proper rites but they did what they could to call for the attention of the gods and their ancestors. They made a small fire and burnt some dried meat and laid a fine leather cap in the grave atop his old wolf pelt. Eventually, they covered him with earth and moved down the hill for the night.

Through it all, his spear-brothers still avoided Herkuhlos. Even Helhena, until full dark was on them. She came to sit beside him as the campfire flickered into life.

"I have never seen anyone move like that," she whispered.

"Like what?"

"The swiftness. You were like... I do not know. A wolf. A real wolf. Or a falcon, falling from the sky onto its prey. How did you do it?"

Herkuhlos shook his head, unwilling to speak of it. "I am tired. Kasos and Dhomyos will stay awake in the first part of the night."

"How did you do it?" she whispered.

It was like a fire roaring inside my flesh. Like my spirit was suddenly set aflame. "I just fought, that is all. Like a warrior."

"Like a godborn," she whispered.

Like a fool, he thought. *If I had attacked them this morning, Sentos might yet live.*

"Go to sleep," he said.

Belolukos sat opposite their small fire, watching in silence. Soon, Herkuhlos lay down and fell into a disturbed sleep filled with dreams of blood and fire and snarling jaws.

In the morning, they led their horses through the bloody battlefield and on toward the river.

14

Kreuhesh the
Bloodletter

"MY LORD KREUHESH," the god's messenger said, raising his voice to rouse the chief warrior in the darkness.

Kreuhesh grabbed his axe as he jumped to his feet, throwing off his furs. "What's wrong?" he growled, towering over the messenger. By the white robes he knew it was one of the acolytes of Leuhon. Dawn was not yet come but those pale robes almost shone even when the earth was in shadow.

"The god summons you, my lord."

"Why?" Kreuhesh said, looking around and listening. Nothing but the usual sound of hundreds of sleeping men and women and animals all around him. The usual stink, too. There was no sign of danger.

"The god sent me to rouse you and relay his command that you attend to him at once."

Sighing, Kreuhesh waved his war axe at the shivering man. "Go on. I am coming."

Ever since they had set off across the plains with the gods, Kreuhesh had made his bed near to his lord the god Leuhon in case he was needed and in case there was an attack from enemies. The relentless wind was cold but at least the masses of men and animals all around them blocked some of it. Still, the nights were bitter beneath the stars and his limbs were stiff as he walked toward the god's place.

Leuhon was unmistakable even in the gloom. The god's shadow was darker than the earth around it.

"You may approach the god," the acolyte said.

Kreuhesh stared at the man, imagining driving his fist into the man's wet mouth and breaking his skull open with the head of his axe. Instead he walked by him and approached the god, kneeling before his master with his head bowed.

"My lord," he said.

"You must find me blood, Kreuhesh," Leuhon said, his voice a low rumble. The mighty god Leuhon stood with his arms crossed looking down at his chief warrior.

Find it? Kreuhesh was confused for he ensured Leuhon received fresh blood every day. He glanced up at the white-robed acolytes that served their god but they looked back impassively. "I will have some brought at once, my lord."

Leuhon made a noise somewhere between a sigh and a growl. "No, Kreuhesh. You must find me blood and flesh. Men and women."

Kreuhesh suppressed a sigh of his own. Ever since the god had found him he had been raiding and capturing in his name. From the forests of the north and the wide vales of the great rivers to the endless grassland of the plains he had conquered all ahead of them. When he found *woikos* and camps he killed most of the men and boys and took the women and girls for his lord. Some of the surviving men swore oaths to serve Leuhon and these men Kreuhesh took into his war band. More than two hundred warriors now. More than any of the eleven other gods had. And he had taken more women captives than the rest of them all added together, even after the hundreds they had killed along the way. Leuhon commanded and Kreuhesh delivered.

"You want me to raid ahead again, lord?" Kreuhesh said, bowing his head once more.

"There is a river ahead," Leuhon said, as still as a sleeping bull. "Wide as the Rasga. Go there. Take the flesh."

"I will, lord," Kreuhesh said, making to rise.

One of the acolytes spoke quickly. "There is more. You will wait until you are dismissed."

Kreuhesh looked up through his eyebrows. The acolyte was a grey-haired, spindle-armed old goat too weak to even lift a spear let alone wield it. The acolytes had been priests of various clans who had submitted to the god when given the choice of service or death. They were nine in all and Kreuhesh wished he could break their skulls in with his hammer.

"Yes, wise one," Kreuhesh said and stayed where he was, his hands clenched into fists.

"We are come to a land of *briya*," Leuhon said. "This I will make my land. Here I will rule. You, Kreuhesh, will find the *briya* to rule all."

Kreuhesh had no notion of what his master was speaking of. "I will do as you command, my lord, but I do not know this word *briya*."

The old acolyte snorted. "That is no surprise seeing as you are a creature of the forest, Kreuhesh. Something like a boar, one might say." A handful of the other acolytes laughed quietly and it took all of Kreuhesh's strength to restrain himself. "A *briya* is a settlement. It is something like a clan's *woikos* only far larger. Instead of twenty or thirty houses or tents there are hundreds. And instead of hundreds of people there are thousands."

"Thousands?" Kreuhesh frowned as he looked up. "In one place?"

"What is more," the grey-hair went on, "the *briya* are built atop hills or mounds and are protected by walls."

"Like a stronghold?" Kreuhesh asked. There were countless places from the mountains to the seas where people had built defensive structures where the desperate gathered to protect themselves in a raid. Sometimes made from logs and other times from stone and they gave the warriors within an advantage. Riders could not charge over them and if they were stone they could not be burnt down by attackers. But every one that Kreuhesh had seen defended he had seen fall. With enough warriors you could overcome anything.

The acolyte scoffed again. "Strongholds are mere sheep pens compared to the *briya*."

"And you wish for me to destroy one for you, lord?" Kreuhesh addressed Leuhon.

"Destroy many," Leuhon said. "But from the greatest I shall rule. All others shall submit to me."

"I will do as you command, lord."

Leuhon used a massive hand to indicate that Kreuhesh should rise. "You will."

Kreuhesh hesitated, thinking about his other duty. "What about the woman, lord?"

The god snorted. "Leave her. Go now."

With a final bow and a glare at the nine acolytes, Kreuhesh strode away for his men. He would take fifty warriors for the first scouting ahead to this great river. There were always rich clans in valleys and fifty warriors on horseback would do terrible damage coming down from the plains unexpectedly. They would cut down the warriors, subdue the herders and servants and then they could truss up the women for the god. A tingle of excitement gathered down low in his guts, almost in his loins.

Before he reached his men he turned away from them and headed through the camp toward the wagons of the captives. Leave her, Leuhon had commanded. Kreuhesh did not intend to defy the god but he found himself approaching. And it was not true defiance. The god had meant that his duty to keep the woman was to be put aside while he took the warriors on a raid not that Kreuhesh should not approach her before he went. All he wanted was to see her before he went away. To see her so that she would know where he had gone and that he meant to return.

Finding her wagon in the predawn murk he hammered a fist on the side boards, the sudden sound waking the women within with a start. He allowed himself a smile as he rounded the rear of the wagon and looked into the darkness beneath the arcing cover.

"Woman," he said.

They would all know what woman he meant and what he was

commanding her to do. There came the sound of muttering within and the women stirred and then she was there, her shadowed face appearing at the rear.

"Down," Kreuhesh commanded.

There was a long pause before she obeyed. He allowed her those small acts of defiance because she understood by now how far she could push him. She understood that she could push him hardly at all. It pleased him to see it.

With a sigh, she slipped over the rear boards and dropped lightly down to the ground. She moved with the grace of a gazelle and he liked to see it. He would like to see her long limbs and her full, womanly body moving without clothing. Moving beneath him. He shuddered to think of it and reached a hand for her. Her eyes widened and she stepped back, suddenly alert.

"You cannot," she snapped.

He dropped his hand and clenched his teeth. "You do not command me, woman."

"It is not I that commands you but Leuhon," she said, shivering in the freezing air. "I am his."

Kreuhesh snorted. "I wonder what my lord would do if I took you here. If I stripped you and took you against the wagon. There is no one here that would stop me. You could not. And what if I killed you after? Would my lord slay me? Perhaps he would. But I would have had you and you would be dead." He leaned in, savouring her fear. "So what do my lord's commands mean really?"

She stared at him, still shivering in the cold. "You would not dare. No man would throw his life away for nothing."

He smiled, then, and almost laughed aloud. "For a taste of your sweet flesh, Alkmene. And I know you do not think of yourself as

196

nothing."

A sound from within the wagon caught his attention. It was filled with women and girls and of course they would all be listening to every word he spoke. Along with those in other wagons around him they were the pick of the herd. The wives and daughters of chiefs and warriors plucked from clans from the forests to the plains. A few were too old for breeding but young women and girls always needed older women to keep them steady. Girls on the edge of womanhood were ripe for use. There was little in the world more valuable than a strong young woman. You could do anything with them. Take them to wife, make them a servant, trade them for horses, cattle, or anything at all, give them as gifts to your own men. But the young ones were also prone to madness. Keep a herd of young girls alone together and they would drive each other into fits of screeching and wailing inside of a day. They would cry themselves voiceless and some lost their wits entirely, staring dumbly even when you slapped them and ripped off their clothes. Many stopped eating and grew thin and sickly and worthless. A few went further and used their nails or anything sharp to cut their faces to ribbons and some even slew themselves before they could be gotten with child or even after. But if you put one or two older women in amongst them it calmed down the lot. Kreuhesh had learnt it the hard way but he had learnt it. Same as making a stew. Mix in a few chunks of old, dried flesh in with the fresh pieces to make the stew go down smooth.

With a smirk at Alkmene, Kreuhesh looked into the darkness inside the back of the wagon. "Come out here and show me your face, girl."

"She is sleeping," Alkmene said quickly.

Kreuhesh glanced at her and hammered his fist on the side of the wagon, rattling the pegs and loose boards. "Out, girl," he said.

She appeared almost immediately, her eyes wide and fearful. "Mother," she said in her quiet, girlish voice.

"It is well," Alkmene said, coming to the wagon and helping her daughter down.

They clung to each other as they looked at him. Alkmene with her eyes glaring defiance and Laonome radiating terror. Kreuhesh knew he was frightening to behold. He had worked hard to make it so. He had his hair shaved to the skin on the sides of his head while the long black hair on the top and back was pulled into a long braid. On his cheeks, neck, and scalp his tattoos were made to scare his men more than his enemies for in battle he wore a helmet and jerkin of leather with flat bone armour sewed onto them. There were few chiefs and warriors fortunate enough to wear such defensive armour and all of them were made with boar's tusks. The tusks were cut into flat sections no thicker than a finger. Kreuhesh had killed a chief in the far north where boar were plentiful and had worn his armour with pride ever since. From his belt and his horse he hung scalps, small bones, and pieces of flesh taken from warriors he had killed. Each one was a talisman. Each one retained some of the power of the dead man it had been torn from. They swayed when he walked and the finger bones he had tied together clicked and rattled. It pleased him to hear the noises and remember the men they had belonged to. Men who had dreamed of living long and winning glory. Men who had believed they would protect their wives and daughters. Men who had thought to slay Kreuhesh. Men who fell screaming to their deaths. Most of their bodies now carrion and food for worms but for the strips of flesh and clattering bones he wore. It gave him power to think of the portion of their spirits trapped within, watching him living, winning glory, and ruling over their wives and their daughters.

Laonome shook as she took in Kreuhesh's terrible presence in the predawn gloom. She was not yet flowered, that much was clear and she was as thin as a hazel switch. But she was almost as tall as her mother and it was obvious she would be a beauty. She had little of Alkmene's fire, though. Perhaps that would come when she began to bleed. Girls had little notion of their power until then but once they discovered their worth it was an endless task to keep them under control. It was said that controlling women was like breaking a wild horse but Kreuhesh knew that was not quite true. Women were fire. You could use them to keep warm and to cook your food but if you held them close they would burn you alive. Better to stamp them out than allow that to happen.

He smiled at Laonome. "Are you well, girl?"

She stared at him and then gave the smallest of nods. She was not fire yet. She was not a wild horse either. More like a quaking foal, still wet from her mother.

"Are you eating well, girl?"

She glanced at her mother.

"We are always hungry," Alkmene said. "If Leuhon wants us strong you should feed us more."

"What makes you think my lord wants you strong?" he asked, relishing her confusion. "What do you think he wants you for, woman?"

Alkmene lifted her chin. "Tell me, then."

Kreuhesh snorted. "I don't have to tell you anything."

The truth was he was not sure why Leuhon had claimed

Alkmene and her daughter after their attempt at escape moons ago. Was it just for the way she looked? Alkmene was a beauty and her spirit burned bright but she was old. More than thirty, most likely, though she might bear five or six more children if she was kept on her back. So perhaps that was what he intended, though if he wanted to breed he could have any one of dozens of younger women and some who were larger. Or was it something else about Alkmene that had drawn Leuhon to her? The god had touched her yellow hair and perhaps that was it. Yellow hair was not unknown amongst men and women but it was somewhat rare. And the gods, those that he had seen, were mostly fair, like Leuhon was. Though some were darker and some had no hair at all that he could see. Did Leuhon want his sons to have yellow hair also?

The thought of Leuhon taking her as a wife filled Kreuhesh with anger, revulsion, and jealousy. But he had to admit he felt lust also when he thought of it. Though Alkmene was tall and strong, he imagined she would be broken by the giant's body and by his seed and though he wanted her for himself he nevertheless found his loins stirring at the thought of her writhing in agony beneath the enormous god as he thrust into her.

Kreuhesh shuddered and licked his lips. He did not know he had reached for her until she drew back and pushed Laonome half behind her. He dropped his hand.

"I am leaving," he said. "I will be gone for many days."

That aroused her interest. "Good."

He smiled, genuinely amused. If she had not been under Leuhon's protection then he would have beaten her bloody for that but she knew just how far she could push him. It was admirable.

"While I am gone I will have men watching you. Do not flee.

200

And do not try any of your tricks or sweet talk with them. I give you free reign with me but my men do not have the strength of will that I possess and if you get haughty with them they will kill you."

"Leuhon will kill them."

She was afraid, now. He fancied that he could smell it on her, rising from the warmth beneath her clothing along with her earthy, unwashed womanly smell. He breathed it in and sighed. "Woman, you think all men are like the chief who opened your legs every night? Most of these brutes are more like animals. Witless, the lot of them. All they know is killing men and taking women. The last raid I led I said to my men before it that none of the clan's wives were to be raped. I said they could do what they wanted with the herder women but the proper women were for the god. Any man here who disobeys I will kill, I said to them. Do you understand me, I said. Oh yes, they all said, looking in my eyes. I even had them repeat what I said." Kreuhesh laughed. "I killed four of my own men that morning. Just couldn't stop themselves once they seen the ripeness of a woman." He stopped smiling and leaned in. "And it's men like that who will be watching you, woman. You understand?"

She looked at him without flinching. "I will stay out of their way. And I will not try to escape."

"I know." He jerked his head at the wagon. "Go on, now. In you get."

Alkmene pushed Laonome up and in and pulled herself up onto the rear behind her. Kreuhesh reached up and grasped her hip with one hand and pushed her backside with the other, propelling her inside. As he did so he dug his fingers through her woollen clothing into the flesh at her waist and squeezed her buttock so hard that it must have hurt her. She was slim and her muscles were hard but she was a mother with a full figure and he savoured the feel of her. She whirled and swiped at him but by then he was already walking away, chuckling to himself and smelling his hand to breathe in her scent. He would miss her. But he would be back soon enough.

He roused his men with a few sharp commands. He had a dozen warriors who through their skill in battle and their wits had risen to be his companions. Each of them commanded the loyalty of a dozen more so that when they all rode together they were an almost unstoppable warband. He chose a few to ride with him and instructed the rest to watch the captives and to protect the god from the warriors of the other gods that rode with them. Each of the twelve gods had their own acolytes and warriors, their own captives and their own herds. Though all marched together they were almost entirely separate from one another. Almost, apart from the occasions when the gods met together for a discussion. And almost, apart from when the warriors and herders of one god attempted to raid the belongings of one of the others. They would wake to find cattle had gone missing or sheep or even horses or captives. Raiding like that was punished by death. The gods proclaimed that the whole of the earth was theirs to raid but the property of a god was sacred. Almost all were caught sooner or later. And the guilty were taken to the god whose property had been raided. That god usually cut the guilty man's throat and drank his blood and ate his flesh. Leuhon had taken a bite out of a man's chest while the man was still living and held him in his grasp while the man screamed and Leuhon chewed. Despite all this there were still raids and Kreuhesh made sure to leave enough warriors to protect his god.

It was two days hard riding to the first settlement. Kreuhesh delighted in the journey, freed of the masses of captives and animals and the noise and the stink of it all. Free also from the watchful eyes of Leuhon and his acolytes. It was a pleasure also to be out of the grasslands and into river valleys once more with woodland and hills all around. Kreuhesh was from a land of trees and scrub in the north and though they had kept cattle on the edge of the grasslands and raided into it, he had despaired at the endlessness of it in their journey south and west. Nothing for days in all directions. Nothing but grass and the wind and the glaring sky above. Hardly any clans to be conquered, either. All were wintering in the valleys. And now, before the coming of spring, he would destroy them all.

His scouts came back late on the second day to report a *woikos* ahead. Thirty houses at least, they said, probably more.

Kreuhesh looked at the setting sun. The days were getting longer but still there was never enough daylight to be had.

"We can camp here, lord," his man Hendros said. "Come upon them before dawn."

Kreuhesh nodded for that was their custom. But he could not bear to wait. "We go now."

"But it will be full dark when we reach them," Weben protested.

Kreuhesh turned his gaze upon him until Weben lowered his eyes.

"Do not kill all the men," he said. "I want one warrior at least taken alive."

"And the women for the god," Hendros said.

Kreuhesh thought of Alkmene and felt his loins stirring. "Do what you will with the women," he said. "And then kill them. Kill them all."

They rode hard and reached the place just the last light of day was dying. It was on a dome of high ground near to a river, as his scouts had said, with houses built close together. Those houses were larger than any he had ever seen. Rectangular with high walls plastered with daub and roofed with dense bundles of reed. Some were so close together that they were practically touching and Kreuhesh saw at once that they formed a kind of defensive wall around the settlement, like wagons parked end to end in a circle to protect a camp inside. Perhaps this was one of the *briya* that Leuhon had told him about, only smaller. It may not have had hundreds of houses but it was a place built atop a mound with high walls. Whatever they called it he knew there would have to be a way in somewhere.

With a wave he ordered some of his men to ride one way around the place and he led the rest in the opposite direction, the hooves of their horses thundering upon the earth. He circled the *briya* at the head of his warriors as their cries and whoops filled the night air. Some of the men wheeled away to light their reed torches and bundled tapers, ready for the attack, and the yellow light of the flames began to spark all around.

"There!" Kreuhesh cried, pointing with his war axe. There was a dark shape between the lighter walls and he knew it was a way in. He turned his horse toward it at once and his men came with him, turning like a flock of birds in flight and charging toward the deep shadow.

Shapes moved within.

Men stood there, ready to defend their homes.

Kreuhesh roared a challenge just as an arrow hissed out of the dark and struck the man on his flank with such force he fell from his horse and was trampled by the men behind. Javelins followed the arrow, striking horses and men and the earth all around Kreuhesh and he bellowed again as he reached the shadows. Once he was close he was surprised to find the houses were even larger than he had thought but he had no time to ponder it for there were spears in the hands of the men before him. Kreuhesh yanked on his horse's reins to turn it aside and used his war axe to smash aside the spears that thrust at him. He slid from the back of his horse as his men crashed against the defenders. Men were shouting on both sides and the thundering hooves behind him shook the earth. A horse fell beside him, its legs kicking and the rider falling beneath the hooves of another. Still, the weight of men and horse forced the defending warriors back deeper into the gap between the houses. There seemed to be more of them all the time, emerging from the darkness to fill the passageway with more bodies. An arrow missed him by a hand's width and then a javelin clattered onto the hard ground by his feet.

Kreuhesh glanced at the men dismounting all around him. He saw Hendros and Horghis at his side and Kelwos and Melo close behind.

"With me," Kreuhesh shouted over the noise of battle. "We kill them!"

Hendros thrust his spear over his head. "Kreuhesh!" he shouted.

All around them the men lifted their faces to the night and roared his name. "Kreuhesh!"

Kreuhesh forced himself into motion toward the wall of spears ahead with his axe raised. His men rushed the enemy with him, filling the enclosed space with their war cries. A flint spear came suddenly at his face and Kreuhesh smashed it aside with the shaft of his spear and brought the head down on the skull of the man wielding it. The man's skull crumpled and he dropped like a stone. Kreuhesh was already moving, swiping at the men either side and beyond. His axe thudded into the shoulder of one man before Hendros drove his spear into his throat, spraying blood over Kreuhesh.

Something struck Kreuhesh on the head. His boar tusk helm helped protect him but still it stunned him for a moment and his vision blurred. Move! He shouted the word at himself, knowing that to be still in such a fight was to be dead. There was no room behind him nor to either side so he ducked low and stepped forward, swinging his war axe before him. He connected with someone, a dull thud from hitting a chest or stomach or back. His vision cleared in time to see a blow coming and he twisted and swung his axe but still the spear hit him a glancing blow in the chest. Again, the boar tusk armour over his body kept him from being impaled but the impact knocked him off balance.

His anger grew. Kreuhesh would not be killed by weaklings of some foreign land. Not after all he had done to become what he was. Roaring defiance he threw himself forward once more and his war axe smashed the face of the man before him, spraying blood and teeth as the bones were crushed. He stepped on the fallen man and grasped the shaft of a spear, turned it aside and brought his axe down to break the arm of the warrior holding it before breaking his skull with a powerful blow. The sounds of battle receded and soon all he could hear was his own breathing and the pounding of blood in his ears. The rest was a distant murmur of blended shouts and clashing weapons. He killed one man and then another. Someone was at his feet, clawing at him. Kreuhesh stamped down, feeling the man's jaw snap. He stomped again, crushing his throat under a heel. A wounded man, blinded by the blood on his face, groped at the air, crying for his brother. Kreuhesh laughed as he shattered the fool's skull.

And then the enemy were gone. Those that yet lived had run. Turning, they disappeared into the maze of buildings. His men chased them but Kreuhesh, breathing heavily, let them go ahead of him. More of his men pushed past him, stepping through the dead and the dying in the passageway and whooping as they pursued the fleeing enemy.

"You are injured, lord," Hendros said between deep breaths. Horghis, Kelwos, Melo and many others stood ready with him.

Kreuhesh looked down but despite the torches around him it was too dark to see himself clearly. "I am well, Hendros." He waved his axe in the direction his men now ran. "Remember I want one alive."

His men nodded and half of them walked into the *briya*, the rest staying with him to guard him and to do his bidding. Kreuhesh was still filled with the joy of battle and part of him wished to rush into the homes and join his men in the slaughter. Already the night echoed with the screams of women as their homes were broken into. But Kreuhesh knew he had to stay apart from such delights. He must appear to be above them now to show his men that he was better than they were. He was a chief in all but name and he had to act like one.

It was over well before morning. Some men continued to take their turns on the few women that survived until sunrise but most lay on the grass outside the *briya*, some dozing and others cleaning the blood from their weapons and trading stories about the deeds done in the night. The food uncovered inside had been brought to Kreuhesh and he saw the baskets of meat and pots and bags of grain and dried fruits were distributed amongst the leaders of the warbands.

Kreuhesh sat with his men as the rest of the spoils were laid out before him. Weapons, furs, even some lumps of copper. It was rare in the north but he knew well that it could be fashioned into spears and daggers. He would have such weapons made for himself from the copper, if he managed to keep it secret from Leuhon long enough.

In the distance, by the walls of the settlement, some men were playing a game and laughing loudly. They had stripped a young woman naked, tied a rope around her ankle and were whipping her along like a cow. Every now and then, on some signal, a man would yank the rope and pull her to the ground. She was filthy and covered in marks from the whips but she made not a sound as they tormented her. Half of the men around him watched impassively at the scene.

"Kelwos," Kreuhesh said to the warlord who was examining one of the javelins they had taken. When Kelwos looked up, Kreuhesh nodded at the men tormenting the girl. Kelwos understood at once and called for his horse before riding across to the men. His shouts could be heard across the valley and the men slunk away, casting looks back at Kelwos as he dismounted and picked up the girl. Picking her up he tossed her over the back of his horse and led it back to Kreuhesh at a relaxed amble. The men all around were in good spirits, Kreuhesh realised, and he knew then he had not been the only one missing the pleasures of riding free from the gods and their enormous clans.

Kelwos dumped the girl beside the other prizes and she curled up on the cold ground with her knees to her chest and lay there unmoving. Her dark hair covered her face but Kreuhesh looked at the weeping cuts on her back, buttocks, and thighs.

"If you wanted a woman, lord," Hendros said, a half smile on his face, "you should have told us last night. We could have found you a fresh one."

A few of the men around laughed but Kreuhesh was not amused. "Bring her to me."

Though the girl yet breathed he could see as they dragged her on her knees to him that her spirit was gone. It had flown from her body in the night and all that was left before him was the flesh. The men held her while he lifted her chin. The girl's face was bruised and bleeding. Warriors that did such things to women were beneath his contempt. They were mindless animals, unable to control themselves. They lacked the will of men and would never achieve greatness. Their names would die with them. Only men of will could win undying glory through their deeds and Kreuhesh knew his will was greater than any other man he had known.

He drove his knife into the girl's neck and pulled it out. She flinched and squeezed her eyes but he knew she would welcome it. He handed over the knife to his waiting man and received an empty bowl in return. This he held to the girl's neck as she bled from the wound. The blood had not half filled the bowl when she slumped. One of the men pulled her head back but Kreuhesh took the bowl and nodded at the men who took the dying girl away. With his men's eyes upon him he lifted the bowl to his mouth and drank the warm blood. He had never taken pleasure from drinking blood but he forced himself to drink it anyway. The gods drank human blood.

Leuhon drank blood and ate raw flesh every few days and Kreuhesh had opened the veins for his god. Eventually he had mustered the courage to ask the god why he did it.

"There is power in blood," Leuhon had replied, amused at the question.

It had taken Kreuhesh days before he tried it himself. It was fortunate that he did it in secret for he had vomited it back up. But he forced himself to finish it and he forced himself to keep it down every time since. He had expected to be filled with power, as the god had said, but that had not happened yet. Still, there was something powerful about it. The gods were the embodiment of will and he felt as though he was emulating the gods in a way that no other man had the will to do. Even before he had drunk blood himself he had been known as Kreuhesh the Bloodletter for the service he provided to the god. And ever since his men had witnessed him doing so the name had stuck. At first he had not liked it for it made him sound like a servant but now it was better for it was an emblem of the manifestation of his will and he knew that when his name lived on it would be as Kreuhesh the Bloodletter.

He wiped his mouth and handed the empty bowl away. The blood felt heavy in his stomach. "Bring me your captive, Hendros," he said.

The warrior had been defending his home inside the *briya* when Hendros had beat him down into unconsciousness. He had stood in his doorway and slain three warriors and wounded two more before then and so Kreuhesh knew he was a brave man and one skilled with a spear. But no man's bravery can survive the destruction of his people and when the bruised warrior was brought before him it was clear his will was broken. He was held by the arms and forced onto his knees. His eyes, staring through Kreuhesh, told of the despair in the man's spirit.

"Do you understand my words, warrior?" Kreuhesh asked.

The man's eyes flicked up. He spat at Kreuhesh's feet. "I understand, *hwergher*."

Kreuhesh was amused. He did not know the word but he imagined it was a grave insult. Perhaps the man was not entirely broken after all. "

"If you tell me what I want to know, I will give you horses and food and you will go free. What you do after is up to you. Do you understand?"

The captive frowned. "So you can follow me to the next *briya*? No. Just kill me." His words had a strange sound to them but Kreuhesh could understand his meaning.

Kreuhesh snorted a laugh. "But you will tell us all the places that you know. That is the price of your freedom."

"I will not trade my life for that. No." He lifted his chin and held the gaze of Kreuhesh for as long as he could before looking away.

Kreuhesh nodded. "Of course. Only a coward would take such an offer." He pointed at the man. "And I know you are a brave man. I have heard how you protected your kin. A man's kin is everything for people like you. I know this." He gestured to Hendros and waited for the other captives to be brought forward. Two women and a string of children were led up the hill. They were bent and sobbing and terrified but when they saw the man on his knees they cried out for him.

"Hesk!" the women cried.

"Pater!" sobbed the children.

The man let out a terrible cry and tried to rise but was held in place.

"You will all ride away from here," Kreuhesh said as the man's family were led away. "I will give you horses and food. I swear it in the name of Leuhon."

The captive who was named Hesk mastered himself, swallowing hard. "What do you wish to know?"

Kreuhesh smiled. "What is the largest *briya* you know? And where is it?"

Hesk's eyes were wide, looking around. "The other side of the Denipa," he said.

"Go on."

"Where this river meets the Denipa, downstream half a day there is a ford. By the marsh land. It can be crossed. Half a day before lies Pelhbriya."

"It is a large place this Pelhbriya? Larger than this?" he gestured at the man's shattered settlement.

"Larger and stronger. A fortress. You will never take it."

"Oh? And why is that?"

"It is defended by a wall of stone. And the men there are great warriors. Greater than you."

Kreuhesh nodded slowly. "I like this place. And it is the largest of the *briya*?"

Hesk hesitated but then shook his head. "North from Pelhbriya is a place named Nemiyeh. Many days. I have never been there but it is the largest *briya* anyone has ever known. The lords there rule most of the Denipa and the lands beyond to the west. They are beyond you, *hwergher*. If you test them they will slaughter you all."

Around them the men stirred and muttered but Kreuhesh was not concerned by the flaring of the man's spirit.

"Where do you get this?" Kreuhesh asked, holding up a copper ingot.

Hesk nodded. "From Pelhbriya."

"Where do they get it?"

Hesk shrugged. "It comes up the Denipa from the sea called the Melamori. Nemiyeh has more copper still. The warriors west of the Denipa all fight with copper spears and daggers. They have never been defeated."

Kreuhesh smiled. "You have been helpful indeed."

"What I tell you only brings your end nearer, *hwergher*. You are weak. If you attack them you will all die."

Kreuhesh stroked his beard and tapped a finger on his lip as he looked at his captive. "What is this word, hwergher? I do not know it."

Hesk smiled. "It is what you are. Enemy. Stranger. Murderer. Liar. Thief. Wolf. *Hwergher*"

Kreuhesh nodded, stepped closer and looked down. "You wish to see your women and your sons die before you? Is that why you mean to anger me?"

The man shook as he glared at Kreuhesh. "You are hwergher. You do not keep your oaths. We shall never leave here. We are already dead, I know this."

Smiling, Kreuhesh held out the copper ingot. "Release him," he commanded the men holding him. "Take it," he urged.

Hesk, confused, took the ingot.

"Stand," Kreuhesh commanded. With effort, the man obeyed and stood stiffly, expecting a killing blow. "Give him horses. Good ones. Enough for them all. And food." He turned back to Hesk. "Tell them that the warband of Kreuhesh the Bloodletter is coming for them. Tell them that the warriors of the god Leuhon will tear apart their flesh. You tell them."

After Hesk nodded, Kreuhesh waved him away. Disbelieving his fortune, Hesk was reunited with his family. After hurriedly sobbing and embracing they were mounted on half a dozen good horses and they rode away to the west.

"I never thought you would do it, lord," Hendros said as they watched them riding through the warbands past the smouldering *briya*. "Why warn our enemies of our coming?"

"Think of the tale they will tell," Kreuhesh said, smiling as he imagined it. "The fear will infest these places and that fear will do half our work for us."

Hendros shook his head, unable to understand it. That was well enough for Kreuhesh. Few men understood that the real battle between men was not one of arms but of will. His will would overcome all before him. His will would shatter that of his enemies.

"What will we do when we reach these places?" Horghis asked.

Kreuhesh imagined the slaughter. Pictured in his mind the streams of captives and the piles of bodies. He could almost taste the blood of those that he would drink. He would like to bring Alkmene along to witness it. He smiled at the thought and decided that he would do just that.

He waved a hand at the family riding away down the valley. "We will destroy them."

214

15

Wodra

THE COLD DROVE THEM on. Bitter wind and thin, freezing rain made them ride close with their heads down. Their horses plodded on through the short days and they all huddled together in the long nights. They hardly spoke to one another and when they did they were often irritable. But they were too tired and hungry to maintain anger for long. The cold drove it out of them.

Herkuhlos dreamt of Gendryon lying dead and cold amongst the ruin of their camp. Somehow, Gendryon was then alive and speaking to him in the darkness. He knew that it was not long before the rites after which he would join the koryos and Gendryon had taken them out onto the plains to sit together under a clear, cold sky.

"Serve Kolnos well, boys, and soon you will be men," Gendryon said. While they shivered even within their thick furs, bare-headed, bare-armed Gendryon seemed not to feel the cold at all. "When the last rite is completed you will have your ancestors within you. You know that the laws of the clan will no longer bind you but you must never forget that your koryos will be bound together and to your *koryonos*. It is your oaths that will bind you." They could just about make out his face in the moonlight. "What is more sacred than an oath?"

"Nothing," Belolukos said at once.

"Nothing upon the earth," Holkis said.

Gendryon nodded. "It is far worse to break an oath than it is to kill a man of your own clan. It is worse to speak a lie than it is to kill. You understand this, I know." He looked up at the moon for a long while and the wind blew hard, slicing into the skin of their cheeks. "Oathbreaking is the worst crime a man can commit and yet it is not always easy to keep an oath. You will be gone until the midwinter sacrifice and you will have no one but each other out there in the wild. Whichever of you is chosen to be *koryonos* the other must serve without question, do you understand?"

"Yes," Holkis said.

Belolukos nodded. "I do."

The wind gusted between them and Gendryon watched the moon for a while. "You must keep yourselves true, as straight as an arrow shaft, for whatever will come. Body, will, spirit as one. But not all of your spear-brothers of the *koryos* will be as true as they might be. Do you understand?"

"Yes," Belolukos replied.

"No," Holkis admitted, drawing a sharp look from his brother.

"All men are body, will, and spirit, yes?" Gendryon said. "You are both strong in body and in will." They heard the smile in his voice as he spoke. "Too strong, perhaps, for your own good. But will you find your spirit out there in the wild? A chief is not only a warrior but he must lead the rites for his people and to do that he must be aligned with the gods. His spirit must match his strength of body and will. How might he do that?"

"By winning glory," Belolukos said quickly.

"Through living true," Holkis added.

"You are both right. Win glory and live true. Never take an oath you do not mean to keep and once your word is given you never break it. Do what is best for your people and understand that a chief must live for himself and for his people while also being above them. You boys must be better than those who serve you."

"But one of us must serve the other," Belolukos said.

Gendryon waved that away. "I speak not only of the koryos. But the spear-brothers who serve you in this will one day be the men of your *tauta* and you must understand that most men will never be in alignment with themselves."

"I do not understand," Holkis said. "Why not?"

With a snort of amusement, Gendryon shrugged. "It is the way the gods made it. Think of Kasos. Already he is a fine singer of songs and he knows his lore better than anyone. One day he will help to carry out the rites for our people. His spirit is strong but what of his body? What of his will? Now think of Dhomyos. He as strong as a man grown, almost as strong as you, Holkis, but he has almost no will. He will follow you without question but can you ever trust him to lead a warband? Wedhris, Hermos, all your brothers can live true and win glory. But can they achieve alignment such as a chief must?" He wagged a finger at them. "Think on this when you are on your *koryos*."

They had nodded, ready to agree with anything if it meant they could ride back to the warmth of their tent before dawn.

"What of Sentos?" Holkis asked suddenly, wondering what Gendryon saw in his friend.

Gendryon had paused. "Sentos is a good boy. Takes after his father, who I have trusted to lead a warband many a time. Yes, Sentos may one day find his true self, if you lead him well." At that, he had stood, stretching his back. "Go and catch your horses. I shall race you home."

With a start, Herkuhlos woke to find the sky cleared of cloud and the wind dropped away to nothing. The air was crisp and after sunrise the sky shone a hard blue that hurt his eyes. With his dream fading, he rose and warmed himself by breaking camp.

"The Sky Father watches us," Kasos said, glancing at Herkuhlos as they rode west. "Something will happen now."

Herkuhlos looked across to Helhena. "What do you see?"

She squinted at black dots swirling above the horizon. "Can you not feel it, Herkuhlos? Something is going to happen."

Soon enough, they found what it was that the Sky Father wished them to see. The tracks of the *yotunan* became a vast mass of frozen mud in all directions. Charcoal and burnt wood lay in depressions here and there. Animal remains dotted the churned earth and every few paces were more piles of dung. Crows pecked at the remains, cawing at each other and squabbling even though there was plenty of death to share between them.

Herkuhlos rode slowly through the waste, looking down at the mess. An abandoned bundle of twigs lay trampled into the mud by a passing hoof. A scatter of seeds fallen from a sack.

"Did they camp here for a few days?" Helhena said, riding beside him.

"It looks that way."

"But why would they stop now?"

"If the *yotunan* are fleeing the gods and the gods have not yet stopped them," he mused, "perhaps they feel safer now. They have come so far from the Sacred Mountain."

"Surely they know as well as anyone that no one can flee the gods." She looked at the sky. "He sees all."

Herkuhlos glanced up but said nothing.

Riding in from his position on their flank Kasos waved a javelin overhead and raised his voice. "The tracks lead away south!"

"South?" Helhena said. "Why change direction now?" She looked around at the featureless horizon in every direction. "What lies south of here?"

Herkuhlos thought of the songs sung of ancestors who had led raids in that direction. "The plains there are rich and the men strong. Gendryon had a guest friend there. The people will not be on the plains at this time of the year and will now be in the vales of the rivers that lead to the two seas. Wherever they are they will not stand against the *yotunan*."

Helhena looked thoughtful. "And beyond the plains the mountains rise between the two seas."

"Great mountains. My ancestor Perseyus once journeyed there. You think they make for the mountains?"

"The *yotunan* have escaped from mountains. Perhaps they mean to return to others."

"Perhaps. But the mountains are passable. Beyond, far to the south, lies a land of strange people and mighty rivers."

Helhena made a face. "Why would they go there?"

"The *yotunan* want nothing but blood and the destruction of the world."

A distant noise made him turn. Belolukos was on the other side of the area of disturbed ground, waving a hand from atop his horse and shouting something.

"I cannot hear you!" Herkuhlos bellowed back.

Belolukos shouted something else that was snatched away on the breeze. He waved at them to come to him. Herkuhlos began to ride to him and then stopped his horse. When his brother was *koryonos* he expected his spear-brothers to come to him to speak. Herkuhlos had almost obeyed out of habit but he now found himself angered by his brother's presumption. Did he think he was still the leader of the *koryos*? Or was he trying to impose himself on the rest of them to re-establish his lost authority? Whatever was the truth of it, Herkuhlos could not allow himself to be summoned by anyone, even his brother.

"If you wish to speak to me, come to me and speak," Herkuhlos said and turned his horse away to ride south. If Belolukos could not hear his words he would understand his actions well enough.

"You mean to antagonise him?" Helhena said softly as they rode away.

Herkuhlos scoffed. "If he believes himself to be leader still then he will have to..." he began but trailed off as he realised it was improper to speak of such things to an outsider and a woman at that. "I do not," he said, finally.

They rode on behind Kasos, following the tracks that led away to the south. At the sound of galloping hooves he turned to find Belolukos charging to a stop, clods of earth thrown up by his horse's hooves.

"Why did you ignore me?" Belolukos said, his face flushed.

"If you wish to speak to me," Herkuhlos began, "you must come and—"

Belolukos spoke over him, blurting out his words as he pointed. "The tracks lead west!"

Herkuhlos and Kasos exchanged a look. "But they also lead south."

"Are you sure, Bel?" Kasos asked.

Belolukos rolled his eyes. "A blind child could follow these tracks, Kas."

After examining both sets of tracks leading away from the vast camp they concluded that the *yotunan* clan had separated. Some portion of them going south while the majority carried on west.

"So we have to go west," Belolukos said when they came together to discuss it.

"Why not south?" Kasos asked. "There are many wagon tracks going that way."

"Most of the tracks go west and there are more animals, more people on foot. The larger group went west, it is clear and there are wagons going that way, too."

Herkuhlos looked south. "We will go south."

The eyes of his followers turned to him.

His brother stared, confused. "But why?"

What could he say? That he could not do what Belolukos wanted without feeling like his authority was being challenged? If he said anything to suggest that was the case then the others would think him weak. If they thought him weak and unsure of his leadership then that would only serve to strengthen his brother's challenge to him and he could not allow that.

"Because I command it," Herkuhlos snapped. "We go south."

He led them on the trail of the *yotunan*. The further they followed the trail into the plains the clearer it became that there were many horses and dozens of wagons but there were few cattle and hardly any sign of people on foot. Surely the captives would be walking. It was possible that the wagons carried the most precious of them but Herkuhlos began to doubt whether he had made the right choice. But still they carried on for days heading south and even southeast, taking them further away from those that had gone west. He urged them on and rode ahead of the others, often passing out of sight of them. If his mother and sister were ahead then he meant to catch them swiftly. If they had gone west with the others then he knew every step only took him further away from them. But he could not let himself think about that and instead rode harder with the cold north wind at his back.

"The tracks are fresher," Kasos said on the third day, prodding the hoofprints with the butt of his javelin.

"We are gaining on them," Herkuhlos said with satisfaction. "We must push on harder now."

"The horses are tired," Wedhris said.

"We are tired," Dhomyos muttered.

"I thought you all wanted to be men?" Herkuhlos snapped. "You do not hear Helhena complaining and she is a woman. She has more balls than the rest of you put together."

"She probably does," Kasos said. "My balls were frozen off half a moon past."

Some of them chuckled and Herkuhlos smiled for a moment before he shook his head. "We can catch them if we push harder."

Belolukos scowled. "But catch who, brother?"

"We shall see!" Herkuhlos cried and turned his horse.

Every day the tracks grew fresher and they knew that the *yotunan* ahead were travelling slower than they had before. Ten times a day Herkuhlos thought they would find their enemy over the next horizon but no matter how hard he pushed his horses and his spear-brothers it seemed the enemy were always just out of reach. It was four more days of hard riding before they caught them up. But then one bitterly cold morning, Herkuhlos smelled smoke and heard faint sounds on the wind.

Excitement and fear twisted a knot in his belly. He turned about and galloped back to the others. They looked miserable and tired, their faces pale beneath the dirt covering them and dark circles beneath their eyes.

"We have done it," he said and told them that there was smoke in the air ahead.

Kasos breathed in deeply, nodding. "Woodsmoke."

Dhomyos reached for the axe beneath his furs and pulled it free. "Let us ride in amongst them and free our mothers."

Wedhris shook his head. "Dhom, you fool. There are hundreds of them."

Dhomyos scowled. "But we have Herkuhlos."

Belolukos snapped. "Put your axe away, you ox-wit. If they so much as see us we are all dead."

"Best keep our voices down then," Wedhris muttered.

"What do we do, Herkuhlos?" Helhena asked.

He nodded at her. "I will go forward alone," Herkuhlos told them. "While you take the horses back north half a day. I will find you when I have laid my eyes upon our enemies."

"And I will watch the herd and the others," Belolukos said, nodding in agreement.

Herkuhlos looked closely at his brother. He wondered if he meant to take them away west once Herkuhlos was gone. He imagined returning from scouting to find the plain empty and then he would be alone and without hope. Even if he did not he did not wish to leave Helhena with him. And the others might find that Belolukos was a better leader than Herkuhlos and wonder whether they should follow him instead.

"No, Bel," Herkuhlos said. "Kasos will tend the herd and command the men while I am gone."

"Kasos!" Belolukos cried. "Why do you insult me, brother?"

"It is no insult," Herkuhlos replied. "You will come with me, Bel."

Mollified, Belolukos nodded.

"And I go with you," Helhena said.

"Not this time. We go close to the enemy."

"I am not afraid of death!"

No, you are not, he thought. If anything you seek it out. "But you would risk bringing about ours," he said instead.

"You speak as if I am a burden to you. A danger!"

"You ride well, Helhena, but you are not a wolf."

She turned away but nodded.

"You chose well bringing me with you," Belolukos said as they rode away. "I am the best of them. As I would have chosen you if I was leader."

Herkuhlos felt the fire in him. "Yes," was all he managed to say.

"We should dismount," Belolukos said. "We may come across the enemy outriders soon."

"Soon," Herkuhlos said.

Coming to a gentle rise in the ground they slipped from their horses, pegged them into the earth so they would not wander into sight of the enemy, and went forward on foot. The rising ground led to a slope on the other side, a stream beyond that and a low plain stretching away to the distant horizon.

"There," Herkuhlos said, lying on his face and easing their way through the grass. The ground was frozen hard beneath his chest and the stiff grass crunched as he shifted his weight and lifted his head a fraction. "There they are."

A mass of horses with wagons parked in the centre with small fires dotted here and there. Men sat at or walked between campfires and chopped wood.

Belolukos wriggled up beside him. "What are they—"

They both froze as a huge figure stood in the centre of the camp. He was shrouded in huge furs and an enormous hood covered his head but he was huge. The ordinary men around him were only as tall as his waist or chest.

"He's even taller than you," Belolukos whispered.

"Tall as Kolnos," Herkuhlos whispered and watched as the figure lumbered past a group of warriors who only came up to his chest. "No, he is taller."

Belolukos grunted. "But how can a *yotunan* be bigger than a god?"

Herkuhlos did not know. They watched as the *yotunan* walked a few paces away to the wagons parked on the far side and ducked to look beneath the cover.

"The wagon looks like a child's toy compared to him," Herkuhlos muttered.

"Brother, this is bad. No man can stand against a monster like that."

The *yotunan* stood and walked through his warriors to where a group of six men were gathered on their knees. Their hands were bound and they wore tattered tunics and their heads were bared. All were shivering. With a blade in his hand, the *yotunan* slit the throat of every man. The watching men stepped in and collected the blood in bowls.

"What are they doing?" Belolukos asked.

Herkuhlos could only shake his head.

From the nearest edge of the camp, a band of men broke off and came to the river.

"Careful," Belolukos whispered. "Don't move."

They were far away but men's eyes were sharp.

"Why are warriors collecting water?" Herkuhlos asked, speaking softly to himself.

"Perhaps they are thirsty."

"There are no women," Herkuhlos said, looking through the camp. "No women, no girls, no boys. Where are they?"

"In the wagons under the covers?" Belolukos suggested.

"Why not send them for water if so?"

Belolukos sighed. "They're fools? The women are..." He chanced a glance at Herkuhlos. "They killed them?"

"We need to see inside the wagons."

Belolukos turned his head. "Yet we cannot."

"It will not be the first camp we have raided."

"You are mad."

"Keep your voice down, they will hear you."

Belolukos hissed. "It cannot be done."

"Mother and Laonome may be in one of those wagons. Or others from our clan or even Helhena's little sisters."

"You would risk our lives in the hope that a seeress will open her legs for you? If you want her you should just take her."

Herkuhlos banged his forehead against the earth in frustration. "What in the name of Kolnos are you talking about?"

"I'm talking about that cursed seeress following us around as if she's part of our *koryos*. What is she doing here? You're not even brave enough to lie with her so what's the point? She has no purpose. She has bewitched your mind."

"Bel, now is not the time to talk about that."

"You are the one who brought it up."

Herkuhlos gritted his teeth. "My point is our mother might be in that wagon. Or that one. What else can we do but try for them?"

"If they are within, how will we free them without being caught? We have but two horses. But we will not need them at all because that demon will catch us and tear us to pieces with his hands."

Herkuhlos closed his eyes for a moment and the thought came into him, no doubt put there by a god. "Let us go back to the horses now and eat and then we shall come back. At nightfall we will go in. Not to find mother and Laonome and to bring them out but just to see if the prisoners are in them. We can get close enough to listen to their words. We go back for the others and then pursue the *yotunan* until we find a way to free them."

After backing slowly away out of sight they turned and ran back to get their packs on the horses.

"They went west, I told you," Belolukos said as they ran. "I was right."

"Perhaps."

"Admit it, Holkis!" he said and then corrected himself. "I am sorry, brother, I forgot that you have a man's name now."

"I forget myself sometimes," Herkuhlos replied. "And you may be right about going west."

"I am."

"Perhaps. But we cannot turn that way without discovering the truth of it."

Belolukos breathed a long breath. "Sometimes I can barely believe this is happening. I hope one of us lives through the night so the story of this madness can be sung."

"Kasos will be the best man to sing it," Herkuhlos said. "It is his fate to sing our song."

"I was hoping it would be me," Belolukos said.

Herkuhlos could not help but laugh.

The horses were glad to see them and they spent some time reassuring them and checking their hooves before stopping to chew some strips of meat and drinking most of what little water they had. They tethered the horses a little closer to the enemy so that there would not be so far to flee back to them and so that the horses could graze on fresh grasses. Throughout all this, Herkuhlos and Belolukos hardly spoke a word to one another but Herkuhlos thought ceaselessly on what was facing them back at the enemy camp. The *yotunan* was enormous. It had slaughtered its prisoners and had their blood collected to drink.

Was that the fate that awaited Alkmene?

Had she already suffered that fate?

Thinking that thought made him feel weak and fearful and so he would not allow himself to dwell upon it. All that they could do now was press forward and so that was what he had to do.

Always his thoughts came back to the *yotunan*. Such a creature could not be fought by mortal hands, he knew that with certainty.

Kolnos himself had said that Herkuhlos was not the equal of even the least of them and so it was beyond doubt. The wolf god had said that one day Herkuhlos would have to defeat them but even if it was ten years from now or a hundred he could not imagine besting so mighty a foe. His only hope was to raid without being caught.

At the edge of nightfall they crept forward once more. At the top of the high ground they eased themselves up until they could look down at the parked wagons, men, horses, and cattle.

"Still there," Belolukos whispered.

It was almost too dark to see but the men had lit three small campfires within the ringed wagons and most of the warriors seemed to be gathered around their meagre warmth waiting for the food to cook. The *yotunan* sat apart from the others, wrapped in furs and hidden by darkness and flickering shadows of the firelight but looming over them all, somehow dominating the camp by his presence alone. Spitted meat roasted above the coals and flames. It smelled like pork.

"I would give anything for a taste of that," Belolukos muttered.

"You cannot drive pigs across the plains."

Belolukos paused, confused. "So?"

"Where did the meat come from?"

"Dried pork? From the wagons?"

"Since when do you roast dried pork, Bel?"

"What are you getting at?"

"The captives, Bel. The ones they slaughtered."

Belolukos breathed out sharply. "By Kolnos."

"Slaughtered for this feast."

"Evil," Belolukos muttered. "They are evil, Holkis."

"They are."

They watched the warriors as the last of the day's light drained from the sky above and full dark descended. Herkuhlos was so cold he could not feel any part of his body.

"Now," he whispered.

His brother took a shuddering breath and together they inched themselves forward over the icy ground. They would have to go slowly but swiftly enough to cover the distance so that they could be in place when most of the warriors turned in for sleep. Men slept most deeply during the first part of the night when the weariness of the day took them down into heavy slumber and this was a good time to raid a camp. They would get close enough to see and hear everything and then when the moment was right they would slip in and look inside as many wagons as they could before fleeing.

Slithering through the freezing grass toward the stream they saw a warrior walking out of the firelight, past the outermost wagons and on down toward the water. The warrior ambled, picking his way slowly with his arms out before him.

"He is fire blind," Herkuhlos hissed directly into his brother's ear while grasping his shoulder. "Let us take him!"

"Take?" Belolukos said but Herkuhlos was already up and running through the darkness.

Herkuhlos ran across the grass toward the river. The ground was sodden where springs emerged to flow into the stream but he splashed on through them without slowing.

The warrior's head jerked up at the sound just as Herkuhlos leapt the stream and drove his fist into the man's belly, folding him in two and lifting him from his feet to slam into the ground. Herkuhlos grasped the writhing man, punched him in the face hard enough to stun him and hefted him over his shoulder. Then he turned and ran back across the stream.

Belolukos reached him on the wet ground and together they ran back into the darkness, up the hill, heading for their horses. May the moon remain hidden beyond the clouds, Herkuhlos thought as he ran. Do not let them see us or our lives will be ended here.

The man in his grasp writhed, coming back to consciousness. Before he could cry out, Herkuhlos threw him to the ground and punched him in the stomach, silencing him as he curled up in breathless agony. Throwing him over his shoulder again he ran on.

"What are we doing?" Belolukos said when they were out of earshot of the camp, looking repeatedly over his shoulder.

Herkuhlos was breathing hard. "Trust," he panted, "me."

They found their way by the faint light of the moon through the clouds and by instinct but still they had to stop and take stock of their position repeatedly. Belolukos clicked his tongue for the horses and listened on the wind for any sound of them.

"There," he said. "Can you smell them?"

"All I smell is this foul dog."

"Trust me then."

When they finally reached the horses the clouds had thinned and the halfmoon travelled across the sky. Their horses strained at the fullest extent of their tethers, coming to meet them as they approached.

"They are pleased to see us," Belolukos said as he patted and stroked his horse's neck.

"Not as much as I am to see them," Herkuhlos said. "Now let us truss our prize and get away."

Belolukos used leather thongs to tie their captive's wrists and ankles and they removed the knife from his belt before tying him onto Herkuhlos' horse.

"Just like a dead pig," Herkuhlos said.

They rode away into the darkness, first heading east until they reached a stream where they turned north and rode on. Whenever the prisoner struggled, Herkuhlos would twist around and thump the man hard on his lower back, silencing and stilling him once more.

"This will do," Herkuhlos said eventually as dawn was on the way.

"Why here?" Belolukos asked, peering around in the grey darkness. To the east the horizon was showing a faint purple line against the black of the earth. "They could still catch us."

Herkuhlos cut the cords binding their prisoner and dragged him off so he landed with a thump on the frozen ground. "I can wait no longer."

Belolukos pulled the captive into a sitting position and Herkuhlos slapped his face.

The bound man took a deep breath and raised his voice to cry for help. Herkuhlos smashed his fist into the side of the man's head and he fell sideways into a limp heap.

"You fool!" Belolukos hissed. "You have slain him!"

"I barely touched him!"

"You do not know your own strength, brother."

They yanked him upright as he came back to consciousness.

"You are dead men!" their prisoner said. His voice was strange. Different to theirs, the words pronounced in unusual ways yet they could understand his speech. "The god will slay you and drink your blood!"

"What god?" Belolukos asked, confused.

Herkuhlos shook his head. "Never mind that. Tell us about your captives."

"I tell you nothing."

Herkuhlos showed him his knife. Held it up to the faint light of the distant dawn. "Can you see this? Look at it! You will tell us or I will carve your ears off."

"And your nose," Belolukos added.

"Then we will cut off more important things," Herkuhlos said.

Belolukos laughed at that, enjoying himself. Both had heard enough as boys of the ways to get a captive warrior to tell you where his herds were.

"Tell you what?" the man said, warily.

"Whether you had captive women in your wagons."

The man sighed, tension leaving his body as he began to understand what was happening to him. "Women? No, no. No people no more."

"He lies," Belolukos said. "Here, I will cut off one of his ears." As he spoke, he pinched the man's ear and twisted it, bringing his knife close.

"It is truth! Truth, I swear it by the god. By all the gods. We have no women, no children. No men. The god gifted them to the others."

"What god?" Herkuhlos asked, frowning.

"The god," the man replied, licking his lips and clearing his throat. "The god my master."

"You serve a god?" Belolukos replied.

"We all serve the gods, friend."

Belolukos rolled his eyes, scoffing.

"Which do you serve?" Herkuhlos said.

"My god descended the Sacred Mountain and chose me to be his acolyte. I serve him now and always."

"You do not mean that *yotunan* back at your camp?" Herkuhlos said.

The man lunged for Herkuhlos' throat, his face twisted in rage. Herkuhlos fell back in surprise with the man atop him but Belolukos was there to reach his arm around the man's throat and lift him away. Together they wrestled him to the ground and held him there until his fury had subsided.

"Next time you try anything," Belolukos said, right into the man's ear, "you get the knife."

"You insulted the god," he spat. "It is you that will get the knife!"

"Let's kill this shrivelled sheep turd, Holkis!" Belolukos said, pushing his knife point against the man's neck.

"Wait," Herkuhlos said, his tone calm. "Just wait, brother." He eased his brother's knife arm away and spoke softly. "There is no need for any of this. If my words insulted you, it was not my intent. We merely want to understand. Tell me. You tell me and I will listen."

Belolukos hissed a warning and Herkuhlos glanced in his direction to silence him.

"Not me you insulted," the man muttered, "but the god."

"Then I apologise. Tell me about the god."

The man hesitated. "You will free me?"

Herkuhlos could not bring himself to lie but he lowered himself to deliver something close to one. "After you tell me everything I want to know, I will have no use for you."

The man scoffed but he appeared mollified. "What do you want to know?"

Herkuhlos did not know where to start with what he wanted to know. "What is your god's name?"

"We call him the god. But the other gods sometimes called him Wodra."

"Wodra. I never heard of a god with that name." Herkuhlos held up a hand. "No offense meant. Is he from your land?"

"He is a god. He is from wherever he wills. But he came from the Sacred Mountain."

"And where do you come from?"

"I am Koss Clan. My people live in the shadow of the Sacred Mountain."

"And how then did you come to serve the god Wodra?"

"Many gods descended the mountain together. A long time they honour us with their presence. They came to choose. Some chose other clans but Wodra chose me and my clan to be his acolytes. A great honour. We have served him in his descent and the sacred journey."

"What is this sacred journey."

"You would not understand."

"Tell me anyway."

"You are not *permitted* to understand."

Belolukos grasped the captive's head. "Time to take our first ear, brother."

The man jerked. "Wait, wait! I will tell it, I will tell. The sacred journey to rule new lands and to make new clans."

"How many gods descended the Sacred Mountain?"

"Twelve gods. Wodra is one of the foremost."

Herkuhlos hung his head for a moment. There was no doubt now that the *yotunan* had deceived this man and his clan about what they were. "Who are the others?"

"I am not permitted to know."

"But you do know, don't you."

Belolukos raised his knife and jabbed it against the man's cheek. "Tell it quickly or I'll cut your face."

"I only know some. The Stag, the Boar, the Lion, the Bull, Geryon, Wodra, Ladon, and the most terrible and glorious of them all, the great god Kerberos."

"And where are they, these others? Why are they no longer together?"

"The gods' paths lead where they lead. It is not for mortals to know the will of the gods."

Belolukos scoffed. "Of course it is, you fool."

Herkuhlos glared at his brother to silence him and spoke quickly. "What happened when they separated?"

"A few days past we stopped and the gods... they... spoke. They had disagreements."

"About what?"

"We are not permitted to know."

Bel grasped the man's ear. "That's it, I'm taking it now."

Their captive spoke rapidly. "Some of the gods wished to go west and others northwest, others southwest. Just three of the gods wished to go south. My lord Wodra demanded to go southeast and so we go now this way."

"What happened to your prisoners? The people your god took on this great raid you have made these many moons past."

Belolukos growled behind him. "We saw how your master slaughtered captives, you worm, so do not think to lie to us."

"My lord Wodra has little desire for captives. Just a few old men and boys that refuse to obey. Refuse my master's rule. These men he must drink."

"Gods do not drink the blood of men, you mad fool," Belolukos said.

"You know nothing!" the man said, shaking.

"Why not take women and children also if your god needs blood?"

"To travel swiftly. We will soon abandon our wagons when the land rises. We need only to cross the great mountains in the south to reach new lands where endless worshippers await his rule and we loyal men shall serve as his acolytes for ever."

"His rule?" Belolukos said, scoffing.

Herkuhlos glanced hard at him before turning back to the man. "So all the prisoners have gone with the other gods?"

"The Lion took the greatest share, for his sacred path leads him to a place not far from the plains and there he will rule over those he has taken. In time, all the gods will do the same in the lands of the north and the west and the south. My brothers and I will serve Wodra in the lands of the south where men now worship false gods. Those false gods will be overthrown and Wodra will rule and we shall be his acolytes and—"

Belolukos struck him hard, knocking him down.

"Ah, I can take no more of this madness, brother!" he cried. "His ravings make me sick to my guts."

"I know," Herkuhlos said. "And we have heard enough. We must go back to the west. You were right, brother. We should never have come here."

"At least now we know we must find the *yotunan* named the Lion above all the other demons."

The man struggled upright. "My god is—"

Belolukos struck him again. "Your god is a monster. You serve a *yotunan*, you witless fool! A vile beast escaped from the Sacred Mountain. Escaped from the captivity of the true gods, the only gods!"

"Lies!"

Herkuhlos stood and looked down. "You have been deceived. The *yotunan* are cunning in their lies. They speak only to conceal truth in order to wreak their destruction upon our world."

The man, wild-eyed, pointed at them. "You are the deceivers! And my lord Wodra will bring down destruction upon—"

Belolukos kicked him in the stomach and he curled up clutching himself.

"You want to kill him?" Belolukos asked, taking his axe from his belt. "Or shall I?"

The man looked up and struggled to rise.

"He has been deceived," Herkuhlos said. "Tricked."

"All the more reason to slay him."

The man got to his knees and shuffled closer, raising his bound hands as if to clutch at Herkuhlos. "You will be merciful, my friend, I know you will."

Belolukos placed his axe on his shoulder. "Dawn comes, brother. We need to be gone."

Herkuhlos looked down at the frightened, cold man. "Why do you serve this... Wodra? What do your people know of him? Your people had worshipped him before?"

"We worshipped him when he came to us."

"Then how do you know he is a god and not something else?"

The man stared as if Herkuhlos was the one who was mad. "If you have seen him then surely you know."

"We saw him from afar. He was big. Is that all that makes him a god to you?"

The captive's eyes shone in the predawn light as he rose higher on his knees. "If you could lay your eyes upon him you would see that he is unlike any mortal that ever lived. And his power is beyond mortal understanding. Once you taste that power, you know the truth of it."

"Taste?" Herkuhlos said. "How did you taste it?"

He restrained his running words then spoke softly. "You are not permitted to know."

Belolukos leaned down. "Speak or I'll hurt you."

"You mean to kill me anyway so why should I tell you anything more?"

Looking at Herkuhlos, Belolukos shrugged. "He makes a good point, brother."

Herkuhlos looked down at the man. "Your lord escaped the Sacred Mountain along with eleven other *yotunan*. Your master is evil. Your master has wrought nothing but destruction since his escape. Destruction, disharmony, disorder. The gods exist to preserve the world, not to destroy it. You serve evil. But I will release you from your service."

He took out his axe.

The captive shook, grinding his teeth. "My lord will find you," he spat the words, "and he will kill you."

"I doubt he will change his course for a single acolyte,"

Herkuhlos said. "Especially one as weak as you. But if he does, I will face him."

The man's face twisted into a savage grin. "He will destroy you."

"Perhaps. But I will not be deceived and I will not betray the true gods."

Herkuhlos hesitated, looking down at the anguished face.

Belolukos sidled closer. "You want me to do it?"

"No," Herkuhlos said, angry at the momentary temptation in him that wanted to accept.

All things die.

He swung his axe down, chopping into the man's skull. The man's spirit left him in a slow sigh that was almost a groan. He slumped and Herkuhlos pulled his weapon free, pushing the man down with his foot. His body lay there on the dark grass, cold and alone. There was no honour gained by his death. No glory in it. Herkuhlos cleaned the blood from his axe and met his brother's eye. Belolukos nodded once and strode for the horses.

Herkuhlos and Belolukos rode north side by side, hurrying to find the rest of their spear-brothers and Helhena.

"So," Belolukos said, smiling as the sun rose and touched them with its light and warmth. "It is to be west again after all?"

"Yes, brother, you were right," Herkuhlos replied. "West. To find the Lion."

16

Pelhbriya

ALKMENE KNEW HER chances at escape had improved. Since crossing the great river the demon clans had separated. The giants had led their warriors and stolen herds away to the south and the west. But Leuhon had led them north along the banks of the river. It was true that there were still more than a hundred warriors and half as many herders around her. All served Leuhon, willingly or not and they all stood between her and freedom.

Despite all that she began to hope.

Kreuhesh the Bloodletter, her captor and tormentor, was away from the clan more than he was with it. He had led many of his warriors away on raids as the clans approached the river and the long crossing began. There were countless animals and horses to be driven across and herders and servants constructed boats from wagons and made coracles from animal skins stretched over green wood cut from the skeletal woods that filled the valleys all around.

Hundreds of trees were cut down and rafts banged together. Boats were carried as prizes away from the peoples that lived beside the river and along the tributaries all around. The people that Kreuhesh and his warbands raided and captured. Many of those people heard of the danger approaching and had fled upriver or across it, leaving their homes and whatever they could not carry to be burnt and taken, but Leuhon's warriors did not appear disappointed when they returned empty handed.

Whenever she had seen him, between raids, Kreuhesh had seemed joyful. She knew well how raiding filled men's spirits with joy for it was what they lived for and once tasted, it was never forgotten. But Kreuhesh's face was ever twisted into a kind of constricted grin and his eyes shone with madness. Never in her life had Alkmene feared a man. Even Leuhon, the giant, deformed monster that he was, did not scare her as Kreuhesh did. His leering made her shiver and his endless threats were not idle ones, she knew that. It was only a matter of time before he or one of his men lost control of themselves and violated her or Laonome and they were capable of killing them suddenly and with hardly any provocation.

When it was their turn to cross the river they were ferried over in one of the handful of boats. It was a narrow, low-sided thing with almost as much water in the bottom as there was outside of it but the herders dragged them across the river over a ford and she was grateful that neither she nor Laonome had to wade through the water as so many others had done. The water would have come up to Laonome's neck, she was sure and it would not have taken much for her to be drowned.

Indeed, there had been countless accidents in the crossing.

Cattle, horses, men, wagons, many had slipped or been dragged away by the current never to be seen again. Trees and the banks and the curve of the river meant it was difficult to see far downstream but she overheard that there was white water down there and rocks in the river that smashed men apart when they hit them. While she was being pulled across in the boat, Alkmene looked at the current and imagined falling into the water and being carried away. It would almost be a relief to be free of the demons and their warriors.

But Alkmene had her arms wrapped tightly around Laonome, kneeling before her in the freezing water in the bottom of the leaky boat. She would never abandon her. Never. Whatever she had to suffer to keep her daughter safe she would suffer it with all the strength she possessed. She had nothing else now but the hope that her line would continue in her sons, safe behind the demons in the east. Great Mother protect them, she thought.

On the other side of the river was a massive and chaotic camp with hundreds of shouting men and terrified beasts being herded into place toward the demon that they belonged to. Alkmene, Leonome, Henu, and the other women were driven north along with a stream of captives toward the area that Leuhon's followers had established. Wagons were now in short supply. Some had been lost down river, others were stuck in soft mud, and others had been disassembled for the crossing and had not been built again. They spent a cold, wet night huddled together amongst the chaos. Alkmene wondered if she could use the disorder to slip away through it all but both she and Laonome were shivering uncontrollably in the darkness and without furs and fire and food in their bellies it would be death even if they managed to get away. At times in the night, when the sounds all around them quieted and the wind changed to the east, she heard the rushing river off in the darkness. The endless waters carrying themselves away southward towards the Melamori. If only she could steal what she needed, steal a boat, and float away on the current.

It was a faint hope but it was something. She resolved to find some way to hide food for their journey. To find another weapon or even a flint from the earth that she could fashion into a cutting edge. And perhaps there would be a way to barter for warmer clothing from one of the herders who rode in the thick furs. All she could offer, though, was her body. She shuddered. No, she could not lower herself. The only good fortune she had been granted thus far was to be spared that indignity and she would not throw that away. She was a descendent of famed Perseyus and had born the child of a god. She would not debase herself for anything.

The next day the demons had led their clans away from Leuhon and Alkmene had felt a thrill that she could not place.

"What does it mean?" Laonome had asked quietly as the word spread.

"That our lord Leuhon means to make his clan here," Henu answered, her smugness infuriating. "You see, Alkmene? I was right. Look around you. This is our clan now. These are our people."

"Do not listen to Henu," Alkmene said to her daughter. "It just means that something has changed but not everything. We are still captives of a demon and his mad, corrupted servants."

Henu hissed at her. "Lower your voice!"

"I will not," Alkmene said, though she did not continue to voice her thoughts.

When the clan moved out again, Alkmene and the other high

value women were once again placed inside wagons for the journey north. Alkmene wondered if it would ever end or if they would wander for year after year to the edge of the world.

"They say Kreuhesh has taken his warbands north," Henu said as the wagon rolled.

"Who says?" Alkmene replied, looking around at the women.

"I heard two warriors talking this morning when we went to make water," Henu replied. "And anyway it is obvious, is it not?"

Alkmene nodded. "Because he has not come to torment me."

Henu shrugged. "You should be grateful for his attention. He is a powerful man. Second only to Leuhon. In our new clan he will be something like a chief. And you might be his favourite wife. Think on that."

Alkmene stared at her, scarcely able to believe it. "You are mad. He has taken everything from us."

"Yes," Henu allowed. "But that is what men do. They protect what they have and take what they can from other men. The strongest are the victors. Women should count themselves fortunate to be protected by the strongest."

"Your own nephews, Henu, your brothers were slaughtered by him and his men. You have lost your wits. I shall never lay with a man as evil as that."

Henu sighed. "I mourn them every day. But that is in the past now. The wheel turns and we move on. Ever on. When the wheel turns again you may find yourself a strong woman once more with the most powerful husband and lord the earth has ever known. Your daughter might make herself a great marriage also and your blood will flow on." Henu looked pointedly at her. "And she carries my blood also." She shrugged. "If you resist the turning of the wheel you may find yourself crushed beneath it."

"I will never submit to evil," Alkmene said, crossing her arms and turning away to signify that the discussion was over. How she wished she had her own tent again so that she could throw Henu out of it.

"You value your own honour over that of your blood," Henu said, unable to let the matter rest. "Over the good of your own people."

Alkmene turned her gaze upon Henu. Slowly she sat up on to her knees so that she loomed over Henu, who looked unnerved. "You will be silent," she said in a low voice.

Henu glared for a moment but looked down. When Alkmene sat back down she found Laonome staring at her with worry upon her brow.

"It is well, dear one," Alkmene said, reaching out to squeeze her hand. "All will be well."

As the wagon rattled on, the axles squeaking beneath her, Alkmene thought about what Henu had said. As much as she hated to admit it there was a kind of grim sense to it. Instead of fighting and seeking escape she could find a path through by cooperation with her captors. They had absolute power over her fate but if they were to be a clan, as Henu believed, then perhaps the women they took would regain some of their traditional power as wives and mothers and even more. The warriors that followed Leuhon had all been recruited from the clans of the forest, the vales, and the plains. They were men just like all the others she had known. They raided, killed, took what they needed and moved on, just as the clans of her fathers had always done. It was only the demons that had corrupted them and forced them endlessly on and on from one clan to the next so that they never returned home and instead always went on, ever growing their numbers. If they were to finally settle in one place perhaps the normal order would be restored. And if that was to happen, would it truly be worse than death to live amongst those men? After all, those men had chosen to submit to a new lord and now they were off doing what men always did. Raiding neighbouring and distant clans.

The wheels turned beneath her on the journey north. Around them the land changed a little to one of hills and wide plains between them crossed by streams and small rivers. The bare trees of the woodlands they passed by and through were oak and ash but also pines standing tall and green through the cold. The worst of the winter had passed and there was no more snow. Indeed, on some trees tiny green buds were already showing though spring seemed far off. She spoke to her daughter about the trees and the birds above them. The women told stories of the gods and the ancestors and even reminisced about their husbands and sons and the others recently slain. Often they wept but sometimes they laughed. It was at times almost pleasant and in no small part that was because Kreuhesh had not returned and the men he had left to watch her did so from a distance.

She began to wonder again about escape. Every once in a while she caught a flash of light through the trees and knew it was the river that flowed south and every time she imagined herself finding a boat and paddling it away to freedom with Laonome before her. Occasionally, she might allow Henu to accompany them in her fantasy but only if the older woman had been quiet for a while.

It was midday when Henu woke her with a jab of her foot. Alkmene jerked awake, looking around in panic for the danger.

"Something is happening," Henu said, nodding forward past the driver and the oxen.

Many of the women were already on their knees looking at something and Alkmene raised herself to see what the fuss was about. Usually it was a fight between herders from different clans or warriors from different warbands or cattle that had taken ill or a lame horse. The sound of galloping hooves filled the air along with distant shouts coming together like the sound of a rushing river. She looked, expecting something tedious but instead gasped.

Ahead, on a great, wide mound with a flat top was a great settlement surrounded by a high stone wall. They had passed similar places either side of the river but nothing so large and never in her life had she seen such a wall. It surrounded dozens of large houses. Men stood on the wall and the roofs of those houses and there must have been hundreds of them.

"What is it?" the women asked the driver.

He scowled at them over his shoulder. "Be silent, women."

They prodded his back through his furs and asked him again. They were not afraid of him because he was just a herder. "Tell us, Boro. Unless you do not know. Old Boro knows nothing, the real men do not tell him."

"I do know," he snapped. "It is a *briya*. They call it Pelhbriya."

"Why have we come here?" Alkmene demanded, staring at the men standing ready to defend their homes.

He frowned and pointed. "They're going to raid it."

Alkmene stood, hunched beneath the canopy, and looked ahead. At the base of the mound hundreds of horsemen rode in either direction around it. Some ranged up the slope to throw a javelin at the men on the walls or just to hurl insults and threats.

The men within stood with their spears and looked out impassively as if they knew that nothing could possibly harm them from within their walls. Alkmene thought they were right. They were taller than a man and were strong enough to stop horses. With the slope on their side the defenders could fight from atop the wall and fend off anyone who came at them with relative ease, thrusting down at those brave enough or mad enough to try scaling the stonework.

"They are mad," Alkmene muttered. "No one can raid such a place."

Henu snorted. "Ride with men on a few raids when you were young and now you think yourself Perseyus reborn."

A couple of the other women sniggered and Alkmene gritted her teeth to still her anger. "I have driven my spear through a man's teeth and shattered his spine and tasted his blood in the air. You know of nothing but weaving and herbcraft and would do well to remember that you are beneath me. Now be silent."

Henu said nothing and Alkmene did not bother to look at her. Instead she watched as the horsemen clattered ever nearer up the slope from all directions. Some arrows were shot from both sides and javelins were hurled. A man was thrown from his horse and the men on the wall ducked and moved about as the missiles flew. But the riders fell back again and again. Some rode away with javelins or arrows in them while horses collapsed under the barrage. The shouts and thundering hooves grew louder as the repeated charges increased their intensity and the driver of Alkmene's carriage leapt down to calm the usually docile team of oxen. Herders and other captives cried out at the sight ahead of them. They were close enough to see and hear but far enough away that they were in no danger. Still, most of them had never seen anything the like of it and were afraid and agitated by the violence. Alkmene had been part of a fifty-warrior raid and even she was stunned by the sight.

Her attention was drawn to the left side of the mound where more warriors clustered on either side. She pushed through the other women and climbed into the driver's bench to better see what was happening. Then she understood why they were there. There was an entrance through the wall. A wide gap in the stones with a wooden barrier across it like a gate in a corral only built solidly from large timbers that had hardly a gap between them. On the wall on either side men stood and hurled down javelins and rocks at the attackers.

A band of warriors rode up close under a barrage of missiles, leapt from their horses and attacked the gate with long handled axes. Not war axes with their blunt heads but the kind used to fell trees. They hacked at the timbers while the men within tried to kill them. Some leaning down from the walls and the gate itself to thrust spears at them, exposing themselves to arrows from the riders circling lower down the slope. One defender leaned over the gate from above and stabbed down at an attacker with a spear before the shaft was pulled, sending the man toppling to earth on the wrong side of the gate where he was brutally hacked to pieces. Some of the warriors tried scaling the walls for in truth they were not much higher than a man could reach at full stretch. But climbing with a weapon in hand was not easy and every time one attempted it he was quickly repulsed by the men within by arrow, spear, or stone.

The warriors attacking the gate had the worst of it, clustered together as they were, and when half lay dead or dying at the gate the rest fell back, ducking low as they ran down the slope with missiles coming after them. The men on the wall cheered and shook their spears in the air.

"What are you doing?" the wagon driver cried, staring up at Alkmene in the driver's seat. "Get down from there, woman!"

She hardly looked at him. "See to your oxen, herder," she said in the most dismissive tone she could muster.

Watching from the corner of her eye she saw him scratch his head beneath his hood before he turned again to watch the fighting while he muttered under his breath.

Another band of warriors rushed the gate and once again they were met with a terrible storm of arrows and stones and thrown spears from the walls and the roofs of houses behind the wall. They hacked at the timbers and kicked and pushed at the gate. It shook hard against their attacks, shaking back and forth but despite their assault it held and the men fell back.

"They will never do it," Alkmene muttered under her breath, delighted to see how many of her captors were falling. A hundred more and perhaps they would give up. She willed them to attack to the last man so that she could take Laonome and run.

She froze.

Everyone around her was staring at the fighting. She could flee now. The driver might raise the alarm but she could slip out the back and take Laonome with her. She looked around the side of the wagon and her heart sank.

Two warriors. Kreuhesh's men. They sat their horses amongst the other wagons but they were both looking at her. One smirked as she saw him register her.

Alkmene sat back on the bench. She almost screamed. How could Kreuhesh be so utterly mad and yet so competent? If she had the power to do it then she would have torn his heart from his chest and forced him to eat it, the vile pig shit, while she laughed and spat in his face.

Taking a deep breath, she calmed herself. The day was not yet over. Things could still go ill for Kreuhesh and those warriors might be needed. She would have to keep watch for an opportunity but even if it did not come then this was still good for her. Her captors, her tormentors, the evil ones, were losing. They were dying before her and she revelled in their deaths. They bled into the earth and each drop was a blessing for the Great Mother.

Gasps and shouts filled the air around her. She leaned forward and looked to the far left beyond the throng to see Leuhon striding forward through his warriors. Alkmene's heart pounded at the sight of him. Leuhon wore a great boar tusk helm and his chest, shoulders and belly were likewise covered. There must have been hundreds or even thousands of tusks used to make his armour. They must have been taken from the armour of slain chiefs and great warriors along the way and with a pang of loss she realised Gendryon's armour must also have been torn apart and rebuilt for the demon. Leuhon's great lion pelt, fastened about his shoulders over his armour, fluttered and flew out behind him like a cloak. In his hands he carried an enormous spear with a polished stone spearhead. The riders surged ahead of him and assaulted the men on the walls beside the gate with their javelins. Other warriors dismounted and ran after Leuhon as he strode up the slope. The defenders were in something like a panic at his approach and at the massive attack but though some fell more and more gathered about the gate to repulse the charge. Arrows flew, whipping down at Leuhon who ducked his head, hunched his massive shoulders, and walked on through the barrage. Some struck him and broke on impact and bounced off his armour. Others stuck in the flesh of his arms and legs or slipped between the small boar tusk plates and though he flinched and thrashed he walked on with hardly a break in his pace until he was at the gate itself. The warriors atop the gate and wall hurled stones and javelins but Leuhon lifted his huge spear and swung it across the top of the wall like he was sweeping dead leaves from the top of a tent in autumn. He smashed them down from the wall and from the gate, knocking some to the ground outside where they were set upon by the warriors and hacked and battered to pieces. The roaring voices rose into cheers as Leuhon's followers sensed he was about to bring them victory. The demon kicked at the gate and a single blow almost shattered it. He kicked again, rocking it back and forth. Spears thrust at him from within and he swatted them aside and leaned down to throw a shoulder against the gate, ramming himself against it again and again until the timbers cracked. With a final kick the gate collapsed and Leuhon smashed it aside to stride within, his spear before him. The warriors gave howls of triumph and rushed in after him shaking their weapons above their heads. The remaining defenders disappeared from view as they ran down to defend the paths into their homes.

Alkmene was stunned. She shook as she listened to the screams that soon filled the air. She had heard that sound before but never from so many. The women behind her had long since ducked back inside the wagon and crouched inside with their hands over their ears.

"Laonome," Alkmene said, seeing her daughter likewise curled up and covering her head. "Come up here and sit beside me."

Henu's head jerked up at once. "No! She does not need to see this."

"She does," Alkmene said, returning Henu's look. "She is a daughter of chiefs. Laonome? Come."

"It is cruel," Henu objected. "Whatever she is, she is but a girl."

Laonome pulled herself away from Henu's grip and climbed onto the bench beside Alkmene who put an arm around her.

"It is not my purpose to be cruel," Alkmene said. "But you must not look away."

"I understand, mother." Despite her brave words, her body shook and her eyes were wet with tears.

As she spoke, the first of the prisoners were dragged from the *briya* by Leuhon's warriors. Wounded men staggered away with their hands bound while women were dragged along the ground by their hair. All were slapped and punched and abused terribly as they were propelled into groups and bound or held under guard.

Kreuhesh appeared from within, striding forth from the shattered gate with his men around him. Even from a distance she recognised him by his size, his armour, his bearskin cloak. He was covered in blood from his feet to the top of his helm but she doubted that much of it was his. He turned and bowed his head as Leuhon appeared. The demon was likewise spattered with blood but it was clear he was wounded. He limped and his left arm hung loose. The great spear was gone and he still had the heads and foreshafts of arrows stuck in his arms and legs. Alkmene prayed that the Mother would cause his wounds to fester and kill him but she did not hold much hope that he could be so easily killed.

Kreuhesh led Leuhon down and across the slope to the clusters of prisoners and pointed to some with his axe, blood dripping from the end. Warriors dragged two women forward and yanked at their tunics, ripping them down to reveal the women's bare flesh.

Laonome turned away and pressed her face into Alkmene's neck.

"No," Alkmene said, her revulsion and anger causing her voice to be harsh. "You must know what our enemies are."

Henu hissed from behind her. "No girl needs to see women violated. Even if they be strangers."

Alkmene ignored her and Laonome turned her head to watch once more.

Leuhon reached for one of the women and grasped her by the upper arm. He nodded at Kreuhesh who lunged forward and stabbed the woman in the neck with a knife. She clutched at the wound, shock and confusion overcoming her terror momentarily. Through her fingers, blood welled and gushed down her white skin. Then Leuhon grasped her other arm and lifted her from the ground. He brought her close to his face and sank his teeth into her neck, sucking and drinking from the wound while she struggled.

Laonome buried her head into her again and the women cried and sobbed. Alkmene felt her own tears welling in her eyes but though she shook and wept she would not look away.

The woman stopped fighting and hung limp. After drinking a moment longer, Leuhon threw her down and motioned for another. His face and blond beard glistened with fresh blood as he reached down and yanked out the arrows from his body. Kreuhesh's men pulled the next woman forward though she fought and thrashed in their grasp. Before he thrust his knife into her neck he suddenly turned and looked and looked at the watching crowd of captives and herders. Alkmene understood then that this was at least in part a display for them all. They all had heard that Leuhon and the other demons were eating the captives but few admitted to seeing it themselves. This now was like a secret rite being performed before the entire clan. Its purpose could only have been to terrify them and to keep them in line. Or perhaps they were now so certain of their power that they no longer cared if the livestock knew what fate awaited them.

Kreuhesh's gaze swept past her and then suddenly snapped back as he saw Alkmene. With a relaxed movement he raised his bloody knife above his head in a friendly gesture and grinned at her. She tensed, horrified. Quickly, he turned back and drove his knife into the woman's neck and drew it out in a gush of blood.

Alkmene turned away, clutching her daughter and wrapping her arms around her shoulders.

"Come away now," she muttered to Laonome, leading her back into the wagon with the screams filling the air behind her along with the taste of blood. "Come away."

There could be no peace with the demon and his followers. They were truly evil, she understood it now as she never had before.

This will only end with our deaths, she thought.

Our deaths or theirs.

1 7

The Denipa

HERKUHLOS SHIVERED in his furs. The river ahead of them was mighty. The greatest he had ever seen. It had to be the Denipa, known from the songs of those who had raided far to the west in days gone by. Its source was somewhere in the far northwest and it flowed into the distant Melamori far to the south.

The winter had been terrible and long. The days of their passage west across the plain blurring together until it grew difficult to tell one from the other or remember how long it had been. The cold was overwhelming. It got into their bones and nothing could make them warm again. The nights were the worst and seemed to last forever and passed in a shivering daze of dreams and half-waking nightmare. They collected wooden detritus and dried dung from the trail as they rode and had a small fire as often as they could, clustered about it while it burned. The day that they came across the remains of a smashed wagon had been bitterly cold and they had built a fire large enough to be seen from across the world but none of them had cared any more about staying hidden. All they had wanted was warmth.

Along the way their food had dwindled faster than any of them had believed. No matter how little they ate and how much their stomachs ached with hunger the food shrank.

"We will slaughter a horse," Herkuhlos said one night over their small fire. "When we need to."

They had all nodded, chewing on their frozen, dried strips of horseflesh.

What to drink was always their concern. None of the mares had milk anymore. The cold had dried it up. When they came to small streams on the plain, the passage of the *yotunan* had often filled them with filth and dung. Whether it was malicious destruction or inattentive herders they did not know but either way they had to break up muddy, stinking ice and scoop up the brown water below to drink. Even springs they found trampled and disturbed.

But the worst of the weather passed as the days got longer. It was still cold and rain fell more frequently but they were no longer struggling for every step. Soon the trail led them into a shallow valley. The springs at its head became streams and they became a river that widened as it wound its way roughly west, growing ever larger until it flowed into the widest river any of them had ever seen.

It had to be the Denipa.

"We have come a long way west," Belolukos said beside Herkuhlos, looking at the distant bank. "Do you remember the song of Heitar the Six-fingered?"

Herkuhlos nodded. "He crossed the Denipa in his raid."

"He did."

"If he did it then we can do it too." Herkuhlos did not feel as confident as he tried to appear. The river was wide indeed.

"Yes but he was a great chief."

"He was nothing when he crossed, Bel. He became chief because of his raid."

"True enough."

"Surely, you do not mean for us to cross that," Wedhris said, riding up beside them with the others.

"We have to cross it," Herkuhlos said.

"If we could find a boat then we could do it," Kasos said, smiling. "Or if we could build a raft, we could do it with ease. But how do we get the horses across?"

"Horses swim," Belolukos said.

"Horses drown," Kasos countered.

"Heitar the Six-fingered did it," Belolukos said. "You know his song better than any of us, Kas."

Kasos nodded. "He captured a man who lived on the river and forced him to show the best way to cross. There will be no one here now to show us. The demon clan will have taken them all."

"The *yotunan* crossed this river," Herkuhlos said. "And so we must. Come."

He led them through the churned earth. Wagon wheel tracks cut gouges into the earth and the mud was mixed with vast quantities of dung. Great herds had been forced across at this point and so Herkuhlos knew it could be crossed.

"There," Herkuhlos said as they reached the muddy banks. "It is a ford."

Dhomyos scratched his cheek. "Deep one, by the looks of it."

"We can ride across?" Wedhris said, looking between Herkuhlos and Belolukos.

"Do not be a fool," Belolukos said. "If you are thrown you'll be off down the river and that will be the end of you."

"Current don't look too strong," Dhomyos said.

"But it is," Helhena said. "The river is wide and though it is slowed by the bend, the water flows swiftly when shallow."

They glanced at her, then at Herkuhlos, and finally at Kasos for confirmation.

"Sounds right," Kasos said, shrugging.

"We can go upstream, look for somewhere better?" Wedhris said.

"Or downstream," Dhomyos said.

"It appears wider upstream," Helhena said. "And, look, you can see the white water downstream. The river flows faster there."

"We could jump from rock to rock?" Dhomyos said.

"One slip and you're dead," Wedhris replied.

Belolukos scoffed. "And what about the horses, you fools?"

Herkuhlos turned to face them. "The *yotunan* crossed here. They forced great herds across. They even rolled wagons across or floated them. We can manage it with our few horses. Let us be on with it."

"But I am so short," Wedhris said. "Where you will walk, I will go under."

Dhomyos laughed. "Hold on to your horse, then."

Wedhris nodded.

Herkuhlos grasped his shoulder. "Have no fear. You are stronger than you think you are. It is what must be done, and so it shall be done."

Wedhris swallowed, looked up and nodded once more. "I understand."

"You stay right behind me and do not stop for anything. All will be well."

They led the horses down into the water, speaking softly and stroking them. The lead mares were steady enough but Herkuhlos' young stallion was agitated and he tossed his head. Grasping the halter, he brought him under control and stroked his neck before they crossed.

The water was freezing. Colder even than he had expected and the feel of it on his legs took his breath away even before it reached his loins. He cried out then and his horse jerked its head up. When they were a few paces from the bank and the water was up to his waist he felt the current pushing at him. It was strong indeed. It tugged at his legs and loose rocks rolled beneath his feet, threatening to send him spilling into the water.

That would be death, he knew. He forced himself to go slowly, feeling the way with each step. His horse was unhappy, blowing hard and tossing his head.

"Steady," he muttered to his horse. "We are strong. You are strong."

The current was so strong that he began to wonder if he had not made a mistake. Perhaps the *yotunan* had crossed moons ago when the water was lower and the current slower. Was he leading his people over a ford that could not be crossed in early spring?

Turning to look at the line of people and horses behind him, he began to veer from the path and found himself stepping down, the water coming up to his neck before he stepped onto the higher ground again. He led his horse further the other way and found the water soon growing deeper on that side.

"Stay on the ford!" Herkuhlos shouted back to his people. "It is not wide."

He turned back to watch the far bank. Bare earth with no grass. The demon clan had clawed their way out there, carving deep hoofprints in the mud and the ground had not yet healed. Suddenly, he felt vulnerable.

If anyone lay in wait for him, they could shoot bows and throw javelins as they came to the water's edge and there would be nothing he could do about it. Nothing but die an inglorious death. His thoughts strayed to his mother and sister. Do they hope we are coming for them? Or have they lost all hope? It struck him again that it was mad for him to hope that they lived, for it was likely they were long dead. He could not bear to imagine the torments they suffered and yet his thoughts went that way by themselves so often.

A shout broke him from his reverie.

Wedhris slipped and went under, coming up gasping for air and spluttering and coughing, yanking hard on his horse's bridle. The horse began to back away and turn. In turning it stepped toward the edge where the riverbed dropped away.

"Wedhris!" Herkuhlos said, turning to wade back, intending to grab his horse to steady it. "Come this way! Follow my voice. Wedhris!"

Instead, Wedhris attempted to leap from the river onto his horse's back, grasping with both arms outstretched and spraying freezing water everywhere including his horse's face.

His horse turned in panic and with his hind quarters knocked Wedhris off his feet.

Wedhris went under before Herkuhlos could reach him and

when he came up again he was already impossibly far downstream, flailing his arms. Beyond reach and beyond all help.

With hardly a thought, Herkuhlos let go of his horse and threw himself into the river.

The cold enveloped him like a giant wrestler's embrace, taking his breath. The current was strong and took him away down the river after Wedhris. Herkuhlos swam after him but he lost sight of his bobbing head. It was impossible to see further. There! He saw a waving hand and heard a faint cry over the rushing water.

The rushing sound grew louder and the current went faster. Swirling him, the river rushed around a rock jutting from it and the water seemed to grow around him, spraying and churning as it gushed between the rocks that were suddenly everywhere. His foot smacked one underwater, making him cry out and water rushed into his mouth.

He tried to swim toward the bank but the water had him in its grasp. All his strength was nothing to that of the river. Herkuhlos knew he should have sacrificed to the god of the river but he had not and now it meant to dash his brains out against a rock.

A cry ahead of him. Wedhris was just there, twisting away in the torrent, an arm reaching out.

Herkuhlos tried to swim but the water was different, almost as light as air, and he could get no purchase on it to drag himself through.

He bumped against Wedhris and grasped a fistful of his tunic. The river tried to pull them apart but Herkuhlos held on. I will sacrifice to you if you save us, he thought. But the river god could not hear a man's thoughts. He was thrown against a boulder, his back cracking hard and the side of his face dragging along it as the river forced him on, bouncing and grinding against it.

For a time, he was insensible. Whether it was but a moment or longer, he could not say but when he regained his senses he felt at once that the water around him was different. Harder, somehow. In his fist, Wedhris's tunic.

"Swim!" Herkuhlos tried to shout, only to swallow a mouthful of water and cough as he struck out across the current, kicking and dragging himself and Wedhris with him.

His feet touched the bottom. He was dragged over again but a few moments later his feet scraped against loose stone and mud once more.

Pulling Wedhris to the bank was the hardest thing he had ever done. It hurt to move and yet move he did, leaning against the river. He could hardly see through blurred vision but he struggled on until he grasped a fistful of mud and reeds.

Wedhris was limp. Herkuhlos pulled him, slipping with every heave, onto the soft low bank.

After squeezing it for so long, he found he could not unclench his fist. Shaking, he used his other hand to pull open his fingers from Wedhris's tunic.

He was cold and limp. His long hair had come free from its knot and when Herkuhlos pulled the strands from his face he found a laceration on his skull near the hairline. The slit was as wide and long as Herkuhlos' finger and the river had washed it clean to reveal the white bone.

Wedhris's eyes were open but they saw nothing.

His spirit had long left his body.

Herkuhlos took a breath and his chest sobbed once before he fell back to lie in the mud and limp grass. His own eyes closed and he dreamed.

Shivering, he opened his eyes. He was so cold, he could barely move. Mustering his will he forced himself up

Around him on the riverbank were pieces of timber. Further downstream a wagon wheel lay lodged between two boulders. An ox carcass lay bloated nearby and a man's arm, likewise swollen and discoloured, stuck up from a trampled reedbed.

Herkuhlos heaved Wedhris onto his shoulder and walked upstream along the bank. More bodies lay twisted here and there. Horses, cattle, sheep, pigs, and people. Discarded by the *yotunan* when they fell in the river crossing.

The river began to churn and froth when it narrowed between higher rocky banks and looking down into it Herkuhlos wondered at his survival.

"Perhaps you did hear my oath," he said to the river. Shifting Wedhris's weight on his back, he wondered at that. "Yet granted but half of it." He looked at the sky and then back to the river. "Did you spare me because of my father, is that it? Do you seek his favour or was it something else?" He shifted the cold body on his shoulder. "Wedhris lived with fear, it is true, but every day he overcame it. He was loyal. He crossed half the world for his people only to..." Herkuhlos trailed off. "This is no way to meet your end."

The river rushed on below him, bubbling and boiling over the rocks as it crashed downstream. Bracing himself, he forced his feet on.

Soon after, Belolukos and Kasos rode along the bank to him with two spare horses in tow.

"Is he dead?" Belolukos asked as they reached him.

Herkuhlos did not answer but Belolukos dismounted and

helped to lay Wedhris's body over the nervous horse's back.

"Did everyone get across?" Herkuhlos asked, his teeth clattering together.

"They did."

Herkuhlos looked between Belolukos and Kasos. "You did not leave Dhomyos in charge."

Belolukos scowled. "He can guard a few horses well enough. He does not need to think to do that." Then his face changed. "Ah, you are worried for your woman." He shrugged. "If she is such a warrior she should be able to fight him off well enough."

"He would never force himself on her," Kasos said. "That is certain."

Herkuhlos mounted, feeling the warmth of his horse beneath him. "You were strong in the crossing," he said, patting his steaming neck. "A more faithful horse could never be found. You should know that I would not have left you if I could have helped it. Ride now. We go to the others. There is something that must be done."

He reached Helhena, Dhomyos and the rest of the horses before the others and felt the heat of relief fill his limbs. Helhena wrapped a dry wolf fur over his shoulders as best she could, leaning herself against him to do so. He grasped her and held her to him, wrapping his arms around her. For the first time in many days, he breathed easily.

"You are as cold as ice," she said into him and rubbed his flanks.

"Wait," he said, pushing her away. "My clothes are wetting you."

"I do not mind." She smiled. "But we must build a fire and get you both warm. I see the others now come up with..." Her voice

266

trailed off as the horses came into view. Two riding, one being led. "Is he dead?"

"The river saved me but took him."

Helhena was shocked, as if she had expected Herkuhlos to save him. As if he had such power.

"Wedhris," Helhena muttered. "His spirit rides to the afterlife."

"We must bury him properly. But first there is something that must be done. The god of the river was not appeased before we tried the crossing."

She tilted her head. "Appeased with a sacrifice? Yes, we should have done so. I am at fault."

"No," Herkuhlos said. "I am."

Taking his axe from his own horse's loops, Herkuhlos led Wedhris's horse back down to the river while the others stood and watched. The horse was afraid and backed away but Herkuhlos hushed it softly and drew it on until its forelegs stood in the water.

"Mighty Denipa," he said, raising his voice. "I have transgressed and took from you by crossing your waters without making an offering. In your anger you took my spear-brother who was called Wedhris. You would have taken me also but for my oath to you. An oath I will now fulfil." He lowered his voice and patted the horse's neck. "You are a faithful horse. You served your master well across half the world. Yet he failed to master himself and was taken by the river. I was sent back after my silent oath to make right my transgression. And now I send your spirit to the air, your blood to the earth, and your flesh to the waters."

He drove his knife into the horse's neck, holding it steady as he drew it across to open the great vein. It fell to its knees and Herkuhlos swung his axe down. The horse slipped into the river and was carried away.

"No! How could you do that!" Belolukos said, running over. "We do not have horses enough as it is."

"I made an oath to the river."

His brother scoffed. "What oath? You made no oath."

"We angered it by not appeasing it before we crossed and it took Wedhris. I swore to put it right and it saved my life."

Belolukos raised his voice. "Wedhris panicked and fell in. It was his own fault, not that of the river. And now you have wasted one of our best horses."

"Horses die. And an oath is an oath."

"If you had any patience we would not have crossed so rashly," Belolukos said. "We could have made camp and looked for a better place to cross. Or done as Kasos said and made a raft and then Wedhris would yet live. But you could not wait, could you? You drive us on without pause and without thought."

"I drive us on because I lead," Herkuhlos said softly. Even if his brother's words were true it was not right to speak them.

"A leader thinks of his spear-brothers. But you are not a leader. You are not a leader you are a man alone and we are your cattle."

Herkuhlos shook his head. "Whatever I have done, it is done. We must dig Wedhris' grave swiftly and be gone. We have crossed now and it is not safe here in this strange land."

"Wedhris does not deserve a burial," Belolukos said, looking back across the river.

"You do not believe your own words," Herkuhlos said, astonished.

"Of course not," Belolukos snapped. "But what a place to lay him, brother. Look at it. Everything is wrong here. So much death.

The rot in the air. The filth. This place is polluted."

Herkuhlos suddenly felt exhausted. More exhausted than he could ever remember feeling before. When he closed his eyes for a moment he felt dreams reaching for him. "When we heard as boys how the *yotunan* are but chaos and destruction, I did not truly understand."

Belolukos looked back across the river and spoke softly. "It seems wrong to bury Wedhris in this land. In sight of the river that slew him."

"We cannot go back now," Herkuhlos said, opening his eyes. "The way is forward."

Belolukos turned away. "Let us do it, then."

As they had to dig with sticks and their weapons, the grave was shallow and irregular and they had no red ochre. Belolukos covered Wedhris with his wolf skin and Herkuhlos laid Wedhris's good spear by his side. Kasos placed a bowl with a few splashes of mare's blood and Dhomyos put strips of dried horse meat in his hand. Helhena was not one of them but no one objected when she placed a twig bristling with pine needles by his feet.

After filling it in and placing some heavy rocks atop it, darkness was almost come.

"Kinsmen die," Belolukos said with a flat voice, looking down at the grave. "But this is a bad place."

Herkuhlos, standing beside him, nodded. "His spirit will go on."

In reply, Belolukos snorted for it was clear that the spirit of Wedhris would not go on in glory but would wallow in ignominy somewhere down in the cold and the dark. Nevertheless, Belolukos did not give voice to the thought. There was no good that could come of that.

They rode swiftly to find a place to camp. As cold as the night was, they dare light no fire for they were in a strange land and had no knowledge of what to expect. Herkuhlos lay in his furs while the others slept.

Beside him, Helhena turned and whispered in the darkness. "You must sleep."

"I will."

She laid a hand on the back of his. "Or you should speak what is in your mind."

Herkuhlos did not know what he was thinking until he began speaking softly. "Wedhris might have had a long life if he had stayed with Orysthos. He would have been a warrior, taken a woman, fathered sons. Instead he followed me here to this strange land. Only to die without purpose and now his spirit will be but a shade never to return in the flesh of his descendants."

Helhena was silent for a long moment before she replied. "I think always of my sisters."

"Haedha and Weita," he said.

She squeezed his hand and he knew she was pleased he had remembered their names.

"I think of them being taken by the demons. I think of what they have suffered since. If they suffer still or if their suffering is long ended. And I curse myself for obeying my mother and hiding beneath the house while the others were taken. If only I had disobeyed I would be with my dear sisters. My mother." She sniffed and swiped at her nose.

He knew that she meant she would be with them in life as a captive or in death as a spirit. "We will save them. We will get them all back."

"I am not a child," she said. "Falsehoods do not comfort me."

"Why come then?" he asked. "If you have no faith in our victory."

"My people came this way. I wish to be near them."

"Before you die?" he asked.

She was silent for so long he thought she had fallen asleep. Then she sniffed and he knew her tears were flowing. "We will be with our people soon," she whispered.

He wrapped his arms around her and held her close. While the wind blew across the strange land, they slept through the darkness.

18

A Taste of Power

KREUHESH SAT ATOP his horse and watched the distant *briya* as the sun rose beyond the plains in the east across the Denipa.

Nemiyeh.

It was true what the prisoners had said. Nemiyeh was the largest settlement in the world. It had to be so for how could anywhere be larger? There were houses beyond counting atop the enormously wide mound that sat huddled against and above the river.

At least it did not have a stone wall like the place they had conquered in the south. Taking the walls of Pelhbriya had cost him dozens of warriors and now they were so few that he doubted they could take so large a settlement as the one before him. He had ridden ahead with the scouts once they reported they had discovered Nemiyeh, leaving Leuhon and the rest of the warriors four days behind him down the river. After Pelhbriya had fallen, Kreuhesh had assumed Leuhon would take it as the seat of his rule but the god was not satisfied.

"There is a greater place. A wealthier place."

"Wealthier in bronze," Kreuhesh had replied, thinking of the magnificent bronze spears and daggers they had taken from the warriors of Pelhbriya. "The captives have admitted as much."

Leuhon had been amused. "No, Kreuhesh. Wealthier in flesh. You will take it in my name."

Kreuhesh had stiffened at that. They would have failed to take Pelhbriya without the god himself stepping through a storm of arrows to break the gate and terrorise the warriors within. For although they hid behind stone walls the men were not cowards nor were they lacking in skill. Did the god mean that Kreuhesh would take Nemiyeh alone without Leuhon's help? He had no wish to appear weak by voicing the question and so he had merely bowed.

Now he was watching Nemiyeh from a low hill in the south as the sun rose and he began to doubt that it could be done. There were thousands of people inside the *briya*, emerging from their houses to walk the streets between them and many were streaming down the slopes and out into the lands beyond. All around Nemiyeh the landscape was covered with ditches and fences and fields with tracks between them all. There were cattle grazing in many of the fields and sheep in others. In the narrow woodlands by the river pigs moved in the shadows beneath the budding trees. Between there were fields of bare earth, the ground disturbed.

He snorted. "So much cattle here and yet these people grow grain. How can any man eat bread and call himself a man?"

The handful of mounted men around him chuckled, their breath steaming and catching the first rays from the sun. If they stayed much longer they would be seen and perhaps pursued. The men of Nemiyeh had horses by the hundred and Kreuhesh had no wish to be caught by a warband before he could flee. He knew also that they would be alert to the danger for he had sent plenty of captives this way to spread the word that the god Leuhon was coming.

Kreuhesh took his gaze away from the groups moving down the slopes and searched Nemiyeh once again. He was pleased to see that there was no stone wall around Nemiyeh. The outermost houses were built touching one another and they formed an almost continuous, distorted circle of wall around the perimeter. The houses were the same as the ones he had seen across these parts. Sturdily and cleverly built from timber with wattle walls coated in thick daub dried hard that were far from easy to break through. Some had stone foundations and the largest had rooms on two floors.

There were at least four places around the perimeter where the houses did not meet and none appeared to have a gate. These entrances led all the way through the houses to a wide, open square in the centre of the *briya*. There was a structure in the middle but nothing else.

Kreuhesh smiled as the rising sun showed him how open to attack Nemiyeh was.

The entire eastern portion of Nemiyeh was protected by the river which ran at the base of a high cliff but his men could attack from the north, south, and west all at once.

Even so, they would be terribly outnumbered by the defenders. If each house was ruled by a warrior, there would be hundreds of them. And there would be other men, young and old, fighting with them. His men would have to slay three or four men each at least to overcome them all. Many would die. It was far from certain without Leuhon's assistance. Surely the god would see that and would lead the attack once more?

If it could be taken then this would be the end of the great raid for him and for all of them. If they took Nemiyeh then Leuhon would rule from here and Kreuhesh would be his chief warrior for the rest of his life. There would be untold wealth. If he took this place for his god then Kreuhesh knew his rewards would be more than any man whose song he had heard. Even his famed ancestor Hasak of Dhonu could never have dreamed of so many cattle, so many women, and men sworn to him.

Kreuhesh thought of the woman Alkmene and wiped his mouth as he salivated. Would Leuhon give him the woman if he took Nemiyeh? Certainly, he would not if Kreuhesh failed. He smiled to himself as he thought about all the wives that he would have. He would lie with them all at once inside one of those large houses about the flat, open square at the top of the mound. Alkmene would hate to be thrown down, naked, with three or four other women, while he forced himself into them all. He was chuckling to himself when a cry went up from near the *briya*.

"We are seen, lord," Hendros said, pulling his axe from its straps. "Do we fight?"

Kreuhesh watched the frantic people running back toward their homes while others ran for horses with spears in their hands. "No," he said after a while. "We will return to the god. I must tell him that Nemiyeh stands ready to fall."

The warriors from Nemiyeh rode after them for far longer than he would have expected. It seemed that they were not weak men

276

although it is easy to be courageous when you think you are chasing off a band of raiders.

It took days of hard riding to get back to Leuhon and the others coming up from the south and when he saw them in the distance he almost thought the other gods had returned with their own warbands. But it was simply that Leuhon's captives had swelled in number since the river crossing and the destruction of Pelhbriya. And there were small settlements all over the land between Nemiyeh and Pelhbriya and most were located atop mounds of varying sizes. All that the warbands of Leuhon had found in their paths had fallen swiftly but still they had lost men that had not been easily replaced. Kreuhesh had offered a handful of his enemies a chance to submit to Leuhon but all so far had chosen death, despite the acolytes' attempts to persuade them otherwise.

"Even if he is a god," one man had said, "he is not my god."

Another, covered in blood, had raged at them before he was struck down. "He has killed my people and now you ask me to swear oaths to serve him. You are all mad!"

The people that lived on the west of the Denipa were a strange lot to Kreuhesh. The leaders amongst them mostly looked like the people of the plains and the language they spoke was close enough to his own that they could be understood. Beneath them were herders and farmers who seemed a different breed altogether. They were shorter in stature, with slight builds and narrow skulls. And then there were those who were clearly a mixture between the two kinds of people who as far as Kreuhesh could tell were entirely of the herder caste and he had no doubt the warriors were fathering these strange offspring on their own servants. There had been a few of the indeterminate types fighting against his men but not many.

The wives of the warriors were strong like women of the plain and like them the women could be dangerous if not watched closely. It was worse when they were first captured, when the deaths of their menfolk were so fresh that they were driven mad and were taken to attacking Kreuhesh's men rather than submit. But once they were beaten into submission most of them gradually came to accept their place, just like all the women of the east.

It was the smaller people who were more numerous and it was they who capitulated with hardly a fight. Like all herders they were used to serving their masters so it made little difference to them who that master was. Servitude was in their blood and so they welcomed it wherever it was offered.

All this together meant that Kreuhesh found himself with hundreds more captives and even fewer warriors to guard them. If they ever managed to overcome their lack of will they would be a problem and he would lose even more men getting them back under control.

Sitting on his horse and looking across the rolling landscape between him and the great mass of people and animals approaching, Kreuhesh resolved to have his men brutalise the captives more thoroughly when he reached them.

"I can almost smell the women from here," Kelwos said and the others laughed for they too were looking forward to lying with a woman. "They are wet with desire for me already." He breathed deeply and sighed.

"It is the smell of their fear," Horghis said. "They see you coming and they remember you."

"No, Horghis, it is not the women who fear his loins," Hendros said. "It's the sheep!"

Kreuhesh listened to their laughter but did not join them in it. His eyes searched the figures in the distance and picked out the wagons. He would see Alkmene soon. He would tell her that soon they would be at journey's end. With delight he imagined her face when he told her that he would claim her as his wife. She would recoil, he knew, and she would resist but that would simply make it all the sweeter when he finally broke her. All women submitted eventually. It was their nature.

There was Leuhon.

The god strode forward above all others, his lion pelt framing his head and his yellow hair catching the light. Around him were figures in white, the acolytes, scurrying around the god and bowing like the weaklings that they were.

Kreuhesh decided he would ask Leuhon tonight for Alkmene to be his prize for taking Nemiyeh and thought of her as he rode toward the approaching clan. Before they were halfway the first of the outriders rode to intercept his approach. They raised their hands as they closed and came to a halt before Kreuhesh and his men.

"Lord Kreuhesh," Hedwol, the foremost of them, said. "You have returned."

Kreuhesh was in no mood to trade greetings. "Curse you, Hedwol. You should be riding half a day ahead of the others, not cowering back here like women."

Hedwol started. "The god himself commanded us to stay close, lord."

That was a surprise. "Why?"

"I do not know, lord. But the god asks that you return to him at once upon your return."

"After I eat," Kreuhesh growled.

Hedwol looked uncomfortable. "Forgive me, lord, but the god says before you eat. Before you do anything you must go to him."

Narrowing his eyes, Kreuhesh replied. "The god himself told you this? He addressed you, Hedwol?"

"No, lord. The acolytes conveyed his wishes."

Kreuhesh snorted. "White robed fools. Soft creatures, weaklings who know nothing of hard riding."

"Yes, lord," Hedwol said while attempting to mask his fear.

"Is all well here, Hedwol?"

"Yes, lord. No trouble that I know of." He shifted on his horse. "I merely speak the words that were spoken to me, lord, and mean no disrespect."

Kreuhesh was pleased to see the man's discomfort and considered defying the commands of the acolytes. They were petty and manipulative, more like women than men, and they would enjoy giving orders that they conceived themselves in the name of the god. It would be gratifying to delay until well after dark or even the morning just to show that Kreuhesh the Bloodletter let no man command him. Not any more. On the other hand, if Leuhon had truly ordered him then he would not be defying the acolytes but the god himself and Kreuhesh meant to ask him for Alkmene as part of his prizes for taking Nemiyeh. No, he would do as they said and go straight to him. It galled him to think that he had been manipulated but there was nothing else for it.

"You men enjoy your food," Kreuhesh said. "I go to the god."

Without waiting he rode straight at the heart of the clan where Leuhon stood. The people were slowing and coming together to make camp for the night by the time Kreuhesh met them. Warriors greeted him with a shout or a respectful wave while the herders drove their animals out of his path as he rode through them. Kreuhesh grunted as he stretched his aching back as best as he could while mounted. He smelt the fires starting and knew meat would soon be roasting. His stomach growled and he cuffed at the corner of his mouth, drooling just thinking about it. Through the crowds he saw the cluster of wagons that held the prime women and felt a different kind of hunger rising. Soon, he thought, all this will be over soon.

The god, his guards, and acolytes were at the rear and Kreuhesh had to slow in order to make his way through the clusters of men and animals. Bound captives, sitting in groups or lying exhausted on the cold earth, glared at him as he passed by and Kreuhesh snorted at their defiance. He was tempted to stop and cut off a couple of heads while the rest watched but he was too tired.

Leuhon saw him approaching from far off and Kreuhesh was about to raise a hand when the god turned and walked away, his lion pelt fluttering behind him as he headed off away from his people. Kreuhesh frowned. Does he walk away from me? Anger kindled. Why summon me and then abandon me?

All nine acolytes approached on foot and blocked his path with their hands raised and spread wide. "Kreuhesh, you have returned as commanded," the oldest greybeard said.

Kreuhesh gritted his teeth as he stopped his horses. "If the god commanded me then stand aside and let me through to him."

"The god awaits you, Kreuhesh," the greybeard said, folding his hands before him along with all the others. "But first you must be cleansed."

Kreuhesh snapped at them. "I find my men, then, and eat and

wash the dirt from me before I return."

The greybeard seemed amused. "Not that kind of cleansing alone, Kreuhesh. Your body shall be cleansed. As will your spirit."

Kreuhesh looked past them at the form of Leuhon, retreating alone into the distance toward a woodland. Beyond the trees was a mound of some sort and he vaguely recalled passing it on the way north to scout Nemiyeh. "What is this?" he said. "What is happening?"

The younger acolytes bristled at this but the oldest stilled them with a look before answering. "The god wishes to reward you, Kreuhesh."

"Reward me how?"

"With a taste of his power."

Kreuhesh had no idea what that meant but he liked the sound of it. Still, he remained suspicious of the acolytes as he dismounted and they led him on foot in the direction that Leuhon had taken.

"We need guards," Kreuhesh said, turning to look at the men who always protected the god. "Mounted warriors to watch us."

"All will be well," the greybeard said.

"It is almost dark, you fool, and these lands are filled with the enemy. At least let us bring horses."

"You think the god is in danger?" the greybeard said.

"Not the god, no."

"And you think the god unable to protect us, his most loyal servants?"

Kreuhesh glowered at them but said nothing. He looked over his shoulder at the camp and smelt meat cooking on the fires and heard a burst of laughter from the men somewhere amongst the throng. Around him the acolytes walked in their white robes, dirtied at the ankle and stained all over but still brighter than any real man could keep them. What did they mean to do to him? He had a sudden urge to take out his knife and kill them all. He did not doubt he could do it. Once they were dead he would run for his horse and ride away clear to the west. Perhaps he could find another of the gods to serve. One who would not drag him into the woods in the evening like a sacrifice.

Reward me how? he had asked. With a taste of his power.

The acolytes were many things but such men were not speakers of lies. What could it mean? Would he be granted some new responsibility? Would it be an official position in the new clan? Would he be named chief? With a sinking feeling he wondered if he would be made into an acolyte. But no, the god would never do something so foolish. Kreuhesh was a warrior and a leader. Whatever this power was it would be something that made him stronger in battle. A new weapon, perhaps?

They reached the edge of the woodland as night was coming. Leuhon was nowhere to be seen and there was no sound amongst the trees other than the rushing wind and the birds calling out as they settled down to roost. Bushes in the undergrowth were budding now and soon the woods would be filled with new green leaves. But not yet.

Onward they led him deeper into the shadows beneath the trees. There was a track of some kind and the acolytes seemed to know where they were going. Ahead, there was a light flickering. Smoke on the air.

"There is someone there," Kreuhesh said, his voice sounding strange to his ears.

"All is well," the greybeard said and they continued without missing a step.

Soon they came to a clearing where a small fire burned. Men stood there waiting. Warriors he recognised and many prisoners bound and seated on the ground. They were captives taken from Pelhbriya and other smaller places in the days since. There were twenty of them and a dozen guards to watch over them. Safe enough as long as the captives remained bound and weaponless.

Behind them and beyond the edge of the trees lay the low mound he had seen from a distance. In the last light of day he saw a shape moving on the hilltop.

Leuhon.

Kreuhesh was baffled. What was the meaning of all this?

"We go on," the greybeard said, gesturing at the hill.

With a final look at the silent warriors and their captives by the fire he went with the acolytes around him to the base of the mound and then up toward the top where Leuhon awaited. Kreuhesh's skin tightened across his body and his guts twisted in knots. He felt almost like a boy again, recalling the times when his father and brothers went off to rites that he had no knowledge of. Somehow he expected his father to suddenly thump him on the head and send him sprawling to the ground as he had liked to do at such times.

"This is not for you, boy," he would say. "This is for the real men of the clan."

But the acolytes escorted him to the flat summit of the mound where Leuhon stood waiting in the darkness. Shivering, Kreuhesh drew to a stop along with the acolytes around him. The wind gusted around his ears and whipped at the robes of the acolytes.

"Kreuhesh," Leuhon said, his voice a rumble in the gloom.

"You have served me longer than any other warrior. You have won for me mountains of flesh and rivers of blood. But there lies another great task ahead of you now. Tell me, Kreuhesh, have you seen Nemiyeh with your eyes?"

"I have lord," he replied, unable to stop shivering.

"Can it be taken?"

"It is a vast place, lord. There are more men there than anywhere I have seen before. It can be taken but it will take every warrior we have. And when we take it we shall lose many men before it is done."

"So you are not certain of victory?"

Kreuhesh flinched. This was not going how he had envisioned it. Why was he so afraid? "I am as certain as I can be, lord. I mean to take it or I will die in the trying."

Leuhon grunted in the darkness. "Kreuhesh, do you understand your worth to me?"

"No, lord," Kreuhesh said, finding himself speaking before he could think.

"What do you desire, Kreuhesh?"

"To serve you, lord."

A shadowed hand waved. "You have this already. What rewards do you seek for this service?"

"Wealth, lord, and glory. Cattle and women of my own. Warriors to serve me. To be chief amongst men." He bowed. "But ever in your service and in your name, lord."

Leuhon grunted.

Was he angered or amused? Kreuhesh could not tell. Perhaps neither.

"All this you shall have, Kreuhesh, once we take Nemiyeh. You will go from this place with all my warriors and you shall slay them all. Nemiyeh shall be mine. My people will worship me and you, Kreuhesh, will conquer in my name. The people to the north and west shall bow to me or they will fall to your axe. You shall take Nemiyeh but I would not have you fall."

"No, lord." Kreuhesh's heart raced. It was as he had hoped. All he had done would come to fruition. "I will not fall."

Leuhon laughed softly, a low rumbling sound coming from his black silhouette before the grey sky. "No mortal may choose his time to fall. But I shall give you strength, Kreuhesh. Strength that you might slay twenty men even though you stand alone. You shall be granted a taste of the power of the gods."

Kreuhesh's heart pounded in his chest. He did not understand. "Yes, lord."

"The power will last mere days. It will fade as the days pass. But live on, serve well, and you may be granted this power again." Leuhon stepped closer. "Do you wish for this power, Kreuhesh?"

"Yes, lord."

Leuhon gestured to the acolytes who encircled Kreuhesh. Together they broke into a low chant, their voices filling the night air with rhythmic words of power. They sang of a battle between the gods and of the betrayal and deception of the evil god of the sky and his wife the earth. Kreuhesh could scarcely follow the words and the story as his head whirled. He was tired, exhausted even, and he was hungry and cold. His wits were overcome with the strangeness of the rite and he felt his spirit rising within him to dominate the weakness of his flesh. While they sang two of the acolytes shifted together in the darkness by Leuhon and bent to the ground at his feet. Kreuhesh was dimly aware of strange smells and a whiff of something burning before it was snuffed out. Then Leuhon grunted and the smell of fresh blood was in the air along with the relentless chanting of the acolytes.

Two of them approached him, carrying something reverently between them. They lifted it to his face and he saw that it was a wide, shallow bowl. When they pressed it against his lips he jerked back in shock. It was a warm, pungent liquid. A pang of fear struck him that it might be poison.

"Drink," Leuhon growled.

Kreuhesh obeyed and grasped the bowl, raising it to his lips again and drinking down the warm liquid within.

Blood.

It tasted of a dozen things, sweet and foul, but the overwhelming taste was that of blood. There was honey also and floating pieces of something soft and chewy and the bitter taste of something burnt. But he gulped it down, feeling the weight of it as it met his stomach and his guts roiling at the sudden intrusion. While the acolytes chanted on, he drank and drank mouthful after mouthful as the acolytes tipped the bowl higher and higher until it was empty. Kreuhesh took a breath, licking his lips and cuffing his chin where the blood concoction had run.

Pain gripped his stomach and he bent over, his arms wrapped around his body. Another spasm wracked him and he fell to his knees, groaning and clutching at himself.

Leuhon stepped closer and looked down. "Not all who drink are strong enough to contain my power."

Kreuhesh groaned and tried to stand. His heart hammered in his chest and his fingers and hands went numb. When he tried to ask what they done to him all that came out was a strangled moan.

Gritting his teeth he forced himself up onto one knee and then with a great effort stood and lifted his chin to look at the dark mass standing over him.

The acolytes finished their chanting and fell silent. Though the wind gusted in his ears, Kreuhesh was no longer cold. Instead, he felt a fire burning within him and spreading through his limbs to the tips of his fingers. He could hear the breathing of the men around him and the deeper, slower breath of Leuhon before him. He looked up to see the moon rising through thin cloud. The muscles of his legs seemed ready to launch him into a leap and it was all he could do to contain them.

"This is but a taste of my power," Leuhon said. "It will fade as the days go by. Prolong it by drinking the fresh blood of your enemies."

"I will, lord," Kreuhesh said, astonished at the feeling growing within him. He looked at his hands. They seemed almost to belong to another.

"There is one more test for you," Leuhon said. He raised a massive arm and pointed down the hill at the fire burning by the trees. "Slay the captives. Then go at once to Nemiyeh. Take all you need. I shall come behind."

"I will, lord," Kreuhesh said again. He bowed and turned, feeling his legs shake as he walked away. They shook not because they were weak but because they were bursting with energy. Without a thought he burst into a run and leapt downhill in the darkness. He had no fear of putting a foot wrong and twisting his ankle for he seemed to be as sure footed as a gazelle and he went so swiftly that he reached the bottom before he knew it and was running into the light of the fire.

The warriors guarding the captives leapt into action, cutting away their bonds with their knives.

"I am to slay them," Kreuhesh said, elated by the feeling of his body and the sharpness of his mind. "I am to sacrifice them for the god."

"We were told, lord," one of the warriors said as he moved to another man and sawed at his bonds. "We are to stop them fleeing but we must not help."

"Help what?" Kreuhesh asked but he already suspected he knew the answer.

"If they slay you, lord," the warrior said, "they are to go free. The god commanded us with his own words."

After freeing the last man, the warrior threw down his knife and stepped back, taking up his spear. The other warriors did the same, throwing down their knives before stepping back to the edges of the trees and the edge of the firelight. The twenty captives stood, snatching up the dozen knives and moving at once toward Kreuhesh. The ones without knives hung back while the others spread out so that they could come at him from both flanks and head on. Their eyes reflected the flickering firelight and their faces were twisted in their hatred for him and in their determination to slay him and so win their freedom.

Kreuhesh took out his own knife. It was the only weapon he had against twenty men.

The power of the god filled his flesh and his spirit soared.

Lifting his face to the moon, Kreuhesh laughed.

1 9

The Dead

IT WAS CLEAR TO Herkuhlos that the land west of the Denipa was rich and filled with wealth. At least, it had been before the *yotunan* had come. The woodlands were dense and tall but many had been cleared for grazing and for farming by the people that had lived there. Their settlements were numerous and some were large. All had been destroyed and the people were gone but they must have been wealthy indeed. Now they were either captives or they were food for the crows and wolves. It seemed as though the *yotunan* were not stopping and Herkuhlos wondered if they ever would or if they would go on until all the peoples of the earth were devoured in their path.

"The tracks go west also," Kasos cried, riding back to them from the hills to the west. "Now what do we do?"

Herkuhlos sighed and looked up at the sky. It was high sun. The clouds cleared a little in the north and he saw the blue beyond. "It seems the *yotunan* have divided once more."

"More than once more," Kasos said. "The tracks in the west divide into three at least."

The damage torn into the earth by the *yotunan* clan had spread in all directions on the western bank of the Denipa. It had taken five days of riding around to begin to understand what had happened. It seemed that the great mass of people and animals had spread out in all directions and made camp all about for days on end. Tracks led away from the area at almost every point. There could be no doubt. The *yotunan* had separated. Dividing the hundreds of people and animals into small groups they had headed away from one another. Most, it seemed, had gone south but many also went west. But each of these groups was smaller and there were few wagons between them.

The greatest single group appeared to have gone north along the bank of the river. It was this group that appeared to have most of the wagons. Though precisely what it all meant was not clear and Herkuhlos did not know which way to go. For days he had refused to make a choice, fearing choosing the wrong direction as he had done before.

But they had looked enough and Kasos had returned from his scouting to the west. His people were looking at him, expecting his decision now.

"What do you think, Bel?"

His brother blinked. "You are asking me?" He sat straighter. "You recall the captive we took from Wodra? He said Leuhon took most of the captives. That he had most of the wagons."

"I remember."

"Well then we should go north, no? Following the river. That is where the largest group went."

Herkuhlos nodded. "Kasos? What do you say?"

He rubbed his face. "That man you spoke to may have lied. He may have been mad. Or what he said may have been truth when he spoke it but everything may have changed since then. How many moons has it been?"

"Dhomyos?" Herkuhlos asked. "What say you?"

Shrugging, Dhomyos pursed his lips as he looked between Herkuhlos and Belolukos. "Whatever you two decide is right enough for me."

"Helhena?" Herkuhlos asked. "Can you see any clear path ahead?"

She was looking at a flock of fowl flying low upstream. "The signs say north." She turned her gaze to him. "But if the signs are wrong we can always turn back and try another path."

Herkuhlos was not sure they would survive any contact with their enemies in order to be able to change their minds but he simply nodded.

"North it is," he said. "Lead the way, Bel."

The land had been devastated just as much as it had been on the plains across the river. On the morning of their second day north they came across a settlement that had been thoroughly destroyed. It had been built atop a slight rise on the ground and had a ditch around the base and a timber defensive wall ringing the houses on the top. But these had not stopped the warriors of the *yotunan* clan. The large houses within had been smashed and burned. The thatched reed roofs had burned away leaving blackened timbers lying at angles beneath. The timber palisade had been thrown down in a dozen places.

It smelled of death. There were half rotted bodies lying amongst the ruins and crows sat atop the timbers, cawing at each other and watching the riders and their horses warily.

"Should we go within?" Kasos asked.

"Why?" Herkuhlos asked.

Kasos frowned. "We need food."

Dhomyos turned away. "I will slaughter my own horse before going into that."

"What if there are survivors?" Helhena asked.

"What if they are diseased?" Belolukos said. "Or cursed? Anyway, we cannot help anyone. We do not even know these people."

Herkuhlos agreed. "There is nothing for us here."

From then on there were scattered buildings every half a day or less along the river. Every place was destroyed. The land they rode through was a mix of woodland and open pasture from the river to the line of hills in the west. Patches of cleared ground surrounded the settlements. Some areas were surrounded by broken fences and were clearly corrals while the others were where the local people grew fields of millet. Everywhere had been trampled and the earth churned by the passages of horses and cattle.

"The people would be planting their seeds soon," Helhena said as they rode by a muddy circle of cleared ground. "And now nothing will grow here."

"Their fault for being bread eaters," Belolukos said. "Imagine not being able to drive your wealth away from your enemies if you need to."

"Our herds did not save our people," Kasos pointed out. "Anyway, horses die. And cattle die.

"The bread eaters are not like us," Belolukos said as they rode past the burnt houses of the slain.

"I like bread," Dhomyos said. He sighed. "I'd like some bread now."

All the houses that they saw on the way north had been destroyed. Those that had not burned had been pulled down. Some they found with one or more intact walls and these would have made good shelters for the night were it not for the corpses that lay rotting within. After a while they stopped approaching the ruins.

"Such waste," Helhena said. "That is what I can never understand. Why must they destroy everything? All this work to build and grow and live only for it to be wasted. Ground under foot and discarded to rot and to ruin. It is just so unnecessary."

Herkuhlos shrugged. "*Yotunan* are destroyers. Devourers. They are evil."

"But *why* are they?" she asked, anger colouring her face. "Why must they be like this?"

Herkuhlos shook his head. "I do not know, Helhena."

The ground grew stonier as they travelled further north and the land rose into isolated low hills with wide plains between them. Atop some of the mounds were low stone walls with broken and burnt houses inside but they avoided them as they avoided all the others.

It was late one morning when Dhomyos rode back to them from scouting ahead. They were all tired and going slowly while a light, persistent rain fell and drenched them to the skin.

"Herkuhlos," Helhena called. The edge in her voice stirred him from his thoughts. "Dhomyos returns."

"There is something ahead," Dhomyos called out when he got

close enough. He waved a hand over his head. "Big walls."

Belolukos rode in from his place on their left flank. "What is it?"

"Another broken house, Dhomyos?" Kasos called from behind.

Dhomyos shook his head and his eyes were wide as he fought for breath after his hard ride. "A settlement. Houses. Many houses. It is surrounded by the biggest wall I have ever seen. And the houses within are not destroyed!"

Herkuhlos sat up straighter on his horse. "The people are alive?"

"Don't know," Dhomyos said. "Didn't see anyone. Didn't smell smoke either."

"There cannot be a place that has defied them," Belolukos said. "Can there?"

"Big wall around it," Dhomyos said, scratching his chin.

"Bigger than a demon?" Herkuhlos asked.

Dhomyos shrugged.

"Might be dangerous either way," Kasos said, leaning down and sliding a javelin from its loops. "Might be warriors there."

Helhena reached for her bow. "Perhaps we are catching the demons at last?"

"Let us look at this place," Herkuhlos said, taking up his war axe. "Be ready to flee."

They picked their way along a track through a woodland that had seen the passage of wagons, perhaps moons ago but still discernible in the dark earth. It was a thin woodland with many trees felled over the years and the undergrowth was cleared all around. When they reached the edge of the wood they saw the mound ahead across flat, open grazing ground. The fortress on the hill was protected by a wall of grey stone taller than a man and the houses inside looked unburnt and unbroken. But all was silent. Only the wind howled through the stones.

"Look," Helhena said. "They did not escape the demons."

Herkuhlos sighed. Bodies lay rotting upon the hillside beneath the walls. Now that he saw them he noticed many more around the base of the mound and even some lying atop the wall. He could smell the decay in the air and felt a sudden wave of sadness for these strangers. He did not know them and now he never would but they had suffered the same fate as his own people at the hands of the *yotunan*.

"What do you think?" Belolukos asked.

Herkuhlos stared across the wasteland. The crops grown by those people had been ripped up or trampled into the mud. The trees of the small woodland toward the river to the west had been cut down in their hundreds and the ground was littered with sticks and splinters.

"I think that the *yotunan* came through. They overran that stone-built place and killed the people."

"I know that much," Belolukos said, turning to spit downwind. "I mean what do you think about us stopping here a while?"

"We cannot stop now," Herkuhlos said. "We are getting closer."

"Listen, brother. Our horses need rest. That brown one will be lame soon if she does not take a day or two. We are all tired, even you, and our clothes are falling off us and need mending. This attack was not made so long ago and we may run into the rear of the demon clan without meaning to. How would we fight or run when we are so tired?"

Herkuhlos nodded. "And if we are to rest then doing so within those walls would help keep us warm and dry if nothing else."

"But surely it is cursed now," Dhomyos said, making a sign to ward against the evil clinging to the hill.

"Cursed for who?" Kasos asked. "For the people who lived there perhaps but not for us."

"Their spirits will be there." Dhomyos nodded at the silent stones. "Their spirits will not want us within. Anyway, it will stink of death. The horses will not like it."

Herkuhlos turned to Helhena. "What do you say? Can we shelter within for a night or two without angering the dead?"

She did not have to think for long. "If we behave as guests, perhaps. We must treat the place with the proper respect. We must share our food with them. The bodies must be treated as if they were our own people."

"I agree," Herkuhlos said and turned to Dhomyos. "You happy with that?"

Dhomyos frowned as he jerked a thumb at Helhena. "What did she mean about the bodies?"

"We will clear them out," Helhena said. "Or else it will stink."

Dhomyos sighed and looked at the sky. "Let us sleep in the woods, Herkuhlos?"

"Come on," Herkuhlos said and led them across to the slope where they found a path leading up the hill into an entrance through the wall.

The fortress had once been home to hundreds of people who lived in dozens of large houses. The stone wall encircling those houses was as thick as it was tall, made from slabs of stone of all sizes stacked cleverly to make a strong defence. The gate that had once barred the entrance was smashed and the pieces lay scattered across the path.

"Strong place," Belolukos said approvingly as they stepped inside through the gateway.

Dhomyos grunted. "Not strong enough."

"Would have kept raiders out," Kasos said, slapping a hand on the stones. "Even fifty or a hundred warriors could not have taken it. More, even."

Inside there were bodies here and there. Far fewer than they had expected. Most of the people had been killed outside or driven away and for the most part those that lay in the streets and houses were men killed in the fighting. The path led into an open area in the centre that had more paths radiating from it. There, too, lay dozens of bodies in clusters.

The dead were putrefying. Their bodies bloated and stinking, their skin soft and blotchy.

"How long have they been dead?" Herkuhlos asked Kasos as they regarded the dead.

"A moon?" he guessed, holding his furs over his mouth and nose.

"If it was a moon they would be rotted down more than this," Dhomyos said through the spare tunic he had tied around the lower half of his face. "But more than half a moon."

Herkuhlos and Belolukos exchanged a look.

"We are still a moon behind them," Belolukos said, shaking his head. "After all this time."

"Less than a moon," Herkuhlos replied. "Either way we must not stay long here. We will cleanse this place, repair our clothing, make more, hunt in the woods, and be after them all the faster now. Come, we cannot delay any longer."

They lashed together poles to make hurdles with which to drag the bodies out beyond the wall. It was foul, stinking work and Herkuhlos thought to himself that he was wasting time in doing it. If the enemy were half a moon or more ahead of them then it was unlikely they would be discovered if they camped in the woods rather than within the walls. But it also seemed somehow necessary. Not for him and his people but for the people who had died. So many settlements they had passed. Ignored. He had done nothing for them and they lay rotting to the bone in their own homes. But they were inside this place now and for all the foulness it somehow felt right to be cleansing it. To treat the dead with some small measure of respect.

It was hard work. The dead were heavy and difficult to move. When lifting them onto the hurdles they left puddles of stinking liquid behind and sometimes the skin and other parts of them came off or their abdomens split open. Still, they worked as swiftly as they could bear.

Their horses were nervous and had to be coaxed inside one at a time and quieted.

Before any was touched, Helhena spoke blessings over them and the men told each one his own name before lifting them.

"If only we could bury them," Helhena said after they laid yet another body in the row they were making outside the walls.

Belolukos, leaning down with his hands on his knees and breathing hard, looked up at her. "You can dig the graves if you wish."

"I did not say we must bury them," she replied. "Only that it should be done if we are to treat them with the proper respect."

"They are strangers. This is far more respect than they deserve and we're only doing this much so their spirits do not cling to our dreams." Belolukos scoffed and shook his head. "Burying strangers. Sometimes, girl, I do not know if you are wise or witless."

"One of the countless things you do not know, Bel," Helhena shot back.

Herkuhlos laughed at the expression on his brother's face. "Come on," he said, his expression souring as he looked up the hill at the walls. "Many more to toss out before we can eat."

"We will have to draw water and wash away the filth," Belolukos said, stretching his back. "After the last of the bodies are cleared."

Together they went inside, passing Kasos as he dragged out another man on a makeshift hurdle they had lashed together for the purpose. "The path is clear now," Kasos said, puffing hard and keeping his face turned as far from the body as possible. "And the open space in the centre. I will lead the horses in."

The houses were larger than any they had seen before and many were so close together that the walls touched but there were paths through the maze of structures, the largest leading to the centre. There were dead lying in the passageways between the houses as well as inside the buildings themselves. Herkuhlos looked down at one woman who had long fair hair twisted into a braid. She had no eyes, as the crows had eaten them, and her woollen tunic was torn and the front covered in brown blood from the wound that had killed her. In her hand was a broken spear shaft. Like the others her flesh was discoloured, corrupted and blistered and her abdomen was bloated

"Went down fighting," Belolukos said at his shoulder. "A good woman. A shame." He bowed to her. "Mother of the stone fortress, you died protecting your hearth. We honour you. I am Belolukos, once of the Kweitos Clan." He looked at Herkuhlos.

"I am Herkuhlos," he said, and bowed. "Though I do not know your name, I will remember your bravery."

Belolukos slapped him on the shoulder. "You take her shoulders and hope her head does not come off like the last one."

Just as they bent to their task, someone began shouting. After sharing a look they raced through the buildings of the fortress toward the shouting. They ran between the buildings and into the open, square-shaped centre of the settlement, Helhena and Kasos not far behind them.

Herkuhlos raised his own voice. "Dhomyos! Where are you?"

He emerged from the doorway of a house ahead of them on the other side of the square, waving a hand and grinning. "Herkuhlos, I found something!"

"Are you well? Is anything wrong?" Herkuhlos shouted as he and the others ran to him.

"You will not believe what I have found," Dhomyos replied, ducking back inside.

"Dhomyos!" Helhena cried, panting. "We thought you were in danger."

"That witless aurochs," Belolukos said, breathing hard and shaking his head. "I will knock his head against the ground for this."

"Not before I do," Herkuhlos replied, ducking inside the building.

It was dark within and it smelled stale. The inside had been wrecked. Broken timbers littered the floor along with broken shards of decorated pots, all covered with loose straw that had been thrown about during the fighting or when the attackers had searched.

"In here!" Dhomyos called from another room further back.

"Imagine living in this," Belolukos muttered, looking up at the high ceiling overhead and the rooms leading off the main one.

The next room, where Dhomyos was, had likewise been torn apart. There were reed mats tossed here and there and plank shelves ripped down from the walls and the pots upon them smashed on the floor. Grain was trodden into the dust.

"Dhomyos," Herkuhlos said as they made their way through the doorway, "you cannot call for us like that unless there is danger."

Dhomyos crouched in the corner beside a body. "It is him!" he said over his shoulder, waving at them to come closer.

Herkuhlos pushed forward and bent to the man lying on his back. Despite a small opening high up on the wall it was dim in there and his eyes had not adjusted to the gloom. "Who is it?"

"It is Makros!" Dhomyos said. "Do you not see? Do you not remember? That man we met back at Helhena's camp. The one we fought and he knocked down Bel and then he ran with us all the way back to—"

"Enough, Dhomyos. I remember him," Herkuhlos said, astonished. "What in the name of Kolnos is he doing *here*?"

Belolukos crowded behind them. "Is he dead?"

Dhomyos shook his head. "He is wounded but he lives."

The man breathed. Old blood stuck Makros' long hair to his scalp. Herkuhlos touched the area around it, feeling the swelling. He lifted the furs covering Makros and searched his body for other wounds.

"He smells dead," Belolukos muttered, holding his nose.

Herkuhlos recalled Makros leaving them to continue his pursuit of the *yotunan* that had destroyed his clan and his *koryos*. It seemed like a lifetime ago. It had been before midwinter when they had last seen him. That had been before Herkuhlos had been captured, and before he had been named by Kolnos. A lifetime ago. To see him here now in this place where they might not have come must have had some special meaning. Surely the gods had brought them together once more for some purpose.

"What happened to you, Makros?" Herkuhlos said softly.

Helhena stepped forward. "Move aside, my friend," she said, placing a hand on Dhomyos' shoulder. He shuffled out of the way and stood over them.

When she knelt by the sleeping man Helhena pulled all the furs right off him and began prodding his shoulders, his arms, chest, and belly. He smelt bad.

"This is not proper," Kasos muttered from the doorway into the back room. "He is not her father, uncle, brother, or husband. Therefore she should not be laying her hands upon his body. It is terribly improper."

Herkuhlos turned. "Why are you all still here? Who is guarding the horses? Who watches the walls? What about the last of the bodies?" They stared at him. "Get out and see to it!"

Kasos and Dhomyos, much hurt to be missing out, slouched off.

"I best keep an eye on them," Belolukos said, nodding to his brother before making his way out.

Herkuhlos nodded back and turned to see Helhena pressing her fingers into Makros' thighs, her hands close indeed to the man's loins. He cleared his throat and spoke softly. "Perhaps you should let me do—"

Makros hissed suddenly, then groaned and twitched, rolling his head. His eyelids fluttered but did not open.

"His leg," Helhena said, lifting the tunic up to expose the bloody right knee and thigh of the injured man. His trousers were torn but the woollen fabric was stuck to the slimy wound.

"By Kolnos," Herkuhlos said before clamping a hand over his mouth and nose. The sudden stench of rot that wafted up to him was foul indeed.

"Yes," Helhena said. "It is bad."

"Can you heal him?"

She looked at him and sat back. "His leg's putrid, Herkuhlos. Nothing can heal him. My cousin had this once. Not bad, to start with. But nothing worked. The fever filled him, the death spread." She shrugged.

"What about cutting off his leg?" Herkuhlos said, thinking desperately for a solution. Something that would mean Makros did not have to die. "That works, does it not?"

Helhena narrowed her eyes. "I remember hearing a song where a chief cuts off his rotten leg."

"That's it," Herkuhlos said, grasping her shoulder. "The song of Dolon."

She sighed. "If you cut off a man's leg, he dies in moments. You know that."

"But the song..."

"In that story Dolon drank a... a powerful potion brewed by the gods that saved him from dying," she said. "I do not know its making."

Herkuhlos sat back and pinched the bridge of his nose. "So Makros will die from this?" He spoke softly.

"Yes."

He could hardly believe it. How could it be that they had come across him like this only for him to die? What was the meaning of it? Simply some cruel trick of the gods? "Can you help him anyway?"

She nodded. "I will cut away his clothes and wash him. Wrap him in something clean and keep him warm."

"Until he dies," Herkuhlos said.

"Yes."

All things die.

"How can I help you? I can bring water. Clean cloth, perhaps."

Smiling sadly, she touched his arm. "I will see to it all. You must keep us safe."

Herkuhlos nodded and stood. "I will."

While Helhena made a fire and boiled water, Herkuhlos found the others and gathered them to him in the square in the centre of the settlement.

"This fortress is so big that even though we searched it we missed Makros lying in there for half a day. Now, we must search this place properly. If we can miss a dying man, who knows what else is in here with us. We must search every house again and search them properly this time."

"What was Makros doing here?" Kasos asked, as if Herkuhlos had not spoken.

"I could not ask him because he did not wake up. And he never will."

They hung their heads for a moment.

"All this way," Dhomyos muttered. "He made it all this way on his own. Running all the way."

"He must have found horses somewhere," Belolukos said.

"Even so," Dhomyos countered. "Could you have done it alone,

Bel? I could not."

They all imagined it in silence for a moment. The moons they had spent together had been hard enough with horses to spare and bags of supplies. Their respect for the older warrior grew.

"Only to die like an old woman in the back of some strange house," Belolukos said, scoffing. "What a waste of his portion."

"He suffered a wound," Herkuhlos said. "It is the wound that kills him. It could happen to any of us."

"Perhaps he was one of the men attacking this place," Belolukos suggested. "Perhaps he was captured and went to serve the demons."

The rest of them scoffed at that. "Makros would have died before betraying his oath," Herkuhlos said.

"You speak as if you know him," Belolukos said. "But he would not be the first warrior to submit rather than die."

"He must have been captured by the *yotunan*," Kasos said in agreement. "They made him help attack this place and he fell in the attack. How else could he come to be here?"

"Never," Dhomyos said. "Not Makros. And anyway they would have killed him rather than capture him," Dhomyos said. "And he would not have allowed himself to be captured. It is more likely he defended this place from attack and was left for dead when the demons left. Yes, that is it. He fought with these people to help them against the demons. Poor Makros. He was a good man. He helped us."

"We will likely never know the truth," Herkuhlos said. "He is insensible with a fever and death will take him soon. If we can, we will bury him with honour and we will remember his name and his deeds. I wish it were otherwise but there is nothing to be done.

From the smell of his wound I doubt he will last the night. Now, be on your guard for we must scour this place for any more survivors and for hidden enemies."

"And food," Dhomyos said.

"Not likely," Kasos said.

They busied themselves with the search and with the last of the bodies. The houses were far larger than any in the homeland of the clans and many had a second floor above the ground level where people slept. Under the floors were stone lined pits for storing food but these had all been found and opened by the servants of the *yotunan* and there was nothing left anywhere. Before night fell, they blocked the gateway up as best they could with the broken timbers and used stones from the walls to hold them in position. It would stop the horses from escaping and no wild animals would get through but it would not hold against any sort of attack.

"Makes me nervous," Belolukos said after they had finished the work.

"What does?" Herkuhlos asked, stretching his aching back.

"Being inside this place."

"The spirits will be appeased fully once we offer up some meat."

"Not that," he said, scowling. "It is not right to be surrounded by walls and buildings. We cannot see out. A hundred men could be approaching and we could not see them coming. No wonder these fools all died."

"Bel," Herkuhlos said. "Do not anger them."

"How could they have suffered to live in this way? Each warrior with his kin and servants in one house, all living this close with the walls touching each other. Hundreds of them all living like this so close that when your neighbour breaks wind it is you that smells it.

They live like cattle."

Herkuhlos shook his head and looked at the darkening sky. It was growing colder. "I am hungry. Come on."

They made their camp in the open centre of the fortress, in front of one of the largest houses. Before eating, they poured out a cup of water and burnt a large piece of horse flesh in the fire. It was not much but they had shared a portion of what they had with the spirits of the dead and they hoped that it would be enough. The smell of death still lingered but already it was fading. They washed themselves thoroughly with water from a well near the centre.

Makros lay insensible beside the fire. The warmth of it seemed to comfort him, or perhaps it was the soft sound of their voices in the dark. All were exhausted by the exertions of the day and soon their heads began to drop.

"I will stay on my feet," Belolukos said, yawning and getting up with his spear in hand, "and will wake you next, Kasos."

Kasos waved a hand, turning over on his furs and tucking his head in. Dhomyos was already snoring. With a nod, Belolukos wandered away across the square and disappeared into the shadowed streets between the houses.

Helhena looked over at Herkuhlos. "Why do you think they did not burn this place?"

He had been wondering about that. "Perhaps they were in too much of a hurry to move on."

She shook her head. "Even when they did not stop moving they still made sure to smash every place we have seen so far. Like my home. They attempted to set it on fire even though the demon clan did not stop riding." She shrugged. "After killing everyone, I mean."

"Why do you think?" he asked her.

The firelight flickered across her face so that her expression appeared to change over and over again though she sat motionless. "What if they mean to return?"

"To live here?" he asked.

"They could be heading back here as we speak. They could be here at dawn for all we know."

Herkuhlos looked at the shadows around them and felt the danger out there approaching. He shook it off. "We are safe now. In here. For tonight at least."

"That makes a change," she said softly. "We have slept in the open every night for as long as I can remember. I have almost forgotten what it is like to sleep beneath a roof."

He looked back at her and their eyes met. They looked at the empty houses around them and Herkuhlos immediately thought of the sleeping lofts inside. For so long he had wanted her but it had never seemed like the right time. Always they had been exhausted, cold, afraid. Not much had changed, perhaps, but it was enough and he was filled with his need for her.

He stood and stepped to Helhena and held out his hand. She smiled and took it before he pulled her upright into an embrace. For a moment, she leaned against his body and he felt her warmth.

"It is cold," she whispered.

"I will warm you," he replied.

It was pleasant to hold her against him and part of him wished to stay like that for longer but he could not suppress his desire a moment longer. Taking her hand he led her away from the fire toward the darkness of the nearest house.

They had not taken two steps toward the building when a great cry split the air. It was a strangled shout of surprise followed by other loud voices. It was close.

From inside the walls.

"Stay with Makros!" Herkuhlos said, rushing to the others. Kasos was scrabbling in the dark for his weapons while Dhomyos slept on, oblivious. Herkuhlos kicked his feet then grabbed his spear in one hand and his axe in the other. "With me!" he shouted at them.

With Kasos and Dhomyos behind him they rushed through the darkness across the square and between the buildings toward the sounds.

"Bel!" Herkuhlos shouted as they came upon the fighting.

Belolukos struggled with two figures. They were not men but boys. Belolukos had dropped his spear and he had an arm around each of the boys he was attempting to restrain.

Herkuhlos rushed in and wrapped his arms around one, pulling him away. The young boy writhed and kicked at him, shouting as he did so.

"Stop this," Herkuhlos said, holding the boy by the shoulders. The boy spat in his face and turned to bite the back of his hand. Yelping in surprise and anger, Herkuhlos slapped the boy on the head. The blow knocked him down and he lay unmoving on the ground.

"There is another," Belolukos said, breathing hard and jerking his head. "A third boy. He got away."

"Catch him," Herkuhlos ordered and Kasos and Dhomyos raced off in the darkness toward the wall. "There may be more," Herkuhlos shouted after them.

"Just boys," Belolukos said, shaking the one in his arms and slapping him about the head until he fell silent and stopped fighting. "Just a group of boys. Came out of nowhere."

"What are you doing here?" Herkuhlos snapped at the boy that Belolukos held. "How many with you?"

The boy kept his mouth closed and turned away. Both him and the one lying unconscious on the ground were wearing tunics and trousers but it was too dark to see them clearly. Were they scouts for the *yotunan*?

"Let us beat it from him," Belolukos said, shaking the boy.

"Agreed. You take them back to the fire," Herkuhlos said and poked the unconscious boy with a foot. "Pick this one up or drag him back and bind them. I will find the others and see you back at the fire."

"We should check the gate. This could be the start of an attack."

"Yes. Yes, tie the boys up and check the gates. But we meet back at the fire. Call loudly if you need me."

"You too."

With a last look at one another, Herkuhlos ran on between the buildings after Kasos and Dhomyos but had not gotten far when he met them coming back the other way. Two shadows looming out of the darkness but still he knew them at once by their shapes and their gait.

"Where's the third boy?"

"Got over the wall, the little turd," Dhomyos said, breathing heavily. "Like a gazelle, he was. Wasn't he, Kasos?"

Herkuhlos spoke quickly. "Why did you not follow him over?"

"It is too dark," Kasos said waving his spear. "Could be anywhere out there."

"Hear anyone else? Smell people? Horses?"

312

"Quiet as the dead," Dhomyos said, drawing an elbow and a hiss from Kasos. "But it is. There's nothing out there. No raiders."

"None that you could see," Herkuhlos said. "We must return to the fire and then check the ways in. We might be under attack." He led them through the narrow street back to the centre where their fire burned low. Beside it, Belolukos was finishing tying the second boy's arms behind his back. Makros lay unmoving by the fire, insensible to the world.

"Where's Helhena!" Herkuhlos cried.

"Wasn't here when I got back," Belolukos said without looking up.

"Helhena!" Herkuhlos shouted, running first one way and then another, panic rising in him. He knew at once that someone had come in and taken her and now he would never get her back.

"I'm here," Helhena said, running from the shadowed path back into the firelight with her bow in her hand.

"I told you to wait!" Herkuhlos said, anger replacing relief almost immediately.

"And I defied you," she said, her voice hard. "I went to check the gate."

Herkuhlos shook his head as he did not know what to say.

"Good idea," Belolukos said, tying a final knot in the second boy's bonds and standing. "So are we under attack?"

Helhena pointed her bow toward the gate. "It seems quiet."

They stood together, listening to the wind and the soft crackling of the fire.

"Just three boys sneaking in alone, then?" Herkuhlos asked, turning to look at their captives. "Why would they do that? Where are they from?"

Belolukos grinned as he turned to look down at the two boys. "Let us ask them."

Both boys were awake and staring at them with wide eyes. While Kasos and Helhena watched the approaches, Dhomyos threw more wood on the fire and blew it back to life. Belolukos squatted before the boys and smiled at them. He selected a thin, long stick from the pile of firewood and waved it at first one boy and then the other.

"What are your names?" he asked.

They glared in silence.

"Talk to us, boys," Herkuhlos said.

"Who are you with, boys?" Belolukos asked and sighed at their silence. "You know, if you carry on like this, I will take offense. You wouldn't want to offend your new master, would you?"

At this they both flinched, the smaller one most of all.

"Tell me the truth now," Belolukos continued. "You serve the *yotunan*, don't you." He peered at them. "Which monster do you serve?"

"They might think they serve a god," Herkuhlos said.

"Yes, yes." Belolukos nodded. "You serve a demon who claims that he is a god, yes? Which one is it?"

"The Lion?" Herkuhlos said. "Ask them about the Lion."

Belolukos poked the smaller one in the belly with his stick. "You serve the Lion, boy? He sent you to spy on us? Slit our throats in the night, is that it?"

"No!" the boy snapped. "Never!"

"Quiet, Yal!" hissed the other.

"Ah, so, the little turd is named Yal. What a strange little name for a strange little turd."

At this, Dhomyos burst out laughing but stifled it when

Herkuhlos glared at him and gestured at Kasos. "You two, go watch the gate."

Sighing, they both drifted away muttering. Helhena moved off toward the street leading to the western wall.

"Wait," Herkuhlos said. "I didn't mean you."

"We should watch all the ways in," she replied without breaking stride. "Easy to climb the walls anywhere."

He watched her disappear into the darkness and thought of what might have been if only these boys had not disturbed them. "Listen to me," Herkuhlos said to them. "Your name is Yal, yes? And whatever your name is, you boys need to tell me everything."

The small one, Yal, glared at him. "We tell you nothing!"

"Quiet!" the bigger one said, swinging his bound hands into him.

Belolukos poked one and then the other with his stick, making them squirm as he jabbed at their bellies and chests. "You are both going to tell me everything. The only question is how much you want to suffer first."

"They won't talk," Herkuhlos said. "You remember how stubborn we were at their age. How many years do they have, do you think? Ten?"

"The big one is ten at the most but this little one cannot be more than six."

"I'm eleven!" Yal snapped.

"Shut your mouth!" the other said.

Herkuhlos laughed. "What is the purpose of this, Bel? They are just boys. Probably their clan was destroyed like ours and now they are scavenging to survive. We may as well let them go."

Belolukos stared. "Let them go? I will not let them go. I took them. They are mine. And now they will serve me."

"Serve you? Why? They will just be more bellies to fill when we have enough trouble now filling our own."

"We need servants! We are the sons of a chief, are we not? We have taken captives and now they will serve us. It is the proper way. We never have anyone to care for the horses or to guard them. They can make the fires, fetch the water."

Herkuhlos pursed his lips. He did like the sound of that. The boys sat motionless, their eyes fixed on his. He wondered if they would be more trouble than they were worth but all captives needed breaking in to start with. In time, when they understood their position, then they would likely prove their worth. Until then they would have to be watched closely, especially around the horses. But overall it would be well to have extra hands around.

"All right," Herkuhlos said, deciding. "You can keep them."

From the darkness across the square, a deep voice spoke loudly.

"No. They are mine."

2 0

Kounos

AT THE SOUND OF the voice, Herkuhlos froze and turned towards it.

The figure that stepped from the shadow into the edge of the light made for a frightening sight. He was a tall old man of forty or more with long, dirty hair. His tunic was leather and his arms were bare. He was as thin as the spear he held but the muscles on his arms were thick and sinewy, veins running all over. Despite his desiccated appearance his hands were large and strong. When he walked slowly forward it was the advance of a wolf before he rushes in for a sudden kill.

In the light of the fire his hooked nose and narrow eyes were pointed at Belolukos.

Herkuhlos and Belolukos jumped to their feet and levelled their spears.

The stranger raised his own spear over his head. The blade at

its tip was shining bronze and beautifully made. "I challenge you."
He addressed Belolukos.

"Do not," Herkuhlos whispered, looking around at the shadows all around him. There was no sight or sound of any other attackers and the fact that the stranger had issued the sacred challenge rather than attacking suggested he was alone. Or else why would he do it? "Bel, do not accept. We can take him together."

"Not with honour," Belolukos said and raised his own spear. "Get back," he said to Herkuhlos without taking his eyes from the stranger. "You challenge me," Belolukos replied to the stranger. "I am Belolukos of the Kweitos Clan. And you will die."

As he spoke, he whirled his spear around above his head, brought it down level to his waist and rushed the older man. Seeming to have expected that very thing, the stranger stepped sideways, brought his spear shaft down onto Belolukos' and whipped it sideways at Belolukos' head. Ducking below it, the shining bronze spearhead swished over the back of Belolukos' skull, close enough to whip up his long hair as it passed.

They came apart but both changed direction and went for one another. The stranger stepped sideways and thrust his spear at Belolukos' chest just as Belolukos' thrust missed. Again, Belolukos' instincts saved him as he twisted away from the blow but the edge of his enemy's blade caught his forearm, opening a cut as he retreated from the old warrior.

Herkuhlos felt the fire rise inside him at the sight of the wound. His instinct was to charge at the enemy and slay him at once but he could not intervene once the challenge had been offered and accepted. There was no custom more sacred for warriors.

Brought by the sounds of battle, Dhomyos and Kasos rushed

from the gates back into the centre of the fortress and stood to watch. Helhena had an arrow ready on her string. She could not shoot down the enemy during the challenge without bringing down a curse upon herself and her entire clan but Herkuhlos wondered if she cared about such things.

The stranger stepped forward, pressing his attack with careful thrusts as Belolukos retreated, bashing aside one jab after another with increasing desperation. It was suddenly clear to Herkuhlos that his brother was outmatched. The old warrior was smaller but his skill was the greater. Herkuhlos gripped his spear, fighting down the urge to step forward.

One thrust slipped through and cut Belolukos' shoulder and the stranger's spear shaft whipped over and down to crack the back of Belolukos' hand before springing back up to crack him on the side of the head. In but a moment, Belolukos found himself unarmed and staggering to the ground from the succession of swift blows.

The old warrior could have finished Belolukos with a thrust to the neck or through his ribs.

Instead, the warrior immediately lifted his own spear over his head and stood motionless, breathing hard and looking at Herkuhlos, Helhena, Dhomyos, and Kasos.

Helhena, about to shoot him before he could strike, relaxed her bowstring. Belolukos, rubbing his bruised skull, scrambled away and stood scowling at the warrior who had bested him. His eyes were still somewhat unfocused.

"I only want my boys," the man said, speaking now to Herkuhlos. His accent was strong but his words were clear enough. He nodded at the captives. "They are mine. I will take them and go."

Herkuhlos looked at the wide-eyed boys sitting bound by the fire. It was the sensible thing to do to let the old warrior take them. He had challenged before he could be attacked and Belolukos had foolishly accepted but now the challenge was over. The honourable thing would be to grant him the prizes that he had claimed. On the other hand they could all attack him together and surely they could kill him. Helhena could put an arrow through him before he could take two paces and she looked like she was ready and willing to do it. Killing him in a fight after his victory over Belolukos, to say nothing of his decision to leave Belolukos alive, would not bring down the anger of the gods but it would be dishonourable.

And yet to let him defeat his brother and take the captives back would be a humiliation that Herkuhlos could not abide.

Herkuhlos raised his spear over his head. "I challenge. I am Herkuhlos of the Kweitos Clan. If you win, you take the boys. If I win, I take your spear and your boys and you leave here never to return."

The stranger sighed, looked at the boys on the floor, and then at the stars overhead for a long moment. "And when I beat you, will the others challenge me?"

"No," Herkuhlos replied.

The old warrior pointed his spear at Helhena. "Will she shoot me dead?"

I have little say over what she will do, Herkuhlos thought. "No," he said. When he met Helhena's gaze he could not be sure what she intended.

After a pause, the old man nodded. "Very well." He raised his beautiful bronze spear over his head. "I am Kounos of Pelhbriya. In the name of the god Wolkanos I accept your challenge, boy."

He lowered his spear and stepped away from Belolukos, who also retreated, still glaring with fury.

Herkuhlos knew the stranger was an experienced warrior. He had far more control over his spear than Herkuhlos did. No doubt he knew a hundred tricks that could catch him out if he was not careful indeed.

They circled each other.

Though Herkuhlos was far taller, the older man had a look of great strength in the rippling muscles of his arms. His movements were steady and precise.

A challenge is not a battle, Herkuhlos heard the words of Gendryon, spoken long ago. *There is no need to hurry. A challenge may last only as long as the first spear thrust or it may run until both men are so tired they can hardly stand. The first blow need not be struck right away and once spears are crossed, it need not be a rush to the end. An experienced chief knows how to keep his strength back when his enemy's may be waning. Remember to breathe, boys. Feed the spirit with your breath.*

The wisdom of experience, Herkuhlos thought, looking at his enemy. But he seems to have it also.

The stranger certainly was being patient. His spear traced circles and whirls in the air between them, the polished bronze gleaming in the firelight. The older man breathed deeply and seemed content to wait until dawn before he would make an attack.

He is yet tired from his last fight, Herkuhlos realised, watching closely as they circled. And means to regain his strength by this delay. The longer I wait, the more time he has to recover his breath. Probably he is also hungry and exhausted from travelling the land without a clan. He grows stronger now while I delay.

Deciding, Herkuhlos stepped forward and thrust one handed at the stranger's chest. A lightning fast jab with his long reach could not fail to hit its target.

His spear hit only air.

The stranger's weapon came curling up from nowhere to strike at his face. Herkuhlos twisted away and grabbed the shaft with his free hand and wrenched it away from his head. The stranger yanked hard but Herkuhlos held on, twisted it from the old man's grasp, and stepped forward to swing his own spear sideways into the man's flank. His spear shaft broke on the stranger's arm, half of the spear spinning away with a clatter, but the old warrior was down on one knee and Herkuhlos stepped forward to level the man's own spear at his neck.

"I, Herkuhlos, have defeated you."

The warrior winced, clutching his arm, and fixed Herkuhlos with a look of fury. "Kill me, then."

Herkuhlos tilted his head. "I will keep this fine spear. And your boys. I have no wish to kill you but I also cannot let you go free. Not yet at least."

Belolukos stepped forward, looking down with an expression of triumph. "Let us keep him, brother. He can serve us as will the boys."

The stranger snorted. "I will never serve you, boy. You might as well kill me."

"Perhaps I will," Herkuhlos said. "But not now."

There was a sound across the square and Helhena pulled back her bow and cried out a warning. "Herkuhlos!" She did not shoot at the figure that stepped from the shadows.

A boy stepped forward with a javelin cocked back and ready to throw. "Let him go!" the boy said, aiming his javelin at Herkuhlos.

Belolukos was closest and he stepped closer still, pointing a finger at him. "You throw that stick and I'll snap your neck, boy." As he spoke he sidled closer to the spear he had dropped in the fight.

"I'll kill him first!" the boy said, his voice high but breaking. He was no more than twelve.

"Kill me, then," Herkuhlos said, holding his arms wide. "Kill me and then die, knowing this man will die and these boys also at the hands of my friends." He looked hard at the boy. "Or lower your spear and you all will live."

Helhena could have put an arrow through him at any moment but her hand was no doubt stayed by the boy's youth. Would she have the courage to shoot him if it came to it? Herkuhlos hoped she would not have to.

The boy hesitated for a heartbeat and Herkuhlos knew then that the boy would not act.

Helhena spoke up, her bow half-drawn with an arrow on the string. "Drop the spear or die."

The boy shook. He lacked the bravery to act but he could not bear to lose face by giving up.

"Bel," Herkuhlos said without taking his eyes from the boy.

At once, Belolukos rushed forward. The boy flinched before turning, intending to thrust his javelin into Belolukos. But his indecision had cost him the vital moment and Belolukos grasped the javelin, yanked it aside, and punched the boy in the jaw, knocking him down.

"Tie him up," Herkuhlos said, angry at himself for being ambushed yet again. "Tie them all up. Then we search for more."

"There is no more," the old warrior said.

"And why would I believe you?" Herkuhlos asked, looking down at the kneeling man.

He grunted. "Believe it or do not believe it. The truth is the truth."

"If I find anyone else then I really will kill you. All of you. Believe that truth."

The old man and the third boy were trussed up tightly and guarded while another search was undertaken. There was no one either inside or outside the walls, as far as they could tell but Herkuhlos said he would sit up and watch the captives for the rest of the night. It had grown cold in the dark of the night and so they fed the fire and laid down to sleep. Makros still lay motionless but alive within the circle of warmth.

"You can have the warrior," Belolukos said as he wrapped himself in his furs. "The three boys will serve me."

"Not sure I want him walking at my back," Herkuhlos said softly, looking at the older man across the fire. The man looked back at him steadily. "And I doubt those boys will be any better. You will find your water pissed in and your food rubbed over dung."

The old man grunted at that.

"Nonsense," Belolukos said sleepily. "I will break them."

Herkuhlos looked at the boys. "When you think them broken is when they turn on us. There is a reason clans take women and girls and boys too young to remember their fathers."

"Our clan has captured men. Merok, Garl, and that one with the fingers, remember him? They were captives."

"They were herders," Herkuhlos said, speaking to Belolukos but

324

looking at the old warrior. "And herders are born to serve, so that changing one master for another does not change their lives overly much. Does this man seem like a herder to you? And these must be his sons. They are killers, even the little one. You want killers guarding our horses?"

Belolukos sighed and rubbed his eyes as he turned over. "I need servants to be a lord."

"True enough."

"I will break them." He yawned. "But I will start tomorrow."

"Sleep well, brother."

Herkuhlos sat feeding the fire. All the others slept here and there. One by one the three boys lay down and slept beside the warrior but fitfully. When one began murmuring in his sleep, the warrior reached out with his bound hands and patted the boy's shoulder and hushed him with soft noises. After that, the warrior sat watching Herkuhlos. His wrists and ankles were bound and a length of rope was tied between them so that he could not stand fully upright. He would be no danger, Herkuhlos thought.

Silently they regarded each other through the heat above the flames.

"Your sons?" Herkuhlos asked, nodding.

The stranger grunted. "No." He looked down at each of them. "And yet in a way, yes."

"Nephews?"

The stranger tilted his head. "Yal is my sister's youngest boy. Drej is my father's cousin's son. Pehur is... a herder's boy."

Herkuhlos looked at the largest of the boys. "The one who threatened me with the javelin? I am surprised. Such devotion in a herder."

Leaning forward to his hands, the stranger pulled a strand of long hair away from his face. "He loves me. They all do."

"Why?"

"You tell me something first."

"Very well."

"How old are you?"

"Sixteen."

A laugh escaped the stranger's mouth before he stifled it. "So young."

Herkuhlos felt his anger rising. "My youth amuses you, captive?"

"I see it now but I did not when we crossed spears. My laughter was at myself. Bested by a boy."

"I am a man." Herkuhlos shrugged. "The rite was performed not long ago."

"You have the strength of one." The stranger smiled a little. "The strength of more than one, I must admit. You are taller than any man who lived here. Taller than any I have seen, I think. Slim, though. Slim as a sapling but as strong as an oak. It shames me to admit that I never heard of the Kweitos Clan. Who is your father?"

Herkuhlos hesitated a moment before answering but he saw little danger in it. "Gendryon was chief of our clan. My mother Alkmene was his wife. Our homeland was the vale of the Kweitos River that ran swiftly into the Rasga. It is far to the east."

"I know of the Rasga. I never met anyone who had seen it before." The stranger glanced at the sleeping boys. "You say your father was chief once. He is dead? Your clan is gone?"

A part of him was wary of speaking too much and of revealing secrets to a dangerous captive and yet it somehow felt right to speak of it. "The *yotunan* came. The demons escaped from the Vale of

Tartaros beyond the Sacred Mountain and since then they have been capturing and destroying all before them. My clan is no more. The men are all dead. My uncles, cousins, all the men are dead. The women... some of the women were taken."

The stranger nodded, his eyes glistening. "Just like here, then." After he spoke he clamped his quivering jaw closed and turned away, tears now brimming in his eyes.

"You know this place?"

Blinking rapidly he tried to smile but pressed his lips together until he had control of himself. "My home. My people."

"If that is true, how is it that you live?"

"How is it that you do?" the stranger shot back.

Herkuhlos was about to tell him to hold his tongue but he held his own instead and shrugged. "If we had been with our people, we would have been killed."

The old warrior nodded slowly and then gestured with bound hands at the people around the fire. "You were all elsewhere when they were attacked?"

Herkuhlos looked at Helhena, curled up and snoring softly at his side and across at Makros who yet hung between life and death. "We are not all the same clan. But our songs are almost the same."

"How is it that you are all together here?"

Herkuhlos nodded at Helhena. "Her father and Gendryon were guest friends but we did not know her until we found her. Alone. All her people gone. Makros there was from the north somewhere. I never even heard of his people. He lost his clan to the *yotunan*, then he lost his *koryos* to them when he attacked the demons. And still he fought on, alone, tracking them halfway across the world. Though he will not fight for much longer, it seems."

"And why are you here?"

"The *yotunan* took my mother. My sister." Herkuhlos gestured at Dhomyos and Kasos. "The others also have lost their families. Perhaps our mothers and sisters are dead but if they live..." He shrugged. "I mean to get them back."

The stranger stared. "You cannot hope to defeat such evil. Have you seen them?"

"*Yotunan* can be slain."

"Can they?"

"So the gods say," Herkuhlos replied, thinking of Kolnos.

"Not by sixteen-year-old boys."

"I am a man."

"Men cannot slay them either. No mortal can. These demons are of the undying ones." The warrior shrugged. "So I have heard."

Feeding another piece of wood into the fire, Herkuhlos watched the stranger. "I think I understand now why you were not here when this happened."

The old man raised his eyebrows. "You do, do you?"

"These boys. They are three. You are an older man. A warrior. You took them into the woods to hunt and to teach them the lore. We have this same rite. You returned to find your people gone. As we did."

The stranger sighed and shifted his position. "My name is Kounos. I am a *kerdos* in service to Wolkanos. Do you know what that is?"

"A weaver of metal."

Kounos pursed his lips. "I suppose so."

"And Wolkanos is your god?"

"He is the god of the kerdos. God of the forge. God of the white fire." Kounos scowled. "You do not know Wolkanos?"

Herkuhlos shrugged. "I have heard of him but there is not much copper where I come from. Perhaps Wolkanos has little interest in us."

"Perhaps. My forge is the temple of Wolkanos and it lies in the woods to the west by a stream that flows from a lake and eventually into the Denipa. I work there always and my work is dedicated to the god. I sleep there, even in winter. The boys are my acolytes and together we serve Wolkanos."

A weaver of metal was a special kind of man. The Kweitos Clan did not work metal and never had but there were some *kerdos* here and there amongst the Heryos clans of the Rasga. Their lore was sacred and was not for the knowledge of all. It was dangerous knowledge and deadly work. Some metal weavers were said to be driven mad by their communing with the spirits of the strange green substance that came from the earth. Such men were precious and they were strange. Not truly a part of the *tauta* like the rest of the men and they lived apart so that they did not pollute the clan with their dangerous knowledge.

"If you truly are a metal weaver then how is it that you fight like a great warrior?"

"You honour me, strong one. All men must fight or they are not men." He sighed. "Though I have not fought for some years and I see now that it was a mistake to neglect the spear dance." He tugged on his bonds. "In my service to Wolkanos perhaps I grew to love the heat and the fire too much and neglected my duties as a warrior. This is the consequence of failing to do as the gods command."

"You beat Bel," Herkuhlos said. "And he is the strongest of us.

He has been besting some of the warriors of our clan in stick fighting and in wrestling since the summer before last. Beating him was no small thing."

"Ah, your efforts to ease my suffering only wounds my honour more," Kounos said, smiling. "I meant it when I said I would never serve you, boy. The moment you cease watching me I will strangle you."

Herkuhlos blinked at the sudden change in the conversation. "You wish for me to kill you. You mean to anger me, is that it? So that I will slay you? Why?"

Kounos held up his bonds. "Better to be dead than a slave. I will never serve you. It is the truth. Never. I am sworn to Wolkanos and I will never be broken. The first chance I get I will kill you. All of you. The girl, too."

Herkuhlos looked closely at him. The man spoke evenly and without emotion, as if they were discussing the best way to skin a gazelle. But his words chilled Herkuhlos. "You speak the truth though you know it will mean your death."

"I am fond of the truth."

Herkuhlos had no desire to kill the man before him. "Tell me then why you came back here."

"It is called Pelhbriya. It is my home."

"I thought the woods were your home."

"The magic of the metal is sacred and it cannot be brought into the land of the living. Often I sleep there, yes. Days and days I stay there to conduct the rites and to teach my boys the lore. But I have a home here. My people are here."

"Your wife? Children?"

He shook his head. "The metal is my wife. The boys my

330

children. When I am gone, if the god wills it, these boys will call down Wolkanos and breathe life into the metal as I have done." Kounos looked at them. "Unless we all die here."

"Unless I kill you all, you mean."

"You will have to kill us," Kounos said. "Or you could release us."

"Why would I do that? You are our captives. Your lives are mine."

"I heard what you said to your brother. You wish to free us."

"Then you heard wrong. He wishes you to serve him. I wish to kill you."

Kounos' lip twitched. "Free us."

"So that you can kill us in our sleep?"

"If you free us then I have no reason to cause you harm."

"But there is nothing you can do for me either. So I will lose the honour of taking four captives in exchange for nothing."

Kounos looked up at the stars. "The gods would look kindly upon you."

Herkuhlos laughed. "My gods would not be pleased. Perhaps you serve different gods here."

"I serve the god of the flame. You favour a warrior god, I know. All boys do." He held up his hands apologetically. "All young men, also. But I know you are a godly man."

"How can you know that?"

"Before darkness fell I saw the bodies of my people laid outside these walls. They were not there two days ago when Pehur watched the place from afar. You did what was right by the gods."

"We wished only to appease the spirits of the dead so that we could stay here for a day or two. It was for us that we did it, not for the dead or for the gods."

"You did what was right. What does it matter who you did it for? You followed the lore. You know what is right and what is not. And you laid the dead out with respect, Pehur said. With gentleness and care. You did not need to do that."

Herkuhlos watched Kounos. Was his friendly, calm demeanour a trick? If he was to untie his bonds would the man still try to kill them all? If Kounos and his boys walked away, how could Herkuhlos be sure they would not return with twenty warriors?

"What would you do if I freed you?"

"Make Pelhbriya our home again."

Herkuhlos scoffed at his words. "You cannot hope to defend this place with three boys as your war band. You will lose it to the first raiders that come here. And the demons are not more than a moon north of here. If they return then you will all be killed."

"The demons are in the north, yes. Closer by far than a moon, my friend. Their war bands still roam the lands all around. We have seen them, my boys and me. And you are right that I cannot hold Pelhbriya against them. But I must attempt it. I must."

"Why?"

"My ancestors came across the Denipa and forced the people of Pelhbriya into servitude and took this mound, their wells, their homes, and built these walls wider and taller. Ever since my ancestors have ruled this place. I will not give up what they won and built while the spirit is yet in my body. Which is why I say you must free me or slay me."

Herkuhlos poked at the fire and laid another piece of broken wood onto the coals. "We go to free our people, Kounos. Your people are there, also. Why not join me? You and your boys.

Together, we will defeat the *yotunan* and free those that were taken."

Kounos looked tired. He shook his head and closed his eyes, hanging his head. "You are truly just sixteen, son?"

"Why would I lie?"

Kounos sighed. "I have trained many boys in my life. Boys who are filled with the urge for greatness can be impossible to contain and some of these are sent to me, out there by my river. Some, if it is the will of the gods, allow themselves to be tamed. But there are some who allow their hearts to rule their wits. These boys get burnt. They find themselves on the end of someone's spear before they are men grown."

"I am not a boy."

"If you think yourself strong enough to face a demon, then you are mad, whatever else you are."

"Go to sleep, old man," Herkuhlos said, angry at him. "I will decide what to do with you when the sun has risen."

"If this is my last night with blood in my body, I shall spend it watching the stars." He looked up.

"Do as you will," Herkuhlos said.

Despite his proud words, Kounos eventually curled up on the ground and slept as soundly as the boys around him. After Herkuhlos was sure the old man had fallen asleep, he woke Dhomyos and warned him to keep away from the stranger and to be wary of any tricks. With that, Herkuhlos, exhausted, fell asleep.

He woke at dawn, ate a little, and went to the gate and beyond to check that there were no enemies on the horizon. A grey mist drifted in the low parts that was driven away when a steady rain began to fall as the sun rose. The others made themselves busy around the camp, building the fire back up and preparing more wood, fetching water, seeing to the horses. The captives sat together in silence, watching everything.

Makros still clung to life.

"He opened his eyes just before dawn when Helhena gave him some water," Belolukos said.

Herkuhlos was excited by the news. "He is getting better?"

Belolukos shook his head. "He is still going to die today but he's a warrior, that one."

Herkuhlos went beyond the wall to pass water. He looked at the grey, wet world beyond. This land belonged to Kounos. The old metal weaver and his acolytes were the only survivors of a strong people and they deserved to carry on in the place their ancestors had built. Walking back inside towards the fire, he knew there was only one problem that he had to overcome.

"Brother," Herkuhlos said. "I must speak to you."

Belolukos sauntered over. "The boys said they know where more food is hidden. Just seeds for grinding but I will make them show me. You see, they are already coming to terms with their new position."

Herkuhlos sighed and drew him away further. "Listen, Bel." He paused. "Brother. You will be angry but it must be done."

Belolukos stared, worry beginning to spread across his face. "What must be done?"

"I am going to free our captives. All of them."

Belolukos gaped. "You cannot mean that. You are insulting me. All three boys are my captives. Mine! I took them. Yours is the old man, free him if you like but you have no right to mine."

This was not going well. "I wish you would not make this difficult, Bel. Anyway, you swore to obey me."

"No chief would take captives from his men!"

"I am not taking them. I am freeing them."

"But why? I can break them. Already they are helping us with food."

"This was their home, Bel."

"I know, they told me. What of it?"

"They are going to stay here. We are going into terrible danger now and even if you do break their will they will likely die in the fights to come."

"So?" Belolukos scowled. "All men die. Servants serve. It is the way."

"It is. But I am not your chief. I am not your *koryonos*. You swore to follow me but what am I, Bel? What are we? This world is wrong now. Nothing is as it should be. We are not a clan who has taken prisoners in a raid. We are not a *koryos* taking captives back to our tribe. We are heading into darkness."

Belolukos took a slow, shaky breath and replied in a low, dangerous tone. "When we rescue mother we will return to the east and the captives will serve me there. You cannot take my honour. I will not allow it."

"It must be done. It will be done."

"Do not do this, Holkis. I will not forgive you."

"I hope that you will."

"You turn me into a fool!"

"How so?"

"All that you do, you make me a fool! All that you are! You are no brother of mine."

At that, he pushed Herkuhlos aside and strode away toward the gate. Herkuhlos wanted to call him back but he knew it would do no good. Anything that he said would only anger him further. Was he doing the right thing? It did not feel that way.

Returning to the fire he ran into Helhena, who looked fearful. "What has happened?"

"A quarrel between brothers," he replied, attempting a smile. "Nothing more."

"It will be something more if you do not rein him in," she said. "His hurt pride will be dangerous if you do not force him into obedience."

"It is not your concern," Herkuhlos snapped and walked past her back to the fire where the others stood watching his approach.

"What's wrong?" Kasos asked.

Herkuhlos ignored him and stood over Kounos and the three boys. "I am Herkuhlos of the Kweitos Clan. You are my captives, taken fairly in battle. And in the sight of the gods I say you are mine no longer, nor do you belong to any of my men. You are free without hindrance."

Kounos looked up, warily. "You ask for nothing in return?"

"Your spear is also mine," Herkuhlos said, gesturing at the magnificent bronze spear. "This I give to you as a gift from one guest to another. You have shared your food with us, and your home. We will share our food in return and part as guest friends." He looked down at Kounos. "If you would have it so."

"By Wolkanos, you will not regret this," Kounos said. "I swear it. I will never do you harm, nor will I harm your people. I, Kounos, swear it in the sight and hearing of the gods. I swear it by the fire of Wolkanos and by my blood."

Herkuhlos nodded to Kasos and Dhomyos who bent to undo the bonds of cord and leather and soon the four captives stood free, rubbing their red wrists. The boys cast sidelong looks at one another, the smallest of them grinning fiercely.

Kounos accepted his spear from Herkuhlos and bowed his head. "Truly, Herkuhlos you have nothing to fear from me. And you may stay here until you are ready. Pelhbriya is yours. You may take one of the houses. Take one each, my friends."

"Perhaps one day," Herkuhlos replied. "But now we must make our preparations to go on. Our people are in danger and they will remain so until we free them."

Bowing again, Kounos smiled, lines creasing the corners of his eyes. "Though I believe that you walk into death, I also know that you are a credit to your people. All of you." He looked down at Makros lying wrapped in the furs. "You mean to take him with you?"

Herkuhlos looked down. "In truth, I expected him to die in the night. Nothing can be done for him by mortal hands. I wonder if you would watch over him until his last breath. He was a warrior. If you bury him as one, the gods would look favourably on you."

Kounos pursed his lips. "Nothing can be done by mortal hands, indeed. But what about immortal ones?"

"If the gods were going to save him, they would have done so by now."

"But the Seeress of Nemos is not a day's ride."

"What is that?"

"Surely, you have heard of her?"

Herkuhlos shook his head. "Our homeland is far to the east. Do you mean there is a healer?"

Kounos nodded slowly. "For the appropriate sacrifice, the Seeress will heal any sickness."

"Nothing can save a man with the green death."

"The Seeress can. I have seen it. Long has she protected our people. She was here before we ever came to Pelhbriya."

"No woman lives that long."

"As I said, she is not a woman. She is the Seeress of Nemos. She is a *wotis*, a goddess who reads the entrails, who sees into what will come to be. But she can heal any ill, by Wolkanos it is true. She lives deep in the woodland by a sacred lake with healing waters."

A goddess? Herkuhlos thought. Surely that could not be. He dismissed that part of it with hardly any consideration but if the rest was true then it might be worth a try.

"Anyone that lives near here will be long dead," Dhomyos said. "The *yotunan* kill or take all in their path."

"They did not find my forge and they did not find her, I am certain. As I was protected by Wolkanos, she will have protected herself. She is immortal, my friends. No one will find her unless they know the path through the woodland to the sacred lake. There is nowhere that a man can stand at a distance and see the lake, for the hills and trees hide it from view."

Herkuhlos shook his head. "Then how will we find her?"

"Pehur will lead you."

They turned and looked at the eldest of the three boys.

Herkuhlos pointed at him. "The herder?"

Kounos frowned. "His father was a herder. One of the Kalekka who serve us. But now Pehur is the best of my boys, as they will all admit."

"But how can that be if he is so low born?"

The boy scowled but held his tongue.

"The god's power is in him," Kounos said. "Wolkanos favours

him. He works bronze like no acolyte I ever had before."

Kasos was interested in that. "But why would your god choose a herder's son for his power? One of foreign blood at that."

"I do not know why Wolkanos chooses those he does but he chose me and he has chosen Pehur. And all that matters is that Pehur knows well how to guide you and your friend to the Seeress."

Helhena spoke up. "But Makros will die if we move him."

Kounos shrugged. "And he will die if you do not."

Their eyes turned to Herkuhlos who nodded. "I suppose we must try. We will make a hurdle and tie him to it and we shall drag him to this seeress, this *wotis*. We must see to the horses and collect our things."

"Before you go," Kounos said quickly. "There is one more gift I would grant you. Come with me, it is hidden deep within my clan house."

"You have my thanks but I must go now or Makros will have no chance at all."

"Son, this gift will help you to slay your enemies."

Herkuhlos stopped. "It is a weapon?"

Kounos smiled. "Come with me."

21

A Mighty Gift

KOUNOS LED HERKUHLOS TO the northern edge of the fortress to one of the smallest houses. It was dark and damp within. No fire had been lit in the hearth for a long time and even the *yotunan's* warriors seemed hardly to have given it any notice. A few decorated jars were smashed and the pieces scattered. Some shallow pits dug here and there about the floor as if their search for hidden stores had been hasty and superficial.

"This is your house?" Herkuhlos asked.

Kounos sighed as he looked around. "No wife to tend to it. Whenever I returned to Pelhbriya I brought my acolytes to serve me until we returned to the grove."

"Where you create weapons?" Herkuhlos said. "Weapons like your spear?"

Kounos smiled sadly and moved to the centre of the house, looking down at the hearth. "It is a sacred place. There is power there."

"And that power goes into your bronze," Herkuhlos said, understanding something of it. "Through you?"

"The god has always favoured me," Kounos said, crouching by the cold hearth. "When I was a boy, the *kerdos* was an old man. He lived at the forge and never came to the fortress. I wanted always to be a warrior but when I returned from my wandering, there was an accident." He began to pull up the flat stones from around the hearth. "It was my fault. My foolishness caused a fire. The fire burned my father's house and might have taken the rest were it not for the rains." Kounos stopped to hold out his scarred arm. "I suffered this. My sister's face was burned. She lived but no right-minded man wanted her after that and so I was sent to the forge."

"As punishment?"

Kounos continued to pull up the stones. "My father thought so, though other men were honoured to see their sons apprenticed to the *kerdos*. I hated it. I hated the *kerdos*. I hated the work. It was beneath me as a warrior to spend my strength in the making of things, like a common craftsman, like a herder. All I wanted was to fight and to win fame and to one day become the chief. Hand me that broken piece of wood there."

Herkuhlos did as he was commanded. "Your father was the chief?"

"His brother was." Kounos began to dig with the stick, driving it into the earth under the hearth and dragging the soil and pebbles out. "I was the best of my generation and I knew it was my destiny to rule my people. But the god decided otherwise."

"What happened?"

"First, I started to hate the work less. Or perhaps I grew

342

competent first. We prepared the ore. We learnt the songs, the lore, the rites, the tools. Gradually, I felt the god in me."

"What does that feel like?"

"Just as I say. When I was taught... well, these things are sacred. But when I worked the fire, I felt the god in it. When I worked the metal, I felt it there, also. The circle of time turns strangely when the god is in you. You lose yourself to the god. You give yourself up to it and... well, these things are not easily spoken. And perhaps they should not be."

"I know of it," Herkuhlos said. "At least, I knew it sometimes when we danced the spear dance. And when we crossed the plains to here, I knew it when I fought against raiders who meant to slay all of us and who did slay one of my spear-brothers. It was something like blind rage that took me and yet I was beyond anger. It was something like you say. My enemies seemed to stand still and only I was free to act. But it was as though I chose nothing at all and my spear seemed to move in a path long decided for it. As though the god moved it with his own hand while I was little more than a witness to it all."

Kounos paused in his digging to turn and regard Herkuhlos. "I knew you were a born warrior but it seems you are also a bear warrior. You know of these men in your lands?"

"I know what you mean. The wolf spirit, some also call it. Warriors who drink the mead of battle and give themselves, their spear, and their enemies to Kolnos. But those men must be inducted into the brotherhood and they must perform the rites before battle. They drink the mead of war and dance the spear dance to lose themselves. But that is not what I am as I did none of that."

"Then you have a gift few warriors are granted. To be so close to the path of the gods that you can step onto it with such ease. When I work bronze I must follow the rites before I feel the god in me but my acolyte Pehur is somewhat like you in that he does it with such ease and almost without will at all."

"But that is the weaving of metal not battle. It is not the same."

"It is not the same. And yet it is."

Herkuhlos rubbed the back of his neck, frowning. "I do not understand."

"If you live long enough, perhaps one day you will." Kounos had dug down a long way and stopped to look over his shoulder. "Truly, the gods favour you, Herkuhlos. And that is why you must have this."

Kounos had dug down onto a stone slab beneath the earth. He cleared away more dirt, grumbling as more fell back into the pit but eventually uncovered a green metal ring, smaller than a bracelet fitted cunningly into the stone itself. Herkuhlos was confused and was about to ask what he needed with a child's bracelet when Kounos heaved on it, his muscles bunching as he strained. Stone grated on stone and the slab levered up on one side to reveal another pit within. It was dark inside but it was lined with stone and filled with lumps of something.

Herkuhlos stepped forward and looked down into it. He almost stumbled in, so shocked was he at the sight.

Dozens of copper ingots piled one atop the other.

More than he had ever thought to exist in the world.

"By Kolnos," Herkuhlos whispered. "How do you come by this?"

"Traders come up to Pelhbriya from the south through the

Melamori and they row up the Denipa. We give them cows and horses from the east and grain from the west. And I make spearheads and daggers with the bronze and send them west and south, mostly."

"Why not east?" Herkuhlos said, thinking how much his people would give to have so many metal weapons.

"Some go east," Kounos replied, shrugging. "But the people of the south bring gold and precious things. Those in the west grow mountains of grain. What can the east offer but cows and horses?"

"There is nothing more valuable than cows and horses," Herkuhlos said.

Kounos tilted his head. "For some people."

"I did not know there was so much bronze in all the world."

Kounos smiled at that. "There is a great settlement north of here along the Denipa. It is called Nemiyeh. There many *kerdos* there and they have more bronze even than this."

Herkuhlos looked hard at him. "North? Then perhaps that is where the demon has taken my people."

"There can be no doubt."

"And you wish to gift me this metal?" Herkuhlos said, wondering how much to pack onto each horse.

"Ah, no," Kounos said, spreading his gnarled hands. "No, this is the most valuable thing in the world for me, you see. And I must work it now with my acolytes. People will come here again in spring and summer and I must be ready to trade for food and everything else we need if Pelhbriya is to grow once more."

Herkuhlos was beginning to wonder if the old warrior was not a little mad. Perhaps he had lost his mind when his people had been destroyed. Or perhaps he had always been mad and that was the real reason he had been sent away as a boy. "You must understand Kounos that this place will be taken from you by the first warband that comes by here. I took it from you without even meaning to do it."

"Perhaps," Kounos said, frowning. A flash of anger passed across his face but it passed and the old man slapped his chest with a dirty fist. "But the god is in me now, Herkuhlos, I feel it and he wishes me to work the forge. Perhaps others will seek shelter with me. Perhaps not all my people were killed and are even now hiding in the woods. They will return and in time we will be strong again. And it would not be so if not for your godliness, Herkuhlos. Which is why you must have this." He reached inside the hole up to his shoulder, felt around, and slowly brought out a long package wrapped in layers of oiled and waxed skins.

Standing before Herkuhlos, Kounos held the package in his arms as a mother might hold a baby to soothe it, and slowly unwrapped the skins.

"My master stood aside and watched me make this," Kounos said, speaking softly. "It took a long time. When it was done, he said he had never seen its like and he knew he could die, for his acolyte had surpassed him. He was as good as his word and he died that winter. As I made it, I knew I would never make its equal. In life, we are granted a single great accomplishment. Mine was this and I have never bettered it, nor will I."

The final layer flopped back to reveal a shining dagger as long as a man's arm. The blade was thick at the base and tapered to a point, perfectly symmetrical. Both edges were sharp almost to the hilt, which was wide with a long, thick handle.

"You mean to give this to me?" Herkuhlos said, almost

whispering. "But why?"

"When it was made, I did not know who I had made it for. I thought perhaps it was for my father but he fought little by then, aged as he was. My uncle would have wanted it more than anything in the world if he had seen it but I knew somehow that it was not for him. My master asked me why I had made the handle so long and so thick and I said I did not know but I was sure it was not a mistake. I reasoned that the handle had to be so large to balance the weight of the blade but now I finally understand that I made it this way to fit your hand."

Herkuhlos was confused. "I do not understand. You made it for me? But when did you make it?"

Kounos nodded. "I made it the same year my master died. The year I became the master. Sixteen years ago."

"Then how could you have known?"

"Ah, I could not have. I did not know." Kounos pointed a finger upwards. "But the god knew."

He held it out and Herkuhlos reached slowly for it. His hand did fit well around the handle and when he lifted it, he was surprised at how light it was. "I never knew a dagger could be so long."

"Most cannot," Kounos replied. "When they are made too long the blade bends or breaks too easily. But the bronze that I used for this was... different. Stronger. I knew that with the right form I could make the blade longer than any before. I have heard from the men of the south that there are other weapons like this there. They call them swords but I have never seen one. All others I have made since have failed. But not this one. It cuts all along both edges and pierces with thrusts."

"The men of the south fight with these? How is it that they have such wealth?"

Kounos shrugged. "They say there are places there where thousands of people live all together, serving strange gods who dwell atop sacred mountains built by the hands of men." He tilted his head. "Perhaps these tales are lies, for foreign people can never be trusted, but they are certainly wealthy with copper and bronze."

For a moment, Herkuhlos imagined these distant places where men could build mountains for their gods to live upon. It all seemed too far away to concern him for now. "I still do not understand why you think this should be mine."

"It was made for you, it is clear to me now. And you will use it to slay those who have slain my people, will you not?"

"I will."

"And you will need a great weapon if you truly mean to slay a demon."

Herkuhlos cleared his throat, almost overwhelmed by the thought of the challenge. "If any weapon can it is this one."

"Then we shall part as friends," Kounos stepped back. "Also, I shall gift my spear to your brother who is named Bel. There is no better spear in the world and perhaps it will go some way to restoring his honour."

"You are a good man, Kounos."

Herkuhlos took a final, admiring look at the sword before wrapping it up once more. After that their preparations to leave were swiftly completed. Makros still breathed but if they were to get him to the Seeress before he died they would have to go quickly. It was a full day's journey.

They tied Makros to a hurdle and gathered outside the fortress where the bodies lay. Kounos had said he and his acolytes would see them all buried. The rain had cleared and the sun was shining between swift, high clouds.

Herkuhlos spoke to the boy named Pehur. "You will lead us to the Seeress of Nemos."

The boy glared, glancing over his shoulder at the walls of Pelhbriya. "I will."

Belolukos had hardly said a word to Herkuhlos though he carried his new spear proudly enough. His face was twisted in anger when he turned on the boy. "You call him lord, boy."

Pehur's lip curled but he looked down. "Yes, lord. I will lead you to the sacred lake of the *wotis*, lord."

With that he set off down the slope with the others riding after him and their pack horses trailing behind.

Herkuhlos looked back at Pelhbriya. Now that Kounos had returned it would not be long before the walls would echo to the roaring of fire and the chants of the metal workers calling down the god. Life of a kind had returned to the *briya*. But for how long?

"We must go," Helhena said over her shoulder, riding away with Makros' hurdle dragging behind her horse.

"Yes," Herkuhlos said, turning away and riding after her. "We must go on."

22

The Seeress

THEY MADE THEIR WAY west across uneven ground and into a hilly woodland. Their young guide Pehur appeared sure enough about the route but it was not an easy ride, picking their way around dense clusters of oak on the higher ground and willow and alder in the damp lowland. Eventually they came to a stream and followed that as it wound its way through the trees, their horses often splashing through the water.

Makros groaned, his face so pale and grey he looked dead already as he bounced along on his hurdle, dragged behind the horse.

"Do not die yet, Makros," Herkuhlos said, riding behind him. "We take you to... to someone who will save your life."

"This is a waste of time," Belolukos muttered, turning around. "He will be dead before nightfall."

It was late in the day when Pehur slowed to a stop. The weather had changed once more and a cold mist seemed to creep from the damp earth to gather in the hollows. The boy sat on his horse and pointed ahead through the trees.

"That is the way in."

"In to what?" Herkuhlos asked.

"To Nemos. The sacred lake of the immortal *wotis*."

Belolukos scowled. "What are you waiting for, boy? Go on, will you."

They could barely see the waters of the lake through the gathering mist. Low hills surrounded it closely on all sides and the mist hung still and lifeless within the depression. The stream they had followed trickled from one end of the vale on its way east to the mighty river. Boulders covered with bright green moss lay jumbled with stunted, strangled trees clawing their way from the gaps between then. The only way through and down to the low ground around the lake was across the soggy earth around the stream.

"The Seeress resides at the other end of the lake," young Pehur said softly.

"How far in is it?" Belolukos asked, staring into the drifting grey clouds.

"Not far," Pehur said. "The lake is small."

Still, they hesitated near the mouth of the vale, their nervous horses tossing their heads and pressing against one another.

"There are raiders roaming the woods," Pehur said, prompting them. "We should go all the way in before any see us. Once we are within we should be safe."

Herkuhlos looked around at the rocky ground rising to either side with the trees of the woodland atop. "Is there a way out of here?"

"Only this way," Pehur said. "As far as I know. It is a sacred place and I came only once before, with my master."

Belolukos shook his head. "We will trap ourselves."

"Better that than exposed out there in the woodland for the night," Herkuhlos replied.

"Perhaps." Belolukos did not seem convinced.

Herkuhlos turned to Makros, lying like death on his hurdle. His skin was as pale as bleached bone. "By Kolnos, we must go on or the journey here is wasted."

"It is wasted anyway," Belolukos muttered.

Leading his horse through the stream, Herkuhlos descended into the misty vale. His brother and the others following behind. Thick stands of reeds covered the edges of the lake where it became soft, marshy ground. The limp brown reeds were showing green spring growth. Beyond, the surface of the lake was still beneath the mists. All around the lake an area of flat, stony ground spread to the surrounding steep slopes that rose higher the further they went into the vale. Atop those slopes the trees of the woodland grew. Looking up at them, Herkuhlos imagined how easy it would be for a heedless woodland traveller to find himself tumbling to his death. Smaller trees grew at the base of the slopes and some bushes clung to the rocky cliffside. Herkuhlos thought he could probably climb to the top if he had to but the mixture of loose stone, earth, roots, and crumbling rock did not make the prospect appealing.

Between the waters and the trees was a grassy path wide enough for four to walk abreast. Loose rocks littered the path and every few paces a hoof or a foot kicked one, sending it clattering across the thin soil or down into the lake with a plop, breaking the perfect stillness of the waters.

"You are certain this is the right path?" Herkuhlos asked Pehur.

He spoke softly in reply but there was no uncertainty in his voice. "It is the only path, lord."

The lake was not large and soon they reached its far side. The rocky ground beyond the lake there rose into higher cliffs of jumbled rock the colour of charcoal and ash. Between the edge of the lake and the cliff face stood a large rock, half the height of a man and twice as long, with a flat top.

Herkuhlos did not have to ask if they were in the right place.

"What happens now?" he asked Pehur. "Where is the Seeress?"

"She lives beneath the earth," he muttered. "Seen by no man." The boy's eyes flitted around as he spoke.

"Then how can she help us?" Belolukos asked, grasping Pehur by the shoulder and turning him about. "Speak, will you."

Pehur glared for a moment and then looked down. "Her acolytes attend the supplicants and always they come out to heal the sick." He paused, chewing his lip. "But now perhaps..."

Belolukos shook him. "But what? Go on, boy."

"But I think that perhaps they are here no longer."

"What? Why?"

Pehur looked down. "My master said the Seeress would never leave this place. The waters here are sacred. The Seeress of Nemos has been here since time began. Perhaps she has but I know raiders have come to these woods. We have seen them riding through. They are everywhere. I think they must have come here. Taken the Seeress and her acolytes or killed them."

Belolukos stared at Herkuhlos. "That faithless snake." He spat on the ground in front of Pehur. "Your lying master just wished to be rid of us and sent us here. Now Makros will die anyway and we have wasted a day coming here and it will be another day going back to Pelhbriya. Did he want us to be trapped, is that it? What is he up to?" With a shove, he sent Pehur sprawling to the ground and he drew his knife. "Well, he cannot hold that fortress against us, no matter what tricks he tries. I'm going back there and I'm going to take his head."

"No!" Pehur cried, scrambling to his feet. "He did not lie, I swear it. He believes in the Seeress' power. He did not lie but I know that there is no one here but women and not even all the warriors of Pelhbriya could stop the demons."

Herkuhlos stepped forward. "Lower your weapon, brother. He is only a boy."

"Old enough that he should know his place. Why not tell us before we came all this way? It is almost night and we shall have to stay out here either in the woods or trapped beneath this cliff. And Makros will be dead before sunrise anyway." He pointed at Pehur. "You, son of a herder, you stay out of my sight."

"What should we do?" Helhena asked Herkuhlos.

He looked at the cliffs above them and the mists over the lake. If they could only remain unseen it would be a pleasant and safe place. "Make camp here and keep watch."

"What about a fire?" Dhomyos asked. "We can make fire, can't we?"

"A small one," Herkuhlos said. "There are plenty of trees and bushes."

A woman spoke from behind them. "Light no fires here."

They jumped and turned to see a woman standing on the other side of the slab of stone.

Herkuhlos stared at her, his heart racing and spear before him, before looking quickly about for anyone else or any other danger. But she was alone, standing still in a long pale dress with her dark hair loose about her shoulders. She was slender and held her hands low before her. It was as though she had appeared out of the mist.

"Are you the Seeress?" Herkuhlos asked, putting up his spear and taking a step toward her. "A seeress?"

She smiled. He noticed she was an older woman. Older even than his mother. "I am merely a servant of the Seeress. You are welcome here as long as you obey her law."

"Then we shall obey, servant of the Seeress," Herkuhlos replied at once. "But what is her law?"

The woman smiled. "First, you must name yourself and speak your purpose."

"I am Herkuhlos son of Alkmene of the Kweitos Clan. This is my brother Belolukos and our people. As you may see we have a man who is near death. In Pelhbriya we were told by Kounos the weaver of metal that the Seeress could heal him. Is that true?"

The woman frowned. "I am Henhi, servant of the Seeress. You have come a long way, Herkuhlos son of Alkmene. What is your purpose in these lands?"

"To find the demon that took my mother and my sister captive." He glanced at the others. "We all have people who were taken and we mean to rescue them." He hesitated and then carried on. "Also, I am to slay the twelve demons that have torn their way across the earth in their escape."

A frown creased Henhi's brow. "You seek death, then?"

"No. But I swore an oath to the god Kolnos and so it must be done. My path is set."

Henhi tilted her head. "A man's path is set but the thread of life twists as he walks it. And some men twist their thread more than others." She looked past him at Makros, lying still in his furs. "However, I am sorry to say that I can smell the death on your friend from here. I fear he is beyond all help. You may stay until dawn but then you must leave. May the Mother protect you all."

She turned and made to leave.

"No!" Herkuhlos said, stepping forward, anger and fear rising. "I do not believe you. Kounos said the seeress can cure any illness. You must help him."

Henhi turned, a frown creasing her face. "The seeress cannot cure death. And I find it troubling that you trust the word of a metal weaver over that of a servant of the Seeress."

"But there must be something you can do," Herkuhlos replied, stepping closer so that he was almost at the great rock, looking across its back at her. "You must at least try. Try and fail but at least do something."

She smiled, her eyes sad. "You have the earnestness of youth. I did not see it until now. How old are you, Herkuhlos?"

"I am sixteen. But soon I will be seventeen."

Henhi's smile faded into a look of compassion. "When you have seen as much death as I have, you will come to accept what cannot be changed."

"You think I have not seen death, old woman? I have seen every man of my clan cold and dead upon the earth." He pointed to Helhena. "I have seen the men of her clan cold and dead and I have killed men with my spear and with my axe. I have seen death and I have dealt it. That man is named Makros and he also saw his clan dead and he took his *koryos* to attack the *yotunan* only to see them fall also. He has crossed the plains as we have but he did it alone and still he fought his enemy. After so long apart, our paths crossed and I found him like this. I may not understand the gods but I know that some god meant us to find him and once found to cure him. Your seeress has that power. If she cares anything for order she must help him."

Henhi looked at him, her expression hard now. "A sacrifice would have to be made."

Did that mean she was going to do it? "Anything. What is the appropriate sacrifice?"

She cast an eye over each of them and their horses. "Whatever is most precious to you."

Herkuhlos looked around at his people. His eyes fixed on Helhena and she saw the uncertainty in them.

"And which god is the sacrifice for?" Helhena asked the acolyte.

Henhi frowned. "The sacrifice is for the Seeress, of course."

Kounos had called her a *wotis* and a goddess but they had not fully believed him. And even if Kounos had believed it, that did not make it so.

"You mean that the Seeress really is a goddess?" Herkuhlos asked. "A seeress, a *wotis*, and also a goddess?"

The acolyte's expression did not change. "What else could she be?"

A goddess, Herkuhlos thought. Was that really possible? It would make a certain kind of sense if it were true but why would a goddess live alone so far from the Sacred Mountain? Perhaps the old woman was lying or mad but if there was a chance to save Makros then it was worth going along with her demands.

Herkuhlos looked around, thinking hard. They could not

afford to give up another horse, especially as they did not know for certain whether the Seeress had genuine power or even if she existed at all. What else did they have that a goddess or her acolytes would want? Not weapons, presumably. "We have meat and furs to offer."

Henhi did not seem to be impressed and she breathed out softly. "Is that worth the life of a man?"

"Nothing is worth the life of a man," Herkuhlos replied, irritated. "Nothing that we can sacrifice. If our food and our pelts are not acceptable then tell me what you want."

Henhi bowed. "I shall consult the Seeress." At that, she turned and walked slowly toward the cliff face behind her. At its base, she turned and disappeared behind a bolder."

"Ah," Belolukos said, holding out his hand. "It's a cave. She came out of a cave. I knew it." Belolukos nodded at the cliff. "We could go in there and force her to heal him."

They all stared at him in surprise.

"The Seeress would stop you," Helhena said. "And you would bring her curse on all of us for violating her sanctuary."

Belolukos scoffed. "How can you all be so blind? Can you not see that *she* is the Seeress?"

They looked at the base of the cliff and back to him.

"She said she serves the Seeress who is divine." Herkuhlos said.

"You believe everyone, brother, because you are ever honest. You believed Kounos when he said this old hag was a goddess who could cure Makros and now look at us. She is an old healer living in the wilderness, nothing more. She practically told us there was nothing she could do. And now, because you would not listen, she asks for gifts to try to heal him when she knows she will fail. Oh, she is a clever one. Cunning."

Herkuhlos tore his gaze from his brother and watched the base of the cliff where the old woman had gone. There was no sign of her.

Crossing the camp, Herkuhlos kneeled by Makros and leaned close. His face was white beneath his thick beard but somehow he still breathed. "You live on when weaker men would have let their spirit go. I believe there is meaning to your struggle, Makros. You have a purpose left unfulfilled and your thread is not meant to be broken."

"Herkuhlos," Helhena said. "Look."

He looked up to see Henhi approaching with a lamp burning in her hand. "The Seeress has spoken. For your sacrifice, the Seeress will accept blood."

While others muttered objections, Herkuhlos approached the acolyte in shock. "Blood? If the Seeress asks for me to sacrifice one of my men to save another who is not—"

"You may bleed without dying," Henhi said quickly. "To heal your friend, the Seeress needs blood, not death."

Herkuhlos nodded slowly. "Very well."

Belolukos advanced on him. "You must be mad. She means to weaken you." He pointed at the old woman. "You are a lonely old healer but even you must know this is wrong. We deny this sacrifice. We can give you a little meat. That is enough for you to work your magic."

Henhi smiled at Belolukos and looked up at Herkuhlos. "Will you grant the Seeress blood from your veins, Herkuhlos son of Alkmene of the Kweitos Clan?"

"Yes," Herkuhlos said at once, taking up his knife. "Should I bleed into the earth?" He looked down at the flat slab of stone between him and Henhi. "Onto this?"

Henhi bowed, raised her hands over her head and clapped once. From the base of the cliff, four women in long plain dresses emerged carrying an enormously wide shallow bowl between them. All were slender and young, hardly more than girls. Their hair was long and loose, the tresses swaying at they stepped carefully closer.

"By Kolnos," Herkuhlos muttered. He heard Belolukos and the others muttering their own oaths behind him. After so long away from women it was as if they were something strange and wonderful and he felt almost as though he were seeing women for the first time. Helhena did not really count as she dressed like a man, was as filthy and stinking as they all were. But the young women carrying the bowl looked like women were supposed to look and it was like drinking from a cool stream on a hot day.

In silence the four young women came to the stone, laid the bowl upon it and stood back with their hands down and eyes lowered.

Henhi looked expectantly at him and he dragged his eyes away from their loveliness to the bowl before him. It was made from copper and though it was tarnished with age it was still a wonder. Although the copper was beaten thin, never had he seen so large an object made from metal.

"I cannot fill that bowl and live," Herkuhlos said, staring at it.

She smiled. "You would be surprised how much blood a man can lose and still live. But it need not be filled. Sacrifice what you can."

He looked around at Helhena and then at Belolukos, who shrugged. "At least you will heal right quickly. That is more than the rest of us can say."

Herkuhlos nodded. "True enough."

A flicker of curiosity passed over Henhi's face but she said nothing as Herkuhlos sliced through the skin of his wrist and held his arm over the bowl. It hurt more than he had expected and he leaned his thighs against the side of the stone when his legs felt weak. Watching his blood pour forth over his hand to patter and pour into the darkness of the interior. He wondered when he should stop and whether if he stopped too early the Seeress would refuse to heal Makros. The blood looked almost black in the shadow and he could see a distorted reflection of himself and Henhi looking back at him. It was not long before he began to feel lightheaded and he found himself breathing deeply.

"It is enough," Henhi said. "Stop now. We shall wrap the wound." As she spoke she nodded to one of the young women who stepped forward with strips of clean cloth in her hands.

"No need," Herkuhlos said to the woman. "See, already the flow of the blood slows and soon enough it will heal." He smiled at her. "All by itself."

The woman frowned and looked to Henhi. The older woman looked down at the cut on his arm. "You should clean it, at least." She nodded at the lake shore behind him. "Even small wounds can go bad."

Not for me, he thought. "I will."

At a nod from Henhi, the young women lifted the bowl of blood and carried it carefully away, disappearing behind the huge rock at the base of the cliff.

"Now," Henhi said, coming around the flat stone and approaching their camp. "Your man Makros will be brought inside."

"We can carry him in," Herkuhlos said, waving his men forward and starting towards Makros.

"No. It is forbidden." She softened her tone. "Together, we are strong and we will treat him as though he is our own son, our brother, our father."

Herkuhlos nodded, looking down at Makros with concern and wishing the young women would return swiftly. "You have sons, Henhi?"

She smiled. "I was sworn to the Seeress when I was a girl and have served her ever since."

"Will she save him?" Helhena blurted out. "Will she save his life?"

"The Seeress' powers are great and yet even she cannot—"

She broke off and turned, surprise on her face, as another woman emerged from the hidden mouth of the cave. They all stopped and stared. Herkuhlos gaped, open mouthed at the figure. He knew for certain that she was a goddess. She was too perfect. There was nothing else that she could be.

A tall young woman in a pure white dress approached with a graceful stride, her fair hair flying free as she paced forward and raised a hand to point a long finger at Herkuhlos.

"You," she said, her voice deep and resonant, "are an immortal."

Herkuhlos stared, his mind overwhelmed by her beauty and the suddenness of her appearance. She called him an immortal. Why would she say that? Gathering his wits, he managed to bow his head momentarily. "I am not immortal."

Henhi had dropped to one knee and glared at the others,

motioning for them to do the same. Dhomyos, Kasos, and Helhena kneeled and lowered their eyes. Belolukos reluctantly bent his knee but stared in astonishment at the most beautiful sight he had ever seen.

The Seeress did not look at any of them and spoke only to Herkuhlos.

"You lie."

"No," he replied, meeting her gaze. Her eyes were a vivid green. "I am mortal. But also... I am..." He could not bring himself to say it.

Belolukos finished his sentence for him. "He is godborn."

The Seeress did not take her eyes from Herkuhlos. Some expression softened her face. Was it relief? Or something else?

"Have you come for me?" she asked.

He frowned at the question, not precisely sure of her meaning. "We came to seek your help," he replied, choosing his words carefully. "Our friend here is dying and we were told—"

She spoke over him, glancing down at his waist. "You are armed? Put down your weapons, now."

Looking around he caught his brother's eye. Belolukos subtly shook his head. Herkuhlos knew that his brother feared some kind of trap or trick but Herkuhlos could not believe that the beautiful woman before him would do him harm. So he removed his sword and knife and gave them to Belolukos.

"Watch your back," he whispered as he took them.

"And you."

The Seeress watched closely. "Come with me," she said.

"Wait," he replied. "What about Makros. He dies even now."

The Seeress looked to Henhi. "You will prepare him and with

the others bring him within." She looked now to Herkuhlos. "Your friend will be seen to. Now, come with me."

She walked back, her hair and dress and body flowing like water, and he trailed in her wake, drawn forward like a tethered bull. Stepping beyond the towering outcrop he found a narrow entrance to the cave beyond and ducked inside. Lamps in alcoves lit the large space and he took in the mats on the floor, the benches and beds at the rear and more openings leading to further caves deeper within. It was high enough that he could stand with room to spare.

"Attend Henhi and bring the injured man here," the Seeress said to the four young women who bowed and slipped out at once.

Alone now, they stood apart and regarded one another.

The Seeress was taller than all but the largest of men and yet her proportions were simply perfect. Her skin was unblemished and even in the lamplight her green eyes shone with life. The curves of her body showed through the tightness of her dress around her hips and her breasts. Her bearing told of her strength and vitality. He felt himself to be some dirty, wild thing before her, like a bear come wandering into a tent.

She spoke first. "Who are you?" she demanded.

"I am Herkuhlos, son of—"

She waved a hand at the wall of the cave. "I heard who you said you were. Who are you really?"

"Just as I said. I am... a warrior from a clan far to the east."

"But you are godborn."

Herkuhlos looked away. "My mother is a mortal woman."

She took half a step forward. "So your father is a god. Which god?"

He hesitated before replying. "I am told that he is the Sky Father."

Stepping back, a frown creased her pale brow. "You said that you have not come for me. Is that the truth?"

"I do not lie," he replied, becoming irritated by her questions and her doubt. "I do not understand. I have come here so my friend may be healed. Please, you must heal him now and then we shall speak later."

Narrowing her eyes, she looked at the bowl of blood on the bench in the centre of the room. "I never thought to meet another one who is godborn. I simply assumed that you had been sent for me."

He shook his head. "I never knew about you at all until I met a man in the—"

"Kounos, yes, I heard you say so. You spoke the truth, I see it now. And of course I will help your friend but you must swear..." she trailed off, tilting her head and frowning. "Something is wrong."

It was silent, as far as he could hear. And then he felt a kind of deep drumming sound through the rock under his feet.

"Is that..." he said, his heart beginning to race. "Hooves?"

She rushed to the front wall of the cave and bent her head to a crack in the rock. It seemed she had a spy hole with which to observe the area outside.

Herkuhlos heard shouting and rushed at once for the passage out of the cave. Before he had taken two steps, the Seeress turned to him, her eyes wide.

"Raiders!"

23

Dehnu

PANIC RISING IN HIS CHEST, he rushed forward to find the four young women rushing inside, blocking the way out.

"Move!" he shouted, shoving the last of them aside and throwing himself down the rock passageway and out into the night.

Horses ran by in panic, their hooves drumming on the ground, and shouting filled the evening gloom. Bows twanged and arrows cut the air. Metal clashed against stone. Men charged out of the shadows with flaming torches of reeds and spears in their hands, thrusting at his spear-brothers who defended frantically.

Helhena was closest to him, standing with her back toward the rock and shooting at the shapes that approached, drawing arrows from the bag at her hip and loosing smoothly. Two warriors fell with her arrows in them one after the other while Dhomyos, Kasos, and Belolukos fought a larger number of raiders over where they had made their camp. Those raiders swarmed them, their spears and axes swirling and it seemed as though his friends would be overwhelmed at any moment.

After Helhena shot her next arrow, which struck a shouting warrior in the throat, he rushed in front of her and charged into the fighting. Only when he reached the cluster of enemies did he recall that he had no weapons.

The first man did not see him. Herkuhlos shouldered him to the ground and stamped down on his face, breaking the bones with his heel and smashing the teeth from his skull. The man behind swung a mace at him and Herkuhlos stepped back before changing direction and punching the man in the head, sending him sprawling and his mace clattering on the stones. Herkuhlos grabbed it and swung it down on the man as he was getting up, breaking his spine with one blow.

Two men were rushing Kasos as he swiped his spear at them and backed away. Herkuhlos stepped forward and cracked the first on the top of his head, dropping him instantly in a shower of pink brain and shattered bone. As the second gaped in astonishment, Kasos thrust his spear into the man's guts and he fell back screaming, a rent torn in his flesh and blood gushing forth to soak his tunic.

Together, Kasos and Herkuhlos charged the four men attacking Belolukos and Dhomyos, falling on them from behind. Realising that they were surrounded, the four men attempted to flee but as they disengaged they were cut down instead. After a few bloody moments, all four lay dead or dying upon the earth.

Herkuhlos turned this way and that, peering into the mist and darkness for more raiders. But for a handful of wounded men writhing on the ground, there were no more. From a glance,

Herkuhlos counted three wounded raiders.

One crawled across the stony ground nearby, his legs smashed and blood covering his head. Herkuhlos dragged him back by the ankle and turned him over. Almost at once, he breathed his last and lay still. The third man lay on his back trying and failing to keep his stinking guts inside his body and muttering ceaselessly, driven mad by the pain and the horror. Belolukos stood over him for a moment before using his axe to finish him with a crunching blow to the front of his skull.

The third man had one of Helhena's arrows deep in his belly and lay propped up against the sacrifice stone, wincing and breathing rapidly. Seeing that he was incapacitated, Herkuhlos ignored him for now.

"Are you well?" Herkuhlos said to his brother and the others. They nodded, breathing heavily and their eyes wild.

"Came out of nowhere," Dhomyos growled. "Just came out of nowhere."

Kasos nodded. "Almost had us ..." he trailed off, staring at nothing.

"It would have been worse," Belolukos said, gingerly touching a bruise on his forehead. "Were it not for that boy." He nodded at the body of Pehur lying face down in the mud by the lake shore. "He warned us. Came running down the path shouting raiders. They bashed him as they came in."

"Catch the horses," Herkuhlos said to Kasos. "Dhom, go watch the way in. Do not go too far, though."

They both moved to obey while Herkuhlos crossed to the boy and turned him over. He was covered in mud and had a gash on the top of his head. Pehur groaned.

Herkuhlos grunted. "He lives." Standing, he lifted the boy. "It seems we lost no one in the—"

He froze, the unconscious boy limp in his arms.

Belolukos stood in the middle of the camp, looking down.

Makros lay on the sled, wrapped up and eyes closed. The old woman, Henhi, lay across him.

Her head broken open.

"She was tending to him when they attacked," Belolukos said quietly. "Happened so fast. She might have run but she covered him with herself." Belolukos shook his head and turned to point with his axe. "It was that one." He walked slowly across the bloody ground and looked down at the man with the arrow in his belly. "You killed an old woman, you worm. You worthless, faithless snake. I will do you great harm, now. I will take off your skin before I kill you."

The man screwed up his face and spat toward Belolukos. He tried to smile but the movement had hurt him and he winced again.

"Do not," Herkuhlos said. "Not yet. I would speak to him."

Belolukos stared. "Wolves do not speak to snakes."

"But if he came from Leuhon he may know where mother is being held. He could tell us useful things."

Belolukos dragged his eyes away. A rage burned there. "Speak to him. And then we kill him."

"Yes, brother."

"I want him to suffer for—"

He broke off as the Seeress emerged from her cave. Her four young servants followed behind her looking terrified. Belolukos stepped back as they went right past to the body of Henhi. The Seeress looked down. There were tears running down her pale cheeks. The four women, their faces contorted in grief, lifted the body of the woman and carried her into the cave as the Seeress walked over to the wounded raider.

She stood over him in silence.

Belolukos and Herkuhlos exchanged a look.

The raider sneered up at her and started to speak but she bent down and grasped him by the throat. He struggled against her but the strength of her grip was inhuman. With one arm she lifted him from the ground, up into the air and brought his skull down hard against the top of the rock, smashing the back of his head into pieces with a sickening wet crunch.

She dropped his body and stared at the pieces of bone and hair and pooling blood on the top of the sacred rock. Her face and white dress were spattered all over with blood.

"Get them out of my vale," she commanded Belolukos, gesturing at the bodies.

He bowed. "Yes, goddess."

She turned to Herkuhlos. "And bring your man to me now."

It took him a moment to register. "You still wish to heal Makros?"

Her eyes were filled with bitterness. "All this will be meaningless if I do not try. Come."

Inside the cave, he lay Makros on a mat while the four servant women built up a fire in the back of the cave and heated water upon it. He watched the smoke as it curled up through a crack in the roof. When they came forward they took the furs from Makros and then his clothes before proceeding to wash his skin. The wound on his leg was foul and his pallor made him look dead already. While the servants cleaned Makros, the goddess stood at a table where stood the copper bowl that held Herkuhlos' blood. She dipped a small wooden cup into the blood and crossed to the women who gently wiped at the dying man until he was as clean as could be. They covered him with a woven blanket and stepped reverently away deeper into the cave where lay the body of Henhi and attended to her.

The goddess knelt beside Makros and touched his forehead with her palm.

"Are you healing him, goddess," Herkuhlos asked softly, "or preparing him for burial?"

The Seeress looked down at the pale figure. "He should have passed but his spirit is yet within his flesh." She glanced at Herkuhlos. "Tell me, is he also godborn?"

The question surprised him. "No. At least, I do not think so. I never met another."

"Then he is as strong a mortal as I have ever seen. I will do all that can be done but you must leave us now. Guard my vale, Herkuhlos, until dawn comes. His spirit will have decided by then."

He bowed. "Yes, goddess."

Her mouth twitched. "My name is Dehnu." She hesitated. "And I am not a goddess, Herkuhlos. I am like you. I am godborn."

Herkuhlos started and took half a step forward, desperate to know more.

"Go now," she said, pointing at the way from the cave. "Later, we shall speak of it. You must go."

Reluctantly, he held his tongue and made his way out. There was work to do clearing the bodies from the vale, retrieving and calming the panicked horses, and organising watches through the night to guard against further attacks. The bodies they dumped in the woods and covered with leaf litter and other debris. If anyone was looking for the lost raiders they would not be especially difficult to find but there was not much that they could do. The raiders' horses were strong and they made fine additions to their own herd. They also looted a selection of weapons from the dead and a few other trinkets besides. One man, presumably their leader, had a boar tusk helm that Belolukos claimed immediately. When he found that his head was too large for it to fit he tossed it to Kasos who took it with pleasure.

The boy Pehur came to before long, though he was dazed and went to sleep after eating a little. They all praised him for his alertness and Belolukos gave him a bronze dagger taken from the dead.

"This is good work," Pehur said. "Made by the *kerdos* at Nemiyeh, I think."

"Nemiyeh," Belolukos said. "Where this Leuhon was heading after Pelhbriya."

Herkuhlos gestured at the dagger. "We can assume that he conquered it."

The night seemed to pass swiftly though what little sleep Herkuhlos had was filled with dreams of blood and battle. In the faint light before sunrise, Herkuhlos paced back and forth between the lake and the cave of the goddess, waiting to discover if Makros had lived. His thoughts were going constantly to the Seeress. She had named herself Dehnu and claimed to be godborn. How was it that she was here in this vale? Who was her father? He longed to speak with her and ask her about her life but equally he was almost afraid to hear it. Besides, what did it matter if she was godborn? It would do nothing to help him find and save his mother and that was all that was important.

One of the young women emerged from the cave and approached Herkuhlos. She bowed and spoke softly. "Makros lives."

Herkuhlos exclaimed and almost embraced the young woman in his joy but stopped when she stiffened at his approach. "He lives? You mean he is healed? Can I see him?"

"He will be healed. And the Seeress will bring him out when it is time."

"Does he know that we are here with him?"

"Have patience. Trust the Seeress."

Herkuhlos nodded. "Very well."

When the others woke he told them the news. They were equal parts delighted and astonished.

"I never thought she would do it," Kasos muttered.

"I did," Dhomyos replied.

Helhena was strangely quiet and she soon drifted away with her bow to keep watch. They made repairs and cared for the horses until midday when Makros stepped, blinking and shielding his eyes, from the cave and into the bright light of day. He was naked but for a woollen blanket wrapped around his shoulders. They cried out to see him and Dhomyos clapped him on the back so hard it almost knocked him over and the others cursed him for a witless fool. But Makros laughed, clinging to Belolukos.

"I dreamed of you all," Makros said, his voice raspy but happy. "And now you are here. You must tell me all that happened."

"The goddess of the lake healed you," Belolukos said, smiling.

"I know that much," Makros said, lifting his face to the sun. "When I saw her I was certain that I had died for she was beauty

374

itself." He caught himself and smiled at Helhena. "As are you, of course, Helhena." She scoffed and turned away.

"By Kolnos," Herkuhlos exclaimed. "Your leg, Makros."

He lifted aside the blanket to show his wound. It was an ugly mass of pink scars but instead of the rotting black flesh there was now a long hollow that was blotchy and pitted, still weeping clear liquid.

"They said they cut away the dead meat," Makros said, "and I had to drink this foul potion. Tasted like blood and old mushrooms." He shuddered. "But there is little pain now and the Seeress says that soon enough I will able to run and ride just as before." He shrugged. "With a bit of a limp, perhaps."

They were all stunned.

"You were near death," Dhomyos said, smiling broadly. "And now you are well."

"The gods have saved you for some purpose," Kasos said. "That is the truth of it."

"The Seeress did it," Belolukos said. "She is a goddess, I know it now, a goddess of great power."

Makros pulled the blanket tighter and nodded, narrowing his eyes as he looked around them at the water and the trees atop the cliffs. "But how did I come to be here? How did you find me?"

As they began to speak of all that had happened, one of the young women caught Herkuhlos' eye and beckoned him. Hesitantly, he left the others talking and followed the servant.

Inside the cave, Dehnu the Seeress of Nemos sat waiting for him on a bench before a long table. She was clean now and wore fresh clothes. A simple tunic of pale green with a belt of red leather. Her slender arms and half of her long legs were bare.

"Sit with me," Dehnu said, offering the bench opposite her. "Your people have seen to it we have fresh mare's milk and we have provided honey. Will you drink with me?"

He found that he was staring at her lovely face and shook himself from his reverie. "Yes, milk and honey. You have my thanks. For saving Makros, I mean. Truly, you have a great power."

She eyed him over the edge of her cup as she drank. "The power to heal is within those with the blood of the gods."

Herkuhlos frowned. "Those with the blood of the gods?"

"Yes. The gods have that power. As do the godborn." She shrugged. "Some of them, at least."

"Ah," he said. "Well, I do not have that power."

"Are you certain that you do not?" Dehnu asked, curiosity knitting her brow.

"I never heard of it before. How do you use it?"

"Did your father not teach you of this power?"

Herkuhlos set down his cup. "I never met my father."

She reached across the table and laid her long fingers against the back of his hand. Her skin was soft and cool and clean. "I never met mine, either."

"Which god was he?"

Dehnu sighed softly. "My father was Kostromtagos, a great chief of the north."

"I have heard his song, I think. When I was young. Yes, I remember it now. Kostromtagos of the Endless Raid. His song is old and his were not my people but we remember him."

She smiled. "It pleases me to hear that." For a moment it seemed as though she would go on but instead she took a sip of her drink.

Herkuhlos held up a finger. "Your father was a mortal. So your mother is a goddess?"

"My mother is Plenwhi."

Herkuhlos narrowed his eyes as he recalled the name. "Plenwhi... the old women in my clan would invoke Plenwhi when we took the cattle to the summer pastures. They called her Plenwhi of the open plain, her blessing brings abundance and health to the herds. How did she come to bear you with a mortal?"

There was pain behind Dehnu's eyes. "My father's deeds in life were so great that he was honoured with the gift of immortality and welcomed by the gods to the Sacred Mountain." A faint smile touched her lips. "My mother and father began to love in secret. The gods do not bear children easily. Some of them do not bear a child in a thousand years. My mother's belly swelled." She looked at him. "Your father was enraged. Such a union between mortals and the undying ones is forbidden, you see. Forbidden, it seems, unless you are the Sky Father himself. For their transgression he slayed my father and cast my mother from the homeland of the gods. It is forbidden for one god to slay another. So, banished, my mother carried me across the world until she was beyond the rule of the gods of the Sacred Mountain. She found the sacred springs here and brought me forth. Here I was raised. And here I am."

Herkuhlos stared. He had so many questions. He had never heard of the gods spoken of in such a way. "My father slew yours? Dehnu, I do not know what to say. I am ashamed."

"There is no shame for you. Because the gods do not easily get with child I am sure they believed they would not be discovered. However, my mother and father transgressed and they were punished for it."

Herkuhlos supposed that was true and yet he felt that the punishment was brutally harsh especially considering that the Sky Father himself had fathered many godborn. His place as chief of all gods meant that he was not subjected to the same rules as other gods and mortals but still it seemed like an injustice.

"You say that the gods do not easily get with child," he said. "I have heard the same is true for godborn, although my ancestor Perseyus fathered many children with his mortal wife before he was slain in battle. What is the truth of it?"

Her eyes searched his. "You wish to become a father yourself, Herkuhlos?"

"Of course," he replied. "But I fear the births can be difficult for the children of... those like us."

"We are godborn but we are no more masters of our fate than are mortals and so my guidance is the same as it would be for any young man. If you wish to become a father you should take a mortal wife and then trust to fate. Your wife will get with child or she will not. Your wife and children will be well or they will not. Walk your path and accept your fate."

He frowned. "Like your mother and father did?"

Her eyes narrowed at that. "Yes."

"Where is your mother now? Is she here with you still?"

"No." She forced a reluctant smile onto her face. "Now, Herkuhlos, you must tell me how you came to be. We godborn are rare indeed and I like to hear every tale there is about our kind."

"Very well, though there is not much to tell. My mother Alkmene is descended from a godborn named Perseyus. In the same year that she became a woman my mother was married to another descendant of Perseyus named Lektros. He was a cousin of hers and a mighty chief of a powerful clan. The largest and most powerful. Their union was celebrated by all the clans of the two great rivers from the forests of the north to the mountains and seas of the south and there was joy at the prosperity it would bring to all. The wedding feast was vast. Chiefs and their men from far and wide drank and swore guest friendships with each other. There were many days of rites, feasting, and competitions and Lektros won the horse race and the wrestling and all the omens were good. The night of their union, of course, mother lay with her new husband. From their coupling she had the seed of Lektros which would become my brother Belolukos." Herkuhlos took a sip of his drink before continuing. "And that was when the Sky Father arrived. Unannounced, he walked through the great camp. Some bowed down to him and let him pass but when he made his way to the marriage tent and made to enter, the spear-brothers of Lektros tried to stop him. The marriage tent is sacred and it is possible that the men meant only to object to the god and meant no disrespect. But it is more likely that they understood the god's intent and meant to spend their lives in protecting the wife of their lord. From the feasting, the spear-brothers of Lektros were filled with mead and perhaps that had something to do with what happened. When he pushed them aside they lay their hands upon him. Perhaps someone threatened the god or drew a weapon. Whatever was the cause of it, the god slew them. Many had gathered by now and were witness to the killing. Seeking death with their lords, or perhaps seeking the glory of battling a god, more of the men attacked the Sky Father. But he slew them also. It all happened quickly. And by then Lektros emerged from the marriage tent and tried to stop the Sky Father from taking his new wife. But he failed and was killed.

The god put his seed into my mother. And that is how I came to be. My brother Belolukos and me grew together and were born together. He is mortal while I am... whatever it is that I am."

Dehnu's face twisted in anguish as he told the story. "Her wedding night?" She held her face in her hands for a moment. "He is cruel beyond measure. Sometimes I wonder if the gods are so different from the yotunan. Why would he inflict such pain?"

Herkuhlos frowned, surprised at the intensity of her reaction. "Who can understand the will of the gods?"

Her gaze was unflinching. "You and I can, Herkuhlos. If no one else. We can understand them and we can judge them for their actions. And I judge what your father did as cruel beyond measure."

"Perhaps. But you do not judge the same god for slaying your father?"

"There were conditions for the gift of immortality that was granted to him. He transgressed and was punished. That is the same as any chief of the plains would do to his men for a similar crime."

"I suppose so. It surprises me that you are not angry about it."

"Do you think me cruel also? Unfeeling? I wish every day that my father was alive and my mother was still with me. But they are gone. We can live on with bitterness at our fate or we can accept what has happened and learn from it as we follow our path into what is to come."

That was obvious, Herkuhlos thought. Everyone knew that. But it was not so easy to do. "Where has your mother gone?"

Dehnu looked off to the side as if seeing something that was not there. "She left. But I remain." She looked back at him. "While you have crossed the plains and the wide rivers to save your mother. She must be a fine woman. Or perhaps it is that you are a dutiful son."

"All men have the same duty when their women are taken by raiders. We must take them back. If they are slain we must punish those that have slain them by taking their women or slaying their sons. The *yotunan* led the clan that took my mother and the others but our duty is the same. Glory may be won that way. Glory that all men seek. I have sworn to save her or to die trying." He cleared his throat. "And I have sworn to do more than that."

"What have you sworn?"

Herkuhlos tilted his head. "Do you know of the god Kolnos?"

"The wolf god. Of course I know of him."

"Have you ever met him?"

She smiled. "I have met no gods other than my mother. I know of Kolnos through her words and from those of the mortals in these parts. Kolnos is a god of the plain and the forest. His territory does not extend this far west."

Herkuhlos shook his head. "No one ever told me that the gods had limits to their power. I thought they ruled all of the earth."

"Between them all, I am sure that they do. But each god is something like a chief, with his own places and his own people that he rules over."

"And yet they are all sworn to the Sky Father."

She breathed through pursed lips, tilting her head. "He rules, yes. He is strongest and all those who opposed him were defeated long ago and were imprisoned or were driven out. Those that remain recognise his authority over them but they also do as they wish. Especially those like Kolnos who do not dwell near the Sacred Mountain."

"Kolnos followed the twelve *yotunan* that escaped from the

Sacred Mountain. He told me that I should be the one to slay them."

Dehnu raised her eyebrows. "Mortals are not required to obey every command from a god. Godborn even less so. You did not agree, Herkuhlos?"

He found himself smiling at his own foolishness. "I swore that I would kill them all."

"Ah," Dehnu sighed. "Do you understand how strong the *yotunan* are?"

Herkuhlos nodded. "Kolnos himself said I was not to try to fulfil my oath yet. I am to follow them and learn where they go. Later, when I am stronger myself I may attempt to fight them."

Dehnu appeared saddened. Herkuhlos realised she pitied him. He felt anger at that. He knew he was not strong enough but that did not mean he was destined to fail. Or did it? Had Kolnos had some other reason for encouraging him to swear his oath?

"And your companions," Dehnu said. "They also swore to Kolnos to challenge the might of the *yotunan*?"

"No. I was supposed to come alone but all who ride with me have lost their own people to the demons. They had the courage to act." He shrugged. "And we are all seeking glory in our own way." He thought of Helhena and Makros. "Or chasing an honourable death, at least."

"You are fortunate to have such companions." Her smile was sad.

"I was fortunate that Kolnos had the clan prepare so many horses and supplies for my journey. If he had not..." Herkuhlos trailed off as a sudden realisation struck him. Kolnos had commanded Orysthos to prepare twenty horses and food enough for Herkuhlos to live on for half a year. The chief had balked at the excessive gift but still he obeyed the god. Herkuhlos had found the spear-brothers of his *koryos* and together they had escaped, taking a few extra weapons and more food, while the wolves of Kolnos had apparently searched for him. If they had wanted to stop Herkuhlos from taking his friends then Kolnos could have sent his wolves and Orysthos might have sent his warriors to ride after them. It would not have been difficult and yet he had not.

Herkuhlos grunted. "I now realise that Kolnos wanted me to take my spear-brothers with me." He snorted a laugh. "And I thought I was defying him."

"Kolnos enjoys his tricks." Dehnu placed her hands flat on the table. "I am pleased that we could speak like this before you go."

Herkuhlos was surprised by the sudden change in the conversation. "But I would stay longer. There is so much I wish to know."

"But go you must. You cannot stay here a moment longer. Already you brought raiders on your trail into this sacred place and now my dearest friend lies dead. It is not for myself that I fear, you understand, but I have four more women to keep safe."

"I am sorry. I know that is a failure that can never be undone but if we can stay for another day or two then while I am here I will guard you. You will be safe with me. I can fight better than any other mortal, I swear it."

"I saw you fighting last night, Herkuhlos. I know what you can do. But I do not require your protection. I am not unfamiliar with combat and I am stronger than any man."

He recalled how she had dispatched the wounded man by grasping his throat and smashing his skull apart with a single blow.

Suddenly he was ashamed of his boyish boasting of his own prowess.

She stood and he stood with her. "We will leave you, then, Dehnu."

"I truly am glad to have met you, Herkuhlos."

"Perhaps one day when all this is done I can return here and we can speak further."

He recognised the look of pity in her eyes when she replied. "Perhaps." She did not expect him to survive his encounter with the *yotunan*.

Herkuhlos wished he could think of a reason to stay longer but he could not. He wished he could stay and speak with her for days and months. He wanted to know all that she knew and he wanted to find out all about her and the things she had done. He desired to tell her everything about himself and to find out what she thought about it. But he could not put the thoughts into words and so he bowed and with a final look said farewell.

When they left the vale Herkuhlos stopped at the place where the stream trickled from the lake into the surrounding woodland. He looked back along the lake at the cliff face with the sacrifice stone before it. The sun was shining on the water but he could see Dehnu, her golden hair gleaming, standing beside the sacrifice stone. He raised a hand in farewell. She did not wave back.

He turned away from Nemos, leading his horse into the woodland after the others. The boy Pehur would return alone to Pelhbriya while they instead turned north towards Nemiyeh.

2 4

Unbowed

FROM THE SHADOWS OF THE houses, Alkmene watched the warriors on the other side of the open space at the centre of Nemiyeh. They were calling out to the women who waited their turn to draw water from the main well in the square and though Alkmene needed water also she was loath to subject herself to such treatment. She stopped and put her jug on the floor. There were still blood stains everywhere in Nemiyeh. The main streets must have been running with it and there had been a great slaughter in the centre of the *briya* by the structure they called the house of the goddess.

Alkmene had been fortunate. She and the other captive women in their wagons had been held far back from the fighting and so they had not witnessed the attack itself but they had heard the screams and they had seen the wounded and the stream of captives brought out. Throughout the whole attack, Alkmene had looked for the chance to escape but Leuhon had stood behind them with his arms crossed, unmoving. His acolytes were ever at his side and a handful of warriors attended them. There was no chance for her to get away.

Kreuhesh had led his warriors from street to street, house to house, killing and subduing hundreds and thousands of men, women, children, farmers, herders, and servants. The men who resisted were slain and those that surrendered were beaten and humiliated. Even before the last of the resistance had been rooted out the spoils were being shared between Kreuhesh's men and instead of burning the houses like they had done so many times before-or leaving them untouched as they had with Pelhbriya-they moved into them.

Late on the second day, Kreuhesh had emerged, covered head to toe in blood, and declared that Nemiyeh belonged to Leuhon. The Bloodletter had presented examples of the spoils to his lord. A group of young women, bronze weapons, fine horses, all were paraded before Leuhon or laid at his feet.

In return, the god had offered much of it to Kreuhesh and the blood-stained warrior had returned to the *briya* with his men dragging captive women after him. Alkmene had felt for those women. Their lives had been destroyed and everything they had was now lost. But it would only get worse for them.

Despite the sympathy she also felt hope that his interest in her would now pass. Certainly, he had not spoken to her in the days since Nemiyeh had fallen and she and the other women from her wagon had been moved into a house near to the centre. It was large, with wattle internal walls dividing it into rooms and a second level above the ground floor where they slept. Always, they were guarded.

Watched. Only one of them at a time was permitted to leave in order to collect fresh water and to dispose of the nightsoil baskets.

Alkmene stood back from the crowds crossing the square and lining up for the well. She would not submit herself to the leers, obscene comments, and groping hands of the filthy, low warriors that were there ostensibly to guard the women.

Two paces away along the wall Alkmene spotted another woman, tall like her but hunched with a dirty woven blanket around her shoulders. Her fair hair was tied back with a length of fraying twine. The woman glared at the scene before her with open disgust.

Picking up her jug, Alkmene sidled along the wall until she was an arm's length away from her. "These brutes," Alkmene muttered. "I would slit their throats if I could."

The woman flinched and glanced at Alkmene. After a moment looking her up and down, she gave a sharp nod. "I would make them suffer first."

Alkmene shuffled a little closer. "You are from this place?"

The woman glanced again. "And you are one who came with them."

In response, Alkmene grunted. "They destroyed my home in the east. Killed my people. Dragged me here." She looked across at the women. "I am Alkmene."

After a moment's hesitation the woman replied. "I am Turnu."

Alkmene saw then that Turnu was younger than she had assumed and her face, beneath the grime, was strong and attractive.

"They let me out to collect water for my companions," Alkmene said, watching Turnu from the corner of her eye. "But I find myself unwilling to go amongst those evil men."

"If I were a man," Turnu said, "I would fight them now. Fight them until I am killed."

Alkmene grunted softly. "You do not need to be a man to die, Turnu."

"But then it would honourable. My spirit could go proudly to the realm of the ancestors." She shrugged. "Yet I never learned the spear. My death will have no meaning, now."

Hesitantly, Alkmene replied. "Your husband, Turnu. He fell when Nemiyeh was attacked?"

The woman placed a hand over her face and sobbed once before taking a deep, shuddering breath. "My husband. My father. Brothers. My..." she could not continue and pressed her lips together, tears brimming in her eyes.

"I am sorry. The same is true for me, also, Turnu. It was moons ago now but I feel their loss every day and every night." She glanced around to ensure that no one was close enough to be listening. "You were claimed by one of the warriors? Which house is yours?"

Turnu glanced up with damp eyes. There was fear in them. Wariness. "I am merely a servant."

Alkmene frowned, looking about her at the women going about their tasks. "We are all servants now, I suppose. Although some of the wives of the lords of this place have been taken already as the women of Kreuhesh's warriors. I assumed that you were—"

"I am not," Turnu snapped. "I am of the Kalekka."

Alkmene narrowed her eyes as she regarded the tall, strongly built woman beside her. "I have little knowledge of the way of things on this side of the Denipa, Turnu. But from what I have learnt, the Kalekka are the people of this land. The Kalekka are the people of Nemiyeh, no?"

Turnu scoffed. "No. No, that is wrong. Once, yes. Long ago, the Kalekka ruled Nemiyeh. They have been here since the creation of the world. But then the Heryos came from the east. The Heryos conquered them. The Heryos rule Nemiyeh now." She caught herself. "At least, they did."

Alkmene nodded slowly as she looked around the square. "I understand now. I have seen how most of the women captured here and in Pelhbriya are different from us. They are short, with thin arms and legs and narrow faces. They are dark of hair and eye." She looked at Turnu. "An unattractive people. Weak looking. I understand now why you were conquered."

Turnu looked away. "The gods mean for the strong to rule the weak."

Alkmene touched Turnu's arm through her dirty blanket. "But you have blonde hair, Turnu."

The woman shrugged. "There are many fair-haired Kalekka." She gestured. "There is one there."

In the line of women standing with their water jugs there were at least two of the small Kalekka with blonde hair. It was easy to recognise them by their distinctive features as well as their stature. Alkmene leaned close to Turnu and lowered her voice. "You can trust me, Turnu. I shall not give you away."

"I do not know your meaning."

Smiling, Alkmene sighed. "It is clear you are of the Heryos. I assume you were a woman of some importance but you have clothed yourself like this in the hope of avoiding too much notice. It is clever. Better to live as a servant than be the wife of one of Kreuhesh's warriors."

Turnu spat on the ground. "Wife. Slave, you mean. To be raped by the murderers of my husband for the rest of my life. I will not do it. I will kill myself before then. Kill them and then myself, no matter the dishonour. Better that than—"

Alkmene glanced left and right. "Keep your voice down."

"You are right. It is useless. And serves no purpose. They care not about servants and masters, we are all equally worthless to them. Nothing but a..."

She was both angry and despairing and Alkmene saw then that the woman was near mad with grief. Some of the warriors were now looking in their direction, catching the tone if not the words of Turnu's outbursts.

"Walk with me," Alkmene said, forcing a smile onto her face and grasping Turnu by the elbow she dragged the woman with her along the edge of the square.

"What are you doing?" Turnu cried. "You will not take me to him?"

"I am saving you from yourself," Alkmene hissed. "Now keep your voice down."

Turnu clenched her jaw and walked beside Alkmene. "Where are you taking me?"

"Away from curious eyes," she replied. "Now, tell me about Nemiyeh."

"What about it?" Turnu was confused.

It was formed in much the same way as the other places she had seen this side of the Denipa only it was far larger. Indeed, she had never known so many houses existed in the whole world and they were there all together in one place. Nemiyeh was built atop a wide mound built right against the river. Even before all the dead were removed the victors had taken the homes of the conquered and filled them with their captives and their plunder.

Leuhon had taken for himself the grandest house in Nemiyeh. Like all the best of the houses it was one of the innermost buildings surrounding the central square and it stood at the highest point of the mound.

"That house there," Alkmene said, nodding at Leuhon's new home on the far side of the square. "The demon lives there now. Had you ever been in there? Before, I mean."

Turnu stifled a sob. "Yes."

"Is there any other way in other than the door there?"

"Another way in?" Turnu was confused. "No. All our houses have one door. Why would we need another? And why do you ask?"

"No reason."

Kreuhesh had taken another house nearby and since then he had rarely emerged. She knew what he was doing in there. Sometimes she could hear the screams though it was quiet now.

"Which warrior claimed you, Turnu? Was it Kreuhesh?"

Turnu shuddered. "His name is Horghis. He is *evil.*"

Alkmene came to a stop and pulled Turnu into the shadows by the wall of another house, looking out at the people and the strange structure in the centre of the square. It was like one of their houses but it had no walls. Just pillars holding up a roof. Beneath that roof was a large, single stone. As long as a man and half as high. "And what is that building?"

Turnu looked at her as if she were a fool. "The temple of the goddess."

"What is it for?"

Frowning, Turnu gestured. "For the goddess. For sacrifices. What else?"

"What goddess?"

"The Mother, of course."

"What about the other gods? Where is their temple?"

"They have none."

Alkmene shook her head in confusion. It was one thing to worship the Earth Mother but to build some great structure to honour her above the other gods was madness. "What about the sun? What about the sky? You do not honour the Sky Father above all?"

Turnu shrugged. "They are nothing without the Mother."

Unable to believe what she was hearing, Alkmene scowled. "I thought you were Heryos?"

"We are."

Letting it go, Alkmene pointed quickly to another house, near to that of Leuhon and Kreuhesh. "I have heard that is where many girls and young women are kept. Those who are claimed by Leuhon. What do you know of it?"

Turnu covered her eyes. "I have heard that also." She lowered her voice. "The warriors call it the blood house. They are kept like cattle for that demon."

Alkmene nodded, looking at the innocuous plain walls. The door was closed. When the *yotunan* wished to drink blood, one of the women was bled before being returned to the blood house. "Then we should thank the Mother that we are not within that place."

"We are too old, I think. The demon wants girls, not mothers."

Alkmene thought of Laonome but forced the thought from her mind. The demon had protected them both thus far and surely he had more than enough young women that he did not need one more. Not yet at least. What would happen though when he ran out of Kalekka? She still had to get her daughter away.

Across the square, the warrior guarding the door to the blood house was watching her. She plucked at Turnu's elbow and walked back the way they had come.

"I shall have to get the water soon," Turnu said. "I cannot delay much longer."

"Perhaps we can fetch water from the river?" Alkmene said.

"The well water is sweet. And clean."

"The river is not?"

"Upriver it is not so bad. But once it flows past the cliff." Turnu wrinkled her face. "Especially now."

Alkmene understood what she meant. Nemiyeh was built atop a wide mound with large houses built hard against each other with the streets radiating out from the open area in the centre. One of those streets led west to the top of the steep cliff above the river. The servants threw all manner of waste off the cliff every day, including basket after basket of night soil, and the great river washed it away downstream.

Alkmene had caught a glimpse of it on the day that she was escorted to the house that was her prison. At the end of the street that led to the top of the cliff were piled the bodies of the slain.

These were tossed over a low stone wall into the river below.

"If I had courage enough," she had thought to herself, looking at the blood-stained low wall as the bodies were tipped over. "I would throw myself in after them."

Though she could not inflict death upon herself while her daughter lived, she wondered if someone could survive the fall. She could not stop imagining leaping to freedom.

"Has anyone leapt from the cliff into the river?" Alkmene asked Turnu.

The woman was shocked. "Not even the strongest of men could survive such a fall."

Alkmene pursed her lips. "Is it really so far? I have seen trees taller than that cliff, I am sure of it. And the river must surely be deep enough so that if a man fell he would be caught by the waters and carried away?"

"Their body would be smashed on the rocks. If they somehow leapt far enough to reach the river," she shrugged, "then surely they would drown."

I can swim, Alkmene thought. But would Laonome be able to make a jump like that? She shuddered to think of it. Imagined tumbling slowly through the air like a corpse and plunging into the waters never to surface. It would be an escape of a kind, perhaps, but no descendant of the famed Perseyus could embrace such a shameful death.

A loud voice penetrated her reverie. "What are you two doing?"

The warrior came towards them, scowling. She recognised him as one of the ones who had been watching her, guarding her, since they crossed the river.

"Fetching water," Alkmene said, pulling at Turnu and making for the well.

"No you're not, you're standing around talking, you lazy bitch," he said. "Get on with it!"

She clenched her fist and fought the urge to turn and smash her water jug over his head. "Keep walking," she hissed to Turnu. "Say nothing."

Behind them the guard muttered something else regarding her

laziness. She knew she should keep walking but she could not resist turning and making a fist at him, thrusting her arm up twice in an offensive gesture. "Go and rut with a ewe!" she said.

A handful of the warriors within earshot laughed while the guard scowled. Alkmene smirked as she turned away once more but cringed when he called out to her.

"Kreuhesh will hear of this!"

She felt sick as she made her way to the well and drew the water. The eyes of the other men and their lewd comments had no effect. She hardly heard them. Instead, she worried over the guard's words. Would he really tell Kreuhesh? What would he do if he heard? Probably nothing, she concluded. He was too occupied with other women to be concerned with her any longer. Still, she had that sick feeling that she had made a mistake and she could not shake it until finally she grew angry. Why should she, Alkmene, descendant of Perseyus, live in fear of a depraved madman like Kreuhesh?

After filling her jug she said farewell to Turnu and turned to go back to the house.

"Thank you," Turnu said quietly. "I shall look for you tomorrow."

Alkmene nodded and carried the heavy jug across the square to the open doorway of the house she shared with the other women. Stepping inside it was warmer but so dark suddenly that she could see almost nothing within.

"What is wrong?" Henu asked, coming to collect the jug from her.

"What do you mean?" Alkmene replied, looking at the shadowy faces within for her daughter. "Nothing is wrong."

Henu snorted as she moved away. "Suit yourself," she muttered.

"You always do."

Alkmene gritted her teeth and went to Laonome. One of the other women was combing her hair but she moved aside with a smile to let Alkmene take over. She gave her daughter a squeeze on the shoulder and began dragging the comb through her tangles.

"I remember you used to do this when I was a child," Laonome said quietly.

But you are still a child now, my dear one, Alkmene thought. "What nonsense you speak," she said. "I have never stopped combing your hair."

"It is well, mother. I mean only to say how pleasing this is to me."

Alkmene smiled. "To me also. Your hair has grown so long we must comb it daily now. And I think it must be cut."

Laonome's shoulders slumped. "How I wish I could wash it."

"I know." She stopped combing for a moment. "Sit with your back straight, Laonome."

Her daughter sighed and sat straighter once more. "It is pointless to take care of my hair anyway."

"What is your meaning?"

Laonome shrugged and spoke quietly. "I do not know."

Alkmene turned her daughter around. "Look at me, child. You shall not be a coward. Speak what is in your heart."

"I mean only that we are here in this place. Before, I liked it when my hair shone and you tied it up with dyed threads. But now I almost wish it was all cut off."

"Why?" She knew what the answer would be but it was important that her daughter said it.

Laonome lowered her head. "So that the men would not look

at me."

For a moment, Alkmene felt her heart break at the hurt her daughter had suffered and was outraged at the future that had been stolen from her. What did her future hold if they were to remain in Nemiyeh? To be wed to one of those evil men? Whatever it was, Alkmene doubted whether Laonome would be strong enough to face it. When Alkmene had been her age she had already been learning the bow and the spear for years and she had not been much older when she rode on her first raid. Laonome had never shown an interest in such things. When she had tried them she had discovered no aptitude for them and it was clear that she would never be one to embrace war. Instead she had always loved other things. Songs and music. Herb gathering and healing. Weaving and the making of clothes. That had seemed well enough to Alkmene and Gendryon for they knew she would make a good wife to a chief or a great warrior one day and would be an asset to any clan. But without her father and other kin to protect her it now seemed more like weakness.

Alkmene put her arms around her daughter and held her close. "I will not let them harm you."

"I know, mother."

Henu spoke from across the room without turning from her task. "A woman should not swear oaths she cannot keep."

"I made no oath, Henu. But I shall keep my word." As she spoke she saw a group of acolytes as they walked by the open doorway of her house. Their pale robes were stained with the blood of those they had bled for the demon. "I have so far."

"Mother," Laonome said, shuffling away from the open doorway. She had caught sight of the acolytes.

"Stay here," Alkmene said and went to the doorway. Outside, the acolytes and a handful of warrior guards stopped outside the house next to theirs.

Leading them was Kreuhesh the Bloodletter.

Kreuhesh stopped by the house along the street and pointed his axe inside it. "Take them."

Women screamed from within and they wailed as the acolytes entered and dragged out two girls that could not have been ten years old.

"So young," Laonome whispered from behind her.

"Get back inside!" she snapped. Laonome did as she was told and Henu welcomed the girl into an embrace.

"They will not come for you, child," Henu said, patting Laonome's back. "You are protected by our lord Leuhon."

The pride in Henu's voice made Alkmene clench her teeth.

Kreuhesh the Bloodletter turned his terrible face toward her as if he had heard the name of his master spoken.

"Mother protect us," Alkmene whispered, stepping back from the open door. "I will celebrate your greatness, Mother, and will sacrifice to you when I am able if you protect us."

Moving from the light of the street into the shadow of the house, Kreuhesh slowed to a stop outside their door, filling it entirely with his bulk. He ducked his head and looked inside. His pale eyes narrowed as he looked from Alkmene to Laonome behind her.

"Here you are, Alkmene," Kreuhesh said, his voice barely above a growl. "Not causing my men any trouble, are you?"

She stepped away from her daughter, drawing his eyes. A terrible foreboding descended and took hold of her guts. She

398

sensed that he was the one who intended to cause trouble. Lifting her chin and looking straight at him, she spoke with all the confidence that she could muster. "I am an obedient servant of Leuhon, Kreuhesh. As are you."

He looked at her for a moment before snorting a laugh. "Who were you speaking with by the well today?"

Alkmene fought down her anger. "Some servant," she said. "I never asked her name."

"And what is it that got you both so excited, Alkmene?" he leered at her, his eyes searching her body. She wished to drive her fist into his face or to turn away but instead she had to endure his penetrating gaze.

"The woman has lost everything. She was grief stricken. As are many in this place."

"They should be grateful. They have a new lord and a new god, more powerful than any they had before. They will grow wealthy and fortune will come to us all." He frowned. "Tell me, Alkmene. Are you one of the grief stricken?"

She hesitated, sensing one of his traps. Whatever answer she gave might anger him, though, so she chose to speak honestly. "Of course. Even you must understand what it is like for those you take."

"Even me?" His tone was low. Threatening. "What do you mean, even me?"

Alkmene tensed. "Even a chief is able to understand the pain of his people," she replied.

Kreuhesh leaned against the doorframe. "The pain of losing everything?" His voice was more relaxed now. That only worried her more.

"Yes."

Sighing, Kreuhesh craned his neck forward and looked into the darkness. "But you have not lost everything, Alkmene." His eyes met hers. "Have you?"

Before she could reply, he lifted his axe and pointed it at Laonome.

"It is time she joined Leuhon's herd. We will take her to the blood house."

"No!" Alkmene shouted and stepped in front of her. "We are *protected* by Leuhon!"

Kreuhesh's mouth twisted into a sneer as he ducked inside and stood upright, blocking the light. "It is his protection that stays my hand. If any other woman spoke to me as you did, she would already be choking on her broken teeth."

"Why then do you take my daughter?"

Taking a step forward he lowered his voice and looked down at her. "I do not answer to you but to the god Leuhon. And it is he that demands to taste the sweetness of her blood."

"He asked for Laonome?"

Kreuhesh smiled, the scars of his face twisting his lips. "The god does not ask for what is already his. Now, stand aside."

She sensed that he wanted her to resist so that he could break her with his fists and his axe, as he had done to so many others. Panic rising, she blurted out the first desperate thought that came into her head.

"Take me instead."

Kreuhesh laughed, the sound as thick as boiling pitch. "The god does not want the dried-up blood of an old woman. You see, a child's blood is sweetest. A young child's blood has the most power.

But they are small things, easily broken. A girl on the cusp of womanhood is almost as good and there is so much more of her to drink." Then he spoke more softly. "We do not take her to her death, Alkmene. I will bleed her often but she will heal."

She glanced over her shoulder. Henu stood with her arms wrapped around Laonome, who had her face buried into her neck. The other women stood back, their faces twisted in fear.

Alkmene turned back to him. "Perhaps Leuhon will find my blood sweeter and more powerful than most," she said, "for I am descended from one who was godborn."

Kreuhesh sneered. "Half the lords of the plain claim such descent as do all those of the forest." He slapped his broad chest, rattling the boar tusk armour. "I am descended from the famed godborn Hasak of Dhonu. You think yourself mighty but you are nothing, woman. Stand aside."

Alkmene's panic grew until her words burst from her. "I also bore one who is godborn."

Already reaching for her, Kreuhesh stopped and tilted his head as he frowned at Laonome. "You claim she is godborn?"

"Not her, no. She is mortal. But one of my sons is godborn."

Narrowing his eyes, Kreuhesh lifted his axe until it touched her under the chin. With steady pressure he forced her head up. "Which god fathered the child?"

Alkmene's heart raced but she slapped his axe aside and held his gaze. "I will tell Leuhon myself. But I will not tell his dog."

The sneer spread across Kreuhesh's face once more. "You think yourself clever."

"No."

"We shall see how clever you are when the god Leuhon has

tasted you." He turned to his men who had gathered in the doorway. "Bring the mother. Leave the girl for now."

After Kreuhesh stepped out the acolytes strode in and grabbed her from both sides.

"Mother!" Laonome screamed.

"Be strong!" Alkmene said as the acolytes dragged her out. "All will be well."

Outside, she was pushed into a group of six young girls, surrounded by acolytes and guards. Together they were escorted along the street. The girls huddled about her as they walked, some sobbing, others silent and dead-eyed as they walked toward the centre of Nemiyeh.

The wide space was almost empty of people now. Their group passed the well and continued across the hard ground up the hill toward the Temple of the Mother. She looked at it closely for the first time. As large as the largest of the houses, it was roofed with reed thatch but it had no walls. Eight great tree trunks served as pillars holding up the roof but between them it was open to the wind. Beneath the roof was the stone of sacrifice.

Leuhon sat perched upon the edge of that stone, his feet planted on the floor and his acolytes, servants and guards around him.

Leaving her and the girls under guard outside, Kreuhesh approached his master and kneeled, bowing his head. She could not hear their words but when Leuhon glanced in her direction she knew what was being said.

At a gesture from Kreuhesh, the acolytes dragged her forward into the structure and thrust her forward.

Leuhon sat on the massive flat-topped stone while an old man with scars on his flesh held a length of cord against the demon's forearm, then his upper arm, and then sidled around to hold the string against Leuhon's back. The string had dozens of knots tied in it. When the old man was done with his string he crossed to a sturdy oak table beside them laden with all manner of weapons. Shafts of all thicknesses and lengths leaned against a nearby pillar but the man ignored them as he sorted through dozens of metal hammers, axes, and daggers. Alkmene had only known chiefs and the strongest of their men to be armed with bronze weapons and this man tossed aside one after another as if they were nothing. She wondered if her husband's axe was amongst the pile and felt her legs weaken.

Be strong, she thought. Be strong.

By his features and his stature she knew that the old man was certainly one of the Kalekka. No doubt he had submitted during or after the attack on Nemiyeh but he seemed unconcerned by his change in fortune. If anything, he appeared excited and engaged in his work. Whatever that work was. From the table of bronze objects he took up a long dagger with a twisted and bent blade. With a pebble in one hand he sharpened a section of the edge of the blade before pursing his lips and shrugging. Placing the dagger on a flat stone he picked up a small chisel and hammered into the blade, cutting pieces of the metal off. Some of these pieces he held up to the light, such as it was, and examined them closely. Clicking his tongue, he tossed some pieces aside before lifting a copper war hammer from the jumble of weapons. Laying the head before him, he used another tool to gouge and slice slithers of shining metal from it. These pieces seemed to please him and he nodded to himself.

"I shall need more," the man said without looking at Leuhon. "Twice as much at least."

Kreuhesh stiffened and hefted his axe. "Face your god before you speak."

The man sighed and turned, utterly unconcerned. "Need I repeat myself, lord?"

Leuhon smiled at the man. "Kreuhesh protects my honour and my dignity. I should do as he says, were I you, Marwes." The *yotunan* waved a hand. "Twice as much you say? You shall have it. Is there anything else?"

"I will need ten more men," Marwes said, raising a finger. "Ten men but no fools, lord. If you send me more fools, it shall never be done and you may as well strike me down now and be done with it."

Kreuhesh would have done so immediately, had his master not laughed and waved him back. Leuhon's laugh was so deep that Alkmene felt it in her guts. "Choose your own men, Marwes. Choose as many as you need."

Marwes raised a hand. "Ten is plenty. Too many men are worse than too few, as my father used to say."

Leuhon seemed suddenly bored and he jerked his head at Kreuhesh who stepped forward and pulled Marwes aside. The acolytes jabbed Alkmene's back and she swiped aside their prodding clubs before approaching the *yotunan*. Leuhon turned his attention to her and looked her up and down.

"You have been well fed," Leuhon observed, his eyes searching her body. "It pleases me to see that you are well. You are well, woman?"

"I am."

Kreuhesh spoke. "You will show gratitude to your god."

Alkmene pressed her lips together. She knew she could be killed at any moment for giving the slightest offense and yet she could not bring herself to speak such falseness. Perhaps Henu was right and her pride would be the death of her. "You feed us well, Leuhon, because you feed *on* us."

Kreuhesh stiffed but Leuhon merely tilted his head, mildly amused. "I feed you because you are my people. It is a god's duty to bring prosperity to those that worship him." He gestured at the roof above him. "The people of Nemiyeh worshipped their god here before I came to them. They worshipped but they tell me they never met their god. That is wrong, is it not?"

She realised the *yotunan* expected an answer. "Yes."

Kreuhesh the Bloodletter spoke up. "Is that how you address your god, woman?"

"Yes, lord," she managed.

Leuhon nodded. "Do you know of this place? Before we came here, I mean, had you heard of it?"

She shook her head. "It is far from the land of my people."

"It is farther still to my lands and yet I had heard of it. Long before you were born, men of the plains and of the forest crossed the river to raid this place and many others beyond. At first it was small war bands of the *koryos*, mere boys, snatching cattle and sheep from the Kalekka and trying to get them back across the river." Leuhon laughed at that. "The Kalekka people were wealthy. More than your people could even imagine." He waved a massive hand at the metal piled on the table before him. "Wealthy and yet soft and easy to defeat in battle. You see the fields and crops across the land here? The grass they grow to eat, as if they are cattle. You know that bread is food for children and old women, yes? Even I have eaten bread and I know how these seeds fill your belly but it makes men soft, like children and old women are soft. The Kalekka were soft but they had all this." He gestured at the buildings around them. "So the men of the plain came, more and more. Great bands of raiders. One chief brought three hundred warriors across the river and he took Nemiyeh. He took it. Three hundred men defeated thousands. But a man of the forest and the plain is worth a hundred men of the field."

Why are you telling me this? Alkmene thought. What is happening? What does he want with me? She glanced at Kreuhesh but he seemed to be as confused as she was.

The *yotunan* breathed deeply and looked about him, out past the pillars at the ring of houses. "That chief of the Heryos never returned to the plain. His sons ruled over the people of Nemiyeh, son after son after son." Leuhon sighed. "But they grew weak. Almost as weak as the people they ruled. When I came they fell like scattered grain. Soft men from a soft land." He slapped the rock that he sat on. "But my men shall never grow weak. My men of the plain and the forest shall never grow old. From this place we shall conquer every people between the river and the mountains, and the wide Danubelos. They shall never grow old and they shall never grow weak. Do you know why?"

Alkmene shook her head.

"Because I shall watch over them. And they will bring me what I need. Do you know what that is?"

She lifted her head. "Blood."

He smiled. "And you think your blood is special."

"I said only that I was descended from one who was godborn."

Leuhon crossed his massive arms. "That is not all you said. Which god fathered your godborn child?"

There was no going back, she knew. Whatever she had started with this she had to now see it through to whatever the end would be. "It was the Sky Father."

Leuhon's eyes bulged. Slowly, he stood. He towered over her, his head close to the roof above. "A lie."

She looked up at Leuhon. "It is the truth."

"And where is this godborn son?"

"I do not know. He was with his *koryos* when... when you came. Either he is in the east or..." She could not say it.

"Or he is dead, yes. Perhaps we killed him already. How old is this child?"

"Just a boy."

"How many years has he?"

"Sixteen, lord."

Leuhon regarded her with his terrible gaze. His face was repulsive and she could not bear to look at it for long.

"I wonder if I can taste him in you," Leuhon muttered, as if to himself. He looked at Kreuhesh. "Bleed her."

Kreuhesh the Bloodletter grinned his twisted face as he came forward. She flinched but the acolytes grasped her and held her in their grasp. Kreuhesh grabbed her and pulled his slender bronze blade across her wrist. The pain lanced through her but she did not cry out. Hot tears burned her eyes but she bit her lip and held her tongue. He held her wound over the mouth of a cup until it was halfway full and took it to his lord. The cup seemed so small in his hand. Leuhon breathed it in, grunted, and threw it back, gulping down her blood and licking his lips.

Alkmene peered at the wound on her wrist. Although blood ran all over her hand the cut was smaller than she expected and the bleeding seemed already to have slowed. She watched the *yotunan* cuff his mouth and shrug.

"Sweet enough," Leuhon said. "But I am not satisfied. I must try the daughter."

"No!" Alkmene cried and struggled against the acolytes that held her fast.

Kreuhesh bowed and smiled as he walked out as Leuhon once more sat on his stone, sighing and stretching his back. Alkmene felt the tears filling her eyes. What had she done? After so many moons keeping her daughter safe now she had failed. It seemed that no matter what she did the demon was going to harm her and there was nothing she could do about it. Their fates, it seemed, were set. They would be bled and eventually they would end up dead. As food for this foul demon and nothing could be done to stop it. She craned her head around, looking at the girls behind her and at those watching from the edges of the square.

She stopped struggling when she saw the weapons on the table.

If she could get free from the acolytes and get her hands on a weapon she might have a moment to kill the *yotunan*. Her eyes ran over the axes and hammers and alighted on the broken, twisted dagger. The old Kalekka man named Marwes had cut shards of metal from it but the point was as sharp and narrow as a needle. If she could snatch it, she could drive it into Leuhon's heart or throat or eye. Would such a wound kill a demon? There was no way to know but she had to try. She would not be just another victim for the demon to slaughter.

Forcing herself to look away from the dagger, she relaxed her body and offered no resistance to the acolytes holding her. She pretended to be weakened and slumped against one. He held her up and she leaned on him further, keeping her head low.

From a single quiet sob behind her, she knew that Laonome had been brought up. She turned and noted how Kreuhesh held her by the upper arm. Laonome looked terrified and so young. So small compared to the men surrounding her. Laonome, I am sorry that I have failed you.

"The daughter, lord," Kreuhesh said.

Leuhon looked closely at Laonome. His desirous gaze turned Alkmene's stomach but she forced herself to be still a moment longer.

"Mother," Laonome said, more of a gasp than a word.

"All will be well," Alkmene said softly. "Be strong."

Leuhon rubbed his mouth. "You made a fine child here. She will make one of my men a good wife when she is grown. If she grows as tall and strong as her mother I might make her one of my own." He looked at Alkmene and narrowed his eyes. "You are young enough to make more children. And you were strong enough to birth a godborn and live. Perhaps your womb will take one more." He licked his lips. "But first I will drink this one. Bleed her, Kreuhesh."

When the Bloodletter grasped her daughter, Alkmene purposely stumbled forward out of the grasp of the acolytes and threw herself at the table, hitting it hard enough to knock the wind from her body. Still, she grasped at the twisted dagger just as fingers dug into her shoulder. She twisted and thrust the knife into the acolyte's neck and ripped it out. Free now, she leapt onto the table and down again on the other side in a single flowing movement. As she landed she jumped forward with the dagger ready to thrust into Leuhon's heart.

A blow struck her in the head.

She fell.

Kreuhesh had knocked her down with a crack of his axe handle against the side of her head. He stood over her and slowly pushed the butt of the axe against her throat.

The blow had knocked the wits from her. Alkmene could see only darkness but she felt the pressure choking her and fought blindly against it. She could not understand why she was so weak. Whatever was crushing her throat was as hard as stone.

"Kreuhesh," Leuhon said. "Do not slay her."

"But she tried to kill you, lord!"

Leuhon laughed. "You think this woman can harm me, Kreuhesh? With that thing?"

Kreuhesh bowed his head. "No, lord."

"That is well, then." He looked at Laonome. "Girl. Look at me, girl. Your mother will live. Her spirit is strong. Strong enough to bear my seed, perhaps. Now, heed my words, little bird. I will drink you but you also shall not die. You will live with the other girls now, in the house of blood. I am your god. You live only to serve my needs. Do you understand?"

Laonome shook but she made herself speak. "Yes, lord."

Kreuhesh the Bloodletter cut her wrist and bled her into the cup. He took only a little. Enough that his lord could taste her well but not enough to harm or weaken her. He smiled at her as he did so but she only shook harder and the tears flowed freely down her pale cheeks.

Leuhon sighed as he finished his taste of her. "Sweet indeed, girl. You shall live well in the house of blood. Remember, from now until your portion is ended, you live only to serve me." He nodded to the acolytes, who dragged her away.

Alkmene turned over, groaning, and pulled herself along the floor until she reached a table leg. She could hardly think straight but she knew she had to do something. She just hoped that they would not see. With an effort she dragged herself upright and leaned against the table of weapons for a moment before turning around. She held her head with one hand, feeling the huge lump growing there. Blood trickled down her face and she touched it before holding out her bloody fingers.

The acolytes, guards, and the demon stared at her. Kreuhesh the Bloodletter poked his stone axe into her belly. "You will bow and thank your god for sparing your life."

Alkmene bobbed her head but Kreuhesh kicked her legs and she fell to the ground once more. "Kneel!" he growled.

Slowly, Alkmene knelt and bowed her head, clutching her hands over her stomach. "Thank you, lord, for sparing me." Her voice came out thick and she slurred as she spoke.

Leuhon sighed. "Take her to the house beside mine. Bind her well, Kreuhesh, for her spirit will recover in time and who knows what mischief she would get up to otherwise. See that no one mistreats her for when she is healed I will put my seed in her. If she survives that perhaps in time I will have a son, Kreuhesh."

Kreuhesh bowed. "Yes, lord."

Alkmene was too dazed even to stand, let alone walk, and she had to be carried into the house. It was a fine one with a floor of flat, smooth stone. There one of her ankles was bound tightly and the other end of the rope was tied about a wooded pillar. There was now no possibility of her escaping. They left her curled up on the floor and closed the door, so that she was alone in the gloom.

When she was certain they had gone, she reached inside her tunic and withdrew a triangular slither of bronze no longer than her finger.

She bent to the stone floor and, scraping it deftly at an angle, began to sharpen the metal.

2 5

Nemiyeh

HERKUHLOS LAY FACE DOWN in the undergrowth beneath a copse of beech and oak and eased his way forward through the long grass. Slowly pushing aside the bright green young leaves in front of his face he had his first distant glimpse of Nemiyeh.

"There is it," Herkuhlos said. "It is just as you said, Makros, but still I do not believe it."

Beside him, Makros nodded. "So many houses. So many people. It is the demon's now."

They had made their way north for half a moon on the trail of the demon clan. Even if there had been no tracks to follow they could have found Nemiyeh with ease as they knew it was on the banks of the Denipa and so finding Leuhon was never in doubt. And yet for much of the way they had also encountered small war bands roaming the landscape. These raiders apparently travelled deep into the country all around Nemiyeh and the one they had encountered and defeated at the lake of the seeress was one of many.

"We should ambush them," Belolukos had argued when they had lay hidden while observing nine men in the distance riding across their path.

"That is a risk," Makros had replied. "There are more of them."

"But we are stronger," Belolukos replied.

"Perhaps," Makros said.

Belolukos shook his war axe. "Let us go after them, Herkuhlos. They are enemies. We must slay them."

The fire in his chest urged him to agree. He wanted to kill them and all those who stood between him and his kin. But he knew it was not as simple as that. "What if we attack and one of them escapes?"

"We killed that last war band to a man," Belolukos replied. "And so what if one does get away?"

Makros shook his head, his long, wild hair flying free in the wind. "The greatest danger is the demon and his warriors discover that we are coming for them, Bel. Our only chance of freeing your people is by stealth and if they know a raiding band is coming for them they will be ready and watching for us."

"Let us be sure we kill them all then," Belolukos replied. "We can do it, brother! Helhena can bring down two with her bow. Kasos can get at least one with his first javelin. Dhomyos will charge another and bring his man down. That leaves two each for me, you, and Makros. We can do it!" He snorted. "Herkuhlos, you could kill six all by yourself, I know you could. Let us do it for the glory of battle at least."

Herkuhlos grinned at his brother as his heart stirred to think of it. "You are right, Bel. We should follow them. Kill them and take their horses. We will track every raider that strays from their new home and kill them all one by one until there are none left to oppose us."

They had grinned until Makros had interrupted their joy. "You men are right to seek battle and glory. But think on this. One day soon they will be missing the warband you destroyed at the lake. The demon may wonder if some enemy slew them but it will also be likely one of his warbands has abandoned him. Ridden home to the east or struck out further west on their own. Or gone to join one of the other demons. But if two warbands do not return to him? Three or more?" He looked at them. "We would find ourselves being hunted down not by nine men or twelve but by twenty, fifty, a hundred. What of your kin then?"

They had fell silent. Herkuhlos did not want to agree with Makros but he could not help it.

After days of slipping by half a dozen warbands they had finally made it to within sight of Nemiyeh. Lying in the undergrowth and recalling Makros' wise counsel he slapped the older man on the shoulder.

"We only got this close thanks to your wisdom, Makros."

Grunting, Makros replied. "What wisdom I have comes from the mistakes I have made." He smiled at himself. "And thanks to the gods saving me from the consequences of those mistakes. The gods and one who is godborn."

"Me?"

"You saved me by taking me to the Seeress."

"The gods brought us together again, Makros. The gods directed both of us to Pelhbriya and sent Kounos there at the same moment so that you could be saved."

"A man's fate is set but still he must walk his own path. And it was my own failure that drove me to that fortress."

Makros had told them how he had slept in a woodland by the river a day north of Pelhbriya while he was hard on the trail of the demon clan. A pair of the demon's warriors, apparently out hunting, had discovered him. Or rather, their dogs had. They sniffed him out and came howling through the bushes. He killed two of the dogs and the hunter who was their master but the other man shot Makros in the leg with an arrow. With more dogs coming for him he had limped to the river and splashed through the marshland meaning to hide in the reeds. But when the dogs found him and the hunter began shooting more arrows, he had thrown himself into the river. The current took him away, faster than he had expected and by the time he had dragged himself free from the river he was freezing and weak from his wound. It had become filthy as he had crawled through the mud and cut the arrowhead from his flesh. Thinking to find shelter and start a fire in safety he had made for Pelhbriya. But by the time he had arrived he was already exhausted and wracked with the fever that had almost killed him.

"All I know," Herkuhlos said, "is that the gods brought us together. There must be some meaning to that. Some purpose that we must fulfil together."

Makros nodded slowly. "Since the demons came I have known it was my purpose to die while I sought to pay them back. I have tried. Been close to death more times than I can count. All I have wanted is an honourable death so that I can join my ancestors and my kin in the afterlife."

Herkuhlos found himself thinking of Helhena. She likewise

seemed to be seeking death above all else.

"It is likely that all of us will find our deaths soon," Herkuhlos replied.

Makros turned to look at him. "Since the Seeress brought me back from the edge of death I am no longer certain about my fate. I thought there was nothing to be done but to die and yet it seems the gods do not want that for me. Not yet, at least. And I begin to wonder if there is not some greater purpose in my path."

"Such as?"

"Most of my clan was destroyed and I knew that those who were captured were lost to me forever. That is why I sought death for what else was there? Find some other chief to serve so that I might live a few more years? No, there was only death ahead for me. But the demons did the same to you as they did to me and yet you set out to bring your people back home."

"The consequences will likely be the same."

Makros snorted a laugh. "Is that why the gods made us, Herkuhlos? Is that why we fight for glory? Because of consequences? All men die. What matters is how we live, how we die, and how we are remembered."

"You wish to rescue your people also?" Herkuhlos asked.

"I wish to serve you, Herkuhlos."

It felt wrong to have a man old enough to be his father offer to serve him. To be his man. "You are wiser in war than any of us, Makros. We are not of the same clan. How can you serve me?"

"The gods have guided me to you so that our paths have crossed once more. You have the blood of the Sky Father in your veins. You have sworn to save your kin and you have sworn to slay the demons. Herkuhlos, you seek a glory greater than all of us. Will you fall as you seek to fulfil your oaths? Perhaps. But I will keep our paths together now until the end. Yes, I will serve you as a warrior serves his chief. I swear it in sight of the sky and the sun and in the name of Kolnos."

Herkuhlos did not know what to say. He nodded once. "Very well."

The old warrior said nothing for a while before he reached out and poked him in the arm. "Here comes the prey."

Two shepherds drove a small flock up the hill toward their hiding place in the trees, whooping every now and then when a sheep made to flee from the herd. One shepherd was old, breathing hard and leaning on his stick as he walked and the other was young, just a boy who bounded back and forth with a smile on his face.

"I will take the father," Makros whispered. "You the son."

"Not yet," Herkuhlos replied, looking past the sheep to the *briya* in the distance. There was a chance that someone looking would see them. Especially if they did not grab their prey quickly.

The shepherds came over the brow of the hill and left their sheep to graze the fresh new grass while they headed for the shelter of the trees.

"Let us do it now," Herkuhlos said.

They both came up running and darted for their prey. The young boy was so startled he froze in place and Herkuhlos threw him over one shoulder and ran back into the trees, out of sight of the *briya*. A few moments later, Makros came puffing after him with the old shepherd before him, wailing. The sheep scattered at the sudden commotion but soon resumed their witless grazing.

They took their prizes deeper into the trees where Belolukos paced impatiently and Kasos, Dhomyos, and Helhena stood guard over the horses.

"Finally!" Belolukos said. "

"Please, lord," the shepherd said when they sat them down in the bushes, holding up his hands in supplication. "Have we not suffered enough?"

They were both small and slight with unusual faces. The old man had a strong accent and Herkuhlos struggled to understand everything that he said. "We have caused you no suffering yet, shepherd."

"But you will suffer if you do not tell us what we wish to know," Belolukos said. "You want us to skin you?"

Makros nodded at the boy. "He will care more when we skin his son. Or grandson, is it?"

"No, no, not the boy, I beg you," the shepherd said, wailing. "I have nothing to give."

Herkuhlos crouched before him and touched the man's outstretched leg. "Is that where you live?" he jerked a thumb through the trees. "In that place with the houses?"

"In Nemiyeh, yes. My home is within."

"You're not a man of the plain," Herkuhlos said. "I can see that and hear it in your speech. Did you come with the *yotunan?*"

His eyes widened. "This has always been my home. Always. We are Kalekka, you see? But we were happy with the Heryos as our masters. You are good people, yes, it is true. Very good to us."

"Tell us about the demon," Herkuhlos said.

"The demon? Are you his, lord?"

"Never you mind who we are," Belolukos said.

Herkuhlos touched the man's leg again. "We are enemies of the demon. You can speak truthfully to us."

"Ah," the shepherd said, his eyes still wild. "Then yes, I will say that they came. His men killed us. Killed the lords. Killed my son. His father." He sobbed once and reached for the young lad. Herkuhlos let the boy shuffle to his grandfather's side. "I can say no more."

"The demon is our enemy," Herkuhlos said softly. "The lore tells us to offer friendship to the enemy of our enemies. Tell me, then, herder, if you are an enemy of the demon."

"Is this a trick?" the old man asked, looking between them. "I will say nothing against our lord Leuhon. I am a loyal follower, I swear."

"I told you kindness would not work," Belolukos said, pointing with his knife. "This fool is too stupid to understand. You hold him down and I will cut his ears off."

The herder flinched and clutched the whimpering boy to him.

"Still your knife, son," Makros said to Belolukos. "This poor man is filled with fear already. Fear of that thing in there and those men that serve him." Makros crouched beside Herkuhlos. "Listen, friend, all we want to know is whether our people are inside. Our women and children. They are our kin, do you understand? Do they live?"

The shepherd looked between them and finally gave a tight nod.

"Where?" Herkuhlos said. "Where in that great place are they?"

"All over," the herder said, speaking quietly. "In the houses that were once ours. But most are kept around the Temple of the Mother. Well, the Temple of Leuhon now. That's what we are commanded to call it. The Temple of Leuhon."

"What is this temple?"

"The most sacred place in Nemiyeh, lord, and once we

420

honoured the Mother there, all men sacrificed the first handful of grain from his fields, the first lamb and calf of his herds but now the god Leuhon takes whatever he will. Now the blood of men and women flow across the sacred stone." Anguished, he shook his head.

"Where is it?"

"The centre of Nemiyeh, lord. All the streets lead to the centre. The houses around it are where the lords of the council lived. All dead now and the homes given to Kreuhesh and the warlords. Their homes are where the best slaves are held. And the blood slaves."

"Blood slaves?"

"Girls, mostly. Some Kalekka, some Heryos. Those that the... that our lord the god Leuhon bleeds. Well, the acolytes bleed them or sometimes it is his chief warlord Kreuhesh who bleeds them."

Helhena stepped forward then. "Girls?" Her face twisted in horror and anger. "He bleeds girls?"

"Yes. As I said, lord, women too and sometimes men."

Herkuhlos clenched his fists. "We knew they were devourers. It is what they are."

"How often does he drink these girls?" Helhena asked, her eyes in shadow as she looked down.

"Every day, I think. I do not see much. I live far from the centre, you see, so as to be near the flocks."

Kasos ran a hand over his face. "He eats one a day? How many days has it been?"

"That is it, then," Belolukos said into the stunned silence, staring at Herkuhlos. "They are dead. We came for nothing."

The herder looked up. "Oh, the blood slaves are not killed,

lord. Well, some are, I think. And many others besides. But the blood slaves are bled and they live on. They feed them and keep them, you see?"

"All the women and children are blood slaves?" Helhena asked.

"Oh, no, lord. He mostly takes the young women. Thank the Mother he takes only girls or he would have had my grandson." At that he squeezed the terrified lad all the tighter.

Herkuhlos fought down the thought of Laonome being subjected to such torments. "What about the women, then? The mothers?"

The herder placed a free hand over his eyes and sobbed once. Makros patted him on the back. "Answer him, friend."

"The women that yet live are put to work. The youngest serve the acolytes and the warriors by day and by night. The old women do what all old women do." He sobbed again, shaking his head as tears ran down his weathered cheeks. "My people. My people."

"It is our people we care about," Belolukos said. "They are all in the centre, he says. And all the paths lead into the middle, is that right?"

"Yes, lord. To the top of the hill and the Temple of the Mother."

Belolukos shrugged. "That is all we need to know."

Herkuhlos pursed his lips. "What is this Mother you speak of who resides in the centre?"

The herder frowned, confused. "The Earth Mother, lord."

"Ah."

"What about the warriors?" Makros asked. "Where are they?"

"They have taken the homes of my people. All over the *briya*, east to west, north to south." He shrugged. "Mostly west. They force

422

many of us now into the east, closest to the river."

"Why?"

"The river stinks of shit, lord."

Makros nodded. "And the acolytes. Where are they?"

"The acolytes serve the god Leuhon who resides in Ocka's house."

"Who is Ocka?"

"He was the foremost of the chiefs."

"How will we know which house is Ocka's?"

"It is the largest of the homes, lord. On the western side of the Temple of the Mother. The acolytes made the doorway larger, so that Leuhon could use it. He is a god, they say."

That made Belolukos angry. "He is no god but a demon, you fool. A deceiver and a devourer."

"Yes, lord."

"Are the ways in and out guarded by the warriors?"

"I don't think so, lord. Used to be we set watch on the horses, sheep, pigs, cattle, everything. But no one raids us now."

Makros raised his eyebrows. "No one raids them, Herkuhlos. They are complacent."

"Even so," Herkuhlos replied. "We can never hope to fight so many. How many warriors are there?"

"Don't know, lord. Always some off raiding but must be a hundred of them still."

"A hundred," Belolukos said, shaking his head. "If even one of them raises the alarm them we shall be dead."

"We are all masters of the shadows," Herkuhlos said. "We are wolves, all of us." He nodded at Helhena. "Even you." He looked at the old shepherd and his grandson. "If you speak a word of this then I will find you and I will kill you. Both of you."

The shepherd nodded furiously. "Of course, lord. I will say nothing, lord. Not to anyone, lord."

Belolukos was outraged. "You cannot mean to let them go."

Herkuhlos shrugged. "We cannot tie them up and leave them here. That would be the same as killing them."

"Let us kill them, then."

The old man sobbed and wrapped his arms tighter around the boy. Herkuhlos stood and faced Belolukos. "We are not killing them."

Makros cleared his throat. "Best we keep them with us for now, then. At least keep the boy to be certain the old man does not give us away."

"I would never!" he said.

Belolukos turned on him. "Be quiet."

"What if someone notices he has gone missing?"

"Who would miss a shepherd?"

Herkuhlos sighed. "I am letting them go."

"The Mother protect you, lord!" the old man said.

"Be silent and hear me. If you speak a word of this, I will know it. And I will find you and I will kill you and that boy. Do you believe me?"

"I do, lord."

"Go, then. See to your sheep."

"My thanks, lord. May the Mother guide and protect you, lord. I shall sacrifice a ram to you this very night."

"No sacrifices," Herkuhlos said. "I forbid it. Now, go."

After they scrambled away, the others stared at him.

"You are too soft," Belolukos said.

Kasos grunted. "Heedless of good advice."

"Enough," Herkuhlos said. "We know where our kinfolk are now. All that remains is for us to go and bring them out. How shall it be done?"

The wind blew through the leaves overhead while the birds sang. One of the horses stamped her hoof and Dhomyos moved to calm her. His companions stared at him and then looked at each other, waiting for someone to speak.

"A hundred warriors or more," Kasos said. "The risk is too great."

"And it must be risked," Herkuhlos said. "We have always known there were hundreds of warriors in the demon clans. Nothing has changed. All we need to do is think of a way to avoid them all while we bring our people free of them. As we are all sworn to do."

"That is not the only oath you have sworn," Belolukos replied. "You are also to slay the *yotunan*. How will you do it?"

"He need not do that now," Helhena said. "He can do that after we free our kin. Or whenever he likes."

Belolukos shrugged. "It seems like a fine opportunity to do both together."

Herkuhlos said nothing and Kasos made a suggestion. "We know the demon now lives in the largest house. One with an oversized doorway. Why could you not sneak in and cut his throat before he wakes?"

Makros whistled softly. "Hardly a glorious act."

"At least it would be done," Belolukos said. "How else can he do it? I have seen one of these demons from afar and I know that no man can beat one in battle."

"Could burn it," Dhomyos said without looking around while he stroked his horse's neck.

Kasos scoffed. "What do you mean?"

"Burn it. Set a fire on his house. Burn him up. That is how you kill demons, is it not? With fire." He looked at Kasos. "In the songs, anyway."

Makros grinned. "Not a bad idea."

"It is a terrible idea," Helhena replied. "How will you make it start quickly enough to kill him? No, a terrible idea."

"Not to burn the demon." Makros nodded slowly. "You ever seen a camp burn, boys? I have. What about these houses that they have in these parts? You know they are built from wood and the roofs are bundles of dried reeds. Inside they have loose straw everywhere. When the demons burn these places they go up easily. And if one of us makes a fire on one side of Nemiyeh, it would bring the men out to fight the fire."

Belolukos scratched his chin, frowning. "How does that help us?"

"Think of it. There will be people rushing everywhere in panic. Men shouting. Drawing water and carrying it. In we walk, find our kinfolk, and lead them back here without anyone noticing. Get as far away as we can and do not stop until we are across the river and heading for home." Smiling, he looked around. His smile dropped. "It is up to you, Herkuhlos."

"Then I say that is what we shall do."

Dhomyos stepped away from his mare. "Someone should guard the horses while we bring our kinfolk out."

All eyes turned to Helhena.

She scowled at them. "I am not staying here alone."

Belolukos shrugged. "She has a point. She can shoot well enough but she will not be much of a guard if a band of raiders come upon her."

She crossed her arms. "Then you stay here and you be the one to fight a band of raiders by yourself."

Makros grinned. "Yet again Helhena makes a good point. Surely, the horses will be well enough for half a night?"

"Someone must stay," Herkuhlos said, shaking his head. "Without the horses at the ready to bear the slowest of us when we flee, we may as well not attempt this at all."

Kasos bowed. "I will stay. My spear is the slowest. My arm weakest."

"But your wits are the fastest," Herkuhlos said. "And though we will miss your wisdom, we could not have a better man guarding our way home."

Belolukos clapped Kasos on the shoulder. "Guard them well for we will have to run like deer when we return."

"Now," said Makros. "Who can make the best fire?"

They once again turned to Helhena. She nodded. "I will help to set the fire."

Herkuhlos faced his people. "Our kin are in that place. Lost and alone without us. This is the reason we came halfway across the earth." He looked at each of them in turn. They were dirty and tired but each of them had been hardened by the trials they had faced and overcome and looked back at him unflinchingly. Their courage moved him. "Let us now make sacrifices and hail the gods so that they may be with us for tonight we shall have victory or we shall have death."

2 6

The Fall

CLOUDS DRIFTED BEFORE THE moon but there was enough light to see the way in. The pale plastered walls of the houses seemed to shine from the hill above them.

"They have been too long," Belolukos whispered.

Herkuhlos hushed him softly but he was thinking the same thing.

Makros and Helhena had circled Nemiyeh in the darkness, leaving him, Belolukos and Dhomyos waiting for flames and panic to fill the air. But there was nothing and the night was passing swiftly by. Wind rustled the stalks of the crops in the fields around them and in the leaves of the trees by the river. The waters rushed past below the *briya*, another constant noise to hide their approach.

"They have been captured or slain," Belolukos whispered. "We cannot wait all night for a fire that will not burn."

Herkuhlos silently agreed with him but still he waited. He

wished now that he had never sent Helhena with Makros. He wished also that he had found some time to lay with her before now. Thinking back on it, there were many nights when it could have happened but it had never seemed like it at the time. Why had he not taken her away from the fire one night to lay her down on his furs? He could think of no reason at all. And now it was too late. They would never have the chance.

It struck him, suddenly, how unlikely they were to succeed.

The *briya* was enormous, filled with enemies and a *yotunan* more powerful than the strongest of men. The chances of finding his mother and sister were so faint that it was madness to even hope. All he could pray for was that a god would bring them together. He looked up at the stars. His father was the shining daylight sky. Would he have any power at all in the night? At least Kolnos would be with him. He thought then of what Dehnu had said about the wolf god's territory stopping at the Denipa and wondered whether Kolnos had any power in these lands. That shepherd had said they worshipped the Earth Mother in Nemiyeh and Herkuhlos wondered if he should have sacrificed to her before tonight. If so, it was too late to do so.

It always seemed too late to do anything, hurrying from one camp to the next with hardly a thought to anything. Everything had happened especially swiftly since they crossed the great river and he felt as though he was being dragged behind a bolting horse with no way to stop it or to cut himself free. Is that simply what it is like to be aware of one's fate? To see the path while being unable to change it?

Belolukos jabbed him hard with his elbow. "There!"

From the *briya*, faint cries could be heard over the rustling crops and the river. The walls and tops of some houses were flecked with a faint yellow glow.

"Smell that?" Dhomyos said. "That's a lot of smoke."

Belolukos grinned, his teeth showing in the moonlight. "I knew they would do it." He slapped Herkuhlos on the back. "Your woman's a wolf, brother. A true wolf. Come on!"

"Just a while longer," Herkuhlos said. "Wait for the panic to take hold."

Belolukos got up. "Come on, you fools. Hurry!"

He jogged forward, bent low, with two spears in one hand and his axe in the other. Growling in frustration, Herkuhlos tapped Dhomyos and went after his brother.

In his left hand Herkuhlos carried his spear and in the right he held the bronze sword of Kounos, sharpened along both edges and its point until it could shave the hairs from his arm. At least he had the weapon of a chief in his hand.

The path into the *briya* grew steeper before they passed between the outermost of the houses. There was no gate there and no gates in any of the paths radiating from the centre. The animals were penned or tethered outside or between the houses but there was nothing to stop Herkuhlos and the others from walking right in. It must have been so simple a thing for the demon's men to take the place.

And when they entered the *briya* it almost seemed that it was being attacked once more, for the people had been roused from slumber into action by the fire. Men and women shouted warnings. A group of old women hurried down the hill between the houses herding small children and large goats before them. Herkuhlos and the others politely stood to one side, pressing themselves against the wall of a house as the strangely domestic scene barged through.

"Mother save you, boys," one of the old women said as she went by.

"And you!" Dhomyos called cheerfully after her. Belolukos slapped him on the arm. "What?" Dhomyos asked.

They pushed on deeper into the *briya*, past house after house. Most of the houses were built right up against another with hardly a gap between each house but each cluster of houses was separated from another cluster by narrow streets.

"Where is this big open place in the middle?" Dhomyos muttered. "Can't see anything ahead but more walls and darkness."

"We must have missed it," Herkuhlos said. "In a moment we shall surely be out the other side."

"What can we do but go forward?" Belolukos said over his shoulder as he strode ahead of them.

"Don't like this place," Dhomyos said, glancing left and right at the walls.

"Quiet," Herkuhlos said as a group of men ran from a side street behind them. The men ran on without stopping, heading for the fire. "Come on."

"Look!" Belolukos hissed from in front of them. "This is it."

Ahead, the path ended in the open square at the centre of the *briya*, filled with moonlight and shadow. The temple of the Mother, as the shepherd had called it. An open, roofed structure took up part of it but the rest was almost empty, bar a few figures who ran across in ones and twos, some struggling with waterskins and buckets. Another group pulled up buckets of water from a well off to one side of the area and rushed after the others. Herkuhlos pushed his companions back into the shadows until they were gone and none paid them any heed.

"Quickly now," Herkuhlos said.

"Where are the women?" Belolukos asked, looking around. "Every building is the same!"

Herkuhlos turned to his right and made his way toward the eastern side of the square. "This way."

"Fire's still burning," Dhomyos said as he hurried after them. "What if it burns down everything?"

"We will be gone by then," Belolukos said. "Be quiet, Dhom."

After passing two buildings with open doors that appeared to be empty, Herkuhlos stopped at the third. Women's voices came from within and he peered through the gaps in the timber door. Shadows moved inside.

"Are Alkmene and Laonome in there?" Herkuhlos said, his voice coming out louder than he had intended.

"Who are you?" came one response, followed immediately by half a dozen questions from other women.

"What did he say? Who is he? Is he a prisoner? Tell him nothing."

"I am the brother of Laonome and son of Alkmene. Are you there, mother?"

He could hear a whispered discussion. "He says he's looking for Laonome. Did he say Alkmene was his mother? How did he escape? What should we say?"

"Please, I have come to save them. If they are with you, please tell them to come out."

"Do not!" one of them hissed. "It's a trick."

"I assure you it is no trick. My name is Herkuhlos. I mean, they know me as Meghaholkis. They call me Holkis."

Belolukos jabbed him. "You are confusing them. Anyway, Alkmene is not in there or she would have come by now."

Hard to argue with that. Herkuhlos nodded. "Do any of you know where my mother Alkmene is?"

After a moment's silence, one voice answered. "Let us out and we will tell you."

This provoked a furious whispered argument behind the door but Herkuhlos, heart racing, did not delay. He lifted the length of wood barring the door and stood it against the wall. The door opened and in the moonlight he saw a dozen young women and girls, with more crowding in the darkness behind.

"We have to flee, now," the first girl said. She was far younger than she had sounded, hardly older than Laonome.

Herkuhlos stood in the way. "First you tell me about my kin. Alkmene? Laonome?"

A girl near the doorway replied. "Laonome was in here with us but yesterday he took her."

"Who took her?"

"The Bloodletter," another girl said.

"Yes," said another, "but he took her for... him."

Herkuhlos leaned down and lowered his voice. "Where is she?"

"Don't know."

"Probably in the god's house," the first girl said, pointing out of the door. "Over there."

"And my mother? Do you know my mother who is called Alkmene?"

One nodded. "She made the god angry and got took away."

The god. It was a repulsive inversion of the truth.

"Where?"

"Don't know."

Herkuhlos growled with frustration and punched the door frame, sending a shower of plaster down over the girls. They screamed and Belolukos hissed at them to be quiet.

"What about Wetela?" Dhomyos asked, the name of one of his sisters. "Or Stera? And Kykas who has red hair?"

"We do not know them," a girl said, emotion in her voice.

"I think Kykas died," someone muttered. "Other side of the big river. Moons past."

Dhomyos ran a hand over his face and groaned. Kykas was his oldest sister who had always seemed intent on marrying Kasos when they came of age. Belolukos squeezed Dhomyos' shoulder.

"Let us out!" the first girl said. "We told you what you wanted."

"Best not," Belolukos said quickly. "They could give us away."

"You agreed!" the first girl said, jabbing her finger up at Herkuhlos.

"I did." He stood aside and the girls, hesitantly at first and then rushing, came out of the building. After twenty had run out, heading down the nearest street clutching each other, a few more milled in the doorway.

"You are free, girls," Dhomyos said, looking at them with eyes filled with sadness. "Go. Live."

"We best stay," one said, softly.

Dhomyos was confused. "Why?"

"Them other girls will get caught. Then they will suffer."

"Do you not suffer now?"

The whispered reply came as they backed once more into the darkness. "Not like they will."

Dhomyos and Belolukos exchanged a confused, horrified look

while Herkuhlos stared across the open space to the buildings on the far side. The light of the fire was now brighter than the moon and he could see that the largest house had an enormous door.

"There," Herkuhlos said. "They said Laonome is there."

"They guessed," Dhomyos replied.

"We must look for her anyway," Belolukos said. "And you could try to kill the demon."

Herkuhlos nodded. "Come on."

He moved along the edges of the buildings, keeping to the moon shadows where he could. People still ran here and there across the space and though none looked their way it was likely that at any moment one of them might notice they had enemies in their midst. A group ran from the direction of the fire back to the well and one man began ordering them to draw water while sending others for buckets and water jugs. Voices shouted in the distance. Cries of alarm and anger. The fire was proving to be a greater distraction than any of them had hoped but they only had so much time before they were discovered and challenged.

A dark figure running in the shadows ahead suddenly changed its direction and came toward them.

"Wait," Herkuhlos hissed and pressed himself against the wall. They readied their weapons.

The figure, bent low, seemed to notice them. After freezing in shock the figure hurried on again, this time angling away across the square away from the buildings. As it loped into the open and was illuminated by the moon and firelight, Herkuhlos first saw that it was a woman. And then with a lurch in his guts he recognised her.

"Mother!"

She flinched and ducked, looking left and right in confusion.

Herkuhlos stepped out from the shadows.

Alkmene stared at him. Absolute shock upon her face.

At a run, she came to him and threw her arms around his waist. With one arm, he held her to him. She was thin but she was alive. After a moment, she pulled back and saw Belolukos. She launched herself against him, squeezing him before leaning back and stroking his face.

"My boys," she said, looking between them. "My boys. My boys. And is that you, Dhomyos? What are you doing here? How long have you been captives?"

Herkuhlos and Belolukos exchanged a look.

"We were not captured, mother," Herkuhlos said. "We came to rescue you."

"All the way from home," Belolukos said, grinning.

She scowled and cuffed away the tears that ran down her cheeks. "You witless fools. How could you be so stupid?" She sighed. "Come on, let us free Laonome."

"We looked in that place," Herkuhlos said. "With all the girls. She was not there. They said the *yotunan* took her to his house."

Alkmene gasped and turned back the way she had come. "But I was just—"

She froze.

Herkuhlos saw them, too.

Warriors. A dozen or more, some carrying torches. Their spears and axes glinted in the firelight as they came out into the open from another street. The men were heading for the well but one of them stopped and pointed at them, calling to the others with him.

"We have to run," Herkuhlos said as they all edged back into the shadows.

"Not without Laonome," she said, panic in her voice. She made as if she meant to rush toward the warriors.

Herkuhlos' heart raced. The fire of battle kindled in his chest and he felt the heat rising.

"We are but three men, mother," Belolukos said, pulling at her arm. "We cannot win."

His mother scowled. "You are not men," she hissed, slapping his hand away. "You are the sons of chiefs and warriors. You are warriors yourselves. And you, Meghaholkis, are godborn. We shall slay them all and we shall find her. Come."

Belolukos and Herkuhlos looked at one another. They knew it was madness. Herkuhlos knew that the men of his clan would have dragged away a woman acting so foolishly and yet he could not bring himself to do so to his mother.

Dhomyos was not so hesitant and he rushed forward and grabbed Alkmene's shoulder. "Do not!" he hissed. "You slay us all, Alkmene. We can return for the others. All of them."

Reluctantly, she allowed herself to be turned back and they started away along the edges of the houses keeping to the moonshadow they cast.

But it was too late.

"There she is!" a voice roared.

Feet pounded on the hard earth as the warriors approached, calling for the others as they came on. A horn sounded from amongst them and then another answered further away.

They had failed. There were twenty men coming for them and more were on the way. It was not possible to fight their way clear against so many and their entire plan had depended on not being discovered. Now that had failed their deaths were certain. He could accept that he was about to die. At least it would be in battle against enemy warriors. But he almost screamed with frustration that he had finally found his mother only to see her fall.

There was nothing to be done and so Herkuhlos planted his feet to stand and fight. Behind him, the others turned and fled.

"Come, Holkis!" his mother cried. With a final glance at the approaching warriors he turned and ran after his mother. It would be better to protect her until the last.

Four armed men emerged from the street ahead at a run, brought into the square by the horn and cries of alarm. Dhomyos veered away from the street, heading east toward another street. The way was clear there and Herkuhlos felt a glimmer of hope. A hope that was immediately dashed.

"Not that way, Dhomyos," Alkmene shouted. "No way out there."

They turned again but more men approached from all directions. An arrow hissed through the air and clattered as it struck the ground near them. Another flew overhead and buried itself in the plaster walls behind them as they ran.

"No, no," Belolukos cried as twenty men came out of the street to the north at a run.

"Take her," Herkuhlos said, moving to intercept them. "I shall slay them."

His mother argued but the others yanked her away to the east again as the men rushed Herkuhlos.

He stood to await their axes.

In one hand he held his spear and in the other he gripped the magnificent sword from Kounos.

The distant flames had grown into an inferno, lighting the leers and snarls of the warriors.

Fear rose in his guts at the sight of them. These were the raiders who had turned the plains into wastelands. The rage built inside him. Outrage that they dared to slay his people, harm his mother and his sister. The imagined sufferings they had inflicted flashed into his mind and he shook with the fury that filled him.

Before they reached him, he stepped forward and drove his spear into the throat of the closest man, destroying it in a shower of blood. An axe whirled at his head but already he was moving, stepping sideways and slashing his spear across the eyes of another man and sending him screaming to the ground. He blocked an attack with the shaft of his spear and stepped back, stabbing his sword deep into a thigh and tearing it out as he changed direction. As he did so he swept his spear around in an arc, driving away two men and catching a third in the side of the head, cracking his skull.

He cut and ducked and leapt forward hacking with his sword and thrusting his spear, killing two more and then another before the rest fell away in panic.

Someone was shouting his name and he turned to see Belolukos and Dhomyos defending his mother from half a dozen jeering warriors. He ran at them and killed the nearest by jamming his spear into the man's back beneath his ribs. To get it out of the falling body he had to rip a great hole in the man's flesh and by then two more men were almost upon him. He slashed his sword down into the top of one man's head, splitting his skull apart. The second was tripped by Dhomyos' spear thrust and Belolukos killed him before the man could crawl away.

"Boys," Alkmene said, her voice heavy with fear.

Stepping away from the carnage towards the wall of a house,

they found dozens of warriors surrounding them, lit by the flames across the *briya*. They stood back now, simply watching and waiting with their weapons ready but not advancing. Some wore expressions of anger while others were apprehensive.

What were they waiting for?

Behind them, near to the Temple of the Mother, stood the demon.

The *yotunan*.

Leuhon.

He was enormous. As tall as Kolnos or taller but far broader. His face was hideously ugly and his body was enormous and strange. Over his clothing he wore a full lion pelt with the head over his own and the mane about his shoulders. His massive torso beneath the pelt appeared deformed and it rippled strangely but darkness and the flames behind him made it impossible to see clearly.

"This is it," Herkuhlos said, tearing his eyes from the demon. "We must die here. I am sorry, mother."

"We get into the house," Belolukos said quickly, nodding at an open door a few paces away. "And kill them one by one as they come through the door."

"Agreed," Herkuhlos said. "Mother will go first."

"You go," Dhomyos grunted. "Think I'm killed already."

Glancing, Herkuhlos saw Dhomyos holding his bloody flank. The young warrior pulled his hand away and the shining blood was almost black in the darkness and flickering torchlight.

"You fought well, Dhomyos," Herkuhlos said softly, his eyes on the demon. "Your father would be proud."

Before Herkuhlos finished speaking, the *yotunan* raised his voice. "Alkmene! Why do you flee?"

Alkmene pushed forward to stand beside Herkuhlos. "Where is Laonome?" she shouted, her voice raw.

"She is here," Leuhon said and held out his hand.

Beside him, Kreuhesh pushed Laonome forward and Leuhon lifted her and held her in one arm, as a man might do to an infant or a sack of grain. The girl struggled against his arm and kicked her legs but she could do nothing against his strength.

"Laonome!" Alkmene shouted. "I am here." She took another step forward, a strangled wail coming from her throat.

Leuhon shook his head. "I thought we had become friends, dear one," he said to Alkmene. "And now you betray me." He looked down at the frightened girl in his arm. "You know that I care for you, little one, do you not?"

The girl was so afraid that she appeared out of her wits.

"What do we do?" Belolukos said.

Herkuhlos shook his head as he looked for a way through the screen of warriors. Perhaps he could kill one or two but the rest would converge on him and he would never make it through to the demon. Even if he could, how would he stop Leuhon?

"Leave her be," Alkmene said, her voice tight and wavering. "I beg you."

"I could not stand to see her betray me as you have done," Leuhon said. "So this is how it must be."

At that, he swiftly slipped a small blade into Laonome's neck. As he drew it away, blood flowed and then poured forth from one side of her throat, soaking her dress and Leuhon's arm. Laonome clutched at her neck, her eyes wide and white as she stared at her mother. Leuhon lifted her to his mouth and sucked at the wound for a moment.

442

Alkmene's cry of anguish split the air.

Herkuhlos stared in horror and his own roar joined that of his mother and his brother. He gripped his weapons and burned to use them on the demon but he was stunned by the shock of what he had witnessed.

Casually, Leuhon passed Laonome's limp body down to Kreuhesh and smiled. Blood stained his twisted, malformed lips.

"Do you see what your betrayal has wrought, dear Alkmene?" Leuhon said. "You will see how your child will—"

Alkmene, her face twisted in fury, grabbed Herkuhlos' spear, took three quick steps forward and launched it overhand with every bit of strength she had.

It was a thrusting spear, not a javelin, and yet her fury gave it wings. The spear flew over the heads of the dumbfounded warriors, arcing up and down toward Leuhon's face. His smile fell and he took half a step back, throwing his arms up in fear.

The spear struck him in the chest.

It had such power that it drove him back another step.

But it did not harm him.

When the spear struck, it made a mighty clang and bounced off, cracking the shaft and clattering upon the ground. It was the sound of metal upon metal, as when two metal weapons clash in combat, only with far greater resonance.

Leuhon stood for a moment in shock before his twisted smile returned. He rapped his knuckles against his chest, banging the metal there. Hundreds of overlapping circles of shining metal that rippled as he moved.

"My new skin of bronze!" Leuhon cried, laughing. "You see? You see that I am truly a god?" His face returned to a snarl as he pointed to Alkmene. "Kreuhesh? Bring her to me."

Kreuhesh the Bloodletter strode forward, the warriors parting for him.

Alkmene looked around to the left and right, her eyes hard with a cold rage. "Dhomyos? Do you see the pathway behind us?"

There were a dozen warriors in a ragged line blocking the path east between the houses.

"I see it," Dhomyos said through gritted teeth. His wound was bleeding freely and had soaked him down to the knee on that flank.

"Clear the way for me and my boys," Alkmene said to Dhomyos, "and I will have your glory sung."

Dhomyos smiled, letting his axe slide through his hand until he gripped it at its base. "A glorious death," he muttered. "Save my sisters if you can."

"I will," Herkuhlos said.

"Do it now!" Alkmene shouted as Kreuhesh came closer with his men around him.

Dhomyos turned and lumbered toward the men blocking the path before breaking into a run. Belolukos ran behind him, then Alkmene.

Herkuhlos turned to follow and as he did so Kreuhesh threw a knife at his back. The small bronze blade struck the back of Herkuhlos' leg above the knee and he cried out, limping furiously away after the others. Behind him Kreuhesh shouted for arrows and javelins.

At a full sprint, Dhomyos crashed to the two closest warriors and brought them to the ground. Getting to his knees he drove his axe into the face of the man under him before launching himself sideways at a third man, burying his axe into the man's chest. Now without his weapon, Dhomyos threw himself, roaring, against the next man and tossed him with his hip to the ground.

His battle cry was cut short when a spear took him in the throat. He grasped the shaft as he fell, tearing the weapon from his attacker in a final attempt to help his spear-brothers to escape.

Rushing through the gap he had opened, Belolukos stomped on a fallen man and smashed his axe into the shoulder of another who came rushing from the flank. Alkmene leapt over the bodies of the dying men and ran on as Belolukos turned to run with her.

Loping behind as best he could with a knife in his leg, Herkuhlos saw it all. He saw Dhomyos fighting, roaring, and dying.

Two of the remaining warriors started after Belolukos and Alkmene but stopped when they saw Herkuhlos and turned to block his path. Herkuhlos swatted aside the spear levelled at him and slammed his sword into the head of the man holding it. The sword bit deep, spattering blood and brains into the air before wedging into the skull. As the body dropped to the ground it pulled the blood-drenched handle of the sword from his grasp.

Before he could retrieve it the next man swung a stone war axe and Herkuhlos, now unarmed, hopped back, grasped the shaft of the axe, and butted the man in the face with his head. Falling back the man released his axe and clutched his smashed nose.

Herkuhlos looked over his shoulder to see dozens of men almost upon him.

He flung the hammer overhand at the closest one, crushing the man's face, before turning and running after his mother and brother. His leg hurt and would not work properly but he forced himself on down the dark passageway with the mass of men crowding behind. A javelin clattered near his feet and an axe flew by his head before hitting the ground and bouncing madly away.

"It's the river!" he heard Belolukos shout.

Ahead, a low wall stretched between the rows of houses. Beyond the wall was an endless black nothing.

With a sickening lurch he realised where they were.

The cliff.

"Jump far!" his mother cried before leaping onto the wall without breaking her stride and flinging herself off.

She disappeared into the darkness.

Belolukos roared in anger and terror and jumped after her, arms flailing as he tumbled.

Hands were almost grasping Herkuhlos from behind. A foot kicked at his heel and he almost stumbled. Men shouted and their feet pounded behind him, their breathing even louder in his ears than his own.

The wall was just in front of him. He knew from seeing it from afar that there were rocks at the base of the cliff and to miss them he would have to jump far out. If he did not then he would be broken by the fall.

All things die.

Forcing himself to run through the pain in his leg, Herkuhlos leapt up onto the wall.

Just then, someone thrust a spear shaft into his ankles. Tripping, he fell forward, missing the wall with his foot and smashing a knee on the stones. Momentum carried him off and tumbling head over heels he spun out into darkness.

He fell and fell.

The air rushed over him and lights whirled around and around farther and farther away before he smashed into the cold black water of the river.

2 7

Chaos

HERKUHLOS CLUNG TO THE muddy bank as the river tugged at him, trying to tear him away once more. The night sky was turning a deep blue and he could see trees swaying above him but their branches were out of reach. Heaving himself up he slid in the sodden earth, pulling out chunks of wet grass and handfuls of mud. His grasping fingers found purchase against a tangle of roots and he pulled himself out of the torrent and crawled on his belly up the bank until he was clear of the water. Flipping himself onto his back he breathed deeply and coughed out the water he had breathed in. The silhouetted branches above him juddered and he realised he was shivering violently.

All he wanted was to stay there and to close his eyes. For a moment he gave in to the temptation and immediately fell into something like a dream where he saw flashing images of weapons and blood.

He was on the first raid that he had ever seen. Still a boy, he had accompanied the *tauta* on a raid from their valley across the plain into the territory of the Tengdus. When they had arrived they found the *tauta* of the Tengdus were long gone on a raid of their own leaving only old men, boys, and women to defend their tents and their cattle. There was hardly any fight at all and young Holkis and Belolukos had been disappointed at the lack of blood and glory. Gendryon had taken half their cattle and carried off three of the young women who accepted their fate with hardly a protest.

"Why only three women?" Belolukos had asked Gendryon as they were preparing to leave. The rest of the women stood in groups by their tents glaring and making curses while their frail fathers and small sons tried and failed to keep them quiet. Above, the sun blasted them with heat and the sky shone like polished stone. "Why not take them all?"

Sitting atop his horse, Gendryon had shaken his head, gesturing at the captives with his war axe. "Hendhesa there was taken from us when she was a girl. Kossine with the red hair? She was a herder in my cousin Hekton's clan and shall be returned. That last one with the full breasts will redress the balance when we get her home. She is a fine woman. I may even put a child in her myself."

Belolukos was still confused. "But take them all and our honour will grow all the more."

Gendryon shook his head. "What honour is there in that? If we had defeated the Tengdus in battle then perhaps we would take more but this is enough."

Belolukos did not reply but Holkis still did not understand. "Why take only half their cattle? When they return they will still be strong enough to raid us. But if we take all their cattle, burn their tents, carry off all else they have then they will be too weak to attack us."

Gendryon looked long at him and Holkis could not hold his gaze for long, looking away to where the women stood.

"You would destroy this clan?" Gendryon's voice was flat and low. A dangerous tone. "Why?"

Holkis had looked back at him. "Because they are our enemy."

Instead of being angry, as Holkis had expected, Gendryon nodded as if considering his words as he might have done with a man of the *tauta*. "It is easy to destroy, son. Any fool can break apart in moments what a wise man built in a lifetime. Wild beasts driven mad by hunger or pain will destroy a camp. Is that what we are, Holkis?"

"No. But we may never get another chance like this. Better to do what we can now so they cannot strike back at us when they return. Our people are more important than theirs."

From the corner of his eye, Holkis saw Belolukos nodding in agreement.

Gendryon rode a little closer to them. Behind him the divided herd of cattle was being driven away across the baking grassland.

"All creation wages an endless war against chaos," Gendryon said. He made a fist with his right hand. "On the one hand there is the side of the gods, the side of the shining sun, of fire controlled, of power wielded by the just man." Dropping his right he held up his left fist. "On the other is destruction, the wild thundering storm, pestilence and starvation, and the endless devouring madness of the *yotunan* and the *dura* that leads to darkness. If the chaos is not battled with all the will we can summon then that darkness will extinguish the light forever. The gods may guide us but it is men that stand between all that is good and all that is wrong and every one of your ancestors fought that fight so that you could be here today. Your body may be strong, Holkis, but this war is fought least of all in the flesh." He placed a massive finger against his own chest. "Your will must rise to this eternal battle and though it may waver it must never be broken. As it is undying, your spirit already knows all of this and it is to your spirit that you must listen. Your flesh, your will, and your spirit must be as one as you stand against chaos. So, yes, we do battle with our enemies and we fight to protect what is ours but you must remember that good men are not destroyers. Good men are the enemy of destroyers." He looked at him as if he were trying to see inside his eyeballs. "Do you understand?"

Holkis thought about it. "No, I do not think so."

Gendryon looked at Belolukos who shrugged, squinting at the brightness of the sun.

The older man snorted, amused. "Then you remember my words, boys, and one day, perhaps when you have sons of your own, you will."

Starting, Holkis jerked awake to find the sun had risen and the world was now bathed in morning light. The sky shone beyond the clouds and he lay still and looked at it. Was the Sky Father looking back at him? Had he called his name?

"Holkis!"

Herkuhlos flinched and sat up, looking around. He was surrounded by a copse of alder and a dense tangle of bushes. There was no one with him.

"Holkis!"

The distant voice was half snatched away by the wind but he

recognised it at once and dragged himself to his feet. He had never felt so stiff and so cold. His body was covered in thick, drying mud and he had no weapon.

Pushing his way through the bushes, he tried to call out but coughed instead. His mother's voice called again but it was far quieter and in a panic he rushed on faster, crashing through the woodland in search of her. He found himself in a small clearing and jumped onto the trunk of the fallen tree that ran across it. No longer could he see the river and was now not sure in which direction it was.

"Mother!" he cried. "Alkmene!"

He stopped to listen but heard nothing but the leaves rustling and the birds singing in the branches. If he could not find her, he did not know what he would do. Where was Bel? He struggled to remember what had happened. They jumped from the *briya* into the river and he had struggled to the surface. Gasping for air, he had called out to his brother who was ahead of him downstream. Once or twice he had thought he heard his mother's voice but it had been too dark to see anything. He had tried to swim for the bank but had smashed into a boulder.

Herkuhlos felt his shoulder. The pain there was beginning to fade but it had hurt badly and the rest of it was hard to remember. The river had carried him swiftly away every time he tried to make the bank and then he remembered hanging on to the muddy roots and climbing out.

Had Bel drowned?

What if it was not his mother's voice he had heard but her spirit?

In a panic, he tilted back his head and roared for his brother.

"Belolukos!"

Two pigeons overheard burst noisily away in terror and the rest of the wood fell silent.

Herkuhlos looked around him and took another great breath.

"Belolukos! Alkmene!"

A noise to his right. Branches crashing and footsteps crunching twigs and leaf litter. Then he saw the shapes through the undergrowth.

"It is you!" Herkuhlos cried, stepping down to embrace his brother and mother.

"Keep your voice down," Belolukos said, scowling. "You want the *yotunan* to hear?"

"I found you," his mother said, clutching his arm. "Are you hurt?"

"No," Herkuhlos said.

They were both wet through and Belolukos had a lump on his forehead the size of a cuckoo's egg.

"You are filthy," his mother said.

"It was not my fault," Herkuhlos replied. "There was mud."

"I can see that. What happened to you? Why did you not get out? We have been looking for you since dawn."

Belolukos scowled. "We thought you drowned."

"I did not," Alkmene said. "I never thought that. I knew you would be well. We have been running downstream looking for you."

"You got out before me?" Herkuhlos said.

"I pulled mother to the bank," Belolukos said. "We called for you but you went flailing past like a log."

"We are together now," Alkmene said, her eyes shining with

tears. "All but—"

She broke off and turned away and Herkuhlos saw again the demon opening Laonome's vein and drinking from her neck. He remembered her limp body being thrown aside like an empty wine skin. An ember of the fire in his heart began to glow.

"We failed," Herkuhlos said. "Mother, I am so sorry that—"

"No, no," she said, waving them into silence. "Not now. Now we must flee. Leuhon will not let us go. He will send Kreuhesh and the others after me and he will not stop until he has me." Her lip curled in disgust. "Come, we must find a way back across the river before they find us. There are river valleys and woods on the eastern side and a dozen destroyed *briya* we could raid on our way back to the plains. There must be some horses left that we could take. But we must get across now before Kreuhesh catches up with us."

"There is a ford somewhere to the south," Belolukos said quickly, pointing downstream. "Or we could swim it if we have to."

"We cannot," Herkuhlos said. "We must find Helhena, Makros, and Kasos. They were waiting for us with our horses. They will be fleeing also."

"Kasos is with you?" Alkmene said. "He is a good boy. A clever boy. He will know that he should cross the river after us. We shall look to meet up with Kasos and your horses on the eastern bank."

Herkuhlos could not abandon the others. "And what if instead of riding for the ford they instead stay on this side to look? Just as you both looked for me."

"That is different," Alkmene said. "Of course we looked for you. We are kin."

"And Kasos is our brother," Herkuhlos said, looking to Belolukos. "And Helhena has no one to protect her but me."

"You have a woman with you?" Alkmene asked, narrowing her eyes.

"He is going to marry her," Belolukos said.

Herkuhlos shook his head. "She lost her clan. Her father Hartkos was guest friends with Gendryon. She has been with us all the way from home. I will not abandon her."

"She is the daughter of Hartkos?" Alkmene said. "Gendryon passed through his territory on raids to the west but they were never friendly."

"They took oaths of guest friendship," Herkuhlos said. "And even if they had not, Helhena is one of us. Even you could not deny that, Bel."

He shrugged. "She is good with a bow, I will say that for her."

Alkmene nodded slowly. "And the other one you mentioned?"

"Makros is a warrior. A good man. Another who lost everything to the demons. To Leuhon. He swore himself to me and so I must not abandon him either."

Belolukos sighed. "He is right, mother. We must not cross without our friends."

She stared at them. "How will we find them?" Neither had an answer. "Did you name a place to meet if you got separated?" Herkuhlos and Belolukos looked at each other and then at the floor. She sighed and shook her head. "How did you two ever make it this far? Come on, then. We shall not find them in here."

They followed her westward away from the river, watching and listening for sign of pursuit. Herkuhlos limped from the knife wound in his leg which was already healing but not yet healed. At least the walking helped to warm him and he soon stopped shivering.

As they picked their way through the trees and undergrowth he was wracked with an overwhelming sense of shame at his failure. All they had done since the coming of the demons had been for nothing. Laonome had been killed in front of him. Dhomyos had fallen to save them and Helhena, Kasos, and Makros may also have fallen already. So much death and inglorious failure that he could hardly bear it. Only the fact that his mother was free gave his actions any meaning and her freedom was tenuous indeed. In fact it seemed likely that they would soon be ridden down and killed by the pursuit of Leuhon's warriors.

Around them the wood eventually thinned out until they reached the edge of an overgrown pasture. Beyond the pasture was a small mound with a low stone wall around the brow. It was not much of a fortress but would have protected the homestead from small groups of raiders in the days before the *yotunan* had passed through. Now it looked smashed and uninhabited.

"I remember this place," Herkuhlos said, brightening. "We spent a night in the woods on the other side of it. We argued about whether to sleep in the ruins."

Belolukos frowned. "South of Pelhbriya?"

"No, this was just a few days ago. After we left the Seeress."

Alkmene frowned. "Seeress?"

"I will tell you about it when we are back on the plains," he replied.

Belolukos yanked them down into the undergrowth and hissed a warning. "Look!"

For a moment, Herkuhlos could not see what had frightened his brother. But then he saw a single horse on the far side of the hill wandering to the farthest extent of its tether, its head down grazing.

"Is it one of ours?" Herkuhlos asked, squinting. He could not see enough of the horse to identify it. "Could Kasos be here already?"

"We came a long way down the river and we did it quickly," Alkmene said. "Your friends would have had to ride fast to get here before us."

"The same could be said for Leuhon's men," Herkuhlos replied. "And surely they could not have gotten ahead of our people."

"They must be someone else," Belolukos said, the look in his eyes full of meaning.

"Neither our friends nor our enemies," Herkuhlos said, nodding in agreement.

"Anyone who is not us is our enemy," Belolukos pointed out.

"True," Herkuhlos admitted.

They looked at each other, a plan of action forming in both their minds as they did so. Herkuhlos raised his eyebrows. Belolukos shrugged.

"It is possible, at least," Herkuhlos said.

Belolukos pursed his lips. "A long way in the open. It will take too long and we do not have the time."

"The grass is long all the way to the mound," Herkuhlos replied. "And we will save time if we have a horse."

"What are you two discussing?" Alkmene asked, frowning.

"There is at least one horse there. That would be useful. The rider may have food, supplies."

"He will also have weapons," Alkmene said. "And there may be fifty more horses behind that hill, each with a rider. It is too much of a risk. We should either avoid this place and go north for your friends or we should go east and cross the river. This serves no purpose."

When she put it that way it seemed simple and he almost agreed. But it was possible that his remaining spear-brothers were at the mound and if so they could not leave without being certain. And if instead the rider was one of Leuhon's then they should not leave him roaming free at their backs. They could find themselves surrounded.

"If it is one rider or even two or three then we can probably take them," Herkuhlos said. "If it is more then we shall slip away unseen."

Belolukos agreed and they looked at Alkmene, seeking her approval.

She looked between them. "We have no weapons. We are exhausted and cold. And you think you can approach and slay up to three riders under the light of the sun?"

Herkuhlos nodded. "If the gods are with us."

Alkmene waved a hand. "Then let us look closer."

Herkuhlos and Belolukos led her along the edge of the trees to the closest part of the wood to the hill. Surely, the rider was within the ring of stones atop the mound but they could not see him. They went deeper into the green shadows of the wood so that any watcher would not see them and when they edged toward the pasture again they could see the rear of the mound.

Herkuhlos hung his head when he saw it. Belolukos cursed.

"That is it, then," Alkmene said. "We go on."

There were at least a dozen grazing horses tethered to the southern slope.

Here and there amongst them was a band of warriors.

They were relaxed. Most were eating, some were sitting on the sloping bank, a few appeared to be sleeping. One waved his arms as he spoke animatedly to another. Herkuhlos counted nine but there may have been more.

"Are they Leuhon's?"

Alkmene squinted as her eyes searched the men. "Could be. His bands raid these lands endlessly. Or they could be from some other clan with some other master. It matters not who they are, we must get back before they see us."

"What if Kasos and the others come through here," Herkuhlos said, "and run into these men? They will be set upon."

"Makros could take half of them by himself," Belolukos said.

That was an exaggeration. "And the other half would kill him and Kasos and they would take Helhena and our horses."

"We must find your people first, then," Alkmene said, eyeing the warriors. "Let us go."

What was the best thing to do? Herkuhlos eyed the sky. A crow circled in the distance before swooping down out of sight into the treetops. Surely it was not possible for him and Belolukos to kill all the men in the warband but he could not bring himself to simply walk away. No warrior could live his life fleeing from every battle.

His thoughts drifted to a night two summers past as he sat with some of the other boys and their fathers around a large fire in the woods. They were on a hunt and Holkis had been determined to bring down a deer with his bow but he had not yet even taken a shot. The men of the *tauta* sang songs of the ancestors and passed around a skin of mead. It was a sacred time where the boys felt keenly the path that lay ahead of them and as the night wore on the men began to speak of the kin who had fallen.

Gendryon told of a raid in his youth when his brother had challenged the leader of another warband and had fallen with a spear through his heart. After the tale had been told, the men sat in silence while the fire cracked and popped, the sparks shooting up into the blackness.

"I would have liked to have known him," Belolukos had said.

Holkis had agreed. "It is sad."

Across the fire, Gendryon had stirred. "Sad? Why are you sad, Holkis?"

All eyes seemed to be on him now and he shifted uncomfortably in their gaze. "I mean only that it is sad that he is dead. And that he died before he could father sons."

There was a long silence and Holkis knew that he had said something wrong.

Eventually, Gendryon replied. "The spirits of the fallen who died in glory will go to fight beside the gods in the great darkening at the end of ages. Glory won in the act of battle itself cleanses the spirit so that it may ascend to one day face the greatest fight of all." The fire popped and sparks flared, illuminating Gendryon's face for a moment so that he looked almost inhuman, like a spirit made flesh. "Hear me, boys, and keep these words in your heart. If you fight and win you will be rewarded with glory and wealth. Yet if you fight and fall, you will attain the highest realm. So, the man who fights with all his strength, all his will, and all his spirit can never fail, no matter whether he lives or dies. We must never feel sadness for those who won such glory with their deaths for there is no sacrifice or rite more pleasing to the gods than that of the true warrior who fights and falls in battle."

Crouching now in the woodland, watching the enemy warband

by the mound, Herkuhlos could almost feel the fire that had warmed him that night long ago.

Herkuhlos looked around. The woodland had been managed by the people living nearby and much of the undergrowth was cleared and some trees coppiced for poles. But the shoots were either too young and green or too thick. A few paces away he noticed a straight young tree that was dead but still standing that was just what he was looking for.

"Where are you going?" Belolukos asked as Herkuhlos got up and crossed to it.

"What is he doing?" Alkmene asked.

He ignored them and went on to the dead tree. It was a beech as were many others still living around it. If the gods had been with him then it would have been an ash but beech would have to do, even though it was likely to splinter. The tree was also thicker than the ideal spear shaft but it would serve. It was rotted at the ground and it was no trouble to push the thing over. The spindly top whipped through the branches of the trees around it as it fell, though it did not weigh much and made hardly a sound as it came softly down to the leaf litter.

"What are you doing?" Belolukos hissed. "You want them to see us?"

Herkuhlos picked it up and cracked the narrow trunk in half where it began to narrow so that he ended up with an ugly, oversized pole with a soft, rotten thick end and a splintered narrow end. After snapping off the spindly branches he kicked away the rot as best he could and rubbed both ends and the sharp knots against the bark of a mature tree to smooth it all off. He gave a it a few swings and grasped it like a spear shaft, testing the balance. It was heavy and thick but it should serve.

"You are not thinking of fighting all those warriors with that ugly stick, are you?" Belolukos asked.

"Not all of them, no."

With that he walked away from them to the edge of the woodland and on into the long grass of the pasture. Alkmene and Belolukos rushed out to stop him.

"You cannot do this, son," Alkmene said, running up behind him. "They will kill you."

"You should stay back," Herkuhlos said, turning and pointing at the trees. "If this goes ill you can still flee."

"I will not watch you die, too," Alkmene said, her eyes filled with fire. "Not after all this. I cannot. I will not. I am your mother and you will obey me."

He looked at her. "I am a man now and I do not obey your commands. If the gods will it then all shall be well. Go now, before they see you."

"He thinks he is an immortal," Belolukos said, scowling. "That is it, is it not? You think that you are one of the undying ones, Herkuhlos. You believe that nothing can harm you."

"No, Bel, I do not think that. I know I am not immortal. I know I can be killed. But we have no food, no weapons, no horses. How far do you think we are going to get without those things? I must act now or all will be lost. Go back."

"We can find your friends," Alkmene said. "Avoid these warriors and find your friends and we will have the horses we need to flee. Let us do so."

Herkuhlos opened his mouth to answer.

A shout from the hill startled them. The warriors were standing and pointing. Already one of them was leaping onto his horse and the others hurried to do the same.

"Get back!" Herkuhlos said. "If they kill me, you should run for the river and swim."

"Wait!" Alkmene said but he did not.

As the warriors mounted and charged across the meadow, Herkuhlos walked toward them and raised his stick over his head.

"I am Herkuhlos of the Kweitos Clan," he cried, "and I challenge you!"

28

Lord of Pelhbriya

IN THE GREY LIGHT OF DAWN, Kreuhesh the Bloodletter returned from the riverbank below Nemiyeh and walked through the streets up to the Temple of Leuhon. Smoke drifted above the rooftops from the houses that yet smouldered.

The raiders from the night before had set a fire that had raged until dawn and had burned almost a score of houses. One entire cluster of them was burned beyond repair and only the streets around it stopped the fire from spreading. That and hundreds of people throwing water on the flames that threatened the neighbouring buildings. Kreuhesh cared nothing for the buildings or for those who were burnt in stopping it but he raged at the audacity of the attack. Three men had walked right into Nemiyeh and had taken Alkmene away. One had been killed and the other two had leapt with Alkmene off the cliff and into the river. Surely, they had died in the fall.

The fact that Alkmene had died annoyed him even more than Leuhon locking her away had done. She was to have been his prize and now she was dead. There were other women, of course. Younger women. But he had wanted her. He had known she was special even before she had admitted she was descended from Perseyus and also that she had given birth to the son of a god. Throughout their journey across the plains she had been denied to him by Leuhon's claim and he had never understood why the god had protected her until she had spoken the truth of her descent and her offspring. Despite Leuhon's protection, for many moons Kreuhesh had still somehow expected that she would be his one day. Indeed, already thought of her that way. When Leuhon had stated his intent to put his child into her it had infuriated him beyond measure. Leuhon was a god, yes, but surely Alkmene had been a prize more suitable for Kreuhesh the chief and not for an immortal. He felt as though a prize had been taken from him and his honour with it.

And now Alkmene was likely dead. Denied to Leuhon by her final, desperate act. At least the god would be denied her, too. There was some justice in that, he thought, as he entered the gloom of the temple. His lord sat upon the sacrifice stone with the acolytes attending to him. Leuhon still wore his astonishing bronze armour beneath his lion pelt and the metal gleamed even in the shadows of the temple.

Kreuhesh approached and knelt. "My lord."

"Rise." Leuhon waved away the acolytes and looked down at him. "Speak."

"Lord, their bodies have not been found. The waters carried them away and so they must be further downstream. I have sent men by horse and by boat to search for them."

Leuhon tilted his head. "You will find them yourself, Kreuhesh. Take your strongest warriors and do not return until you bring Alkmene and her sons to me."

That surprised him. "Sons, lord?"

"The warriors with her." Leuhon's bright eyes wrinkled at the corners. "Had you seen them before?"

"No, lord."

"They came for her." Leuhon nodded. "From the plains. They wore the clothes of the Heryos and bore their weapons but for the bronze dagger." The god flicked a hand at one of the acolytes who bobbed his head and stepped forward, lifting the long weapon. It still had blood on it and the blade was now bent from use but it was a magnificent thing. "The tall one who wielded this, the man that slew so many of your warriors, was Alkmene's son. The one she spoke of. The one who is godborn."

Kreuhesh gritted his teeth as he looked at the weapon. The young man had been taller even than he was and despite the slimness of youth had fought as well as any warrior he had ever seen. When the alarm had been raised, Leuhon had commanded that none of the raiders were to be harmed and were instead to be taken alive. That command had cost the lives of many good men and the raiders had all died anyway. "You knew this godborn warrior, lord?"

Leuhon scowled as he stared into the distance. "I know his father."

Of course, Kreuhesh thought. "His father is the Sky Father, lord?"

The god snorted. "The Sky Father. Absurd. But then he always did think himself above the rest of us. Yes, that is his father. He has the look of one of his bastards."

Not knowing what to say in response to such a thing, Kreuhesh nodded once. "I will return with their bodies, lord."

Leuhon fixed him with a sudden glare. "They may yet live, Kreuhesh. The woman is strong and the godborn son at least would not be killed by such a fall. If you find them alive then you will return them alive. Do you understand?"

Kreuhesh thought they would surely be dead but he dared not contradict Leuhon. "Yes, lord." If it had been difficult to capture them when they were seemingly trapped and surrounded by dozens of warriors he imagined the difficulty he would have in taking them alive out in the open. "All three of them, lord?"

"No," Leuhon said, waving a huge arm, "I care nothing for the mortal son."

Kreuhesh nodded. He could at least have that one shot at a distance. "I will gather the men, lord. If it can be done, I will bring them to you."

Leuhon narrowed his eyes. "Kreuhesh, to face the godborn son and bring him to me alive alongside his mother, you may require another taste of my power."

Before Kreuhesh could respond, Leuhon waved to the acolytes who stepped forward with a bowl and stood ready at Leuhon's side.

"This will again grant you power for many days."

Forcing himself to remain calm, though his heart sang, Kreuhesh nodded. "Thank you, lord."

"You have served me well, Kreuhesh. Better than any mortal ever has. Tell me, my chief warrior, why do you believe I spared Pelhbriya from destruction?"

"I do not know, lord."

"It shall be yours, Kreuhesh. You will rule Pelhbriya in my name."

"Lord, you honour me."

"If you continue to serve me well, I will grant you the gift of immortality."

His heart pounding, Kreuhesh bowed once more. "Immortality, lord?"

"It can be done, Kreuhesh. You will serve me for a thousand years." Leuhon waved his hand as if to suggest that was to be discussed later. "For now, you shall take my power."

At that, Leuhon nodded to the acolytes who brought forth a bowl and held it aloft for their god. There was dark liquid sloshing within. With a bronze blade, the god sliced into his flesh at the wrist and bled into the bowl. The shining red blood ran freely down his hand and spattered from his fingers until he was satisfied. While two acolytes washed the god's skin clean, two others bore the bowl to Kreuhesh.

Kreuhesh could hardly contain his greed for the power of the god's blood but forced himself to take it slowly. Raising it to his lips, he poured the warm substance into his mouth and drank it down, each mouthful immediately nourishing and the warmth spread through his stomach and into his limbs. By the time he was tipping the bowl high to drain the last drops, he felt the god's fire in his arms and when he stood he felt it pour into his mind. The world was clearer now. Every movement around him discernible, every sound sharper, all colours brighter. He smelt the sour breath of the acolytes as they declared that it was done.

Leuhon looked down at Kreuhesh. "This is but a taste of

immortality, Kreuhesh. A taste that will fade before long. Bring Alkmene and her godborn son to me and perhaps you will know this feeling for eternity."

"Yes, lord."

"The godborn son has great strength. But now you do too. For a time. I suggest you capture them before the power of the sacrament fades."

"Yes, lord."

Kreuhesh bowed and backed away before turning to find his men. He chose the strongest twelve warriors and twenty of the best horses. It was not long before they gathered on the track south of Nemiyeh and Kreuhesh looked at his followers. Hendros, Horghis, Host, Kelwos, Gelu, Kreps, Tweks, Hok, Melo, Wedhris, Hedwol, Weben. All good men. He felt a sudden urge to tell them that he had the power of the immortals in his blood and he was going to be lord of Pelhbriya and best of all an immortal. But he said nothing. It would be weakness to seek their approval and admiration through his words. Only his deeds mattered.

"We will find the woman. We will find her sons. If any of you harm her, you will die by my hand. Do you understand?"

One of his men stepped forward.

"Lord," Gelu said, bowing. "I must tell you that a war band was seen riding away before dawn."

"Where?" Kreuhesh said, turning to him. "The woman and her sons had a war band?"

Gelu shrugged. "Cannot say, lord. But ten or so horses were seen. Not half had riders."

"Why were they not pursued?"

"I only just heard about it. Tweks and Melo saw them." He

waved over the two warriors he had named. "Tell the lord what you saw."

Tweks nodded. "We was running down for the river like you told us to and we saw horses riding over the hill." He gestured at the rise across the fields. "Going that way."

"South," Kreuhesh said. "You did not go after them?"

Tweks looked at Melo.

"We was going to the river to look to see if the woman washed up," Melo said, shrugging. "Doing what we was told, right?"

Gelu frowned. "It is too far between the river and them horses for the woman to be riding them, lord."

Kreuhesh nodded. "But the warriors who came to free her left men with their horses. When they saw their master had failed, they fled."

"Do we go after them too, lord?"

It was possible that these riders would lead them to wherever Alkmene was. But Kreuhesh had seen the woman go into the river and that meant she would have to come out of it somewhere, whether she was dead or alive. So the best way to find her was to follow the course of the river and to search for her body or for signs that she got out. If there was nothing on this side for a day or two he would lead his men across to the eastern bank and come back upriver on that side. Surely, that was the best way.

"The riders mean nothing," Kreuhesh said to his men. "We follow the river."

When the sun came up fully, the rain came with it, falling and swirling like ashes in the wind. They rode along the river and Kreuhesh repeatedly sent his men down to the overgrown banks to search in the long grass and tree roots for sign of anyone, whether dead or alive.

By midday, Kreuhesh began to understand that his was a difficult task. The river was vast and the current swift. Their dead bodies could have washed far away already or they could have climbed out on either side or onto one of the narrow islands that dotted the river. If they lived they could have made their way up one of the many streams that fed into it. Here and there along the river were marshes with reeds that could hide a hundred men or more with ease.

Yes, it was a difficult task but the reward would be worth the effort.

If you continue to serve me well, I will grant you the gift of immortality.

Long had Leuhon hinted that he would bestow such honour on him and now he had offered it.

There were many warriors walking the earth and many more beneath it but how many of them had been granted immortality by a god?

As an immortal, Kreuhesh would be stronger than any warrior he faced. He could heal any wound he received. And he would not age. At least, not like mortals do. His ageing would be as slow as that of the oak tree. He would endure. When all men upon the earth were rotted to dust, he would go on.

"Nothing here!" Horghis shouted from the marshy ground by the river.

In the trees further along, Hok waved a hand over his head to show they were also clear.

"It grows late, lord," Gelu said. "We can make camp by the trees there."

Kreuhesh looked at his men. "The woman must be found. If

you fail me, I shall slay you all before returning to Leuhon."

Gelu raised his voice. "We go on!"

They searched all afternoon, breaking into smaller groups and then each man searched a section of the banks by himself to cover as much ground as possible. Each of them poked their spears into bushes and kicked down clumps of long grass and sedge and waded into reed beds.

I should have brought more men, Kreuhesh thought as the day wore on without finding any sign of them.

When darkness fell, they lit bundled reeds for torches and carried on along the banks but it was madness to drive the men harder when they would have to keep it up for days and so he called a stop. They camped within sound of the river and soon his men had a small fire going. Some lay in their furs and slept immediately but Kreuhesh was not tired. The god's power was in him and he felt as though he could run forever. As he knew the strength would fade as the days passed he savoured the feeling of it. Many times, he had seen Leuhon crush a man's head with his bare hands and Kreuhesh felt as though he could do the same thing in that moment. If this was but a taste, what was it like to be a true immortal?

"Will you eat, lord?" Gelu asked, approaching and holding out a length of dried beef.

"You are a loyal man, Gelu," Kreuhesh said, chewing on the meat until it loosened up enough to swallow. "You have served me well."

"I am honoured to serve you, lord." Gelu cuffed his mouth before continuing. "And the god."

Kreuhesh stared at him. "Who did you serve before we took

you?"

"I'm Meldhonu Clan, lord. You know Koss the Boar, my chief? My old chief, I mean."

"He refused to bow to the god. You were one of his warriors."

Gelu nodded. "I was nothing before the god came through. I am an eighth son and my father was no great man. No great warrior. Good hunter but never killed many men before you honoured me, lord."

Kreuhesh shook his head. "You are the best man with a spear I have ever seen. I saw your worth. The god sees. No man should serve a weak chief or one who is blinded by lies and refuses to see a god when one is before him. And no man is beholden to brothers and fathers who do not see his worth." Kreuhesh took a deep breath. "Rest now, Gelu. You must all ride again before dawn."

"I can stand watch, lord, if you would like to sleep."

"Do as your lord commands, Gelu, if you value your life."

Gelu bobbed his head. "Yes, lord."

In the darkness, his thoughts ran to his own father and elder brothers. Or rather, his half-brothers. His father had whelped Kreuhesh on a herder girl he had stolen on a raid. Apparently she had been well-built but ignorant and very young and she had died when Kreuhesh was so small that he did not remember her at all. His father had been chief of the clan and claimed descent from Hasak of Dhonu a son of Ekwa, one of the horse gods. Despite that, the clan was small and had to fight constantly to retain their patch of territory between the forest, the plain, and the river valley below the distant mountains of the north.

His father's other sons were cruel, bitter men, jealous of Kreuhesh's size and strength from his youngest days. His brothers would steal his portions of food and mock him, saying he had eaten enough already. They would call him a worthless herder and command him to serve them. Always he would fight but they were older and even if he got the best of one, another would join in against Kreuhesh. The women of the clan were crueller even than the boys and the wives of his father were worst of all. They denied him access to their tents and forbade him from eating their food. When he was driven by hunger and anger to stealing food from the clan's stores he would be caught as often as not and then his father would beat him bloody.

"Fetch the stick," his father would say to one son or another and they would bring to him the thick spear shaft he used to discipline them. It was shiny and blood stained from decades of use.

When his brothers were taken into the woods for their training, Kreuhesh had often followed them, keen to learn hunting and fighting. But he was always caught in the end and beaten bloody.

"You have the spirit of a herder," his father said when Kreuhesh was twelve years old and desperate to accompany the men on a raid as his brothers and some of the other boys were doing. "It is for you to lead the cattle on the plain in summer and to cut wood in winter. Submit to your nature and accept your place."

"I am a warrior," Kreuhesh had protested. "I would one day take my place in the *tauta*."

His father had sneered at that. "You are too clumsy to be a warrior. You have the look of your mother and you have her spirit in you." His father ran a hand over his eyes. "I should have left you for the wolves when your mother died but I was weak and the gods have punished my weakness by afflicting you with madness. Go see to my cattle!"

Instead, he had taken a horse and ridden after the war band as it went south on a long raid. When he was caught his father had watched in silence while his brothers beat him until his bones had broken and the blood flowed from his wounds. They left him to die and went on with the raid, taking his horse.

Kreuhesh had not died. He had made his way home. He had made his own spear and learnt to hunt and trap by himself and eventually he had eaten as well as any of them. In time, the men of the clan developed a reluctant respect for him and even feared him a little for he was one who dwelled apart. Some assumed because of this that he could read the signs and asked him to interpret them which he often did, though his interpretations were usually dire.

The women of the clan, though, never respected him even when he was a full-grown man. If anything they became more repulsed by his presence, even if he bathed in the river first and tied his hair into a knot above his right ear. To speak to them at all he would have to watch, unseen, until they were alone or in pairs and he would get close before they noticed him. Often he would watch them as they went to the river to fetch water or to bathe and then he would go to them when they could not swiftly flee. Herder girls would sometimes let him kiss them and touch them but they were cowardly and easily hurt and he found them contemptible weaklings.

"You are like a wild animal, Kreuhesh. Wild and untameable like a bear. I see now that the gods meant for you to be a seer," his father said on one of the last times they spoke. "And that is why they stayed my hand when I should have exposed you."

"The gods mean for me to be a warrior," Kreuhesh had replied, looking down at his father now and angrier than he had ever been. "That is my spirit and my flesh. I will be a man of the *tauta* and I will take a good wife and lead raids and spill the blood of my enemies onto the earth."

His response had angered his father but by then there was no bigger or stronger man in their clan than Kreuhesh and he had not called for someone to fetch the stick.

When Leuhon had come down from the Sacred Mountain, his father and brothers and the other men had called him a demon, a false god, and a *yotunan*. But Leuhon had defeated them with such ease that Kreuhesh had known the truth at once. No being of such might could be anything but a god. While his beaten father and brothers lay broken in the snow beneath the pines, Kreuhesh had emerged from hiding, walked to the god, and bowed.

"I will serve you, lord," Kreuhesh had said.

His wounded father had cursed him and said Kreuhesh was never his son and promised nothing but evil would ever come to him.

The god had smiled. "Slay these men and you may serve me."

His hands shaking, Kreuhesh had picked up his father's stone war hammer. For so long, he had dreamed of killing him and the others but had never had the courage. Now, with Leuhon looking on, he raised the hammer over his head and brought it down, crushing his father's skull. While his brothers screamed, Kreuhesh had laughed.

"Lord?" the shadow said softly, disturbing his dreams. "You were... speaking in your sleep."

"Gelu," Kreuhesh said, sitting up and looking around. In an instant he was wide awake, feeling the power of the god in his limbs and in his mind. But he felt ashamed for falling asleep and foolish also.

"It is almost sunrise, lord," Gelu said. "I kept watch while you rested. Now I shall wake the others."

"You are a good man, Gelu."

There was great relief on his face. "Lord."

The river ran swiftly on and they rode with it, searching the bank for sign of anyone or anything at all. Copses they searched and abandoned places that stood here and there. Shepherd's huts, stone enclosures, hunter's shelters.

His men began casting sidelong glances at him, waiting for his anger at their continued failure to burst forth. But Kreuhesh merely continued to direct the search. In his heart, though, the frustration was building and he could feel the beginnings of desperation on the horizon. Leuhon had given him the power to accomplish anything and was offering the greatest prize imaginable if only he could complete this task. If he never found their bodies then what would happen to him? Would he never be offered immortality again? Would Leuhon punish him? Would some other warrior take his place?

These thoughts grew to fill his mind throughout the day as the men continued to search. Kreuhesh told them to spread out further and to ride faster and away they went again riding with the river on their left and dismounting when they had to. The lower ground was often crossed with streams and wide patches of marsh.

Then they smelled smoke coming from a dense part of the woodland close by the river and rode back to him at a gallop to tell him.

Kreuhesh soon smelt it on the air but doubted it was Alkmene.

"Why would they build a fire?" he asked. "Even the sons are old enough to know better."

Horghis shrugged. "Drying themselves out. Cold today."

Weben agreed. "Women suffer always with cold. Probably she complains and the boys do whatever their mother says."

Not Alkmene, Kreuhesh thought. But he ordered his men to spread out and to go in on foot with their spears ready while he advanced behind. The sons were both dangerous despite their youth and it would be best to be cunning about their capture. "Kill none of them," he reminded his warriors before they set off. "Break their limbs if you must but no killing."

The undergrowth was thick with new growth in the woodland and they were far enough from any *briya* that where trees had fallen they lay rotting and covered with mould. It almost reminded him of the wooded valleys of his home and he looked for signs of boar as he walked. When I am lord of Pelhbriya I will rule over pasture and woodland and I will spend my days hunting boar and my nights with a dozen women. He smirked as he thought of it but then a shout from ahead brought him running, crashing through the trees until he found his men surrounding their prey.

A single warrior of about forty years with a young boy around seven looking terrified. They had a small fire and were skinning a young buck. Its carcass hung from a branch, twisting slowly. The man's hands were bloody but he had dropped his flint knife. A wood axe, bow, arrows, and two spears lay on the ground beside the fire.

Sighing, Kreuhesh advanced through the ring of his warriors while the man stepped in front of the boy.

"What are you doing here?" Kreuhesh asked the man. "This is

Leuhon's land."

"Just showing the boy the ways," the man said, shaking with fear and trying not to show it. "Singing him our songs."

Nodding, Kreuhesh looked at the half-skinned buck. "Where did you come from? Are you of Nemiyeh?"

"From there," he said, jerking his hand toward the river. "I am of the Heryos. We winter high on the Piksos."

"Down your river and across the Denipa? But why come here?"

The man frowned. "We have always come here. This is where my father brought me. Teach me the river. Teach me the trees."

Kreuhesh nodded. He could understand that. "This is your son?"

"Brother's boy. My own sons died."

"How did they die?"

Anger flared in the man's eyes and he had to unclench his jaw before answering. "Raiders come through not long ago. Lot of raiders."

Kreuhesh stroked his chin, seeing the rage and the grief and the fear in the man's eyes. The god's gift made the smallest details incredibly clear. The man's neck flushed red and he breathed faster. His pupils shrank and he shook almost imperceptibly. Kreuhesh knew that the man meant to either fight him or to run. Probably he would go for his spear and tell the boy to run for the river. Neither would live more than a few moments no matter what happened, no matter what the man chose.

"I was amongst those raiding your lands. Perhaps I killed your sons."

The man shook and when he spoke his voice was tight. "Perhaps you did."

Kreuhesh leaned forward and smiled. "Would you like to kill me?"

"If you killed them, I would." The man glanced down at the terrified boy and back to Kreuhesh. "You serve the demon, don't you?"

Though his men growled their anger, Kreuhesh smiled again, for he appreciated the man's courage. He was resigned to his fate and the fear was melting from him like snow in spring. "The river is wide," Kreuhesh said, his tone mild. "How is it that you cross?"

The man hesitated before answering. "The ford, downstream a ways, across to the long island with the alder. Other side it is deeper. No ford there so I use my boat, pole across to the bank. Where we can we pole upstream in the shallows and across the marsh or else we carry it. That way we get back to the Piksos."

A ford almost across the river to an island covered in trees. Is that where you are, Alkmene?

Kreuhesh smiled no longer. "Tell me this one thing truthfully and I will release you and your boy. Have you seen a woman and two young men by the river?"

The man frowned. "Not seen anyone."

Taking a step forward, Kreuhesh took a long dagger from his belt looked down at the shaking man. "You should know that if you lie to me, I will kill the boy right now."

His eyes flicked between the dagger and Kreuhesh's face. "I never told a lie in my life and I will not do so now. On my word, in the name of the gods, in the name of Kolnos, I seen no women, no men. Just us."

Kreuhesh stroked his chin as he looked at the man's eyes and the creases in the corner of his mouth. "I believe you."

The man's relief lasted but a moment before Kreuhesh drove his dagger beneath his chin, punching the tip into the brain. With a twist he yanked the blade out and the man fell into the leaf litter.

Behind him the boy screamed in a wordless cry of anguish and rage and he threw himself toward the spears on the ground. Hedwol was closest and he stepped forward and thrust his spear into the boy's guts, pinning him to the earth. The boy wailed, clutching at the spear shaft.

"Kill him!" Kreuhesh snarled.

Hedwol jerked his spear free and drove it into the boy's chest.

Kreuhesh turned on Hedwol. "What is wrong with you?" he said. "They were harmless. They were good people." He looked around at all of his men. "You kill children quickly, you understand?" They all nodded and he scoffed. "Come on."

He pushed through the small campsite and continued through the trees, heading for the river. When he reached the rushing water he went downstream, looking for the ford across the river.

"You think they got out on the other side, lord?" Horghis said, coming up beside him to look at the rushing water and the wooded banks beyond.

"When I was a boy, I caught a beaver in one of our traps. As I pulled it out to skin it, the thing wriggled free and slipped into the water. My father told me I could not come home without it and so I went to where the creature lived and pulled its house apart, piece by piece."

"Lord?"

Kreuhesh spoke over the sound of the river. "The woman and her sons are Heryos of the plains, Horghis. If they are alive then they are there."

482

2 9

F i r e

"I CHALLENGE!" HERKUHLOS repeated, holding his makeshift spear aloft as the warriors galloped toward him.

He glanced behind him to see Belolukos half-dragging Alkmene back toward the relative safety of the trees. If they kept going they could still hope to lose the riders in the wood and make it to the marsh and the river without being caught.

His heart hammered in his chest as the riders crossed the ground toward him. They began whooping and brandishing their weapons over their heads as they closed the distance. The earth shook with the drumming of hooves. They spread out as they came up. Most encircled him without stopping while a couple more rode on to the edge of the wood and called out jeers at Belolukos and Alkmene who retreated deeper into the trees.

Mighty Kolnos, Herkuhlos thought as he fought to control his fear, give me strength.

"Who is your leader?" Herkuhlos shouted over the jeers of the riders that circled him. "My name is Herkuhlos and I challenge your leader to cross spears with me."

"Look at this," one of them called. "It is a sapling holding a sapling!"

The others laughed and mocked him for his useless weapon.

"Why would I allow a challenge from you, boy," one man said, riding slowly closer and stopping before him while the horse tossed its head. "You're no chief. You're no *koryonos*."

"But I am," Herkuhlos replied. "I am leader of a war band."

"What," the man said, gesturing at the woods, "that other boy and the old woman?" He laughed and the others laughed with him. "Do not tell me that's your mother, boy. That is not a war band, that is your kinfolk. And you're nought but a wet bow cord."

The rest of the band rode around and around, grinning and laughing. One man rode closer and shook his war axe at Herkuhlos before swerving away.

Soon they will tire of this and then they will kill me.

"If I am nothing then why not fight me?" Herkuhlos said.

"Because it demeans me, boy," the man said. He was a tall man, sitting straight atop his horse with a faint look of amusement on his features. There were tattoos covering his muscled arms and more across his face and neck. His long hair was tied into a large knot on the side of his head.

This man is a true warrior. A dangerous foe.

Herkuhlos raised his voice so that all of them would hear him over their cries. "Only a coward declines a challenge."

The man's face fell. "No man who knows my name would call me a coward." He shrugged. "So I am not insulted. You are a brave one, I give you that. Or are you just desperate? You hungry, boy, is that it? Go and hunt in the woods. You can set traps, can't you? Leave us be or I will kill you."

"I cannot hunt as I am being hunted myself," Herkuhlos said, glancing over his shoulder. He cursed to see his mother and brother still at the edge of the wood looking back at him. "I am being hunted by the *yotunan*. The demons. If you serve the demon Leuhon then you should accept my challenge and take me back to him."

They turned back. "You escaped him, did you?"

"I raided him," Herkuhlos said, standing tall. "And his warriors will come for me."

The man's face hardened. "You raided Leuhon? How did you do this?"

Herkuhlos fixed his eyes upon the mounted man. He would not flinch. "I set fire to Nemiyeh and while they were distracted I went within and killed a score of his men. Also I freed one of his captives and got away. Now he will be hunting me."

The warriors scoffed and jeered until their leader silenced them with a look.

"You are a liar, sapling. And it is because of your lies that I will accept your challenge.

He will fight me. But he thinks me a weakling. "If you had been there last night, you would have fallen to my spear as did your friends." Herkuhlos held out his arms. "Now I give you the chance to avenge them."

The man sneered, unimpressed. "Did you kill them with that twig?" He looked at the man next to him. "Give the sapling your spear."

All the riders moved back but one who leaned down to hand his spear warily to Herkuhlos before riding away.

The leader dismounted and pushed his horse's rump so that it walked away, taking his spear from the loops on its harness.

"What did you say your name was, sapling?"

"Herkuhlos. Yours?"

"I am Korvic, son of Tornu. You know my name?"

"No."

"No?" Korvic shrugged. "Ah, well. Are you ready to die, Herkuhlos?"

His arms were weak and his stomach empty. The man across from him stood with the easy stance of a trained and seasoned warrior and he would know moves of attack and defence that Herkuhlos would not.

But if the gods are with me then I will have over him my strength and my speed. And my will to be victorious.

Korvic thrust his spear forward, darting it rapidly high or low with each thrust. Herkuhlos stepped back and sideways, ducking and blocking with his borrowed spear. The older man knew more tricks and feints but Herkuhlos stepped inside the spear point and batted the shaft aside and drove the spearhead into Korvic's arm, slicing through the flesh below the shoulder.

Grunting with the pain, his eyes wide with surprise, Korvic leapt back and swung his spear at Herkuhlos' head, chopping it in a tight arc that would have felled any man. But Herkuhlos ducked the blow and thrust his own spear shaft between his enemy's legs and twisted it, tripping him up. As Korvic was already moving backwards his momentum brought him down and he fell hard onto his back, his arms flailing wide and Herkuhlos was over him with the point of his spear against his neck.

For a moment, there was silence but for the blood pounding in his ears.

"All I want," Herkuhlos said, breathing hard. "Is three horses." He looked around at the mounted men staring open mouthed at him. "And some food, if you have any."

Korvic looked more surprised than angry. "You shall have the horses. But if you want food then you will have to eat them."

Herkuhlos glanced around at the scowling mounted warriors. "You swear that you will stand by your words? If I let you up you will not harm me and my people?"

Slapping the spear point away, Korvic scowled. "I have spoken it, have I not?"

"Speak it again." He jerked his head. "Loudly, so they all can hear."

"You and your people will not be harmed by me or by my men. I will give you three horses and you will ride away unharmed, I swear it in sight of the gods." Korvic scowled. "You won, sapling. Now, stand aside."

After hesitating a moment, Herkuhlos nodded and put up his spear as he stepped back.

Korvic stood up, his head hanging low in his shame. "You are a fast one, sapling. And stronger than you look."

"Herkuhlos. My name is Herkuhlos."

Korvic looked around at his men. "Herkuhlos." He nodded. "We will remember it. Come, join us for a while." He turned and walked toward his grazing horse.

Herkuhlos looked at the woodland where Alkmene and Belolukos stood in shadow. Even at this distance he could see Bel's grin. "Give me the horses and we will go. As agreed."

Turning back to him, Korvic spread his tattooed arms wide. "I make an invitation, fast one. There will be no treachery here." He looked at his men for a moment. They sat on their horses in silence, their faces grim. "You are hunted by the *yotunan?*" He slapped his chest. "We also are hunted by the *yotunan*. Perhaps you can tell us your story and we can tell you ours. Come. Bring your mighty war band from the trees there. You shall be my guest, Herkuhlos, and we shall share meat and water and none of us shall commit treachery or we will be cursed by the gods as oath breakers."

"I thought you had no food."

Korvic snorted a laugh. "We will let you eat with us if you tell me how you move so fast. Did you see him, brothers? He was as fast as fire." He turned back. "Oh and keep Ker's spear. You won it, I would say."

With that they walked their horses back toward the mound. Thinking for a moment, Herkuhlos waved for Belolukos and Alkmene to come out. They hurried across the open ground to him and he explained what Korvic had said.

"We cannot trust them," Alkmene replied, hardly letting him finish. "They will kill you boys and try to take me."

"I do not agree," Herkuhlos said. "They could have killed us all already if they wished it but they offer us food. We need food. We must stay strong. Come, mother. Trust me."

Alkmene looked from him to Belolukos. "What do you think?"

Belolukos shrugged and gestured to Herkuhlos' new spear. "It seems that the gods are with him on this."

She did not like it but she allowed them to lead her across the meadow to the shadow of the wide, low mound where Korvic and his warriors lounged once more in the long, trampled grass.

"You truly raided Leuhon?" Korvic asked as they sat by him. He passed Herkuhlos a waterskin and a leather pouch packed with dried horsemeat. These Herkuhlos passed to his mother.

"We did," Herkuhlos said, nodding at Belolukos. "Our mother and sister were captives. We got mother out."

"Ah," Korvic said, smirking. "So your war band is merely your kinfolk after all." He looked at Alkmene. She had been washed down a river and lost in a wood. Her hair was wild, her face dirty, and her clothes were stained and torn but her beauty was there beneath it all. "You are a woman worth risking all for, it seems."

She lifted her chin as she stared unflinchingly back at him. "And what manner of man are you, Korvic?"

He pursed his lips, returning her gaze for a moment. His men looked on impassively. Korvic shrugged. "Your son thought that I served the *yotunan*. Well, in a way I suppose that he was right."

Belolukos' head jerked up and he glared at Korvic while Herkuhlos slowly reached for his spear. Korvic stared impassively back at them and his warriors made no move. Slowly, they relaxed.

"You do not serve Leuhon," Alkmene said. "I think I would recognise you if you did."

He smiled. "Yes, women do not easily forget Korvic." Some of his men chuckled. "No, I did not serve Leuhon. After our clan was attacked we were enslaved by the Stag. You know him?"

Alkmene nodded. "How could I not? He has great antlers growing from his head."

The warriors laughed and Korvic waved a hand to silence them. "We do not laugh at you, woman, but at ourselves. Once, we believed his antlers were his. After all that is what his acolytes told us and why would we not believe it? A demon with antlers growing from his head. Why not?" He snorted. "After serving him a while we saw it was a deer skull he has tied to his head with strong leather straps. At night, his acolytes remove this great headdress and lay it by his side. He calls himself a god but he is a deceiver and a devourer."

"You ran from him," Belolukos said, chewing now on a piece of dried meat.

Korvic turned to him. "He slaughtered our people and brought us here. We survived that journey by serving him. But now we shall go home."

"Why?" Herkuhlos asked. "What happened?"

"Nothing happened. When there were hundreds of warriors and all the other demons together there was little chance for flight. But since the Stag went off on his own there were fewer other warriors to watch us and I knew it was time. Then we were sent on a raid to bring him more slaves." Korvic's expression darkened. "More blood to feed his hunger. But we rode hard away from him and we shall not return. That is all."

"What of the other *yotunan*?" Alkmene asked. "Some went south before we crossed the river but after we crossed Leuhon took us north along this bank while the others went on."

Korvic nodded at her. "They kept fighting with each other. Arguing and fighting ceaselessly, none would follow the others. There is a river southwest of here even wider than this one but it runs from west to east. Most of the demons turned south then and crossed it but not all. The Stag said he would go on and on, driving his slaves to the rim of the earth where it meets the endless sea in the west. And there he would rule."

490

"Are you afraid he will come for you?"

"I fear nothing," Korvic said, flatly. "There is nothing that can be done to me that has not been done already. But the Stag will not come for us. He drives ever westward, destroying all he finds and enslaving these strange peoples."

"Why?" Herkuhlos asked, shaking his head. "Why do they do this?"

Korvic looked at him as if he was simple minded. "They are evil, lad. They are *yotunan*. They are *dura*. It is what they do. It is all they are."

"They call themselves gods," Herkuhlos asked. "Why do they do that?"

"They are all mad and they are all deceitful. The *yotunan* are liars. They turn truth upside down."

His answer did not satisfy Herkuhlos but he did not know why.

"You mean to cross the river now?" Alkmene asked. "Where do you go after that?"

"East and north and north and east all the way to home on the River Herdus." Korvic looked at her, smiling. "Do you have a husband, woman?"

"Do not speak to my mother," Belolukos snapped.

"It is well," Alkmene said to him without taking her eyes off Korvic. "My husband was slain by Leuhon."

His smile wavered. "My wives were slain by the Stag Demon and the Boar." His men were listening closely, their eyes dark with rage and loss. "My spear-brothers also. Our women and our daughters slain for their blood by the Serpent, the Stag Demon, and the Boar." When he looked up at Alkmene his eyes were damp. "Did you see the Bull?"

Alkmene snorted mirthlessly. "The demon with the aurochs pelt over his head? I saw him."

Korvic nodded. "He is the worst of them."

His men protested. "The Dog Demon is stronger. More dangerous."

"Kerberos?" Korvic waved a hand. "We are free of them all now."

Herkuhlos frowned, looking at the warriors. "These demons have slain your women but kept you alive? That is not how it was with us. They killed our men and took the women."

Narrowing his eyes, Korvic scratched his tattooed cheek. "What are you saying, boy?"

"I am no boy," he shot back. "I am asking how you came to be captured and not killed in a fight?"

Korvic snorted. "We were killed. My father, my brothers. By the time me and the men here rode back from our hunt we found our women captured. Perhaps we should have fled but we could not abandon them. The demons took us. One by one they killed our women for their blood but kept us to do their bidding. But no more."

Herkuhlos shook his head. He could not believe they would allow the *yotunan* to do all of that only to flee for their lives.

But is that not what I am doing?

"You could come with us, you know," Korvic said, looking at Alkmene. "When I get home, I will need to take more wives. You can be the first of them."

Herkuhlos and Belolukos felt insulted but the question had been asked casually enough and was not meant to offend and so they sat grumbling for a moment before their mother answered.

492

"When I return to my own people, I will find a husband," she looked him up and down. "One who is worthy."

Korvic stared and his men scowled.

Then Korvic scoffed. "You think you are special, woman? You think to reject me? You who has nothing but your long years."

Alkmene silenced her sons with a hard look and smiled at Korvic. "I have the blood of my ancestors in me. I have the strength of my body and the wisdom of these long years. And I have sons strong enough to knock you onto your backside. I have everything I need."

Korvic laughed and slapped his thigh. "I think I want her more than ever, brothers."

"What about our horses?" Belolukos said, growing angry.

Korvic looked up at the darkening sky and nodded. "Three horses, as I said."

He spoke to his men and shortly they separated three of their mares and brought them forward. One was going lame with a swollen knee and another had some sort of weeping sore in its left eye that smelt bad.

"You asked for three horses. Here are three horses." Korvic shrugged, laughed, and slapped Herkuhlos on the back. "Next time be more careful with your words."

Belolukos was angry and wanted to argue and Alkmene wanted them to demand good horses but what Korvic said was true. The warrior had fulfilled his oath and Herkuhlos knew he should have been more specific. The songs of the ancestors were filled with stories of men who had come to bad ends due to badly worded oaths.

"It is fair," Herkuhlos said. He looked toward the setting sun.

"We must find our companions. It is possible that they will come this way."

"You will not find them in the dark. And they will not find you. Why not stay here tonight? We will leave for the river at dawn but tonight we will go inside the wall there for the night and light a fire."

"Is that safe?" Alkmene asked. "Leuhon's men will also be looking for us."

Korvic shrugged. "The stone wall around the top of the mound is not high but it will hide the light of the fire. No one will find you."

Herkuhlos nodded. "We will stay here and keep watch for Kasos and the others tomorrow."

His mother's face darkened. "Leuhon's men could find us first."

"Then we will fight," Herkuhlos said. "We will not abandon our spear-brothers out of fear."

"You mean you will not abandon Helhena," Belolukos said, raising his eyebrows.

"I mean all of them."

"Are you risking all of us because of a woman?" Alkmene said.

"No," Herkuhlos replied and walked away from them to the top of the mound. The houses and animal pens within were no more than burnt ruins, the black timbers lying jumbled in piles. It was a cursed place and he walked through it to the drystone wall on the north side. It was chest height there and he climbed atop it to look at the trees in the distance beyond the pastures and fields with long shadows lying like spears across them. Birds circled high while others flew through the treetops to their roosts. Through the trees to the east was the river. Close enough to make a run for it if they had to, even with a lame horse. He would put his mother on the best mare and give Bel the one with an infected eye. If the last horse could not run then Herkuhlos could dismount and run for the river or he could hold off pursuit while the others made for the Denipa.

But that was only if Leuhon's men found them before Kasos and the others did.

He watched the northern horizon as the sun lowered to the west.

"Where are you, Kasos?" he muttered. "You cannot be dead, brother. It is your destiny to sing of our deeds."

When darkness fell he stayed there watching for any light and listening for the sound of hooves. His thoughts drifted to Helhena. Would he ever see her again? Had she even escaped from Nemiyeh after setting the fire?

They had spent so much time with each other but he had squandered it and now he may well never see her again. From the first time he met her she had attached herself to him. He had known she was merely trying to protect herself by doing so but she had always seemed to believe that he was special. Even before she had known he was godborn.

"Come and warm yourself by the fire," Alkmene said softly from behind him. She came closer to the wall and looked up at him. "They will not be riding at night."

"I must keep watch in case they are."

She took half a step closer. "Do you truly believe that they will find us? Even if they have not already been captured, this land is vast. The river is long. There are woodlands and vales everywhere that could hide a thousand men. We could pass either side of a hill and never know each other was there. How long can we afford to look before our enemies find us?"

"I must do everything I can to find them. What kind of man would I be if I did not?"

"A chief must make hard decisions. He must decide what is best for the whole clan. And now your clan is us. Your brother and your mother. We are all that are left."

He heard the break in her voice. She had always been strong. When he was young he had almost been afraid of her hardness and her unflinching justice. Whenever he and his brother had argued as children she had punished them both. Her message was always the same. Fight not at all or resolve it between yourselves. Even after their seventh year when they left her tent to begin their rites of passage to manhood he had remembered her lessons. As he got older he had realised that his mother was respected by the other women but she was not liked by most of them. She was an outsider from a grand lineage who had stooped to wed their chief only because she was half cursed by her godborn child.

Herkuhlos leapt down from his place on the wall and embraced her. After resisting for a moment she put her arms around him in turn. She felt small to him now.

"All will be well, mother."

She pushed herself away from him and touched his cheek so that he looked down at her. "Wishing for something does not make it so. A leader must make decisions."

"After dawn if they are not here we will make for the ford. We will ride with Korvic and his men for the time being. Perhaps all the way across the plain. They will help to protect us with their numbers and I will protect you from them. Bel and I both will."

Alkmene sighed. "It is the right choice. Come to the fire now.

Warm yourself."

"I am not cold," he said but allowed himself to be led there.

Soon, all of them were sleeping but Herkuhlos lay awake on his back staring at the stars behind the clouds. There seemed to be lumps everywhere beneath him and no matter how he shifted he was not comfortable. Sitting up he stoked the fire and lay more wood upon the embers. Soon, the flames roared and warmed him.

The eastern sky was touched with colour. It was almost morning.

Would the gods bring Kasos and the others to him?

They were sworn to him and he was sworn to protect them. Would the gods bring them together?

Looking up at the stars, he knew suddenly that they would not find him. By doing nothing he was being cowardly. By doing nothing he was ensuring he abandoned his friends. After everything he had done he still felt like a failure. His sister had been killed before his eyes. Saving his mother had cost the lives of so many others.

What was more, he had sworn to Kolnos himself that he would slay the *yotunan*. He had spoken the words and yet he had run from Leuhon instead of fighting. If he had faced the *yotunan* he would have died. But he would have kept his word. By fleeing he had abandoned his oath and so the gods would not reward him. If anything he would be punished.

He feared being caught by the warriors of Leuhon but that fear was also keeping Kasos, Makros, and Helhena from him. By lacking the will to act he was compounding his failure to face Leuhon when he had the chance. He was breaking his oaths all over again.

After all his failures, the least he could do was to try to find his friends. If they yet lived then they would be out there searching for him in the lands all around, riding from north to south, but his mother had been right. How would they ever know where he was unless the gods led them to one another?

Herkuhlos stared into the fire, looking for the answer.

And it came to him.

Deciding, he tied together two bundles of long sticks. One of the men lifted a head and looked at him while he worked but turned over and went back to sleep. When his bundles were tied, Herkuhlos took a burning stick from the fire and took it and his bundles to the north section of wall and climbed up. He lit the twigs and stood with one bundle in each hand, waving them up and down over his head. The flames roared as they burned bright, dropping tiny coals and sending showers of sparks up into the black sky.

There came a commotion behind him and cries of alarm.

"What is he doing?" Korvic cried.

Belolukos woke and leapt up, running to intercept Korvic and the other men, brandishing Herkuhlos' new spear. "Stay away from my brother!"

Korvic jabbed a finger. "He will bring the servants of the demon down on us!"

Belolukos stood with his back to the wall and held his spear ready. "Leave him be."

"It is nearly dawn," Alkmene said, coming up upon them. Her voice was calm but as hard as polished stone. "It is time for you to go to the river."

"We are going," Korvic said, spitting on the earth. He pointed his finger at all three of them. "You put the lives of my men in danger."

"You are right," Herkuhlos said from the wall. "And I apologise. But this had to be done."

Korvic's men were already packing up their camp. "This is not how guests behave."

Another oath betrayed. Will I be punished for this?

"I wish you well, Korvic," Herkuhlos replied, the bundles burning out. He dropped them still burning to the top of the wall.

Korvic spat once more and went for his horse. His men rode for the river in the predawn light, the hooves of their horses drumming softly and fading as they entered the woodland. Soon, colour began to creep back into the world and still there was no sign of Kasos and the others on the horizon. Singing birds flitted through distant branches. Herkuhlos stared at the trees, walking back and forth atop the wall, looking west, north, east, even south. Nothing.

"We must flee now," Alkmene said.

"It did not work," Belolukos said, irritated. "And it never would have done. Why would they have been looking this way before dawn? If I were Kasos, I would have crossed the river by now."

"And how will we find them across the river if we cannot find them now?"

Belolukos shrugged. "The longer we stay the more likely we are to die."

"Is that all that matters?" Herkuhlos asked. "Living and dying?"

Belolukos stared at him. "Of course it is not but what else did we come all this way for?" He pointed at their mother. "We have her now. Finally, we have her. And now we must go."

"I know that we must," Herkuhlos admitted. He touched his chest. "But I feel that we must not. The gods want me to fight, Bel.

I feel it."

Belolukos climbed upon the wall. "That is the immortal part of you, brother. And yet the mortal part wishes you to live." He gestured to himself and Alkmene. "Listen to your mortal side, brother."

Herkuhlos nodded slowly, thinking how right his brother was.

Alkmene stepped forward. "You do know what these warriors are capable of. They are evil. Leuhon is evil. He will send Kreuhesh the Bloodletter after me, I know it. You cannot fight him. Do not give up your life for this when you will have the rest of your days to find glory. It is time to go."

"I remember what you said to Korvic, mother, and I too have the blood of my ancestors in me. Would they have fled from what they had sworn? What if Perseyus have gone home when his men were slain by the acolytes of the servant demon? No one would sing of his glory."

Alkmene's shoulders dropped and she ran her hand over her face. "I just want to go home."

He felt a lump growing in his throat at that. Never had he seen her look so tired or sound like an ordinary woman. Of course she wanted to go home. But there was nothing in the Vale of the Kweitos River for them. Nothing but the graves of the dead. Home may have been a place but it was nothing without the people that belonged to it.

"Mother, I—"

"By Kolnos," Belolukos muttered from the wall. "Look."

Herkuhlos stood beside his brother and followed his gaze to the distant trees. Shapes moved in the shadows between the trunks and branches, approaching swiftly. "Riders."

"Enemy?" Alkmene asked.

"It is them," Belolukos said, a grin spreading across his face. He waved his spear overhead. "Kasos, Makros, and Helhena. They see us! They are coming here."

The three of them rode hard from the shadows of the woodland into the dawn light of the meadow.

At the sight of them Herkuhlos likewise waved his arms over his head, his face hurting from the size of his grin. The gods had heard him. They had seen his actions and rewarded him.

Alkmene climbed up beside them, a frown on her face. "Something is wrong," she said. "They are panicked."

Herkuhlos looked again. The frantic riding that he had taken as joy on their part was in fact a desperate gallop and their horses laboured, running with tired strides. There were no spare horses with them now, only the three that they rode. Their entire herd was gone, along with the supplies and weapons they carried.

"They are fleeing from someone," he said.

As he spoke, more riders burst forth from the treeline and galloped into the meadow close behind the three tired horses.

It was a warband. Hooves drummed upon the earth as the nine enemy warriors whooped with their weapons held high.

Belolukos stopped waving. "Ride!" he shouted.

Herkuhlos shook his head. "They are not going to make it."

3 0

Immortality

IT TOOK KREUHESH the rest of the day to get the horses across
the ford, through the wooded island, and across the deeper channel
to the other bank. Once through the trees there and riding to the
top of a long rise in the ground, they could see a wide pasture
leading into the distance. At the horizon the ground rose to a wide
ridge. Kreuhesh's elation at crossing the river was replaced with
despair when he considered the size of the plains. It was possible
they were already far from him, lost in the endless grasslands and if
that was true then he would have failed Leuhon. And in failing him
he would never be granted his reward. Immortality was in his grasp
and yet it was slowly slipping through his fingers.

"You will find them," he snarled at his wet and tired men.
"Search the bank, north and south. Find their tracks. Find them!"

Half the men went one way and half the other but the light was
soon fading and they made camp in the trees. All night long

Kreuhesh cursed himself for not bringing more men. He wondered whether he should send someone back to Nemiyeh to summon more to the search but that was close to admitting failure and he could not risk his chance at immortality.

Well before dawn he had his men up and searching once more, this time taking them all south along the riverbank looking for the bodies of Alkmene and her sons or signs of their passing.

Their efforts were rewarded when the men found the tracks of a dozen horses in the soft, shingly mud of a sloping beach on the outer curve of a bend in the river. There were sandbanks out in the river, dividing it there into many smaller channels and it was easy to see it as a good crossing place. Horses could be swum across and rested on the sandbanks in between.

"Their war band must have found them, lord," Gelu said, calling from the sloping mud to Kreuhesh up on the bank. "The one that escaped from Nemiyeh. Crossed the river like we did and found the woman. You can see the footprints as well as the hooves. Must be six people at least here."

"The tracks," Kreuhesh said from atop his horse, his heart pounding. "Fresh?"

Gelu shrugged. "A day?"

"Less than that," Host said, correcting him. He poked a pile of horse dung with a stick. "They were here this morning."

They raced after their prey away from the river over undulating soft ground until the sun was high. There, on a low hill on a rise just beyond the one they stood on, was a little stone enclosure. Once, it would have protected the houses of two or three families and their animals but it had been destroyed, as so many places had been when the gods had come through on their great sojourn.

"Smoke," Weben said, pointing. "The fools have lit a fire."

"Something moving beyond the wall," Horghis said.

"A horse, I reckon," Wedhris said, grinning.

"Do we wait until dark, lord?" Gelu asked.

This is it. I will capture Alkmene and the godborn son and return them to Leuhon. Let him have Alkmene if he wishes, why should I care about her if I am to become immortal?

His thoughts drifted. The god would make him into an immortal and then he would rule Pelhbriya for a thousand years. Or even to the very end of the world when the great destruction would come to all. And if he ruled one place then perhaps he would rule more. He would have strength enough to lead his warbands against other places and he would conquer them also and they would worship him as Leuhon was worshipped.

Leuhon would not like that, he knew. To reward a mortal with the gift of immortality was the greatest gift that the gods could bestow but he would not become a god and so always he would be subservient to Leuhon, no matter how much wealth and glory he brought to himself.

An idea sparked into flame.

Once the god had granted him immortality he would need Leuhon no longer. Could he truly slay the god? Not in a fair fight, of that he was certain. Not even with the god's blood could he match him for strength and even the gift of immortality would not change Kreuhesh's stature. But Kreuhesh had achieved everything he had through the strength of his will. He would have to strike the god when he was not looking. And he would have to have his men ready to help with the guardian warriors that were loyal to Leuhon and the acolytes would have to be slain but those were small details to be overcome later. Once Leuhon was out of the way then there was nothing to stop him from demanding worship from those he conquered.

He smiled to himself, seeing it clearly. There was a path ahead where Kreuhesh, the unwanted son of a herder slave would become a god.

All that he needed to do was to bring back Alkmene and the godborn son.

He wondered then what Leuhon wanted with the son. It made sense to want Alkmene but why the boy? Did he mean to offer the godborn his life in exchange for swearing an oath to serve Leuhon? And if so, what if the boy accepted? Was it possible that Leuhon intended to reward the boy with status as a warrior or worse to elevate him above Kreuhesh? Whatever Leuhon planned, having a godborn warrior around would be an unnecessary complication if Kreuhesh was to become a god.

Perhaps it would be better if both the sons were killed during the capture of the mother.

Kreuhesh turned to his men. "We take them now. Ready your weapons. They will flee when they see us. Hendros, Horghis, Host, Kelwos, you ride to the north." He pointed out each man. "Gelu, Kreps, Tweks, Hok, you ride with me. Melo, Wedhris, Hedwol, Weben, you ride to the south. Stop their flight. And remember!" He glared at each of them in turn. "Do not harm the woman. Kill the others."

Though he wished to gallop all the way, Kreuhesh fought to keep his horse at a walk to allow the others to get around the flanks. His eyes on the hill and the thin line of grey stone ringing the top, he thought of what he would say to Alkmene when he had her. He hoped she was alive. She was a beautiful, tall, strong woman and he had such desire for her that he would struggle to restrain himself in the face of her. Still, for all her beauty she was old and Kreuhesh would let Leuhon have her. For now, at least. When Leuhon was dead he could take her himself and perhaps she would bear his child instead.

Perhaps once Kreuhesh had her as a captive he could toy with her a little. He would have to be sure to leave no obvious marks upon her flesh and Kreuhesh could not lie with her. But surely he could squeeze her body and hurt her a little. It would be a joy to see her writhing in pain and he decided as he came closer to the enclosure that he would do it in the dark where the men could not see and then they would not be able to betray him to the god.

Unable to resist any longer, he began to ride faster and his four men raced to catch up. With his eyes fixed on the wall at the top of the hill, he held his spear ready and felt the handle of his axe slapping against his thigh. When they reached the base of the hill and their horses slowed, a head poked above the wall and disappeared again.

"For Leuhon!" Kreuhesh cried, throwing himself off his horse and rushing up the hill to the tumble of stones and the gap in the wall beyond. "For Leuhon!"

An arrow hissed by him as he ran and then another bow twanged and the arrow struck his head with a sharp crack, knocking him senseless for half a moment. His boar tusk helm had turned the arrow aside and saved his life.

Ahead, Gelu and his men were forcing their way through the wall into the enclosure. A rage built in him. He was supposed to be the first one in, not any of his followers. He had the god's power still in his blood and he would not be beaten by any mere mortal. Growling, he charged up and shouldered his way inside behind them.

There was a frantic battle taking place. His warriors fought a dozen men in a roar of shouts and weapons clashing and the screams of the dying. Spears thrust at them from all directions and two men standing atop the walls shooting down at Kreuhesh and his men with their bows.

Kreuhesh was confused.

Was this Alkmene's war band? How many men did her sons have with them? He peered around at the swirling mass of enemies. Alkmene was not among them and neither was the tall godborn son.

Kreuhesh knew then that he had made a mistake by charging in so suddenly. They were not Alkmene's men but some other warband out on a raid. Perhaps even the servants of some other god.

But it made no matter who they were now. Battle had been joined and the only way to end it was by victory. The god's power yet filled him and the rage at his own foolishness drove him on.

He thrust his spear into a man's face and swiftly ran it into the neck of the man beside him. Stepping forward he killed another with a thrust that shattered the man's ribs and drove him off his feet. Then he stepped through the gap he had created and turned on the others, crashing his axe into a man's skull.

Something punched into his leg and drove him to one knee. Growling, he forced himself to stand and looked down to see an arrow foreshaft sticking from his thigh. The bowman on the wall was already nocking another arrow but Kreuhesh launched his spear. It struck him in the guts and carried him off the wall.

Kreuhesh limped toward another cluster of fighting but the enemy warriors understood by then that they had lost the fight. After two more fell the remaining men fled for their horses. All were swiftly cut down in flight.

Suddenly, it was over.

Breathing heavily, Kreuhesh looked around the blackened timbers of the buildings inside the enclosure. "Search for the woman," he growled.

As he had well known, Alkmene was not there.

Kreuhesh ground his teeth and fought to control his rage. He wanted to kill his own men but he knew that it was he who was at fault. He had made poor decisions and now his chances of achieving immortality were rapidly diminishing. His leg began to throb so he grasped the arrow foreshaft and pulled. It was slick with blood and his hand kept slipping. Every time he touched it, pain shot through his entire body.

I will not be beaten, he thought, sweat dripping into his eyes. By will alone I will overcome everything that the gods do to me. By my will I will become a god myself.

He took his knife and cut into his leg, making the wound longer and wider. The pain was excruciating and though he tried to be silent he had to roar to cover his whimpers. Blood flowed freely down his thigh but the next time he pulled on the arrow it slid out with a wet sucking sound. He grunted and tossed the arrow away.

His men stood watching him in silence.

"Give me something to drink," he commanded.

"Lord," Gelu said, dragging forth a badly wounded man by the hair. "I know this man." He threw him down and pulled his head back so that Kreuhesh could look upon his face. "He was one of the Stag's men, I think."

"They all were," Hendros said, poking a dead man with his spear.

Kreuhesh stared down at the wounded warrior. His tunic had been torn off to reveal his broad chest and back which were covered in intricate swirling tattoos, as were his arms and face. He had a wound on his head and another low on his belly. He had a deep cut in his hand that poured with blood.

"Is this true?" Kreuhesh asked him. "Do you serve the stag god?"

The warrior snorted and spat a mouthful of blood. "I serve demons no longer."

Kreuhesh frowned. "What is your name?"

"I am Korvic, son of Tornu. And I know you, Kreuhesh the slave to *yotunan*."

"I serve a god, Korvic. So do you."

Korvic tried to laugh but winced. "Gods do not eat children. They are devourers, you mad fool. All of you are slaves to evil."

"You know nothing of the gods."

"I know that the gods protect us. Bring fertility, rain, wealth. The *yotunan* bring only death to our peoples. All they do is destroy." He sneered and spat again. "And you do it for them."

Kreuhesh looked down at him in disgust. "You are fleeing your god?"

"Returning to our people! If any yet live. To our land if not."

Kreuhesh gestured to the west. "Your god has provided new land. New people."

Korvic snorted and spoke bitterly. "We need no new land. Nor new people."

"Tell me, then, traitor, if you have seen a woman and two young men in your flight. Both the men are tall, one of them taller even than me."

Their captive laughed again, briefly. "You are a witless fool if you search for them here."

Kreuhesh grasped Korvic's chin and yanked his face up. "You have seen them."

"I have seen them." Korvic's eyes closed for a moment before they snapped open again. "If I tell you where, will you give me a swift death?"

"I swear it in the name of my god Leuhon." He released the man's face and nodded at Gelu, who eased the restraining hold he had on him.

Korvic nodded. "Back across the river but further downstream a little. There is a mound like this one but smaller. It has a ring of stones around it but not as high as these. They were there when I was."

"A woman was with them?"

"She was."

"Did you speak to them?"

Korvic nodded. "Spoke to them. The tall one one..." Korvic shook his head. "Good with a spear, that one."

I know he is. "You fought him?"

Korvic coughed a mouthful of blood and spat it before him. His face creased as he examined the wound in his trembling hand. A gouge had been cut between his fingers almost to the wrist, perhaps where he had tried to catch a bronze dagger or spearhead. The wound in his gut would kill him slowly. Already the man's face was pale as ash beneath the drying blood.

"I told you truthfully where they are. Now, you kill me quick. Axe in the head, right?"

Kreuhesh looked around at the bodies and at the broken timbers and then down at his captive. His anger at himself was almost more than he could bear. Back across the river but further downstream a little. If he had not crossed the river he would have had them by now.

"You told me truthfully," Kreuhesh said slowly. "And I believe you."

Korvic shivered, nodding. "Good, good."

"But then you are a traitor, Korvic. You betrayed your god. And if I was a god then I would see you punished."

Korvic's head jerked up. "You swore in the name of your god. It is you that will be punished if you break your oath."

Kreuhesh leaned down and lowered his voice. "I like the patterns on your skin, Korvic. I shall have your flesh made into a cloak." He nodded to Gelu. "Hold him down and flay the skin from him in one piece."

Korvic roared and launched himself up at Kreuhesh but the men dragged him back and pinned him in place. While they carefully cut away the skin from his chest and peeled it off, Kreuhesh climbed the wall and looked back toward the river. Korvic's screams stopped eventually but by then Kreuhesh was smiling again. His reward was still within his reach. All he had to do now was grasp it. And his will would not be denied.

"I am coming for you, Alkmene," Kreuhesh promised. "I am coming."

3 1

Challenge

HERKUHLOS STARED AT the nine hostile riders chasing Kasos, Makros, and Helhena and attempted to judge the distance and speed of both groups.

"Will they make it here in time?" Alkmene said beside him.

Herkuhlos did not know but he was unwilling to take the chance. "I must ride out to meet them." He looked over his shoulder at their three horses. Only one was up to the challenge.

"No, they will reach us before those riders catch them," Belolukos said, pointing with his spear. "I am sure of it."

Helhena rode in front while Kasos and Makros rode behind her, their mouths working as they shouted encouragement to their horses. Makros looked repeatedly over his shoulder at the pursuing warriors, no doubt making his own calculations on whether to keep running. If they got too close they would have to turn and fight but they would not last more than a few moments. The enemy riders were well armed and they rode as expertly as any warrior from the plain.

"But then we will all be trapped in here while they attack us anyway," Alkmene said, speaking quickly. "We must all flee for the river now while there is time."

Herkuhlos looked east toward the river beyond the woodland. It had seemed close enough to run for but he knew now that they would not make it with such close pursuit and his companions' horses already exhausted. "Their horses will barely make it to these walls," Herkuhlos said.

"We could fight them off as we run for the river," Alkmene suggested.

"Mother," Belolukos said. "It cannot be done."

"We will have to fight either way," Herkuhlos said. "With these walls we have a better chance. They will have to dismount and come through the entrance or over the wall to reach us. We will fight them here."

"So we do nothing," Alkmene said, her face set hard. "Holkis, you cannot simply wait for things to happen. You have to decide what to do and then do it."

"I have decided," he snapped. "We get them in here and then we kill those men!"

They waved and gestured at the gap in the wall and the exhausted horses slowed to drag themselves up the slope. The hooves of the enemy horses drummed as they reached the base of the mound and Herkuhlos felt the familiar rage building inside him at the sight of the warband. He felt keenly the loss of his weapons and he knew it would be a deadly fight.

"Come on!" he roared at his friends as Kasos and Makros and

Helhena slid from their horses' backs and pulled them through the narrow gap into the enclosure. Their sweating horses shook and their mouths were flecked with foam and there was a good chance they would soon die from their exertions or at least never fully recover.

Helhena staggered to her knees, breathing hard but she forced herself upright with her bow stave. Makros was flushed red and his long, wild hair stood out like a tangled mane. He took up his spear and his war axe and ran to the gap in the wall with Kasos, who nodded once at Herkuhlos as he and Belolukos joined them.

"Come and die!" Makros roared, shaking his spear and axe.

The enemy riders rode hard a little way up the mound but turned aside from their charge at long javelin range and instead rode around the enclosure in both directions, shouting insults and shaking their spears and axes as they whooped and jeered.

Herkuhlos' heart raced as he tracked the riders riding both ways around the mound. They could climb the walls at any point. If they rode up close they could leap from their horse's backs almost onto the top of the wall and if they charged the entrance together then surely they could do nothing to stop them.

But the warriors did not attack. Instead they continued to circle and shout.

"Bastards are enjoying themselves," Belolukos said over the din.

Herkuhlos looked then at his friends. They were all exhausted but seemed willing and able to fight.

"You are hurt," Herkuhlos said to Helhena, moving to embrace her briefly before holding her at arm's length to look at her properly. She shook from her exertions and took deep, ragged breaths. A deep cut over her eye had bled down her face even to the neck and shoulder but it had stopped flowing and her eyes were focused and clear. Indeed, she seemed ready to kill the whole warband by herself.

He could not resist pulling her back into his arms and holding her tight. Until that moment he had not realised how terrified he had been for her, above even Kasos.

"I am well," she said, her voice muffled as she buried her face in his chest. She pulled away and looked at the distant riders, her mouth turned down in disgust.

"Some god's hand turned aside a javelin," Makros said, shaking his head as he continued to watch the enemy beyond the wall. "Otherwise it would have killed her."

"What happened to you?" Belolukos demanded. "Are these the demon's men?"

Kasos stood with his feet planted in the entranceway, still breathing hard and watching the enemy riders. "They came at us late yesterday when we stopped to camp. Sons of dogs got most of our horses. Thought we lost them in the night. We saw a light on the horizon and we knew it was you. It had to be. They must have seen it too. Caught up with us in the morning. Chased us all the way."

"My fire," Herkuhlos said, feeling foolish. "My fire brought them here."

"We found you," Kasos called. "Because of that fire."

"I knew it was you," Helhena said, glancing quickly at Makros as she said it.

The pounding of Herkuhlos' heart was beginning to slow but still he expected an attack at any moment. The enemy were slowing but still they circled the mound, looking for ways in, counting them

516

and looking at their weapons and their horses.

"They do not attack," Belolukos said, holding his spear ready. "They are cowards."

"No," Makros said, watching the riders. "Not cowards. They are cunning. And ruthless. They will come when they are ready."

Kasos shook his head. "If they are truly cunning then they need not attack at all."

"What do you mean?" Alkmene asked.

Kasos looked over his shoulder and grinned. "It is good to see you, Alkmene."

She smiled at him. "And you, Kasos. Your loyalty to my boys will never be forgotten." Her smiled faded. "What do you mean they need not attack at all?"

He looked at the ruined timbers within the enclosure. "How much water do we have?"

"Not much," Belolukos said. "There was a well here but the demons threw the dead into it and now they are in there rotting."

Kasos shrugged. "Then they could wait out there until we are weakened with thirst. They need not attack us. They can wait for us to die."

"That will never happen," Herkuhlos said. "We will attack them before we grow so weak."

Kasos nodded. "Exactly. So if I were them I would wait for us to attack or to try to run. Why risk charging in here if they do not have to?"

Belolukos scoffed. "You are so clever, Kasos, that you have become foolish. We have the horses. Milk, blood, meat, as much as we wish."

Turning to him, Kasos scowled. "Blood is not water."

"And anyway, they do not look like patient men," Belolukos said. "Nor are they as clever as you. They will come. There must be a fight."

Herkuhlos stepped close to Alkmene. "Are they Leuhon's men?"

She frowned as her eyes tracked the riders, who slowed and grew quieter as they continued to circle them. "I do not recognise them but Leuhon has many warriors."

"We should attack them," Makros said, stretching his back and rolling his shoulders. "They are but nine men. They must have left one or two to guard the rest of the horses and perhaps they will come up soon. Better to attack now when they are fewer, no? I know I would slay one before I fell and if the gods are with me I could take two."

"As could I," said Belolukos, scowling.

Kasos shrugged. "I have killed men. I could probably kill one, if I did it right."

"Leaving four or five for me," Herkuhlos said. "Perhaps more."

"I can fight!" Helhena snapped, fire in her eyes.

Makros nodded. "She can."

"As can I," Alkmene said. "If I have a weapon."

"How many arrows do you have?" Herkuhlos asked Helhena.

She shook her head, angry now. "I shot the last of them this morning." She looked at the bow in her hand as she spoke.

"Do we have javelins?" he asked Kasos.

There were none.

Herkuhlos looked at the riders. They were drifting closer together on the flat ground beyond the base of the mound, speaking to one another as they looked up. Makros was right. They were not afraid and were simply taking their time before attacking. One man even dismounted and began brushing down his horse with a handful of dried grass ripped from the meadow.

"Even if we defeated them and drove them away, some of us would fall," Herkuhlos said. "And that is if the fight goes well. The women are strong but we would have to protect them. How could it be done?"

"What is there to consider?" Belolukos said, raising his voice and pointing his spear at the enemy below. "We go at them. Go right at them and fight until one side is victorious. That is the way that it is done."

Herkuhlos looked at his mother and turned to look at Helhena. He could hardly imagine one of them dying because he had made the wrong choice.

"I will challenge the leader," Herkuhlos said.

Makros raised his eyebrows. "These men have no honour. They will shoot you with arrows and javelins if you stand before them and offer the challenge."

"How can you be sure?"

"I know it." Makros looked over the wall. "There is not much that I am certain of beneath the wide sky, Herkuhlos, but I am certain of that."

"Makros is right," Helhena said. "You must not offer the challenge."

"It is worth a try," Herkuhlos said, smiling. "If they kill me then you are not much worse off than you are now."

Alkmene scoffed at his courage. "This is no time for jokes."

"I was not joking."

"We should all go," Belolukos said, hefting his spear. "Let us all go at once. If we die here then so be it."

All their faces glanced between the warriors outside and Herkuhlos, waiting for his decision. He did not know what was the best thing to do but he could not bear to see his mother facing those men out there. Dying to their spears when they had fought so hard to get her away from them.

"Do you think they are here to take you back to the demon?" he asked his mother.

"It is possible."

Makros jerked his head at them. "They do not seem particularly interested in her." He looked at Alkmene and bowed his head in greeting. "My name is Makros and I am honoured to meet you. Your sons saved my life and I am sworn to serve Herkuhlos."

She smiled at him. A warm, genuine smile. "I am Alkmene and I am honoured to meet you. You are a man of honour, Makros, and a great warrior I am sure, with the experience of many raids and battles. What is your advice to my son?"

Makros looked warily from Alkmene to Herkuhlos and back again. "It is no easy thing to be a leader of men. No man makes the right choices every time. But your son led a warband across the world to save you and whatever choice he makes is good enough for me."

Alkmene looked disappointed but she nodded her thanks nonetheless. Eyes again turned to Herkuhlos while he looked at the enemy beyond the walls. They had slowed to a stop and were now milling around in the meadow, speaking to one another and apparently content to wait. He took in their weapons. Some of them had javelins, all had at least one spear and most had a polished stone war axe. If he led his people down the slope against them they would be hit with half a dozen javelins even before they closed the distance.

"You say that they will not accept my challenge," Herkuhlos said to Makros. "But I shall try it." He held out a hand to Belolukos. "My spear."

His brother frowned as he passed him the weapon. "I know you will beat their leader, Herkuhlos. You are the best man with a spear I have ever seen. You would beat even Old Kelh, I am sure of it." He jabbed a finger at the enemy. "But you cannot trust them."

"I know," he replied and clapped his brother on the shoulder. He turned to the entrance.

"Herkuhlos!" Helhena said and stepped closer to him, her eyes wide as they searched his face. "I..." She trailed off.

He nodded and smiled. "I know. All will be well."

With a glance at the rest of them he walked through the entrance and made his way a few paces down the slope toward the warriors, his heart racing and his throat tight with fear. He held his spear over his head as the raiders saw him and leapt atop their horses.

"Challenge!" Herkuhlos roared. "I am Herkuhlos and I challenge your leader! I am—"

He froze as the closest dismounted warrior took two rapid steps and launched a javelin at him. He watched it cutting through the air, rising and falling. His instinct was to run but the words of Gendryon came to him. *Wait until its path is clear!*

At the last moment he leapt aside and the javelin sank into the earth a pace behind where he had been standing. His friends began shouting warnings and he looked up to see another javelin coming for him. Again he waited as long as he could and darted aside as it sank into the ground. Ahead, the warriors were racing toward him on foot and on horseback.

Herkuhlos turned, yanked both javelins from the earth and ran back up the hill and into the entranceway. There he handed the javelins to Kasos and turned to defend against the assault.

The enemy turned away and retreated down the hill, shouting insults as they went.

"Those bastards!" Belolukos shouted. "Sons of dogs!"

Makros raised his eyebrows at Herkuhlos. He said nothing but those raised eyebrows conveyed his meaning eloquently enough. *I told you so.*

Herkuhlos shrugged, breathing hard. "At least I got us two javelins."

"What now?" Alkmene asked.

"They will attack us soon enough," Herkuhlos said. "Our chances are far greater in here than out there. We must remain ready for their attack but it will come."

Belolukos was angry and his mother frustrated but the others seemed relieved. They had been riding hard and needed time for rest. Makros nodded, indicating that he thought it was a good decision. Herkuhlos appreciated the older man's approval.

While they waited for the attack they stood behind the wall at intervals and guarded the entrance into the enclosure, always watching the warriors outside. Their enemies stood close to one another and conversed, often casting hard looks at the enclosure as they did so. After a while they spread out a little and dismounted to sit beside their horses. A few chewed on dried meat as they watched. It grew quiet and the two sides watched each other.

"Getting their strength back just as we are," Makros muttered beside Herkuhlos. "They are in no rush. They are dishonourable bastards but they are no fools."

"Makros," Herkuhlos said quietly. "Did I make the right choice? To wait, I mean."

The older warrior shrugged. "Hard to say. We shall see soon enough. My people say that each man has a certain portion of life that the gods served up when he was born."

"My people say the same."

"Well, there you go then. It is all decided already. All we do was decided long ago. So why worry?"

Herkuhlos nodded though he still was not content. That was not all there was to it. A man has a path to follow but he must also utilise his will to shape that path.

Makros slapped him on the back. "I'm going to watch the other side. That one with the tusks on his hood has a mad look about him."

The day wore on. By the time the sun rose to its highest point it was obscured by grey clouds and a chill wind whipped through the trees before rain came, soaking them all quickly. Their horses stood with their heads down, miserable and Kasos went amongst them, rubbing them down and speaking to them. He crossed to Herkuhlos and told him that three of them were exhausted and would not run that day. Also they needed food and water soon or they would all be good for nothing except meat.

Herkuhlos nodded. They could not wait within indefinitely, he understood that. If the enemy did not attack before dark fell then he would have to lead his people against them and then it would be in the hands of the gods.

Alkmene approached and leaned on the wall beside him. "I do

not like this waiting."

Yes, mother, you have made that clear, he thought. "Me either. I would rather fight."

"I have had enough of waiting. Of being trapped. I will not go back to him, Holkis."

"Mother, Kolnos himself named me Herkuhlos."

"I know that, I apologise. It is hard to remember but of course you are a man. I see it. You are so different to when I saw you last. Before they came."

"Back at Nemiyeh, mother. That *yotunan* called you by your name."

"He did."

"And he called you dear one."

She scoffed, turning her head away from him. "He is revolting. A vile creature. His mind is twisted into madness. His words are just as twisted."

"How did he know your name?"

"He... liked me. When I tried to escape with... when I tried to flee he caught us and then he claimed me for his own. I feared that he would rape me but he never harmed me at all. Not physically. Even when I tried to kill him he simply bound me and had me held alone in a house. That was where I escaped from when I heard the cries and the running from the fire that your friends set."

"You tried to kill him?" he asked, astonished.

"Twice." She shook her head. "It was foolish. He is strong beyond imagining. I do not know if he even *can* be killed."

"Kolnos says he can. They all must be killed."

"Perhaps only a god can kill a *yotunan*."

Herkuhlos shook his head. "How did you get free?"

She waved a hand. "I hid a piece of bronze sharp enough to cut my bonds and waited for the right night. It seemed as though they were always watching me. I could have cut my bonds at any time after they tied me up but there were always men in the building and it was only when the fire drew them away that night that I escaped." She shook her head. "I waited too long. If I had been more courageous I could have killed the men and freed Laonome before..."

"I am sorry. I got here as soon as I could."

She shook her head, dismissing his apology. "You came all this way, the both of you. I never expected it. In fact, I hoped that you would be far away. Back home, making a new clan. You and your brother and the others of your *koryos*."

"There was not much left at home. Not just our valley but so many of the clans were destroyed and the rest scattered by the great demon clan." Herkuhlos snorted as he remembered. "But Orysthos survived. His clan was whole."

She nodded once. "Good. Then he will welcome us when we return. If his clan survives when others have fallen that will only increase his strength. That will all but ensure our safety. Yes, Orysthos will be a good lord to shelter us."

Herkuhlos smiled. "I will not serve Orysthos, mother."

She frowned. "My cousin can be a brutal man but he is not an evil one."

"Perhaps. But I think I would prefer not to serve any man."

She frowned. "All men serve until it is their time to lead. You are young but your time will come."

"What about Bel?"

"The same is true for him."

He gritted his teeth, recalling his mother's words before they had left the clan with the *koryos*. *Obey your brother in all things. He will need you if he is to be clan chief when you are grown.*

"You told me when Bel was chosen as *koryonos* that I was to serve him loyally."

"I did." She frowned. "And I see I have angered you in some way because of it."

"When we left with the *koryos* your words to him were to lead well and to be a strong leader. You told him he should not be friends with the boys because one day he would be their chief."

A frown creased for forehead. "Yes."

"Mother, why him? Why was he chosen as the *koryonos*? Why did you expect Bel to be chief but not me? I was always the stronger and I am—"

"The son of a god," she finished for him, speaking softly. "And that is why. His father was a chief. Yours is a god." She lowered her voice further. "And I have always known that your fate would be the greater."

"Greater?"

"Belolukos will make a fine chief. He is strong. But he is not godborn. Always he has felt himself to be in your shadow. When I told you to serve him I knew, at least I thought I knew, that it would be for the time of the *koryos* only. Gendryon and the other men of the *tauta* knew that if you were made *koryonos*, your brother would never have a chance to make his mark. Do you understand?"

"I do not know." He frowned. "I always thought that... you were meant for his father. But my... my father robbed you of that and he hurt you. Destroyed what you would have had."

Alkmene gripped his arm. "I have never doubted you. I never

doubted that you would win glory. Your fate is there before you if only you would take it. Do you see? Do you hear my words?"

Herkuhlos nodded slowly. "I think so."

She smiled and stroked his cheek. "Your beard is coming through. You are a man, now. I see it. You are Herkuhlos."

He grinned.

Behind her, he saw Helhena standing a few paces away with one eye on the enemy and the other on him. Or was it Alkmene she was looking at?

Following his gaze, Alkmene turned. "She is your woman?"

"No."

Alkmene snorted. "It looked that way when she was in your arms." She raised her voice. "Come here, girl."

After a moment's hesitation, Helhena warily approached. "My name is Helhena," she said, her voice flat.

"And I am Alkmene." She looked the younger woman up and down. "You wish to speak to my son?"

"To you," Helhena replied, seemed about to say more and then hesitated before going on. "One of your horses is lame. Would you hold her steady while I see to her?"

Alkmene hardly hesitated before nodding and going with Helhena toward the horses, after a glance at Herkuhlos. With a look at the enemy he followed to where Helhena crouched by the horse, touching the swollen knee and lower leg. The mare tossed her head and stamped a foot. All of the horses were tired and on edge, their mood low.

Alkmene grasped the harness and opened the horse's mouth. She made a disapproving noise in her throat. "Almost chewed through this old bit," she said. "It is leather, not bone."

"These three are poor horses," Helhena agreed, her fingers touching the hot surface of the leg. "But let us see if the gods will improve this one." She closed her eyes and breathed deeply as she held her hands around the knee. "Fleet-footed Ekwa, lord of horses, may your strength flow forth through me into this flesh." As she spoke she worked her hands up and down and around the knee, rubbing and squeezing the inflamed joint, causing the horse to toss her head. Alkmene held her firmly in place. "Bone to bone, blood to blood, joint to joint, may they be healed. Fleet-footed Ekwa, lord of horses, may you knit bone to bone, blood to blood, joint to joint, may they be healed."

Letting her hands drop, Helhena stood and patted the horse's neck. She glanced at Alkmene and nodded.

"Did you feel the god in you?" Alkmene asked her.

"No," Helhena admitted. "But perhaps he will heal her all the same."

With a glance at the men beyond the wall, Alkmene rubbed the mare's nose. "Why have you come across the earth to this place, Helhena?"

Helhena glanced at Herkuhlos who was nearby but facing away, watching the enemy. "The demons took my mother. My sisters. All my people." She held Alkmene's eye. "We are Udros Clan. My father was Hartkos. My mother... Adreha."

Something passed across Alkmene's face. "I met your father once, years ago. Your mother Adreha I met briefly when we were both prisoners." She held up a hand to forestall Helhena's excitement. "I am sorry but she is dead. Leuhon took her life a moon past."

Helhena stared through her and then closed her eyes. She

nodded once and opened them. "She had two daughters. Young. Haedha and Weita. Did they also..."

Alkmene shook her head and spoke softly. "I have not seen them for some time. Not since Nemiyeh fell or perhaps before. I am so sorry. It does not mean that they do not live for Nemiyeh is vast and perhaps they are simply elsewhere within all those houses."

Without intending it, Herkuhlos found himself going to Helhena and he wrapped his free arm around her, pulling her close to him. There was nothing that could be said. No words would carry any meaning in the face of such grief.

A cry from behind him shook him from his sadness and he jerked away, fearing a sudden attack. There was noise rising, fear in the air.

"What is that?" Makros cried and pointed at the woodland that lay between them and the river.

From it burst a dozen riders. Mounted warriors riding in a rough line from the trees into the meadow and heading straight for them.

Herkuhlos knew then that they were finished. The nine warriors were not simply biding their time but had been waiting for another warband to join them. Around him the others despaired for all knew now that their deaths were at hand. They could run or they could fight but the outcome would be the same.

"We will stop them here," Herkuhlos shouted, stepping to the entrance. "No matter how many they are we shall kill them as they come at us."

Makros, Belolukos, and Kasos came to stand beside him. He felt like a fool for delaying as long as he had and he felt shame for failing his people. All that remained was to die fighting with as much honour as he could win.

"By the Mother," Alkmene exclaimed behind him. "It is Kreuhesh."

"You know these men?"

"Yes! The one in the centre, the big man with the long-hafted war axe and boar tusk armour. He is Leuhon's war chief, Kreuhesh the Bloodletter. I will not let him take me. I will not!"

The man she had identified looked like a demon himself and even at this distance it was clear that his face was twisted into an expression of rage as his horse accelerated into a gallop. He lifted his weapon and roared at them, his men joining his war cry.

The nine warriors that had been laying siege to the mound had leapt into action at the sight of the charging warband. They mounted their horses and came together and raced away from the mound, charging at Kreuhesh's warband.

"What is this?" Belolukos said over the noise.

"Do they mean to fight one another?" Kasos asked.

"Yes," Makros said. "They ride to battle."

The two sides closed rapidly and they clashed with shouts and the smacking sound of weapons hitting flesh. One man fell but the others passed each other and wheeled about. Some fought from horseback, thrusting their spears and swinging their axes at one another but most leapt from their horses and sought other men to fight. The battle swiftly formed into small clusters of two or three men aside and immediately men began dying.

Kreuhesh stayed atop his horse, crushing men's skulls with his long-handled axe with every mighty swing.

And Kreuhesh's warband was winning. The nine warriors were soon five and then four who fought back to back as the others closed on them. Kreuhesh pushed his horse through his men and brought his bloody war axe down onto a warrior's skull.

"What do we do?" Helhena shouted at him.

Herkuhlos shook his head. They would not escape now and he did not know what else could be accomplished. "We stand and fight!" he said.

The last of the defending men were killed in quick succession.

Not one of Kreuhesh's warriors was killed.

Some picked over the corpses of the men they had killed. Some of them lie wounded and screaming on the ground. A warrior began sawing at the ears and nose of one of the wounded men who screamed as his face was cut to pieces. Another cut into a dying man's scalp, ripping off a ragged disk of skin and hair until he held aloft the bloody scrap by its plaited tail. The scalped man tried to fight back but was stabbed in the chest and brought down with casual brutality.

"Do we run?" Kasos asked.

"No time, son," Makros replied. "This is as good a place to die as any."

Kasos nodded, his lips pressed tight.

At the base of the mound, Kreuhesh rode toward them, threw himself from the back of his horse and snatched up a spear from one of the dead men. He came closer, looking up at them with his axe in one hand and the spear in the other.

"Alkmene!" he roared. "Come down here."

She pushed forward and raised her voice. "Come up here and die, Kreuhesh."

A grin spread across his face while his men laughed. They spread out at the base of the mound behind their leader, leaving the dead bodies and the horses behind them.

"I swear in the name of Leuhon that you will not be harmed if you come to me now."

"Are you afraid to come and fight us, Kreuhesh?" she shouted.

He shrugged. "Yes." He smiled but the smile was not a kind one. His eyes were mirthless and entirely cold. "I could kill you all with ease but my god commands me to bring you back alive."

She scoffed loudly. "Ha! I will slay myself before returning to that demon."

Kreuhesh scowled. "The god also demands to meet your sons. He does not want their deaths. He wishes to meet with them."

Alkmene glanced at Herkuhlos and Belolukos. "You lie."

"I know what you think of me, woman. But you know I am no liar. Come down and you will see."

She muttered. "He is mad and utterly evil. He cannot be trusted."

"It matters not," Herkuhlos said. "None of us are going down there anyway."

Alkmene nodded.

"I see your godborn son beside you," Kreuhesh said, pointing with his spear. "He is strong, I think. I wonder if he is stronger than I am..." A sly look came onto his face and his tongue shot out to lick his lips. "He leads your little war band?"

Before she could reply, Herkuhlos stepped a pace beyond the wall. "I am Herkuhlos. Enough talk. Fight us. Let the gods decide."

"The gods will decide nothing," Kreuhesh replied. "All that remains to be seen is whether my will is stronger than yours." Kreuhesh raised his spear. "I challenge you, Herkuhlos. Cross spears with me and if you kill me my men ride away and leave you all alone." He turned and raised his voice, addressing his warriors. "You hear my words? If I fall, you return to Leuhon without harming these people. You understand?" They nodded and muttered their agreement. Kreuhesh turned back. "But if I beat you then you and your mother come with me back to Nemiyeh. I will let the rest of your men go free."

"Never!" Alkmene shouted. "I will never return, not for anything."

Kreuhesh sighed. "Very well. If I beat you, Herkuhlos, then I will not kill you but I will take you captive. You will return to Nemiyeh with me while the rest of your people including your mother will go free." He shrugged. "I will bring my god half of what he wants, at least. I see no other way."

Herkuhlos looked around at his people. "I am going to accept."

Alkmene shook her head. "You cannot trust his word. He has no honour. Trust me."

"I can kill him," Herkuhlos said. "I know I can. The chance alone makes it a worthwhile chance to take." Without waiting for further argument, he raised his spear. "I accept your challenge. Let us cross spears."

Kreuhesh grinned. "Come on, then."

Herkuhlos might have accepted but he was still wary. "You come up here. We will fight within these walls, safe from your men."

"You think me a fool, boy? Let us fight on the hill. My men will wait down there and yours wait in there. That is fair, no?" He smiled.

"If I win, your men will leave us."

Kreuhesh laughed and his men laughed with him. "I have said

it already but I will say it once more. If you beat me then in the name Leuhon, my men will go. You hear me, dogs? You will go. And if I win, I take you to my god. The rest of your people may go."

"He lies," Alkmene said. "He is a deceiver. You must not trust him."

"I must win, then," Herkuhlos said, turning to face them. "And if the gods are with me I will."

Makros spoke softly but loud enough so that Herkuhlos could hear. "He will be a tricky one, son. A man like that. He will fight like a demon. Look at him. Look at the size of him."

"I have half a head on the man."

"And he is twice as wide. He will know strikes you have never seen in the spear dance."

"It must be done." He looked at them all, his gaze resting on Helhena.

She did not return his smile but she nodded once. "You will beat him, Herkuhlos. You can beat any man who walks this earth."

Alone, he stepped out of the enclosure and down the slope toward Kreuhesh. In the sky above the clouds had parted and the sun warmed his back through his tunic. He rolled his shoulders as he walked and rotated his wrists to loosen his joints.

He heard Gendryon's words coming to him from the afterlife. *War separates the strong from the weak, the heroes from the cowards. Some fall, others assert themselves.*

Kreuhesh stood waiting with a mocking smile on his face as if this were nothing but a joke that only he understood. It was clear at least that the man believed he would win. And why would he not? He was huge and obviously strong and he had killed many men before and while Herkuhlos wore old and worn woollen clothes

Kreuhesh was protected by his boar's tusk helm and the armour protecting his chest and back. To be sure of wounding the man he would have to run his spearpoint into his face or neck or underneath the arm perhaps. Another killing blow was to sever the great vein inside the top of the thigh and the rows of boar's tusk plates hung only as low as Kreuhesh's hips.

It can be done, he thought as he came to a stop two spear lengths away from his enemy. It must be done.

Kreuhesh smiled at him, perfectly relaxed. "Are you ready, boy?"

As Herkuhlos opened his mouth to answer, Kreuhesh struck. His spear shot out before him as he also propelled himself forward. Although he was not entirely deceived by the attack, the speed of it was shocking. Only by the hand of the gods did he react in time to slip aside as he retreated so that the spearpoint hit only the air beside his cheek instead of crashing through his face.

Before he could get his balance, Kreuhesh was striking again, his spearpoint jabbing at his face and chest with relentless speed. Herkuhlos retreated in something close to panic, blocking with his spear shaft as he stepped backwards across and down the slope of the mound, the wood clacking and his breathing filled his ears.

Never go straight back.

From the afterlife Gendryon's wisdom filtered into his mind and at once he angled away with his next backward step and so opened Kreuhesh to a swift counterattack. Herkuhlos' spear cracked him on the side of the head, rattling the boar's tusks. His heart leaping, Herkuhlos pressed his attack while Kreuhesh was off balance and stabbed at his chest, his head, his thighs as their roles as attacker and defender switched. Kreuhesh retreated down the mound, accelerating in order to give himself a moment to compose himself but Herkuhlos stayed with him down into the long grasses of the overgrown pasture.

Without warning, Kreuhesh attacked again, flicking his spear up and nicking Herkuhlos' cheek before he could block. The blow had been intended to take him under the chin and he knew the gods had saved him once more. Herkuhlos found himself retreating again, stepping obliquely and trying his own counterattacks but Kreuhesh was faster and stronger by far than any other man he had ever faced.

He was better with his spear and he was faster. It would not be long before a blow got through.

As if the gods had heard his thoughts the bronze spearhead sliced though his forearm and then the next blow slid up his bicep to the shoulder. Blood gushed forth from the wounds and Kreuhesh's dark eyes shone with joy. The man's smile was more like the snarl of a wolf.

Herkuhlos was filled with disgust for the warrior. Disgust for a man who had submitted to the demon and done the bidding of evil instead of fighting it. There was no fear in him as the disgust was replaced by a deep rage that welled up like the blood from his arm. The fury was like fire filling his limbs with power and he threw himself forward, grasping his enemy's spear behind the bronze head and forcing it aside as he thrust his weapon into Kreuhesh's chest. It was a powerful blow, connecting square over his chest with enough force to knock the man off his feet.

But the boar's tusk plates stopped the flint spear from penetrating and the shaft splintered as the flint head exploded into shards of stone. Kreuhesh fell back, ripping his spear from Herkuhlos' grasp. He hit the ground hard, crying out in pain but still he rolled and got his feet under him. As he rose his face was contorted with the agony of the blow that had destroyed Herkuhlos' spear.

Before he could recover, Herkuhlos rushed for him in a headlong charge and shouldered him to the ground. They fell together, Herkuhlos on top with his legs astride his enemy's hips and he jammed the splinted shaft of his spear beneath Kreuhesh's arm, trying to drive it from his armpit into his chest.

Kreuhesh roared and slammed his elbow down to his side, ripping the spear shaft from Herkuhlos' grip. He brought a knee up hard into Herkuhlos' groin. The pain was excruciating and for a moment he was stunned. The older man took advantage and grasped Herkuhlos around the back of the neck and head with both hands and yanked him down at the same time as he drove his own head up. He butted Herkuhlos in the nose with the hard tusks covering his forehead, breaking his nose. As Herkuhlos pulled away, blood gushed and he was blinded by the tears and the pain. Kreuhesh threw him to the side and rolled away as Herkuhlos reached to hold on to him. Kreuhesh slipped away.

Conquering the pain and disorientation, Herkuhlos threw himself at Kreuhesh, bringing him down by the legs before he could get to his spear. Squirming, Kreuhesh rolled and kicked, hard. The blow smashed Herkuhlos in the head but he held on, still pulling Kreuhesh toward him. The next kick caught him in the mouth, splitting his lip against his teeth. A third and Kreuhesh was free, scrambling to his feet.

If he gets his spear I am dead.

With immense effort, Herkuhlos stumbled upright and staggered toward the bronze spear lying in the long grass. He reached it and pulled it into his grasp as in triumph he turned to face Kreuhesh.

He was not there.

Blinking away his tears, Herkuhlos saw Kreuhesh running at full speed away from him, making for his horse.

It was only then that he saw how far he had come from the mound where his people stood watching the fight in the pasture.

Between him and the mound, stood Kreuhesh's warriors.

"Take her!" Kreuhesh shouted as he caught his horse and threw himself onto its back. The wound under his arm was bad and blood soaked his flank. "Take her alive! Kill the others!"

He felt sick. His head swam and the blood gushed down his arm and from his broken nose. He understood then that the fight had been a trick to separate him from his mother and he felt like the greatest fool that ever lived.

While Kreuhesh watched from afar, his men advanced up the slope with their spears and war axes in hand.

"No!" Herkuhlos roared and raced for the mound, ignoring Kreuhesh.

He ran as fast as he could but he saw with horror that they would reach the enclosure before he even came to the slope. If only they could hold them for long enough he could take the eleven men in the rear.

It was eleven hardened warriors against three. Makros was superb and Belolukos was strong despite his youth but Kasos was likely equal to none of them. His mother and Helhena could both fight but even together they could hardly hope to beat one man.

His vision blurred and juddered as he ran, flying through the long grass and up the hill. Above him the sounds of battle filled the air and the fight was bloody and swift.

The enemy burst through the entrance. The weight of their numbers and their skill overcoming the defenders in mere moments. The voices roared and spear shafts clattered.

One of the attackers fell and then another staggered away down the hill with blood pouring down his face.

He was almost there when he felt the thunder of hooves beneath his feet and he turned to find Kreuhesh bearing down with a javelin cocked back ready to throw. He was so close that he could not miss. The rage in him, Herkuhlos changed direction and in just a few steps threw himself across the horse's line of approach, ducking under its neck and thrusting up at Kreuhesh with his spear. He ruined the javelin throw but the charging horse clipped his shoulder as he thrust, sending the strike into the air beside Kreuhesh rather than into him. The impact knocked him sprawling as the horse charged past with Kreuhesh clinging to it. The horse took a bad step, staggered, and bucked and Kreuhesh was thrown, dropping the javelin. He fell hard as the horse stomped away, tossing its head.

Herkuhlos had dropped his spear. He grasped around desperately looking for it in the trampled grass but he could not see it anywhere and so he scrambled to his feet, ran up the last part of the slope and burst into the desperate fighting within the enclosure. His spear was gone but he would not let anything stop him from saving his companions, his kinfolk.

Kasos lay dead in the entranceway, his eyes staring and his skull chopped apart.

A woman screamed and men cried out from the far side of the enclosure.

Herkuhlos dragged his eyes from Kasos.

And then it was as though the world came to standstill as with a horror the depth of which he had never known before he saw that his mother was dead.

Through the legs and thrusting spears of the warriors attacking his friends he saw her on the ground, face up, head twisted. His mother's eyes stared lifelessly and her mouth hung half open as her spirit departed her body.

The rage took him. The fire burned so bright and hot that he lost himself in the battle rage.

Enemy warriors, oblivious to his presence behind them, continued to pen in his friends on the other side of the enclosure with their attacks. Herkuhlos lifted a huge stone from the wall and marched forward at them. With a massive swing he brought it down on top of a man's head, caving in his skull and dropping him instantly. The man beside him Herkuhlos dragged down off his feet and drove the bloody rock into his face again and again until his head was no more than shattered bone and pulped flesh and brain.

The surviving warriors were on him by then, rushing with their axes held high. Stepping close he grasped one by the neck and caught his wrist with his other hand. With a roar of fury he crushed the man's throat with his bare hand and ripped the axe from his lifeless grasp before throwing down his corpse. Shrugging aside a spear thrust he drove the axe through the skull of the next man, splattering blood over his face.

The others tried to flee, then, but he caught them before they could escape and struck them down. Finding the shaft of his axe had snapped in killing one man, he drove the splintered shaft into the mouth of another, smashing through his teeth and driving it out the back of his skull. The last man crawled away through the blood and bodies but Herkuhlos caught him by the neck and drove his head against the stones of the wall over and over until there was nothing left of the man to break.

Breathing heavily, he wiped his enemy's blood from his eyes and looked around for more of them to kill.

There was none left alive.

Kreuhesh.

Covered in blood, Herkuhlos climbed the wall of the enclosure and looked for the man who had caused all of this. Down in the pasture, Kreuhesh gaped up at him from the back of his skittish horse.

Herkuhlos pointed a bloody hand and raised his voice to a roar. "I am coming for you, Kreuhesh!"

At that, Kreuhesh the Bloodletter turned his horse and rode away at a gallop without looking back.

3 2

Darkness

HERKUHLOS FOUND HIMSELF standing alone on the ground, breathing heavily. He looked down at his blood-soaked hands and felt the ache of the wounds on his arm and face.

Someone was calling his name.

He turned to find Helhena nearby. Her face was pale and her eyes stared intensely at his. She spoke but he could not hear her words and shook his head.

She stepped closer. A cut bled freely across her upper chest, soaking her tunic. "Herkuhlos," she said, reaching for his arm. She touched him with her fingertips. "It is over. They are dead."

"Yes," he said. It was as though the spell was broken and he suddenly saw the death all around him.

Across the enclosure, Belolukos held Alkmene's body in his arms, tears streaming down his contorted face. Makros leaned against the wall, his ashen face stricken with anguish. Herkuhlos remembered Kasos had fallen and saw his body lying in the entrance. He picked his way through the carnage to his brother.

"Mother," Herkuhlos said and found himself kneeling beside Belolukos. Alkmene's skin was almost white and was already cold to the touch, her clothes heavy with her blood and clinging to her body.

Belolukos looked at Herkuhlos through bleary eyes. "We failed," he said, sobbing. "All this. So close. We failed."

Herkuhlos reached across and squeezed his brother's shoulder with a bloody hand.

Makros coughed, clutching his stomach. "I failed. I am sorry."

"No," Helhena said, stepping in front of Makros with her hands held up. "He did not. I saw him. He fought them all back. If it were not for him we would all have been killed."

"What happened?" he asked her.

"Makros put himself in the way of an axe meant for her and it knocked him down. When your mother might have fled, or at least stepped back, she did not. She killed one man and another killed her. Then Makros threw himself at them, standing over her to fight again beside Belolukos." She looked down. "Tell him, Bel." She raised her voice. "Belolukos!"

Still holding his mother, Belolukos nodded. "It is true. There is no fault with him. I failed to protect her."

"While I was lured away," Herkuhlos said, his voice thick with fury. "Like a witless fool."

"There is enough blame for all," Helhena said. "We are all at fault. And none are. Blame the gods if you must blame anyone but it is done. Two of us have fallen. And they must be given back to the earth."

Herkuhlos nodded. That was something that could be done. That had to be done.

Together, they removed the corpses of the enemies from the hill and cleared the area of their remains and the filth. In the centre of the enclosure they dug a large grave and divided it with the timbers from what had once been houses. Into the largest division they laid Alkmene. In it they laid two spears and an axe. Into the other they placed Kasos with his weapons.

By then, night was falling. Herkuhlos felt numb, as if his spirit were not fully within his body. His wounds were healing, as they always did, but the hurt he felt at the loss had not even yet fully registered. Even when he looked down at the bodies in the graves his sadness was distant somehow. But his body went on.

As they now had two dozen horses Herkuhlos sacrificed one at the graveside and spilled its blood into the graves before butchering the carcass.

At the base of the mound they made a camp and built a fire to roast the meat. In the darkness they ate its flesh and feasted their fallen into the next world. At some point, Herkuhlos fell asleep on the grass and dreamt of fighting until dawn, when he woke shivering beside a cold fire.

The next day, they placed the horse's skull and hooves in the grave along with its burnt heart so that its spirit would go with her to the afterlife.

"Do you remember what Gendryon said about those who fall in battle?" Herkuhlos asked his brother.

"I remember everything he said," Belolukos replied.

"There is no sacrifice or rite more pleasing to the gods than that of the true warrior who fights and falls in battle," Herkuhlos said.

"The spirits of the fallen who died in glory will go to fight beside the gods in the great darkening at the end of ages. Glory won in the act of battle itself cleanses the spirit so that it may ascend to one day face the greatest fight of all. If you fight and win you will be rewarded with glory and wealth. If you fight and fall, you will attain the highest realm. So, the man who fights with all his strength, will, and spirit can never fail."

"Yes, I remember them," Belolukos said. ""Why do you repeat them now?"

"What about women?" Herkuhlos asked. "What happens to their spirit if they die in battle?"

Belolukos shrugged. "The same. You think the gods would not want Alkmene to fight beside them?" He nodded down at her. "Her spirit is where it should be, brother."

Herkuhlos was relieved to hear those words for he knew them to be true.

They filled the graves with earth and then they dismantled the wall, piling the stones over the graves to make a mighty cairn taller even than Herkuhlos. Both he and Belolukos worked from dawn until dusk without rest to shift the stones.

When it was done, he walked through the trees toward the river. In the woodland he found a brook in the wet earth flowing from a spring and crouched naked in it, washing the blood and filth from his body until the spring was black and red, as if the earth itself bled.

Returning as the sun touched the horizon he saw the cairn silhouetted against the sky, the edges of it shining with the reflected glow.

"It will be seen from afar," Helhena said beside the fire as they roasted horsemeat. "All will know someone of renown lay within."

"They will not know of Alkmene and Kasos," Herkuhlos said, "so it is not enough."

"We will remember," Belolukos said. "We will have their songs sung."

"It was supposed to be Kasos singing," Herkuhlos said, barely suppressing a sob. "He should have lived. He would have been a wise old man."

"He was like an old man from his first name day," Belolukos said, smiling.

"True enough," Herkuhlos said. "But I failed him just as I did our mother. We could have been away across the river and heading home now if I had not been so foolish. So cowardly."

"There was no cowardice in it," Belolukos said, shaking his head. "None could ever think that of you, brother. But now we must return to our own lands. Our own people."

"I do not want to leave her," Herkuhlos said, looking at the shadow of the cairn atop the mound. "Not yet."

"But that bastard will return," Belolukos replied, bitterly. "The Bloodletter will be back here in a day or two with more men and this time we will not live to remember our people. None of them will be remembered."

Herkuhlos nodded slowly but did not speak.

The others lay down by the fire while Herkuhlos sat up to keep watch. He could not sleep. All he could think of was his failures. He had found his mother only to see Laonome killed by Leuhon. Her blood drunk and her body discarded. Abandoning his oath to slay the demons, he had fled in the hope of saving his mother's life. They had survived the fall and the river but his choices from then had been disastrous.

If he had stayed with Orysthos all those moons ago and denied the will of Kolnos then all the brothers of his *koryos* would be alive. Kasos would be spouting lore and singing in their new clan. Dhomyos would be filling his belly and eyeing the young women, Sentos would be on his way to becoming a respected warrior, and Wedhris would be safe from harm.

Instead, he had thought himself a great man, blessed by the gods, and had gotten them all killed.

Worse than that was the knowledge that Laonome would not have been killed if he had not attempted his rescue. His mother only escaped when she did because of the noise and chaos he had caused with the fire. If he had never come, she might have escaped quietly in the night, freed Laonome and been away before anyone noticed. She could have brought her home all by herself and Herkuhlos had spoilt it with his incompetence.

The shame was almost more than he could bear.

When they sang the song of Alkmene, if anyone ever did, they would say that her godborn son was the cause of her death.

He stood and walked away from the fire. For a moment he made to approach the cairn glowing in the moonlight atop the hill so that he might beg his mother's forgiveness but he could not bear the thought that she would not grant it. Instead he turned and walked toward the total darkness of the trees. The leaves rustled overhead. Deeper into the woodland an owl hooted and fell silent.

A noise made him whip around in fear.

Helhena stood in the moonlit pasture.

Slowly, she approached once more and put her arms around him. He held her. She was cold and he rubbed her back to warm her. Soon, she was rubbing his back in turn. The heat rose in them both until they were breathing heavily. At last, he took her hand and led her a few paces into the trees and laid her down atop his furs. He caressed her face and her neck and ran his hand down her body. She shuddered and pressed her lips against his, pulling him on top of her.

For a time, he was lost in the warmth of her body and the softness of her lips. Her fingers raked his skin and she bit his shoulder and his neck. She gasped in pain and pleasure and he knew nothing but the sound of their breath and the heat of their skin and intense joy as the glow of their pleasure rose to envelope them both in overwhelming desire.

When he came back to himself he breathed heavily and his heart raced. Their heads were still together and her breath was on his face. Their eyes met and after a moment they both laughed lightly.

It had felt sacred. And now his spirit felt somehow cleansed and filled with light.

Soon, they lay together in the darkness beneath the rustling branches with her head on his shoulder and his arm around her. Neither spoke. They were together in a way that they had never been before and indeed in a way that Herkuhlos had never known before. It was companionable silence, their bodies entwined and sharing warmth but their minds were going their own ways.

Herkuhlos realised that his thoughts were clear for the first time since the coming of the demons. The tension and uncertainties that had descended on him since the day he had first met Helhena had lifted and he felt both like his old self and like a new man. He had led a war band and he had killed many enemies but he had not felt like he had yet passed into manhood until now. It was not the act of laying with a woman in itself but the sudden clarity that it had brought. Perhaps it was also that the failure that he had been fearing for so long had now completely come to pass.

"I did not obey my oath," he said, softly.

"What oath?" she asked, running a hand across his belly and up to his chest. Her hand was warm.

He laughed softly with his throat. "I swore to Kolnos that I would defeat the *yotunan.*"

She was quiet for so long that he wondered if she would reply. "No man could do such a thing," she said.

"It does not matter if the thing can be done. Even if it were impossible, if a man has sworn to do a thing, it must be attempted with all his will. And I swore it before the god himself."

"But you did attempt it," she said. "I heard how many you faced at Nemiyeh. You were thrown back."

He had not attempted it but he knew what she meant. "My mother would have fallen if I fought. And Bel and Dhomyos, too." Helhena stroked his skin and said nothing. "But at least I would have done what I said I would do." He shook his head in the darkness. "Instead of cleverness and stealth, I should have walked in there alone, looked Leuhon in the eye, and challenged him to fight me to the death."

"Do you believe you would have defeated him?"

Herkuhlos thought about the size of the *yotunan* and his armour of bronze. "No. But victory is nothing compared to an oath."

"But..." she said, trailing off before continuing in a whisper. "Death is nothing compared to life." She buried her head against him.

His shoulder and neck felt wet. She was crying. He did not know what it was that made her weep but it could have been anything or more likely it was everything together. She did not speak of it and so he knew that she did not wish to give voice to her pain and instead he held her close while she wept. Soon, they fell into sleep. They rose before dawn, woken by the singing of the birds overhead. As they rose and pulled down their cold clothes and wrapped their furs about them they shared glances and smiles. It was cold and the lightening sky was clear overhead. Before they left the trees, he held her in his arms and kissed her. It was not like their kisses in the night and Helhena was subdued. Perhaps she was thinking of his words in the darkness. He certainly was.

Returning across the damp grass of the pasture they found Belolukos feeding the fire, watching over Makros who muttered and thrashed in his sleep.

Belolukos smiled at Herkuhlos, glancing at Helhena. "Are you well, brother?"

"I am," Herkuhlos replied. "Are you?"

"Of course," Belolukos said, smile wavering. "I always am." He stuck a foot out and poked Makros in the shoulder. Makros muttered and rolled over, falling silent. "He has been like that all night."

Helhena touched Herkuhlos' arm and nodded at Belolukos. "I must see to the horses," she said and walked away.

"So," Belolukos said as Herkuhlos sat beside him. "You and her." He raised his eyebrows.

"Yes."

Belolukos seemed ready to make a jest but instead he pursed his lips for a moment and nodded. "Good for you. I am happy for you."

His mouth twitched. "Though your manhood may yet rot away from the god's curse."

Herkuhlos sighed, looking at her as she walked away in the half light. "If only I could be happy. I wish she could be, also."

"That is how it works, brother. Men and women." Belolukos made an obscene gesture with his fist and his open hand. "Make each other happy." He grinned.

Herkuhlos laughed quietly. "I cannot see a future like that."

"What, you are a seer now? It is simple, brother. We go home." He nodded toward Helhena who was stroking the neck of a tethered horse. "You can marry her." He held up a hand as if to forestall any objection. "And yes I know she is often miserable, with good reason, but when you win more wealth you can take more wives."

Herkuhlos watched Helhena as she lifted one of the horse's hooves and examined the underside. "You do not have to be a seer to know she seeks only death."

"Once perhaps but surely not now," Belolukos said, giving him a knowing look. "Not when we take her home. She will not be a death seeker with a babe in her belly nor one at her breast."

"Home. I do not know if there is anything for me there."

Belolukos stared at him. "What do you mean? Because Orysthos will take us in?" He held up a hand again. "Yes, brother, I know you do not want that. I understand. Do not go to him. Make your own clan. You will be a great man, you know. A great chief."

Herkuhlos shook his head. "No, I think it is you who will be the great chief."

Belolukos spread his arms and shrugged. "I will, yes. But you will be the greater."

Herkuhlos stared. "Why do you speak like this?"

"It is the truth. It always has been."

"You never said so before."

He glanced at the cairn atop the mound. The light from the rising sun was falling now on the stones. "I never wished to admit it before. All my life, you have been bigger than me. Stronger, faster, better at wrestling. You remember your lore, you know the songs, you never put a foot wrong in the spear dance."

"Now that is certainly not true."

"It's true enough. I... I hated you, I think. For a while." He looked down. "It shames me to admit that. It angered me to see you best me at everything. To have a godborn brother... I thought it nothing but a curse. But when the *tauta* made me *koryonos* I could not believe that I had been chosen over you and I wanted to do everything right so that they would see I was not lesser. I wanted to be better than you at something. Do something you had not done. And I wanted you to think well of me. Respect me."

"Respect you?" Herkuhlos shook his head. "We have fought side by side as we crossed half the earth together. You are my brother." He held out his hand and Belolukos stood and grasped it for a moment. "I would not have chosen to be what I am, you know."

"Godborn?" Belolukos snorted. "Thank the gods that you are or else we would never have gotten this far." His face clouded. "The way you fought that bastard Kreuhesh was like nothing I have ever seen." He glanced at the cairn. "And then you tore through those warriors as if they were lambs to be slaughtered. If only the gods had not allowed Kreuhesh to escape."

Herkuhlos nodded slowly. "And yet it will not change his fate."

Belolukos frowned and was about to ask what he meant when Makros yawned and sat up.

"What in the name of Kolnos are you boys jabbering about?" He yawned again, stretched his wounded arm, and broke wind loudly. "Any of that roast meat left or did you eat it all?" He winced as he got to his feet, scratching his beard.

"There is and you had best eat as much as you can," Belolukos said. "We all should if we are going to cross that river again."

"We are not crossing the river," Herkuhlos said as Helhena came back to the campfire. She met his eye and did not seem surprised by his words.

Belolukos though was both surprised and confused. "But how else do we get home?"

Herkuhlos looked at each of them in turn and then at the cairn on the hill behind them. The sun illuminated it fully now and he understood what the gods were telling him.

"We are not going home." He turned to look north. "We all came here for something and we cannot go home until it is done. The people of our clans that yet live are in Nemiyeh and they need us to free them. And I swore an oath to slay all twelve of the escaped demons. I will start with Leuhon."

They stared at him.

Helhena's eyes shone, accepting it at once. He had known that she would not object.

Makros smiled and nodded. "It will be a glorious death."

Shrugging, Belolukos agreed. "I was looking forward to going home." He looked at the cairn. "But you are right. This is how we regain honour." He turned back to them. "We will be killed, you do know that, brother? We four against a hundred warriors and that demon have no chance of victory."

"I agree," Herkuhlos said, turning to face the south. "Which is why we will need help."

33

Slayer of Yotunan

PELHBRIYA WAS SILENT. They had observed from a distance for half a day and then approached the great walled settlement cautiously when the sun was descending toward the horizon. It was a fine day with a shining sky above them but there were dark grey clouds gathering in the south beyond the mound.

Herkuhlos led his reduced warband to the gateway. It had been rebuilt since they were last there and it was closed and barred on the other side. Peering through the gaps in the timbers showed an empty, quiet street within.

"We will tether the horses here," Herkuhlos said to the others. They had more than twenty horses in their herd now. "If we have to flee from here we want them close."

"Someone to guard them?" Belolukos asked.

Herkuhlos looked at Makros, Helhena, and his brother. "We stay together now."

They climbed the gate, working together to pass their weapons up and over, and found themselves in the empty street on the inside of Pelhbriya.

"I knew it," Belolukos said, his voice echoing from the high walls of the houses on both sides. "That old man was a fool to stay here with none but a few boys to help defend the place. Of course someone was going to take it from them. We will probably find them dead in there."

"Kounos and his acolytes most likely returned to their sacred place in the woods," Helhena said. "There was never any chance of holding this place."

"The gate is barred from the inside," Makros said, holding his spear ready.

"Stay close," Herkuhlos said and led them along the street into the centre of the *briya*. It was deserted. Since their last time there it had been cleaned up, the remains of the campfire were gone, blood stains on the ground were washed away.

"Where are you, Kounos?" Herkuhlos called. His voice echoed from the walls. "Come out!"

They crouched with their weapons ready, scanning the doorways and streets around them.

"They left," Helhena said. "Let us look for them at their sacred place in the woods. It was somewhere between here and the Seeress' lake."

"We will not be able to find it," Belolukos said, standing up straight. "If all the demon's warriors did not uncover it then what chance will we have?"

"We will find it," Herkuhlos said.

"If we can find it that means some war band already has,"

Belolukos said. "The *kerdos* and his boys are lying dead somewhere."

A voice echoed loudly, startling them. "Not yet, Belolukos."

They whipped about to see Kounos standing in the doorway. He stepped out and approached.

"You were hiding from us," Herkuhlos said. "I am glad to see that you are alive."

"We watch always for riders," Kounos replied, nodding at the boys emerging from side streets and doorways. "When any are spotted we take to our hiding places."

"What hiding places?" Belolukos asked, looking around at the three boys.

"Ah," Kounos said, smiling. "Secret places are best kept secret, no?"

"I suppose that is so," Belolukos said. "But that is no way for a man to live. Hiding in a hole when enemies approach your home."

Kounos frowned. "Better to live like that than to die. It is not for me, you understand, but for the boys. There is no glory for a boy dying in battle or being enslaved and if I die then they would be lost without me to lead them." He turned to Herkuhlos. "But why have you come back here? I take it you turned back from the *yotunan?*"

"Will you offer us food and drink, Kounos?" Herkuhlos said. "We have both to offer you, also."

"Of course. We are guest friends. Come, we shall eat." Kounos snapped his fingers. "Boys. Bring their horses in, close and bar the gate behind them, then keep watch again."

They ran off to do just that and Kounos led Herkuhlos and the others into another house close by. It had been tidied and cleaned and was now clearly lived in. There were benches for sitting and low tables, decorated pottery on the shelves, furs and fabrics on the floor and beds. While it was pleasing to see that domesticity had returned to the house it was still wrong without the women that gave a home its heart. And it only served to highlight the eerie emptiness of the rest of Pelhbriya.

After they had shared their food they sat and spoke. Herkuhlos told the tale of their journey since they had left them. Recounting the events aloud only reinforced his awareness of his failures and strengthened his resolve for what he had to do next.

"I am sorry to hear this," Kounos said when Herkuhlos finished. "The *yotunan* bring nothing but destruction. Now you return emptyhanded to your homeland but at least you have your lives. Not all who find the *yotunan* are so fortunate."

Herkuhlos tilted his head. "We are not returning to our homeland, Kounos. Carrying that hope was what we did wrong." He smiled. "Rather, what I did wrong."

Kounos frowned. "I do not understand. You mean to stay here?" He nodded to himself. "I am delighted to hear it, you would all be most welcome, of course." He smiled.

"We are not staying here, Kounos."

The older man frowned, obviously disappointed. "Where do you go, then?"

Herkuhlos searched Kounos' eyes, looking for some sign that he would do what was needed. "You are a man of a proud lineage, Kounos, and when you work in the sacred forge you are close to your god. I know that you are a devout man. You know and understand the lore of your people." Frowning, Kounos nodded and Herkuhlos went on. "So you know also that gods tell us to destroy what is evil. Not to turn our backs on it but to destroy it.

And the *yotunan* are the embodiment of evil."

Understanding spread across Kounos' face. "You mean to go back?" he shook his head. "Son, you are a fine warrior but you must understand that they are too strong. The demon himself need not lift his hand to destroy you. His warriors will slay you if you return."

"His warriors serve evil and so they must be destroyed also."

Kounos looked at all of them. "You four alone? You are nowhere close to being strong enough."

"The lore does not say to destroy evil only if you are strong enough. It does not say to destroy evil as long as the evil is weak. It simply says it must be done."

Kounos was unmoved. "It means death."

From the end of the bench, Belolukos stirred himself. "It means glory."

Herkuhlos nodded. "We are warriors. We are men. I know you are a *kerdos* also and perhaps that is where your greatness lies but you are a warrior also. You are a man. And a man has duties. Duties to his people, yes." He gestured to one of the boys. "But he has a greater duty to win glory."

Kounos was unmoved. "Glory is a young man's pursuit."

"Never have the gods told us this, Kounos." Herkuhlos turned to look at his companions. "And I learnt this from you, Makros."

"From me?"

"You knew always what had to be done and you did it. When your clan was lost, you took your *koryos* against the *yotunan*. You did not weigh the consequences, you did not even expect to live, and yet you did it without hesitation. When you found yourself alone and wounded, you did not hesitate. You went after the *yotunan* and you did not stop until they nearly killed you again. And when we saved your life you did not hesitate to swear yourself to me. Even though your spirit desired either vengeance or death your honour came before all."

Kounos ran a hand over his face. "That is not right, son. It concerns me that you would take his actions for your guidance." Kounos pointed at Makros. "He is alone. The deaths of those young men that followed him are a result of his sense of honour. If he had taken them away to some other land after his clan fell, then they all would live now. And if you wish to take your people back to face death then that is what you will get. Death and no more."

"It is not about death, Kounos. Or life." He glanced at Helhena. "Life is always better than death. But honour is above all. Honour, glory, following the path of the gods."

Kounos sat up straighter. "It is so easy for you to say it. But honour comes and goes. Once a life is lost, it is gone for ever. Do not throw yours away. Or if you must, do not ask your people to follow you into death."

Helhena spoke up. "I go there gladly."

Kounos tilted his head. "Then your spirit is ill, young woman. It must be healed, not destroyed."

"Think of this, then," Herkuhlos said. "You will never have peace. You will never have safety. You will never have life. While evil rules over you."

"We are still here," Kounos said, quietly.

"Living in holes in the ground at the first sign of strangers approaching. You have no life here. You have an existence. And even that will be ended by the first warband that comes through in force."

"No. No, we are keeping this place alive for when others come.

They will come. And some may settle here with us."

"Kounos, we have travelled the lands on this side of the Denipa. There are no good people left here. All that live in these parts serve Leuhon."

Kounos scowled. "I do not serve him."

"You know, Kounos, that a servant lives in fear of his master. He dares not raise a hand against him even when his back is turned because he knows his place. And that is right and proper but it is not how great men of the Heryos should be."

Kounos pushed himself away from the table and stood. "I see you came back here merely to insult me. Well, now it is done. You may now leave."

Herkuhlos did not move. "I came all this way because I need you."

"You need me for what?" Kounos narrowed his eyes.

"First of all, I need you to make a weapon for me."

Scowling, Kounos shook his head. "I already gave you a weapon. The finest weapon I ever made. And I see you bear it no longer. You wish me to give you another? I have a dagger you can have. I will gift it to you if you gift me four of your horses."

"Your sword was good but it got stuck in a man's skull. Some other man must have it now, back in Nemiyeh. I will take a dagger from you but I did not come to take a weapon you already had. I came to have you make a weapon for me. Something new."

Kounos stared in astonishment. "And why would I do that?"

"Because your people are destroyed. You are the last man of your clan. You are here with three boys, one of them merely a herder, pretending that one day all will be well. That somehow more people will come and you will build your clan once more. But

I do not think you truly believe that. I do not think that you are mad, simply that you have not accepted the truth. And I know what that is like because I was the same as you. I thought that I would pluck my kinfolk from bondage and return to my homeland." Herkuhlos shook his head. "That was never going to happen but I could not accept the truth that I can never go back. My clan is destroyed. Just as yours is."

Scowling, Kounos threw up his arms. "You think I do not know that? I live in this ruin with the spirits of my people around me. I know what I have lost. Why should I choose a path that leads to my destruction when I have three young ones who will die without me?"

Belolukos spoke softly. "You will all die here eventually."

"Why not take your boys to the sacred forge?" Makros asked. "You might be safe there."

Kounos was about to answer but Helhena cut him off. "Because you depended on the people of Pelhbriya to supply you with food and you cannot live there without it. And if you mean to go on here you will have to grow your grain in the fields and you will have to find cattle, sheep, pigs to keep. But you could never guard what you have. Perhaps instead you could survive in the woods, hiding from passing raiders that serve the demons, keeping pigs and collecting acorns. Is that the life you mean to live for the rest of your days, Kounos of Pelhbriya, lord of the Heryos?"

Kounos was moved by her words but still he resisted. "From the moment I saw you, girl, I knew you were a seeker of death. You mean to make me one also."

"You are a warrior, Kounos," Herkuhlos said. "You are the last man of Pelhbriya. Help me to destroy the demon that has done this to your people."

He held his gaze. "For all your grand notions this is simply a matter of vengeance for you all."

Makros growled. "Yes."

"Vengeance and glory," Belolukos said, shrugging.

"Vengeance, glory, or death," Helhena said. "What else is there?"

Herkuhlos nodded. "If you refuse to make my weapon, we will fight anyway. But I would have your answer."

Kounos sighed, shaking his head. "I am minded to agree simply to shut you all up." He looked at Herkuhlos. "I can make you a sword. But it will take many days."

"Take as many days as you wish. But I do not want a sword. You see, Leuhon now wears a skin of bronze."

"A skin of bronze?"

Herkuhlos motioned with his hands as he described it. "Like a boar's tusk cap and a leather tunic but instead of the tusks it has overlapping bronze discs about this big. They cover him from neck to groin. When a thrown spear hit him it did not penetrate. It was remarkable."

Kounos cursed. "Marwes, you godless bastard."

"Marwes?" Herkuhlos asked.

Kounos waved a hand. "Marwes is the best *kerdos* in Nemiyeh. He is Kalekka but for some reason the god put his skill into him. Just as he did with Pehur. So he made bronze armour?" He laughed ruefully. "Some of us *kerdos* have spoken of such a thing over the years but who would ever have so much bronze to make it?"

"You have your answer," Belolukos said. "The demon has carried away every bronze weapon from a hundred clans."

"However he has done it he is now protected by armour strong enough to turn aside a spear with ease. And no doubt a sword also, no matter how finely made."

"What do you want, then?" Kounos asked, confused.

"When you gifted to me your magnificent sword I saw that in your secret place you had vast amounts of copper ingots."

"Aye," he said, warily. "I will use it to make weapons and tools and exchange them for food and other goods with the traders who will come up from the Euxine in summer." He glanced at Helhena as he said it. "But I shall gift you some for this weapon. One or two ingots."

Herkuhlos shook his head. "I will need all of them."

It took them eight days to prepare the fuel and to make the mould and prepare everything else that they would need. The forge had been built in what was once Kounos' own house on the other side of Pelhbriya. The wall on the entire front of the building had been cut away leaving only the posts holding up the ceiling on that side. The acolyte Pehur explained this was to let in the light so that they could see as they worked. All the interior had been cleared out other than long benches on the sides with the tools and other equipment necessary for the forging of bronze. In the centre was a kind of clay tower of waist height and in the base was made a fire. The three boys took turns in blowing air into the base of the fire through long hollow tubes.

"You must not be here," Kounos said to Herkuhlos as the fire grew hotter. "It is a sacred place and soon we must call the god."

"I understand." He looked at the huge block that was to be the mould for the weapon. "Will it work, do you think?"

Kounos scowled. "Leave now. I will send for you when I need

you."

While they worked, Herkuhlos, Makros, Helhena, and Belolukos tended to the horses, prepared meals, and watched for the coming of the enemy. Always, their minds were on the forge. Smoke and heat billowed forth, along with chants sung by Kounos and the boys, occasionally rhythmic banging and every now and then curses and shouting. They seemed to go through a huge amount of wood.

Night fell and still Kounos worked. Herkuhlos paced back and forth within the centre of Pelhbriya or walked the empty streets thinking about Leuhon, about Nemiyeh, and Kreuhesh. He thought also about his own people and about what might be done for them, if any survived what was to come.

Before dawn, he woke to the sound of shouting and grabbed his spear. Along with the others he ran toward the noise but they were met in the street by Pehur, who held up his hands.

"All is well!" he cried, glancing over his shoulder. "But I think we will have to start again."

"What is wrong?" Makros asked, rubbing the sleep from his eyes.

"Nothing, lord." He lowered his voice. "You must understand that nothing like this has ever been done."

"Pehur!" Kounos roared from within the forge. "Where are you, you witless herder? I need you!"

Herkuhlos grabbed the boy's shoulder. "What can I do to help?"

Pehur shook him off. "Nothing, lord. All will be well. But it may be some time." He turned and ran back toward the forge as Kounos shouted for him again.

Belolukos and Makros muttered in annoyance as they returned

to the house to sleep.

Helhena stepped close to Herkuhlos. "You have not slept all night."

"Someone has to keep watch."

She stepped closer. "Let the gods keep us safe until dawn."

They retired to the empty house that they had been sharing and knew only each other until long after the sun rose. Every moment seemed imbued with greater meaning because he knew it might well be the last time he experienced it, with her or even with any other woman. Lying back with his arms around her, he watched the motes of dust swirling in the sunlight before the window and idly stroked her shoulder. What was it to lie with a woman who was not your wife nor a captive nor a servant? There was no precedent for it, as far as Herkuhlos knew, only that to lie with a woman who belonged to another man was a terrible transgression. But Helhena belonged to no man and so how could it be wrong?

"Marry her, then," Belolukos said the next day when he spoke aloud his thoughts. They sat together on top of the northern wall of Pelhbriya, looking out for sign of Kreuhesh or any other warriors. "You will marry her eventually, why not now?"

Herkuhlos shook his head. "I do not think that is what she wants."

Belolukos shrugged. "So?"

Behind them the forge still burned hot and the sounds of metalworking filled the air above the roofs of the houses.

"It seems unlikely that we will all live through what comes next."

His brother was irritated. "Why are you even talking about it, then?"

He looked at him. "You know, Bel, in your own way, you can

sometimes be quite wise."

Aware he was being mocked but not understanding how, Belolukos narrowed his eyes. "And you, brother, can take your finest spear and you can shove it up your—"

"Lord!" Pehur said, sliding to a stop in the street behind them, his voice echoing off the walls of the houses. "Kounos needs you, lord. For the weapon, lord."

Herkuhlos jumped down from the wall. "Lead the way."

"First, you must be purified. No man can enter the god's presence without cleansing himself. And you must leave your weapons."

In a water trough outside the forge, Herkuhlos stripped naked and carefully washed his hands and face and then the rest of his body. The water was cold but he took his time scrubbing his skin carefully and while he did so he slowed his breathing and recited the spear chant to Kolnos. When he was cleansed he put on his tunic and stepped into the forge.

The heat hit him like a wall. Standing beside the column of clay, Kounos wore nothing but a leather apron while two of the boys knelt beside the fire and rhythmically pressed bladder bellows, the fire roaring like some wild creature. While they worked, Kounos peered into the top while he chanted words to his god and the boys repeated the chant at certain places. The boys and Kounos ran with sweat while they worked.

"Come forward, lord," Pehur said.

He did so and Kounos noticed him, stepping away from the fire to meet him in the centre of the building. Only when they were close did Herkuhlos note the dark circles beneath his eyes and the wildness in them. It was a look he had seen in the men who danced the spear-dance for days after drinking the mead of war in the midwinter rites.

"You must give me your blood," Kounos said, looking up at him.

"Why?"

Kounos scowled. "The god demands sacrifice. He has refused to come into our work. Now, bleed yourself."

He nodded at Pehur before returning to the fire and the boy came forward with a small knife and a bowl. Herkuhlos took the knife from him and did as he was bid, slicing across his thumb and bleeding into the bowl. It dripped in rapidly but Pehur was not satisfied.

"More, lord," Pehur said. "The god demands more."

Bracing himself for the pain, Herkuhlos sliced his wrist and the blood welled out and poured forth, spattering into the bowl until Pehur nodded and gave him a cloth to cover the wound and stepped away with the bowl. He passed it to Kounos who poured it into a trough while Pehur mixed it in and both spoke the invocations to the god.

"Now," Kounos said, glancing at Herkuhlos. "Stand on the other side of the mould and do not interfere. This weapon must slay a *yotunan*. It cannot bend. It must not break. The magic must be strong. My spells faultless. When we sing we will speak of our enemy. We must tell the metal what is required of it so that it will know it is a slayer of *yotunan*. You must call to your spirit and with your blood your spirit will enter the weapon. Do you understand?"

Herkuhlos nodded. The sweat poured from him in streams while Kounos peered at the molten metal. When he was satisfied he motioned for Pehur to join him and together they lowered two long, sturdy pieces of wood into the top of the furnace and with great skill and attention lifted the glowing crucible. It was enormous and so heavy that their arms shook but even young Pehur did not falter as they moved a few paces sideways and poured the liquid fire into the mould. As they poured they chanted words to honour the god and the glowing metal was so filled with the god's power that it hurt to look upon it. They spilled hardly a drop and as the last of it went in the liquid metal sputtered and bubbled, spitting forth spurts of flame that cooled and solidified as they hit the outside of the mould and the floor. With great relief, they lowered the crucible to the ground. Pehur fell to his knees in exhaustion while the other two boys stopped their work and stood, peering at the mould.

"Did it work?" Herkuhlos asked, staring at the mould. It was hissing as though it was alive.

Kounos shook his head. "We can never know until the mould is broken open."

"What if it does not work?"

"Then the god was not pleased by our sacrifices."

Herkuhlos was impatient to see whether it had worked. "How does the liquid become the weapon?"

"The bronze finds its shape from that which is around it," Kounos said. "Just as men do to the world. But the bronze must be formed properly before it goes into the mould. Just as men must be."

"True enough." They stared at it. Herkuhlos could hardly contain his excitement. "Should I take it from the mould myself when it done?"

"The transformation will already be done but if you were to

touch it now the metal would melt your flesh." He nodded at the trough beside them. "In a moment we shall quench it in pure water, mead, and the blood of the wielder."

Taking a large wooden mallet, Kounos knocked the mould apart and gripped the weapon by the handle with layers of rawhide. Taking it quickly he lowered it into the trough. The water hissed like it was some dying creature and fizzled and flames burst from the surface before turning to smoke and steam.

Kounos pulled out the weapon and slammed it onto a sturdy table with a mighty bang. The weapon was blackened and covered in bumps and sharp flakes.

Herkuhlos' heart sank to see it. "Did it not work?" he asked. "It looks wrong."

"Do not curse it, you fool," Kounos hissed. "It is not finished. Go now. I will bring it to you when it is done."

"How long will that be?"

"Get out!"

Herkuhlos stepped outside. The cold was a welcome relief. It was later than he had expected and he suddenly felt tired, thirsty, and hungry. He left the forge and went to find food, trying to put the weapon out of his mind but always he wondered if it had worked. And if it had worked whether it would be as he had envisioned and described or how it would feel to wield it. He felt sure the gods had put the idea in his mind but if he had not pleased them in the meantime then they might cause the weapon to break or be malformed. As darkness fell, Kounos had still not emerged though there had been some metallic banging sounds from the forge and more singing. After pacing under the stars for a long time, Helhena came to find him.

"All will be well," she said, watching him pace.

"Perhaps." He shrugged. "Or perhaps it will not."

"Is there anything that you can do about it now?" she asked.

"I could make a sacrifice," he replied.

"Or you could come inside with me," she said, stepping in front of him.

He stopped pacing and nodded. "I could. I could do that."

In the morning he went to see if the weapon was ready but Pehur rushed out, blocked the way and told him to leave.

"He is still working?" Herkuhlos asked, incredulous. "Did it not work?"

"Please, lord," Pehur said. "My master will bring it to you when all is done."

Herkuhlos ducked and peered into the shadows of the forge. "Can I help with anything?"

"Please, lord," Pehur said, unmoved and holding out a hand to indicate that Herkuhlos was welcome to go away.

Grumbling he went to the wall to watch the horizon. There was still no sign of pursuit and no indication that raiders were out there but he knew from experience how quickly things could change. At any moment they could burst forth from the trees. Twenty or fifty or a hundred of them. Would Leuhon send Kreuhesh out again with more warriors? Or would he be satisfied with the damage already done? He almost hoped that they would. He wanted a fight.

"Lord?" Pehur called from the street behind him. "It is done."

Herkuhlos leapt down and ran through the streets to the centre of Pelhbriya.

Kounos was there. He carried before him the long weapon wrapped in sheep skin, cradling it against his chest. It was obviously heavy.

All the others came and watched from a respectful distance as Kounos laid it at Herkuhlos' feet.

"Did it work?" Herkuhlos asked. "Is it done?"

Kounos was exhausted but there was triumph in his eyes. "See for yourself." He drew back the sheepskin and stepped away.

It was remarkable.

Herkuhlos reached down and lifted the long club by the handle, grunting at the weight of it. The war club was exactly as he had imagined it only better. Longer than his arm, narrow at the handle and widening gradually to a heavy, thick end. It had been polished so that it almost glowed with the reflected light of the sun.

"Solid bronze," Kounos said, shaking his head. "The first two I made bent and broke. I tried to keep the weight down but they were too thin. This one, I am afraid, is now too heavy but I tested it every way I know how. If the gods are kind, it will not bend and it will not break."

"It is perfect," Herkuhlos said, his voice barely above a whisper as he ran his fingers along its surface.

Kounos sighed. "As I say, it is too heavy. It will tire you to use it, mark my words. You will hardly be able to control it and soon you will be too tired to lift it. And it will be slow, any fool with a spear will kill you before you can swing this once."

Herkuhlos lifted it up in both hands. It was heavy but he liked the feel of it in his hand. More than that, it felt *right*.

"Heavy is good. With his bronze armour I cannot easily cut him or pierce him. But with this I will break him. It is a slayer of *yotunan*." Herkuhlos hefted it onto his shoulder and held out a hand. "Kounos, you have done as I asked. But now I hope that you will do more."

Kounos stared at him. He looked exhausted, ready to sleep for days after his exertions. "More?

Herkuhlos nodded. "I want you to come with us and face the *yotunan*. A warrior of your strength and skill may bring us victory." He gestured at the three acolytes. "Your boys will come but they shall not need to fight."

Kounos closed his eyes for a moment. "I knew you would ask this of me." He opened his eyes and looked around at each of them. "You were right, all of you. When the traders come up from the Euxine they will slay us and take my weapons and my bronze." He nodded at Herkuhlos' solid metal club. "What little remains with me. We cannot go on here. If there is a hope that some of my people could be saved then I must put myself into the hands of the gods." He looked at Herkuhlos. "I am coming with you. For death or undying glory."

Herkuhlos smiled.

"Finally it is done," Belolukos said. "Now we can return to Nemiyeh. For death or glory."

"Not yet," Herkuhlos said. "We are all of us skilled in battle but we face so many foes that we need every advantage we can find."

"That is well." Makros looked around them at the quiet houses. "But what else is there?"

"We need the Seeress."

34

Days of the Spear

THE LAKE WAS STILL. It was quiet. The midday sun shone down on the water and birds flew from the trees atop the cliffs to the green reeds on the lakeshore. There were deer tracks on the mud underfoot as Herkuhlos led his people and horses through the stream and onto the path that led around the lake of Nemos. On one side the bushes and trees at the base of the cliffs were bright green with spring growth and on the other insects buzzed over the water that shimmered in the sun.

When they reached the stone of sacrifice they stopped and made a camp where they had before and Herkuhlos stood patiently by the stone.

"Hello?" Herkuhlos called. His voice echoed from the sheer cliffs around the lake. No one came out.

"Perhaps they want you to make a sacrifice again?" Helhena said. "Bleed onto the rock."

Herkuhlos frowned. "I would rather not." He looked at the base of the cliff. Though he could not see it he knew there was a hole there that enabled those within to look out without being seen themselves. "They will come."

Birds chirped and flitted around them. Kounos' boys collected water from the lake and began collecting wood for a fire.

"It looks as though no one is here, brother," Belolukos said. "Perhaps they left."

Kounos scoffed. "The Seeress has been here always. She is here now."

"Just go into her cave again," Belolukos said, gesturing at the base of the cliff.

Herkuhlos could not admit that he was afraid to do so unbidden. There was no knowing the limits of her power. "I would not violate her sanctuary."

"What is it?" Belolukos said, narrowing his eyes. "Are you afraid?"

Herkuhlos ignored him as he looked at the trees above them. If raiders stood on the cliffs they could shoot arrows and throw javelins to kill them all before they knew they were being attacked. "Listen, I will not have us ambushed again," Herkuhlos said, turning to Kounos. "Send your boys to the tops of the cliffs to keep watch. They are to come running if they see anything. If they cannot reach us they must shout a warning and flee."

Kounos called out to them and they ran back along the path, seemingly thrilled with their responsibility.

"The entrance needs watching, too," Belolukos said, jerking his head. "I will go back and guard the way." Taking his weapons, he went alone along the path.

"I will try the sacrifice," Herkuhlos said to Helhena. With that he took out his knife and laid it on his arm.

The Seeress's voice echoed the cliff face. "That is not necessary, Herkuhlos."

She stood by the entrance to her cave, half obscured by the wall of rock. Dehnu was as tall and beautiful as he remembered, if not more so. And yet there was something in the way she stood that made him uneasy.

"You are here," he replied, stepping in front of the stone of sacrifice. "Where are your servants?"

She did not smile, nor did she frown, but something passed across her face.

"Come," she said simply and slipped back inside.

Herkuhlos stood staring at the place where she had been. "Something is wrong," he muttered.

"Are you sure you can trust her?" Helhena asked. When he raised an eyebrow she went on. "It may be a trap. What if there are enemies within who have already captured her. Perhaps we should go with you. Take Makros at least."

Herkuhlos frowned. "I am sure that is not the case. You saw how strong she was when she killed that raider and I do not imagine she would allow herself to be captured or manipulated by captors." He touched her cheek. "All will be well. Watch for enemies."

"I will," she said, her face set hard. "I always do." With a last glare at the cave she turned away.

The cave mouth was darker and narrower than he remembered but he squeezed himself through and stepped inside. She stood alone in the chamber, facing him.

"Dehnu, I am glad to see you." His smile faltered as he glanced around. Everything was as he remembered it except for the apparent lack of acolytes. "Do you fare well?"

She smiled but there was pain behind it. "I am well. Though I prayed often for your safety and your health I had not thought to see you again. What has brought you to me, Herkuhlos?"

"It is a long tale. Perhaps we might sit together and eat or at least drink?"

"I can offer you fresh water drawn from my lake and some venison. I took a deer a few days ago." She gestured to the small fire in the rear of the cave where haunches and strips of meat hung on frames and stepped to the table where she poured water from a jug into two cups.

She took the deer herself? He noted then that two flint spears leaned against the front wall and beside them was an unstrung bow. A large and powerful one. From a peg hung a bag of arrows. He smiled to see her weapons. That was good.

"Where are your girls?" he asked.

"Will you sit with me?" She indicated the bench and sat opposite.

Herkuhlos eased himself down, the timbers beneath him creaking at his weight. "What has happened here, Dehnu? Were you attacked?"

"Not since you were here. But my servants could stay no longer." She looked through him. "They went back into the world."

"I do not understand. You mean they left you?"

She looked at him. "Our patrons are gone. Pelhbriya and the other places are all destroyed. And so they are no longer able to support us with gifts and sacrifices."

"But you can hunt," he said, gesturing at the bow and the meat.

"And butcher and preserve meat. These woods can provide all you need."

"Nevertheless, without the patronage of the people we have no purpose here. And it is only a matter of time before Leuhon's warriors find us. I sought to spare them from that fate."

"By sending them away? To where? Nowhere is safe out there, Dehnu."

She nodded. "They went south and west. Sari has kin there and perhaps none of these *yotunan* will control that place. For now, at least."

"But they are sworn to you, surely. How can they abandon their oaths?"

Dehnu tilted her head as she regarded him. "You are angry at them but in fact I am at fault. It is my duty to protect them. But the foremost of them was slain because I failed to protect her. The people of these lands look to me for guidance and wisdom and healing but I did not foresee nor forewarn nor protect them and now they are all dead, slain by the *yotunan*. The raiders and war bands prey upon those that survive including us here in my sanctuary. My women began to doubt my power." A sad smile tugged at her mouth. "To speak truly, they lost all faith in it. In me."

"Their duty is to remain with you no matter what. To die with you. They made an oath."

Dehnu smiled. "You think like a warrior. Not all oaths are alike."

"Of course they are. An oath is an oath. It is sacred and must never be broken."

She sighed. "In any case, I freed them from their oaths to me."

She drank from her cup. "I have been tending to my own needs this last month. It is quieter than I would like it to be but I do not mind the work."

"The work?"

Dehnu looked around. "Drawing water, collecting firewood, making the fire, hunting, preparing the food, cleaning." Her hand reached out and gripped the back of his. "Now, tell me why you have returned. What has happened to you? You are different. Older. There is more grief around your eyes but you are more like a man than you were before."

"Grief ages a man, they say."

She frowned, her eyebrows making a small crease above her nose. "They do but I think this is something else. Tell me, then, Herkuhlos. Did you find the *yotunan?*"

He told her the tale as he had to Kounos, except that he found himself softening the events for Dehnu. Where for Kounos he told of the blood and the battles he found himself telling Dehnu of his hurt and his anguish. Listening with the whole of her being, she seemed to feel it as much as he had, her eyes darting over his face as he spoke, her cheeks flushing in outrage and her tears almost brimming over when he spoke of his mother. Finally, he told her of returning to Pelhbriya, the making of his weapon, and his recruitment of Kounos.

"And so I will return and this time I will slay Leuhon and all those that serve him."

"You believe yourself strong enough to do this?"

"To beat Leuhon? I doubt that I am stronger than him. Nor do I have nearly as many men as he does."

Her fair eyebrows knitted above her nose. "How then do you

intend to beat him?"

He shrugged. "I have a sturdy weapon now."

Dehnu all but rolled her eyes. "While I know little of battle I do know that a metal stick is not enough to slay a hundred men and an ancient devourer."

"Surely, as my cause is just, the gods will look favourably upon me?"

Dehnu stroked her cheek with a long finger as she looked at him. "This is why you came to me? To hear me speak aloud the signs of your fate?"

"You may tell me if you like," he said and shrugged, "but that is not why I came."

When he did not continue she smiled and asked the question. "So why did you come?"

"Firstly, I wish for you to tell me more about the *yotunan*."

Her face clouded. "What is it you want to know?"

"Something that will lead me to victory. I do not know what it might be but you know more about them than I do."

Dehnu raised her eyebrows. "What leads you to think that?"

"You must know. You are wise. And you are godborn."

"As are you."

"Not like you. I am young but you are older than any mortal. And you knew your mother. She is a goddess and she raised you, taught you all you know. She must have told you all about the *yotunan*."

"Perhaps. But you have seen one closely now with your own eyes. Surely you know them well enough to fight them?"

"But there is so little that I know." He placed his hands flat on the table. "Some of it was told to me by Kolnos and some by you. I know that they are evil. I know that they were imprisoned by the gods somewhere on the Sacred Mountain. They are enormous, hideous creatures that devour and destroy all they touch. Leuhon is powerfully built, with broad shoulders and thick arms. His face is monstrously twisted and he girds himself in the pelt of an enormous lion. And he is not the only one who calls himself after a beast. Of these twelve that escaped there are some that call themselves Stag, Boar, Dog, Bull. It seems that they mean to travel to distant lands and rule over the people that belong to those lands. Leuhon has taken Nemiyeh far to the north and he will extend his rule far and wide." He trailed off. "You must know more, Dehnu."

She sighed. "There is little I can add."

"But there must be more," he said, reaching for her hand for a moment before stopping himself. "How is that they could flee so far without the gods stopping them? Why were they kept as captives and not killed or banished?"

"Some were banished. Long ago."

He sat up straighter. "Which of them? You mean some of these twelve or others? Why were they banished? Who were they?"

"I do not know their names." She sighed and rubbed her stomach. "Perhaps you would like to share some of my food now?"

He smiled. "With pleasure."

"You should take some out to your friends," she said, standing. "I fear it is rather plain and there is hardly any fat in the meat but at least there is plenty of it."

He did as she said and carried out a basketful of it. The contents were shared out and Makros volunteered to take some to Belolukos and the boys.

Helhena nodded suspiciously at the cliff. "Is all well? Are you still talking?"

"Talking, yes, although we have barely begun." He glanced over his shoulder and lowered his voice. "If I can persuade her, I think she may even come with us."

"Oh," Helhena said. "I suppose that is good."

"If the gods are with us, at least." He smiled, patted her on the shoulder and hurried back. Dehnu served the smoked, dried venison with a pot of fat mixed with herbs both dried and fresh. It was remarkably nourishing and savoury and he ate with as much restraint as he could bear. It struck him as a strangely domestic activity and he felt suddenly closer to her than he had before. Her beauty was distracting and her wisdom intimidating but beneath all that she was a woman in her own home serving food to a guest and that was something familiar and comforting.

"You said when I was here before that you wonder if the *yotunan* are so different from the gods," he said after draining his cup and cuffing his mouth. "You spoke as if it was nothing to say such a thing but I have not stopped thinking about it since last I saw you. I know that you would not lie about anything and so you must help me to understand."

She nodded slowly and paused to collect her thoughts. "When my mother spoke of the gods it was with longing but also bitterness. They are powerful but they can be cruel." Herkuhlos understood that. He knew the songs of the gods and the stories of their interactions with one another and with mankind. "Despite their cruelty and despite everything they did to her she always longed to return to them. And in the end that is what she did. She preferred a life with them over a life with me."

"How did it happen?"

She shrugged as though it was no great story. "After many years together, teaching me the ways of the gods and men, she told me she could resist it no longer. She left."

"Why did she not take you with her?"

"Never could I have gone with her. If she had taken me she would have been thrown out once more."

"I do not understand. Your father was a mortal and yet they allowed him to stay until his transgression was discovered. You are half a god, surely you would be welcomed."

She pursed her lips before answering. A curiously girlish expression. "It is not only what you are but what you do that matters to the gods. Your blood alone is not enough. Your spirit must align with the potential of your birth. My father was made into an immortal because of his greatness in life and the undying glory that he won by his deeds. But when he transgressed they slaughtered him without mercy." She pointed at him. "Your immortal father did." She gestured at her breast. "And I am the product of that sullied union. My mother claimed we would never be allowed in together and so it was better that I stay behind. She claimed that it broke her heart to leave me but ultimately she simply missed her people." Dehnu smiled sadly. "She missed her kinfolk."

"Kinfolk?" Herkuhlos was confused. "What kinfolk?"

Dehnu narrowed her eyes and looked sidelong at him. "The gods. The gods are her kin, surely you know this?"

Herkuhlos scratched his head, frowning. "The gods are... the gods. They live on the Sacred Mountain together but I do not know that I have thought about it. You mean that the gods are one family?"

She shrugged. "Well, they are a clan. A great family. They are all kin. Your father is not the eldest but he is the strongest and has fathered many of the others with many goddesses. And some mortals."

For a long moment Herkuhlos put his head into his hands and leaned on the table. He looked up. "So Kolnos is another son of the Sky Father?"

"A brother, I think. Or a nephew. I am not certain of every relationship."

"Mighty Kolnos is... my uncle?"

"Or a cousin, yes."

Herkuhlos stared through her, recalling their conversation at Orysthos' camp. "He said as much to me when I met him. He said he thinks of me like a distant relation. But he never said the whole truth." He focused on her. "That means we are kin. You and I, Dehnu."

Dehnu tilted her head as she met his gaze. "We are cousins of one degree or another. My mother is the Sky Father's younger sister."

He was astonished and yet also unsurprised. It felt obvious now that she said it. "And your father was mortal. You said they *made* him into an immortal? By what power is such a thing done?"

"There are ways," she said, seeming for a moment that she would say no more before continuing. "I suppose that as we are kin I can speak of it. It is to do with the blood."

"The god's blood?"

She chewed her lower lip for a moment. Another remarkably girlish gesture. "It is sacred lore that must not be shared with mortals."

"You mean you will not tell me?"

"You are not mortal, Herkuhlos. Not really. Of course, we are not gods but neither are we mortal. We are godborn. And our blood also has power."

He nodded slowly. "How do we use this power?"

"Your friend Makros was near death when you brought him to us. It was our blood that healed him."

"I sacrificed my own blood when I came here."

"I did not know you were godborn until I tasted your blood."

"You tasted it?" he frowned. "Why?"

Her cheeks flushed as she spoke. "In order to heal those who are brought to me I must bleed myself." With a long finger she tapped the pale skin of her wrist. "It weakens me to do it but drinking the fresh blood of a mortal brings me strength. Yet when I tasted yours I tasted the power in it. The same power that I have but even stronger. It was as powerful as my mother's immortal blood. That was how I knew you were more than mortal. Makros was so close to death that I doubted whether my blood would heal him. Having your blood also was like a gift from the gods."

Herkuhlos shook his head as if to clear it. "*Our* blood healed Makros? He drank it?" He pinched the bridge of his nose. "Does this mean that I could have given him my blood to drink when I found him and he would have healed?"

She spread her hands. "The potions I make have many ingredients. The water from the springs here are health giving. Some potions include mare's milk or the blood of a stallion or an antelope. Mead makes for a most potent potion as does a certain kind of mushroom that grows in the pastures and in the woodland." She waved a hand. "Many other herbs, also. There are different potions for different ailments. Some will heal. Others, such as the *keudos*, fill a man with great strength and vigour."

Great strength and vigour. His heart began to beat harder. They could certainly do with more of that.

"But always it is your blood that makes the magic? That gives it its power?"

"All power comes from the gods. But yes, it is our blood that carries this power."

"My blood can heal the wounded?" Herkuhlos' mind raced. "So that if my spear-brother is wounded in battle I could give him my blood and heal him? And before we even go into battle I can fill my people with some of my power?"

She held up her hands. "You must understand that it is not to be used lightly."

"But if it helps us to defeat Leuhon then I must do it."

"It does not do to make the mortals overly powerful."

"Did you mother teach you that?"

"She did. Amongst many other things."

Herkuhlos thought that making mortals powerful sounded like a good idea. "What about your father? Is that how he was made immortal?"

"I do not think so. It was something else. Something permanent. Some other rite."

"Your mother never taught you about that one."

"No."

That was a shame. Herkuhlos tapped his fingers on the table. "We must use the power of our blood to defeat the *yotunan*."

"And how would we do that?"

"If all of my people drank one of your potions, ones made from my blood or yours, it would give them strength in battle?"

"A bowl of my *keudos* potion would give them strength and resilience. They would fight for longer without tiring and any wounds taken would heal faster."

Herkuhlos grinned. "Then that is what we must do." He paused. "You know, I came here for you, Dehnu."

"To ask me about the *yotunan*."

"That was one reason. But I want you, Dehnu. I need you."

She stared at him, her cheeks colouring. "I will make potions for your men. And your woman."

"I want you to come with us."

"I cannot."

"You cannot mean to stay here alone."

"I have decided that I will go out into the world." She smiled. "I will go from place to place. I will heal the sick and prophesise. People will welcome me. Give me food. I will find a place wherever I go."

"The world has been overrun with *yotunan*. Eventually you will be caught and brought to one."

"I am strong. I know how to fight. My mother taught me well."

"So I saw. You are immensely strong and quick. That is why I want you."

"You want me to be a warrior in your warband."

"Yes. But I also want your wisdom and your skill as a healer."

Her eyes narrowed. "I think you are afraid of facing Leuhon alone. But you have no need of me, Herkuhlos. I suspect that you still have no true notion of your strength."

Herkuhlos shook his head. "I am afraid, I admit it. But I will face him alone if I have to. I want you because we will do better with you. And because I want to learn from you. You can tell me about the gods. About the godborn. Teach me." He ventured a smile. "And it sounds like I might be the closest thing to kin that you have in the world. Would you not rather be with me than alone?"

"With you I will go towards death."

"We all go towards death, Dehnu. But we can face it together."

"You want me because I am useful to you. Once you have killed the *yotunan* you will not need me."

"We are kin. Somehow, I felt it from the moment I first saw you but I understand it now and I see it in you as I know you see it in me. We are the only godborn either of us know and we should be together. We belong in the same clan."

She smiled. "I belong only here and only to myself."

He rubbed his eyes. "You agree that Leuhon must be destroyed before the proper order can be restored here."

"I do."

"But you expect me to slay him while you do nothing."

She stared at him. "You swore an oath. I did not."

He looked at her face. The smooth translucent skin was flushed pink over her high cheekbones. She was breathtakingly beautiful and quite unlike any other woman he had ever seen. Not merely more lovely but her features were subtly different to the people of the Heryos or the Kalekka. He had no doubt that those features had come from her immortal mother and he wondered if there was something similar in his own face, inherited from the Sky Father. Did others likewise see at a glance that he was different from other mortals, not only in his stature but also in his features?

"Our bodies are different from those of other mortals," he said, surprising her by the change in direction of their conversation. "We are taller than mortals, shorter than gods. We are stronger, faster, our wounds heal swiftly and our blood carries great power."

She frowned at him. "Yes," she said, hesitantly. "More than mortal, less than a god. That is what we are."

He nodded. "And there are three parts to all of us, Dehnu. Our flesh, our will, and our spirit. Our bodies are different from mortals but what of our will?"

Dehnu sat up straighter, tilting her head. "I would say that our will is more vigorous than that of mortals. Look at what you have done while you are yet so young. And I also have endured what would have broken many a mortal."

He nodded, having concluded much the same. "Our spirits, then, must also be greater than those of mortals."

She touched a finger to her lips and cast her eyes upward before answering. "Perhaps. The spirit which is eternal dwells for a time in mortal flesh." She touched her own arm and reached forward to touch his hand. "The spirit is eternal and true while what is physical is temporary and illusory. All flesh fails, even ours, but the spirit goes on forever. The spirit that possesses each of us comes from our ancestors and when our flesh fails that spirit goes on to our descendants. But I do not know whether the spirit of one who is godborn comes from their mortal or their immortal ancestors."

He looked at her hand, still touching his, and then he searched her bright eyes. "How then can the likes of us ever be in true alignment? Body, will, spirit, if we are this in between thing, neither one nor the other? How can we go to our deaths if we cannot be sure our glory will lead to the attainment of the highest realm?"

She took her hands away and clasped them before her on the table. "All mortals know which actions and thoughts are right and

592

which are wrong. And though we are godborn we are surely no different." She placed a hand over her heart. "But there is more. There is a source from where the spirit comes and a place to where the spirit goes. That source is most high. And though they also walk amongst us this source is the essence of the gods. The gods of flesh who are our ancestors carry within them a portion of this source and through them it has passed into us. I feel it in me, Herkuhlos. I always have. Do you feel it also?"

He stared at her. "The fire. The fire in my heart."

"Yes!" she said, reaching for him once more. "Yes, yes, the fire. You feel it as I do!" Her excitement faded and she grew solemn. "The fire of the gods. The divine fire that crashes from the heavens is also within us. That fire creates the strength of our body and our blood. That fire guides our spirit. Just as the fire from the sky crosses the air to find the earth, you must let that fire travel through you, let it guide you along your path."

He looked into her eyes and could almost see the divine fire in them shining out at him. The fire of the gods was also in him and it always had been. He could feel it even now, a spark inside his heart ready to ignite and roar into flame.

"You say all mortals know which actions are right and which are wrong." He tried not to plead with her but he urged her to hear him and to understand. "Surely your own fire rises, Dehnu, when you think of the yotunan. Do you not want revenge over the demon who destroyed the people of these lands? His men penetrated this sacred place and slew your friend. His actions have driven away your acolytes. He is evil and must be opposed. Tell me that your arm does not yearn to take up your bow and your spears, Dehnu? Surely you desire to test your will against your enemy." He ducked his head in order to meet her lowered gaze and searched her eyes. "Now you have spoken of it, I see the fire in you now. Come with me and put an end to this."

She looked at her weapons for a moment. "There is still much I do not know about battle. When we were attacked by raiders, you rushed out without hesitation and threw yourself against those men, killing them so swiftly. By the time I joined you it was almost all over. Your will, your fire, is made for war. Mine, to my shame, is not."

"You must not be shamed. This was a peaceful sanctuary until I came and you were taken by surprise." He gestured at her spear and bow. "You have since decided never to be caught unprepared again."

She replied with a firm nod. "I admit that putting an end to this evil with my own hand would be a restoration of the balance. If only I had spent more days with the spear than gathering herbs."

"We must all dance the spear dance together until we are ready for this battle. Makros will teach us all and we will reach the greatest heights of skill. When we have become a true warband we shall travel to Nemiyeh and together we shall slay our enemies. With your *keudos* in our bellies and the gods looking favourably on us we shall prevail." He paused, watching her closely. "What do you say, cousin?"

Slowly, Dehnu smiled.

3 5

All Things Die

FOR A WHOLE MOON, the cliffs of Nemos resounded with the clacking of spear shafts as they honed their skill. They hunted in the woodland and ate well to build their strength and preserved much for the coming journey north. Their horses were taken for exercise through the woods and out into the pastures and brought back to safety before sunset. At night around the campfire they spoke of their plans, discussed possible flaws, and made improvements.

Kounos and his acolytes built a new forge between the lakeshore and the cliffside and used the last of the bronze to make powerful spearheads and daggers for them all. There was enough left after that for a dozen smaller javelin heads and a score of bronze arrowheads. Bronze was so precious a substance that none of them had ever seen such a thing as a bronze arrowhead before and Kounos admitted he had never made them until now.

"Better to leave them in our enemies' throats that lying here unused," he said with a shrug.

They reshaped and fitted the armour of the warriors they had defeated and carried away on the horses of the slain so that Belolukos and Makros soon wore boar's tusk helms. There was not enough for more. Herkuhlos insisted that he had no need of it and refused all arguments to the contrary. When he had suggested that Helhena bear one instead of his brother she had sharply refused.

"If I fall, you will all go on to victory. If Makros falls or Belolukos then all is lost."

Makros smiled at her affectionately. "My head is harder than a slither of boar's tusk anyhow." He rapped his knuckles on his head to prove his point.

She laughed at him and looked down while Makros grinned at his own joke.

"We will all fall," Kounos said without turning as he bent over his work. Their smiles fell. He paused and peered around, shrugging. "There is no need to pretend otherwise."

"Our fates are in the hands of the gods, Kounos," Herkuhlos said. He gestured to the helm that Belolukos was sewing together. "But we shall do everything we can to bring victory."

They cut poles for new spears and javelins and carefully shaved down arrow shafts until they were faultlessly straight. It was long, tedious work but each one represented the death of an enemy and they had a great many enemies to slay.

Kounos' three acolytes worked harder than anyone, tending to the camp while also carrying out their work for their master. With every spare moment they could find they disappeared into the woods to practice fighting. The sound of their weapons clacking echoed across the lake and sent birds crying into the air.

"They will bring our enemies right to us," Belolukos grumbled the first time it happened.

"Worry not," Makros said with a grin, "the boys will fight them off alone."

"Do they think they will be joining us in the attack?" Helhena asked.

Belolukos scoffed at that. "They would not survive the first swing of the axe."

It was obvious that they were too young to fight but like all young boys their spirits had grown too large for their bodies to contain them and they were bursting with desire for war. A few days later, Pehur came to Herkuhlos after they had danced the spear dance and knelt before him.

"Lord, I wish to fight beside you against the demon. They killed my kin, lord. Took my sisters away. I have as much right as anyone to seek vengeance against them!"

Herkuhlos sighed and cuffed the kneeling boy across the face. Shocked, he fell sideways and stared up with a hand on his cheek. The blow was hard enough to sting but no more.

"Do not disrespect your master by addressing such a question to me, boy." Herkuhlos gestured at Kounos.

Pehur glared at him, tears welling in his eyes as he got up and went to Kounos. "Master," he began.

"No, you young fool," Kounos said. "Now, see to your work."

Wounded beyond words, Pehur ran off with his head down. The other boys ran after him.

Helhena turned on Herkuhlos. "That boy practically worships you. And now you have broken his heart."

"I know," Herkuhlos said. "I hope that his broken heart keeps him from me."

"You hope to save his life with your cruelty," she replied. "But he has as much right to seek death in this fight as any of us."

Belolukos rolled his eyes. "He is a boy."

"You are barely four years older than he," she snapped.

"And he is a herder," Belolukos shot back. "He is born to hold a stick not a spear."

Kounos would not accept that. "However he was born," he said, fixing Belolukos with a hard look, "the god chose him to work bronze. He made that fine dagger in your belt, son. I would not be so quick to dismiss his low birth."

Belolukos was unmoved. "Working metal is hardly the same as battle." He nodded at his brother. "We have been learning to fight since our seventh year with bow, spear, axe, and our bare hands. We were born for this and we have lived for this. That lad is not even Heryos, he is Kalekka. He can work metal but he should not fight. It would be wrong."

Kounos pursed his lips. "What if his spirit is that of a warrior?"

Scoffing, Belolukos waved a finger in the air. "That is not the way of the spirit, Kounos. Herders are born with herder's spirits. They must aspire to be the best herders that they can be but they cannot be anything more."

"Have you never known a man of your clan to be weak in spirit? A man well born but who lacks the will to fight?"

Herkuhlos thought at once of Wedhris and by the look on Belolukos' face he did too. "No," Belolukos said. "But even if I had that is not the same thing. A boy of Kalekka blood cannot have the spirit of a warrior of the Heryos."

Kounos went very still. "I have Kalekka blood."

Caught off guard, Belolukos frowned. "How can that be?"

"My mother's mother was Kalekka." Kounos shrugged. "Many of the *tauta* of Pelhbriya had Kalekka blood." He spread his hands. "Even before my ancestors conquered Pelhbriya they had raided across the river and carried away Kalekka women for their wives. We are still Heryos."

Belolukos shook his head. "Your spirits were still passed through the blood of your ancestors to you, yes." He nodded down the lake path along which Pehur had earlier fled. "How could he have a warrior's spirit?"

Kounos laughed aloud. "The Kalekka had warriors amongst them. Of course they did!"

Herkuhlos nodded as he thought of it. The people who had built Pelhbriya and Nemiyeh and other places must have been strong once. Not as strong as the Heryos but still there must have been men of will and spirit amongst them.

"Would you allow Pehur to fight?" he asked Kounos.

Kounos frowned. "He would fall."

"Perhaps. But what happens to them when you fall? None of us may be coming back from this?"

"Better they have a chance of life than none at all."

Herkuhlos was not sure that he agreed but he let it go as it was not really his concern. There was enough to think about with their preparations for the journey north.

It was vital that they fought with the power of Dehnu's *keudos* in their veins. She gathered the ingredients she needed and made a concoction meant to enhance the strength, speed, and health of those who drank it. They sat together in a circle and passed the bowl of *keudos* around, each taking a sip.

"Imagine how strong you will get after this, Herkuhlos," Belolukos said as he waited his turn. The firelight reflected in his wide eyes.

Dehnu looked at him across the circle. "Much of its power comes from his blood and mine. We shall not find our strength growing from the *keudos*. We have the power already and you will experience but a fraction of it. However, the *keudos* is not blood alone. It will bring our spirits alive and we shall all see and hear with great clarity."

Herkuhlos drank. It tasted earthy and sweet and he knew there was mead and milk and honey and the sacred mushroom within. It warmed his belly by the time he passed the bowl on and soon he felt it spreading through his limbs and into his eyes. The others around him gasped and looked at their hands and flexed their limbs, their eyes shining with joy.

"Come," Herkuhlos said, standing. "Let us dance the spear dance."

Taking up their weapons they chanted the words of the dance, stepping and thrusting their spears as one, turning and striking again and again. Herkuhlos' heart raced as he slipped from one form into another, flowing through the manoeuvres as he never had before. Around him, the others did the same. All of them now danced with precise rhythm as if they were a single being with many limbs. When the dance was completed, they stood in silent wonder at their new abilities.

"It brings on the wolf spirit," Makros said, his voice deep in the darkness. "My ancestors were within me. I feel them still. Never have I stepped into the wolf skin with such ease."

Dehnu, tall and magnificent with her shining spear in her fist, turned her gaze upon him. "The wolf skin? The wolf spirit?"

He shook his head. "In battle there are some warriors who lose themselves in the fighting. The spirits of the ancestors possess him and he fights without thought, without his own will. In my clan I led the chants for my spear-brothers and the young men of the *koryos* to help them to give up their spirits." He nodded at Herkuhlos. "There are a few warriors who slip into the wolf skin every time they fight. With others it comes upon us when we fight for our lives, when our ancestors deem us worthy. For most of us we must sing their spirits down before battle is joined. But this *keudos...* it is as though a door is opened and the ancestor spirit slips straight through."

"These songs," Dehnu said. "Can you sing them for us?"

It was late spring when they left the sacred lake. On the morning they left the sun was warm and blossom was bursting forth at the edges of the woodland as they rode into the pastures around Pelhbriya. Throughout the journey they watched for raiders and set up sheltered camps every night with two or more of them on watch until dawn. There was little talk. Even when they were at rest they were mostly alone with their thoughts. All knew they were likely riding to their deaths and they each had to find their own peace with what was to come.

Belolukos was determined above all to slay Kreuhesh the Bloodletter before he died. "If the gods grant me that much I shall not complain about the shortness of my life and I will stand proudly to receive my judgement."

Herkuhlos nodded though it was almost too dark to see anything in the woodland. They sat apart from the others who lay sleeping by the dying fire. "He shall pay for what he and his men did. And so will Leuhon."

Belolukos slapped his shoulder. "I believe in you, brother."

Herkuhlos snorted. "You think I will fall?"

He felt rather than saw his brother's shrug. "He's big. And he's ugly." Belolukos grinned. "But so are you."

"Thank you."

Belolukos laughed quietly.

"I have been thinking often of Gendryon these past few days," Herkuhlos said.

"Oh?"

"He is often in my thoughts. I still hear his words. His advice."

Belolukos snorted softly. "As do I."

"Neither of us knew any other father. But I think now how it must have been for him. We were not his. When he married our mother we were babes in arms and she was considered cursed."

"Lucky for him she was or else he never would have had the chance to marry her. Kweitos Clan was hardly powerful. He was fortunate. Blessed."

Herkuhlos smiled. "You were the son of Lektros. A descendant of Perseyus and a man whose destiny was to one day unite the clans of the Heryos and rule as chief of chiefs. And I was the son of a god."

Belolukos grunted. "Not just any god."

"Indeed. And yet he never seemed to resent us. He never treated us as anything but his own sons."

"He certainly beat us like we were."

"He did what was right and what was good. Our blood never mattered to him."

602

Belolukos shifted beside him. "We always knew he was a good man. If we die well perhaps we can see him soon. You can give him your thanks then."

Herkuhlos was silent for a while. They looked out at the darkness, seeing little, listening to the breeze in the branches and the occasional scurrying of small animals in the undergrowth. Far away an owl hooted once.

"We have a strange clan now, do we not," he said, gesturing with his head toward the others.

Belolukos chuckled silently at that. "None stranger."

"And not one of them are of our blood. But I would die for all of them."

"So would I. And we probably will." Belolukos turned in the darkness. "Why do I feel as though you are saying something without saying it? State your meaning, brother."

"No meaning. Not really. I am thinking a little about what might come after. If any of us survive."

"Little point in that."

"Perhaps. But a leader should look ahead. Even far ahead."

Belolukos shrugged. "I would not know."

"But you will be a leader, Bel. You will be a chief. You do want that?"

"I have always wanted that and I want it still. These trees, Holkis, this land. It is wrong here. We should be out on the plains now and planning the summer raids. I miss the sky. Yes, I want to be chief of my own clan but I do not see a path from here to there. And anyway, we have a hundred men and a demon to slay before we need to think of such things, do we not?"

"We do," Herkuhlos said. "Yes we do."

They made their way north through many days of spring rains without meeting any of the enemy. When they drew closer they slowed and went ahead more carefully, one or two of them riding ahead to scout the area while the others came behind with the spare horses. Just a day southwest of Nemiyeh, if their reckoning was accurate, Herkuhlos rode ahead with Helhena on fresh horses. They left the camp before dawn and went slowly and carefully, going easy on their horses in case they needed to ride hard away from enemies. It was not long before they spied a gap in the thinning trees ahead and picked their way toward it. When they reached the edge of the woodland they saw Nemiyeh in the distance. A steady rain fell across the pastures and fields from a low, dark grey sky. Herds moved in the pastures and people bent to the earth in the fields. It was remarkably peaceful.

"There it is," Helhena said, her face dark. "I wonder if any of those people are ours."

"If they are then soon they will be free."

She looked at him. "You believe the gods are with you."

He nodded. "I do."

"I think they are, too." She said. She did not smile. "They are not with me."

"Would you prefer to stay back with the boys when we attack?"

Her head whipped around. "Nothing will stop me fighting."

He wished that he had been able to ease her pain. "Your kin may yet live, Helhena."

She turned her horse around. "Come on. We must tell the others that we have arrived."

They stopped in the woodland before midday, established a camp and made their preparations. They lit no fire and they took turns to watch. Mostly, they were silent as they worked. While they prepared their clothing and checked their weapons, Dehnu prepared the *keudos*.

Herkuhlos thought about Leuhon. The sheer size and power of the demon. Was it even possible to defeat him?

"It is late," he said to his people. "We must eat well, rest, and marshal our strength and prepare ourselves. Sleep early. We shall begin in the dark of the night and cross to Nemiyeh as the sun rises."

Despite the knowledge that he should take his own advice and rest his body for the coming fight, Herkuhlos could not calm himself enough for sleep. He lay on the cool earth and closed his eyes but his mind raced with images of battle. Again and again he saw Leuhon struck by the spear thrown by his mother. He thought of his contest with Kreuhesh and the inhuman speed and the strength of the man. His thoughts drifted to Kolnos giving him his name and he hoped that Gendryon had seen it from the afterlife. He thought then of Orysthos in the east taking the best of the pastures for himself now that the demons had cleared the vales of the clans of the Heryos. The demons themselves filled his mind. Enormous, destructive, terrible, evil, spreading out into the world and he had sworn to slay them all. The weight of his oath was heavy enough to take his breath away.

Unable to rest, he got up and stepped away from the camp, walking thoughtlessly towards Nemiyeh. The sun had set but its light was yet shining from the sky above. It was dry now and the clouds were thinning. Through the trees he could make out faint light in the *briya* from many lamps in and amongst the houses.

A sound from behind startled him but it was just Dehnu,

picking her way closer through the trees. She had long since changed from her long robe into the woollen tunic and trousers of a warrior. She wore a bracer on her arm, as if she expected to be shooting her bow at any moment. A close-fitting leather cap hid much of her braided hair. For all that, she was still beautiful. The light of dusk making deep shadows of her eyes.

"Do I disturb your preparations?" she asked as she drew near, her voice clear and calm as a still lake.

"I am prepared," he said. "And you are always welcome."

She smiled. "Your mother gave you good manners, Herkuhlos."

He shrugged. "The truth does not require prettying. I want to speak to you. I wish that we could have spoken more but there never seems to be enough time. And now..."

"And now we may never speak to each other again? Yes, I too have been thinking of mortality." She smiled. "My own, I admit."

"If you wish to avoid the battle then I understand."

She looked hard at him and he knew that she was a little insulted. "Nothing will turn me aside now. My decision was made when I was still in my home. No, I mean only that I have not thought overly about my own death before these times. I knew I would go on for many mortal lifetimes. My world was safe and constant. Until the *yotunan* came. And now he must be destroyed. It is an undeniable fact, is it not, that devourers cannot be appeased, submitted to, or permitted. Nor can they be ignored. Destroyers must be destroyed. No, nothing will turn me aside now."

He nodded, looking out at the faint lights of Nemiyeh, seemingly brighter now that the cloak of darkness was spreading across the land. "It must be strange for you to be so far from home."

She nodded. "I have been out in the world before. My mother

and I walked often from place to place, north, south, east, and west. We met many people."

"Was that not dangerous? Two women alone?"

Dehnu smiled. "My mother is as tall as you and even stronger, perhaps. Mostly, people welcomed us. Many worshipped us on sight. My mother is terribly beautiful and it was not uncommon for men to throw themselves at her feet on sight."

Herkuhlos stared in disbelief. "She cannot possibly be more beautiful than you. It is all I can do to resist throwing myself at your feet right now."

Laughter burst from her lips before she clamped a hand over her mouth, looking around guiltily. "We are both of us fortunate to bear the blood of a god in our veins."

He nodded, thinking that she meant only his strength. "You said before that there were gods all across the earth. Far from the Sacred Mountain, beyond the plains, beyond the two seas and far to the south. Did you meet any on your wanderings?"

She sighed. "My mother was careful to avoid crossing into lands ruled over by gods or *yotunan*."

"The *yotunan* are out there also? Did they escape from the Sacred Mountain? Why do the gods not destroy them?"

Dehnu looked over her shoulder toward the camp. "There is much I do not know. Most of it happened before I was born and my mother spoke of it but rarely. There are gods and there are *yotunan* that left the north long ago but who they are and where they went she either did not know or she did not tell me."

Herkuhlos looked through the trees. "We were not taught about that. Kolnos did not tell me either." He shrugged. "And there is nothing to be done about it now. We know where our enemy lies."

Dehnu looked at him but in the darkness he could not read her expression. She reached out as if to touch him but then pulled her hand back. "I should sleep for a while now. We must rise soon and begin the rite. You should rest also."

"I will," he said and he smiled. "I have been glad for your company."

She nodded and slipped back toward the camp. Full dark came soon and settled heavily beneath the trees. His thoughts circled about the gods and the *yotunan* until frustrated he returned to the camp. Makros sat up with his back to a trunk with his war axe in his hands. One of the boys stood close to the horses. Herkuhlos joined the others who were lying either in sleep or at rest and he pulled his furs over him. Soon, Helhena came to him and slipped beneath his covering to lay against him, one leg over his, her head on his shoulder. He held her tight and tried not to think that this might be the last time he held her or held anyone at all.

Someone shook him.

"It is time," Makros muttered.

The halfmoon was up and bright beyond the swaying branches but the darkness was deep beneath the trees. They all woke, collected their war gear and followed Makros through the trees to the edge of the woodland where Dehnu awaited them. The three boys stayed back with the horses, watching them in silence.

Dehnu motioned for them to stand in a circle and this they did. Herkuhlos glanced in the direction of Nemiyeh. It was dark there now but the distant sky beyond was touched with the first light of the coming dawn.

Lifting a large bowl before her, she drank deeply from it and passed it to her right. Herkuhlos, Belolukos, Makros, Kounos, and Helhena all drank down the draught.

When all had drunk, Makros took up two spears and clacked them together. Slowly, he beat a rhythm with his spears upon the earth and while he did so he began to chant the words of the spear dance. None of the others moved but instead breathed with him, in and out, holding their breath with a lungful of air at the right moments and expelling hard when compelled by the chanting.

Herkuhlos felt the power of the *keudos* spreading from his belly into his chest and then into his legs and arms. His fingers tingled and when he looked up the stars seemed suddenly brighter overhead.

Rocking back and forth, Makros sang steadily, calling down their ancestors. His words were low, projected from his belly and he now exhorted the others to repeat his words, leaving space in his chant for them to do so. They breathed and chanted with him to strengthen their spirits as the might of the *keudos* awoke in their bodies. Around them the world glowed brighter and the trees almost seemed to breathe with them and birds sang overhead.

His singing grew louder and the spears beat faster as the chanting ebbed and flowed but swelled ever more. The world grew lighter. The blacks and greys became touched with vivid blues and purples and then the swaying grasses became green and yellow. Makros turned to the east and raised his spears high.

They turned and sung with him as the dawn broke over the treed horizon. Beyond the great river, beyond the plains of their distant homeland, the sun rose and they greeted it with a roar, shaking their spears. When their roar died away the silence was overwhelming. No birds sung. Surely even the people of distant

Nemiyeh had heard their roar of defiance.

"Our ancestors are within us," Makros said, looking at each of them. "Their power beats within our bodies and our spirits sing with their strength and with the will of the gods we will defeat the evil in that place." He pointed over the hill with a spear.

Herkuhlos knew it was true. He had never felt such strength. Had never known such clarity. His eyes were wide and the world poured into them.

"We go to death and to glory," Herkuhlos said suddenly, his face hard and his eyes focused. "All things die. Kinsmen die, cattle die, and horses die. There is but one thing that never dies. The gods watch us now and the glory we win today shall never die."

Kounos called out and the boys led six horses forward through the trees and out onto the hillside where they mounted.

They saw Nemiyeh clearly now on its mound hard against the river. A light mist drifted along the river beyond the trees lining the bank and figures moved within and amongst the penned herds around the base of the mound.

Herkuhlos rode out with the others coming hard behind him and he led them quickly down the hill onto the pasture and across the fields, their horses' hooves drumming on the dark, fertile earth. It was not long before they were spotted by the herders and a few muted cries went up. They carried on, riding toward the entrance between the walls of the clustered houses as herders stepped out of their way or cringed amongst the animals inside their pens. No doubt they thought one of Leuhon's own warbands was returning from a raid and were not unduly alarmed.

But then when they were close to the bottom of the mound a cry of warning split the air. A warrior stood in the street, frowning

610

at them and he turned to call to others deeper within. Four warriors ran from the shadows and leapt atop horses tethered in a long row beyond the houses.

Herkuhlos pulled his horse to a stop and the others did the same behind him. He pulled his weapons from the loops, pushed his horse around and slapped her rump to drive her away. Soon all six of them were on foot with their weapons ready on the muddy track leading into Nemiyeh and the four horsemen charged toward them, kicking up dirt before coming to a stop in front of them.

Herkuhlos walked forward and the others spread out beside him as if they meant to walk slowly into the *briya*. In his left hand he carried his thick bronze spear and in his right was his solid bronze war club. He felt invincible.

The leading horseman scowled as he looked down at them. "Who in the name of Leuhon are you?"

Herkuhlos did not stop as he replied, raising his voice. "I am Herkuhlos. I am here to slay the demon Leuhon. Stand aside or be slain."

They gaped, astonished and confused.

"You will stop!" the leader of them said, turning his horse sideways in front of Herkuhlos to block the path. Behind him more warriors were emerging on foot from the street.

Despite the racing of his heart and the closeness of death, Herkuhlos felt suddenly calm as he looked at the men before him. It seemed to matter nothing whether he fell and his muscles quivered with the *need* to fight.

Exploding into movement, Herkuhlos leapt forward and stabbed his spear through the man's neck and pushed his horse aside. The horse turned and fled in panic, throwing the dead rider as it went. The other men hefted their weapons but Makros and Belolukos ran forward and speared two while Helhena put an arrow through the throat of the last man.

Herkuhlos stepped over the bodies and went on toward the warriors gathering ahead. Now that the smell of blood was in the air the herders were fleeing while the warriors were readying themselves for combat. Cries of warning and anger echoed from the buildings.

"Quickly now," Herkuhlos said and jogged along the track with the others behind him, the shadows of the trees extending long across the fields.

The dozen warriors gathering at the mouth of the *briya* soon increased to a score and then more warriors appeared behind them. They were confused and many were only half-dressed, rubbing sleep from their eyes, and a few were unarmed. Although they were angered by the deaths they were not afraid of only six raiders.

Not yet.

A handful of the most daring came down the track and spread out across it beneath the outermost of the houses. A small man commanded them, calling at them to be ready and to stay in line. Then they shouted a warning and shook their spears.

Hooves drummed behind Herkuhlos and he turned, ready to fend off an assault.

Instead, he cursed.

It was Pehur, riding hard on one of their horses. Barely slowing, he threw himself from its back with a spear in one hand and three javelins in the other. He staggered as he landed and came after them. Kounos shouted at him to get away, to flee, but Pehur refused.

"I can fight!" he said, his voice breaking.

"Leave him," Herkuhlos snapped. There was no chance that the untested boy would live through the day but it was too late to do anything about it now. "He has made his choice."

"Bowmen!" Makros shouted, pointing with his spear.

On the slope three men stood with bows in hand and even as he saw them they were bending their bows ready to shoot.

Almost before Makros finished speaking Dehnu and Helhena shot two of the men and Kounos ran forward a few paces and launched a javelin. The bowmen fell before they could get off a single arrow.

The sudden violence drove the enemy on the track into a frenzy of rage and they rushed forward. Herkuhlos went forward to kill the men in the centre of the line. The small one was the leader, the bravest of the enemy, and he was an older man with scars on his face and tattoos on his arms. His face was twisted in a battle rage and he thrust his spear low at Herkuhlos' loins. Herkuhlos turned it aside with a flick of the wrist and stabbed his spearhead through the man's open mouth, shattering teeth and driving the point out of the base of his skull. Without stopping his forward advance, he ripped his spear free and brought his war club down atop the head of the man on his right. The weight of the weapon and the power of the blow crushed the man's skull and felled him like a sacrificed bull.

On both sides, the other enemies were brought down in moments by Belolukos, Makros, and Kounos. While they fought, Dehnu and Helhena shot arrows into the mass of warriors ahead with incredible rapidity.

They advanced over the dead a few paces before more warriors rushed toward them. The shouting filled the morning air like a storm and then a big man with a long-hafted war axe was coming right for him with a snarl on his bearded face, the man's braids bouncing wildly as he ran.

Herkuhlos leapt forward and rammed his spear through the man's heart, shattering ribs and driving him to the ground. The impact was immense, travelling through the spear shaft and down his arm to rattle his teeth but he did not stop. Instead, he pulled his spear free in a shower of blood and bone and he swung down his club at the next man, smashing the warrior's axe aside and kicking him in the stomach, doubling him over. He swung his spear in an arc into the face of another man before smashing his war club onto the back of the doubled over warrior, breaking his spine and sending him crashing to the mud.

Then there was space before him. They were close to the houses and the funnel of the street ahead was packed with shouting warriors. The foremost of them edged forward with their weapons ready. On one side of him Belolukos slammed his spear deep into a warrior's belly while on the other Makros roared a wordless battle cry as he crushed his enemy's skull. More arrows flew overhead and then javelins smashed into the men ahead.

Herkuhlos advanced quickly across the open ground where the warriors crowded one another. Though his heart hammered in his ears he was filled with the calm of the battle rage and he knew that his ancestors were in him, giving strength to his arm. He broke into a run for the last few paces and with a roar he crashed into the men before him, stabbing out with his spear to kill a man, clubbing another, shouldering aside a third before his momentum slowed. Then he was pulling his spear back, thrusting again.

This was glory. To fight with such skill and purpose was the path to glory. To breathe and strike and step with body, will, spirit, and immortal fire all in alignment brought the favour of the gods and the ancestors and he felt them within him now. He almost laughed aloud, such was the joy of battle.

Something smacked into his head and he saw stars for a moment but he did not stop and his spear thrust and stabbed ahead, left, right. He ducked a spear thrust, took a glancing blow from a war hammer on his shoulder, and killed the man who had wielded it. Blood filled the air along with the screams of the dying and the cacophony of the men ahead of him.

Beside him, his brother and his friends fought their way through. There were no more arrows now nor javelins. Dehnu and Helhena fought at the flanks with spears to stop any warriors who sought to get around behind them.

They advanced one step at a time while the mass of enemy warriors backed away or fell and soon they were in the shadowed street with buildings rising up close on both sides. Still, they advanced. Herkuhlos was dimly aware of men shouting at others to back up and to give them space and he smiled, knowing that they were too close together to fight properly.

His spear cut down one and then another. His club brought down the next. He swung it down onto the skulls of those who faced him and they fell. Some who stood before him now wore helms of boar tusks but these were no defence and they fell also, the tusks breaking and flying to the ground, stained with the blood of the wearers.

Now sticky with blood all along its length, his spear suddenly splintered and he dropped it, using only his massive war club. It was heavy and his shoulder ached from swinging it but swing it he did, sweeping it left and right to clear a space. All who were struck were killed or wounded or knocked down. It broke bones and split open skin.

He was cut on the arms and a spear cut a gouge into his thigh and another sliced along his skull above his ear but he felt no pain despite the blood leeching from his wounds. It was terrible and yet he almost laughed with the joy of it. It was as though the enemy were wading through water while he struck with the swiftness of lightning. His club crashed left and right and he drove a path through the enemy. He walked on corpses and the dying, the earth soaked with their blood.

Around him and ahead, the enemies thinned. Those at the rear of the mass of warriors were fleeing and then, quite suddenly, those before him turned and ran also. The last of them, those that hesitated in indecision, he brought down without mercy.

And then the street ahead was clear. There were corpses at his feet and the heels of the fleeing men ahead but there were no more facing him.

From somewhere a horn sounded.

Again, the horn echoed from the top of the hill. From the centre of Nemiyeh. A horn recalling the warriors to fight in another place. They had not broken, then.

Breathing heavily, Herkuhlos glanced around to see how many of his people he had lost.

They were spattered with blood, most of them were wounded and their eyes were wild.

But all of them lived. Even young Pehur still stood, blood soaking his hair and his face grim. Behind them all the way down the slope the street was filled with bodies. Some still writhed and groaned. A blood-soaked hand waved slowly in the air.

Catching his eye, Belolukos nodded once.

"We go on," Herkuhlos said.

On shaking legs he led them into the *briya*. The street was clear ahead but for a small group of warriors at the top of the slope who kept a watch on their approach, backing away carefully and silently.

"We are being led into an ambush," Belolukos said, growling with the rage that filled him.

"On," Herkuhlos said, knowing it was true. "We go on."

"They will fill us with arrows the moment we clear these houses," Makros muttered.

"Let it be done, then," Herkuhlos said, feeling despair and hope and rage and acceptance. "Let us not fear but go on to the end. Stay with me, brothers. Stay with me, my people."

He broke into a run, charging the group of warriors ahead. Their enemies turned and fled, pushing and shouting. In their panic to get away, some fell and these were speared or clubbed as Herkuhlos and the others ran through them and on up the hill.

They burst out into the centre of the *briya*, ready to fight and ready to die, the warriors ahead of them streaming away in every direction.

This is it, Herkuhlos thought. This is where we will be filled with arrows and attacked.

But they were not.

There were warriors at the edges of the open square, in groups here and there with their backs to the walls of the surrounding houses. They watched but they did not attack. The only noises were the shuffling feet and clattering weapons of the slowly retreating warriors.

In the centre of the square, standing before the huge temple, was Leuhon.

The mighty *yotunan* wore his bronze armour and the shining scales over his chest flashed in the dawn light as the sun crested the buildings. On his forearms he wore bronze strips from wrist to elbow. On his legs from knee to ankle he wore gleaming bronze greaves and protecting his head was a helm of bronze. Atop it all was his huge lion pelt, the lifeless eyeholes staring out.

Leuhon smiled.

He turned to Kreuhesh the Bloodletter who stood at his side.

Pointing a shining arm at Herkuhlos, Leuhon spoke to Kreuhesh.

"Kill him."

3 6

Undying Glory

HERKUHLOS GLANCED AT his brother as Kreuhesh came down the hill at a walk, smiling from beneath his boar's tusk helm. The warrior hefted a long war axe in one hand and a heavy spear in the other.

"I will kill you now," Kreuhesh said, his voice echoing from the walls around them.

Belolukos stepped forward two paces ahead of Herkuhlos and raised his bloody spear. "You will face me, demon slave."

Kreuhesh stopped his advance and sneered. "Stand aside, boy."

"You will fight me, you worm, you dog," Belolukos said, his voice loud in the silence. "I challenge you!"

Kreuhesh gestured with his weapons. "You are nothing. You are not worthy to cross spears with me, boy. I will kill your master and only then shall my axe take you."

At that, Herkuhlos stepped forward and raised his voice so that all in the square could hear. "This is Belolukos, son of Alkmene and Lektros, and he is my brother. You are right to fear him!"

Kreuhesh shook his head and turned to look at Leuhon. The *yotunan* stared implacably for a moment and then gestured at Kreuhesh who turned back to Belolukos.

He nodded and stalked forward once more. With a final glance at his brother, Herkuhlos stepped back to the others. He caught Makros' eye. The older warrior shook his head slightly, indicating that he thought Belolukos was about to die. Herkuhlos thought he might be right. But he was not prepared to stop him from trying to avenge their mother.

Shifting his hand along his spear to shorten his grip, Kreuhesh grinned. "You should know, boy, that I am filled with the power of my god."

Herkuhlos glanced up at Leuhon in surprise as Belolukos threw back his head and laughed, shaking his spear. "As am I!" he roared.

Before Belolukos finished speaking, Kreuhesh threw his spear.

Too late, Belolukos threw himself to the side. The spear ripped through the muscles in his shoulder and staggered him. Someone was shouting warnings and he looked up to find Kreuhesh rushing forward and the Bloodletter chopped with his long war axe. Belolukos danced back, ducked under the next chopping blow and came up to butt Kreuhesh in the face with his head, sending him reeling. With two hands on his spear, Belolukos smashed the shaft against Kreuhesh's arm with a terrible crack and he dropped his axe. The blow split his skin and brought forth a cry from Kreuhesh as he staggered to the side. But the strike cracked the spear and the head fell clattering to the ground. Without hesitation, Belolukos rushed forward against the off balanced Kreuhesh and swung the broken end of the spear shaft down onto his helm.

Kreuhesh hardly seemed to feel it and as the blow fell he drew a long dagger from his belt and slashed up at Belolukos' face. Though the younger man turned away, the blade ripped open a gash in his cheek. Before he could recover, Kreuhesh stabbed his blade into Belolukos' belly, grinning in triumph as he twisted the dagger.

Herkuhlos shouted in horror.

With Kreuhesh's blade still in his belly, Belolukos jammed the splintered end of his spear sideways into Kreuhesh's neck.

He staggered back, grasping the shaft, confusion on his face as Belolukos pulled out the dagger, limped after Kreuhesh and stabbed the blade into his chest. Kreuhesh dropped to one knee with his hands now around Belolukos' wrist, his mouth working soundlessly, bringing Belolukos down with him so that they knelt before one another. With a final burst of strength, Belolukos yanked the dagger free before plunging it into Kreuhesh's eye.

Leuhon's chief warrior fell into the dirt.

Breathing hard, Belolukos slowly stood. The wound bled freely and the hot blood soaked his belly and loins. He looked down at the body at his feet for a moment before looking up at Leuhon. Herkuhlos thought that he would speak but instead he turned his back and limped toward him. His brother's face was grey but still he managed a smile.

Herkuhlos clasped him on the shoulder and glanced at Dehnu. She nodded once and Herkuhlos stepped away from his friends, walking past Kreuhesh toward Leuhon.

Suddenly, he felt all the wounds he had taken in the fighting so far. The gash on his head was worse than he had thought and the wound on his thigh stopped him walking properly. His shoulder was a mass of agony where a blow had struck him and he could hardly raise his arm without jarring pain. He found his loins were drenched with blood and he touched a wound low on his belly that he did not recall receiving.

Please, Sky Father, give me strength.

"Now you fight me, Leuhon," Herkuhlos said, raising his voice to a shout.

The *yotunan* surprised him by shaking his head. "We must not. It is forbidden."

Herkuhlos stopped. "What?"

Leuhon tilted his head. "We are gods, you and me. And the gods are forbidden to kill one another. There are few rules for gods. But that one is sacred."

Herkuhlos almost laughed. "I am no god. And neither are you."

Leuhon shook his head, the lion's mane shaking and the fur catching the light of the sun. "We are the sons of gods. That makes us gods, cousin. You should stay, we can speak together. Come and eat with me."

Scoffing, Herkuhlos stared in astonishment. "You are not the son of a god."

"Two gods." Leuhon held up two fingers. "My mother is the goddess Ekidna. My father is the god Typhon, brother of the Sky Father. We are kin, you and I."

Herkuhlos shook his head, though there was doubt creeping in. "I do not believe you. The *yotunan* lie."

"*Yotunan*, yes." A smile spread on his twisted face. "That is what the gods call us. Demon, *dura*, *yotunan*. They are insults, words to unmake our glory by deceiving the minds of men." He raised his arms and his voice. "I am Leuhon the Lion God!" He dropped his arms, his bronze armour clanking. "Once, I ruled alongside my brothers and my sisters the Stag God, the Boar God, the Bull God. Men brought us their sacrifices and we ruled them. And I doubt you have even heard the names of Geryon, Ladon, Wodra, or mighty Kerberos? Of course not. Your father could not slay us but he slew our people and so our glory was no longer sung." He smiled, gesturing at robed men behind him and the warriors all around. "Until now."

"You are mad," Herkuhlos replied, confused and unnerved. "Your words have no meaning."

Leuhon tilted his repulsive head. "Did you know that my father and yours fought a great war? If my father had won, it would have been the Sky Father who was imprisoned and we would have ruled the world of men." He spread his huge arms and breathed deeply. "But now we are free once more and now we take our rightful place as the rulers of men."

"You may have escaped from the Vale of Tartaros and crossed forest and plain but you cannot flee from me," Herkuhlos said.

Leuhon sneered. "Escaped? We did not escape." He pointed a huge hand. "Your father finally did something right. He freed us."

"No," Herkuhlos replied. "I do not believe your lies. The god Kolnos sent me to stop you all."

Leuhon threw his head back and roared with laughter, the deep sound echoing from the walls. "So, Kolnos sent you to your death? He must despise you, cousin, to give you this task." Leuhon's smile faded. "Kolnos is a sly one. You should not heed his words. Him and his brothers and sisters are jealous of us and fear that our power will rival theirs. And they are right to fear us for we will cover all the earth with our rule." His eyes shone from beneath the snarling jaws of the lion's head. "We twelve are but a portion of our clan and the others have long been abroad in the wide world. We will make our most faithful acolytes and warriors into immortals and one day we will each will bring ten thousand mortal warriors filled with our power against those who name themselves gods. Kolnos and all those who worship him will fall. None of them will resist our might. Ekwa, Welnos, Heusos, Plenwhi, Heros, Manu, Yemo, all of them will submit to us or they will die." Leuhon's deformed lips pulled tight. "And then, when all his kin are ground into dust, even the Sky Father will bow down to our rule."

A hundred questions flashed through Herkuhlos' mind. Had Kolnos lied to him? Deceived him? Used him? If so, he would not be the first god to manipulate the actions of a man but still the thought stung like a wound. Did that deception somehow unmake his oath to slay the *yotunan*? No, it could not. The oath was spoken and so he was bound by it until the end.

But Leuhon also claimed that the *yotunan* had not escaped from the Vale of Tartaros beyond the Sacred Mountain. Rather that the Sky Father had freed them. That could not possibly be true.

Even if it was, Leuhon had declared his intention to make war upon the gods and those that worshipped them. No matter what Leuhon said, no matter whether he spoke truth or lies, he had to be slain. They all did.

"You are not a ruler but a devourer," Herkuhlos said, lifting his club. "The gods bring order but you and your kind bring nothing but destruction. This land is not ruled it is emptied and broken. You have killed so many of my people. Your men slew my mother. You slew my sister. You destroyed my people. And I challenge you.

624

Let us fight now."

His voice echoed. Scores of men watched in silence.

Leuhon nodded slowly. "I hoped you would understand. You have a great strength in you, cousin, I see it. None could doubt that you are your father's son." The *yotunan* affected a sad tone. "In time, you might even have become as strong as one of us but alas you are not yet fully grown. You look like a new born foal, boy. It is a mistake for you to fight me. Come and sit with me a while and I will tell you all about your father and his kin and of the evil they have done."

"I am strong enough to fight you. To defeat you." He raised his voice. "But I see the truth that you are afraid to face me!"

Leuhon turned and waved to someone behind him in the shadows of the temple before turning back to Herkuhlos. "Such crimes you accuse me of. I claim them all with pride. They are my glory. Glory is won through great deeds. Through actions that change the world of gods and men. But there is one crime I did not do."

He turned, reached down, and dragged someone forward to stand at his side.

A young woman with long fair hair.

"Laonome!" Herkuhlos cried, his heart pounding.

He stepped forward, unable to believe his eyes. His sister. She was alive.

"Go to him, child," Leuhon said, almost affectionately.

Laonome walked slowly across the open space until she stood before Herkuhlos. There was muttering around him now but despite the eyes of so many on him he saw only her.

"Is it you?" he asked softly. "Is it truly you?"

She smiled. "It brings me joy to see you, brother. You have grown even taller."

With one arm he pulled her into an embrace, though he was coated in blood. After a moment he held her away from him and looked down. "How is it possible? I saw you die."

"I was bled, yes." Laonome's eyes welled with tears. "Bled to the point of death. But he came to me. He gave me his blood to drink. It healed me." She hesitated. ""Leuhon says he will make me immortal. He says he will make me into one of the undying ones, like him."

"He has hurt you."

She shook her head, frowning. "He can be... kind. He calls me daughter."

He glanced up at Leuhon who stood watching, his face expressionless. "Laonome, I am sorry but you must know about our mother. We escaped but we were caught by—"

"I know," she said, tears flowing freely. "Kreuhesh told Leuhon. He told me." She screwed up her face and shook her head. "Leuhon was angry and he punished Kreuhesh somehow."

"It is my fault," he replied. "I did everything wrong."

"No," she said, looking up sharply. "No, it was *them*." There was fire in her eyes, drying her tears. "I want you to kill them."

"Yes. And I will free you, Laonome," he said softly and kissed the top of her head.

Keeping his eyes on Leuhon, he embraced her again with his free arm and held her for a moment. "Makros," he said over his shoulder, and pushed Laonome gently away into his friend. "Take her to Bel."

Makros led her away to the others behind Herkuhlos. Dehnu

had given Belolukos blood from her veins to heal his terrible wound and though he was not fully healed he swept Laonome up into his arms.

Now there was nothing between Herkuhlos and Leuhon.

"You are no god!" Herkuhlos shouted. "You are a demon. A destroyer. And you are a coward. Fight me before your men or they will know you for the weak deceiver that you are."

Leuhon stared at him for a moment. Slowly, he nodded his great head, the mane shaking above his shoulders.

"When I have killed this one," Leuhon said, raising his voice as he addressed his warriors. "You will stop his followers from fleeing and then I will drink them. No one harms the girl."

"You are evil," Herkuhlos said, walking slowly toward Leuhon. "You are a monster. Devourer. Destroyer."

Leuhon smiled as he turned his eyes upon him. "Boy, you cannot harm me. My skin is bronze. My strength far the greater." His smiled dropped. "I shall break your bones and tie you to the stone of sacrifice. There I will flay you. It will take you many days to die, I will see to that." He looked past Herkuhlos. "That one is magnificent." He was talking about Dehnu. "I will take both of your women and if they are strong enough to bear my sons I shall make them my wives."

Herkuhlos snatched up Belolukos' broken spear, took a step and hurled it at Leuhon. He aimed for the *yotunan's* neck where there was no armour protecting him but the spear was unbalanced without its full shaft. The giant braced himself, tucking his head down to protect his face, and the bronze spear hit the bronze armour of his chest with an almighty clang and bounced away.

By then Herkuhlos was already running at Leuhon with his

bronze club in his hand, crossing the open space between them in a few swift strides. When Leuhon looked up from beneath the rim of his helm, Herkuhlos was already swinging his club in a wild arc. Leuhon stepped back and the blow landed on the armoured forearm of the giant with a loud clang as he swatted it away, sending Herkuhlos staggering. His arm rung from the impact but he swung again, aiming for the giant's head.

For all his size, Leuhon was faster than a man and he punched a massive fist into Herkuhlos' face before the blow could land. It broke his nose and for a moment he could see nothing but a cloud of silver boiling up from the depths of his blindness. Stepping back with his hands up his vision cleared just in time to see Leuhon's kick coming. It was aimed at his belly but he darted to the side and swung his club sideways at Leuhon's body. The impact clanged against the scales of the armour and Leuhon grunted but swung his fist backwards, catching Herkuhlos on the side of his head, sending him staggering once more.

This time he found himself sprawled in the dirt and scrambled to get up as Leuhon took two great strides toward him. Herkuhlos swung his club, aiming for Leuhon's head but the giant turned the blow aside and stepped back as Herkuhlos swung again and again, each time the *yotunan* blocked the blows with his armoured forearms.

He caught the club in his hand and wrenched it from Herkuhlos' grasp before punching him in the face again. By the time the blow landed, Herkuhlos was already throwing himself back from it. This saved him from the full force of the strike but the impact sent him reeling back four paces and he fell hard with his arms spread flailing. The impact knocked the wind from him and

628

he smacked the back of his skull on the hard earth.

Leuhon looked at the club in his hand, grunted, and cocked his arm back.

Herkuhlos rolled aside just as the thrown club smacked into the ground where he had been lying before bouncing away. He jumped to his feet and with one eye on Leuhon he scrambled after the club and grabbed it as it rolled to a stop. It was a relief to hold it once more.

Leuhon's lip curled up in disgust as he turned to his acolytes. "My spear."

One ran forward with the weapon and held it out to his god before Leuhon snatched it away. It was taller than the *yotunan* and topped with an enormous broad shining spearhead. He levelled it at Herkuhlos.

"You could have been a god. Now you will not even be a man."

Leuhon walked forward and brought his spear back. Breathing hard, Herkuhlos fought down the urge to run away and instead forced himself to close with his enemy.

He had to get close.

It was his only chance.

The *yotunan's* spear came flying forward without warning, Leuhon rifling it through his hands with a flick of the wrist. By instinct alone Herkuhlos swatted the shining spear point aside with his club but the strength behind it was immense and it moved hardly at all. Enough to avoid piercing his chest but still the edge of the spear carved a gouge through his shoulder.

Herkuhlos yelled in agony and fear as he leapt away, feeling the hot blood gushing forth down his arm. He did not even have a moment to glance down at it before Leuhon's spear came at him again, flicking sideways at his face and then his chest and low at his thighs and loins.

Retreating and fending the strikes with his club, his breathing was heavy and his heart raced. Sweat poured into his eyes and he felt sick, the blood from his wound running down to his hand and flying off in droplets as he defended himself.

The spear nicked a thigh above the knee and he jumped back, fearing to take another wound. The shining spearhead came up from nowhere and raked his chest, ripping through his skin.

It was only a matter of time before he was killed.

His vision blurred as he fought for breath through his exhaustion. It had been madness to face a *yotunan* in combat, he knew that now. Especially one with a skin of bronze. Even if he struck him with his club, he could not do him harm. It was hopeless. The only vulnerable part of him was his throat and he could not get close enough to land a blow there. He wished he had brought a noose instead of a club.

The spear sliced across his belly and Herkuhlos fell backward and found himself staring up at the bright blue sky.

His hatred for Leuhon filled him completely as he thought of his impending death at his hands. The *yotunan* would slaughter his companions and his sister would forever be a slave to a monster. Leuhon would soon have wiped out his entire clan and the demon would go on, ageless, as the lord of Nemiyeh and many other lands.

The rage at the injustice drove him to his feet just as Leuhon thrust the spear for the killing blow.

Roaring, Herkuhlos smashed it aside with his club, breaking the spear shaft with a mighty crack. He swung the club into Leuhon's head, crashing it against the lion's pelt and the bronze helm beneath so hard that Leuhon dropped to one knee.

The stunned *yotunan* blindly grabbed at Herkuhlos but he smashed the bronze club once more onto the lion pelt and sending the giant down onto his hands and knees. Herkuhlos hit him on the back through the lionskin but it seemed to have no effect as Leuhon began to get up.

In desperation, Herkuhlos dropped his club, threw himself onto the giant and wrapped one arm around his neck. The lion's mane was in his face and he could hardly breathe but he grabbed his own bloody wrist and squeezed with every ounce of strength left in him, throttling his enemy.

Leuhon reached back to grab at him but Herkuhlos buried his face into the lion pelt back and squeezed harder. Grasping Herkuhlos' forearm with both hands, Leuhon heaved down and loosened Herkuhlos' grip, giving him a moment to take a breath.

Herkuhlos redoubled his efforts and pulled his arm back across his throat but Leuhon got to his feet and stood with his legs planted, pulling against the arm around his neck. Leuhon's head was bent back, his spine arched, but his massive fingers fought to prise the grip off his neck and he was almost succeeding.

Now with his feet off the floor, Herkuhlos knew he could not resist the *yotunan's* efforts much longer. He could hardly breathe through the stinking lion pelt. Already, he had gone beyond his endurance. His heart raced and he could not get enough air. His strength was leaving him.

It would all be for nothing if he failed now.

Before his grip failed for the last time, he braced his dangling legs against the giant's back and heaved with everything he had. All his hatred, all his rage, all his desire to live, all his yearning for glory he put into it, leaving nothing inside himself.

There was a mighty crack.

Leuhon went limp and fell backwards, toppling like some ancient forest oak and crashing to the earth on top of Herkuhlos.

For a moment, he could not get a breath but then he forced the great weight off him and scrambled out from under the motionless *yotunan*. Sweat ran down his face and stung his eyes but he saw through blurred vision that the monster was still breathing. In terror he lurched across the ground looking for his weapon. Instead he found the head of Leuhon's broken spear and grabbed it, turning back on shaking legs to defend himself.

Leuhon lay on his back, breathing heavily, with his eyes open and flicking left and right. But he lay still with his arms out to either side.

Herkuhlos limped over to him and looked down. The demon's neck was covered in bruises and the whites of his eyes were filled with blood.

"For," Herkuhlos said, between breaths, "Alkmene."

Leuhon opened and closed his mouth but no sound emerged other than a gasp as Herkuhlos pushed the spear into his throat. The skin there resisted for a moment and then parted as the blade slid through all the way to his spine. When he pulled the blade free, Leuhon's blood welled up and flowed down onto the earth, soaking into it. His eyes fluttered closed, a faint look of confusion on his hideous face.

Fighting for breath, Herkuhlos looked up through blurred vision at the hundreds of silent faces all around him.

The warriors stared between their fallen god and the god killer. They could kill him with ease, he knew. As exhausted and wounded as he was even one of them alone could do it. He waited, not knowing how to stop them. It was in the gods' hands now.

Makros broke the silence, stepping forward into it and lifting his spear high over his head. "Lay down your spears for godborn Herkuhlos!" he roared. At that, he tossed down his own weapon and knelt, bowing his head.

All around him, the warriors stared at Herkuhlos. The wind swirled the dust of the earth. High above, crows cawed as they circled in the warm air rising over the hill.

A hundred spears and axes crashed to the ground.

And they knelt.

3 7

Return

HERKUHLOS WATCHED THROUGH blurred vision as Makros and Belolukos shouted and waved their arms at the warriors, commanding them to stay.

"The godborn will not slay you," Makros cried. "He seeks no vengeance. You need not flee."

He noted then how some of the warriors were slipping away but others stayed, looking at one another, at Makros, at him.

Belolukos clutched his gut with one hand but with the other he shouted that they had submitted and so would not be harmed. Herkuhlos almost laughed aloud at the notion that he was even capable of harming anyone right now but then that was no doubt why they were saying it in the first place. It was in the hope that they would not realise they could still overwhelm him with their numbers.

Then again, they had kneeled. Perhaps their will was broken.

Then Helhena rushed toward Herkuhlos, her bloodied face filled with concern, and grasped his arm. "Come here."

She pulled him toward the temple building. After taking a few steps he felt himself stumbling but then Dehnu was there to hold him up and she half carried him into the shade of the temple.

"Sit here," Dehnu said, easing him onto the edge of the stone of sacrifice. She raised her voice and spoke commandingly to someone. "Bring water."

"Will he die?" Laonome asked. She was with them and Herkuhlos wanted to tell her that he was well but all he could do was groan.

Dehnu smiled. "Of course he will not die."

"You can save him?" Helhena asked, her voice high.

The Seeress was unconcerned. "His spirit is strong and so is his body. He will save himself."

Laonome shook her head. "He has saved all of us."

Soon, Dehnu raised a cup to his lips and he gulped down cool water. It was the sweetest thing he had ever tasted and at once his vision cleared. Laonome, Dehnu, and Helhena stood before him, concern on their faces.

He smiled. "You are all alive." He frowned. "Or am I dead?"

Dehnu laughed. "We live. Nemiyeh is yours." She glanced over her shoulder. "And I think that these warriors are yours. Now, lie down for a moment."

He looked down at the great stone under his backside. His blood flowed across it and collected in the shallow depression in the centre. "I do not need to lie down. I need to command these men. There is still danger here."

Gesturing at the crowds with a sweep of his hand, he saw

Makros pointing at a group of men on one side of the square and Belolukos ordering more on the other side, waving his spear as if herding sheep. Kounos directed a handful of others to gather up the weapons lying on the floor. Young Pehur, somehow still alive, was at his side.

"You are in command," Dehnu said. "And your men are doing your bidding. Victory is yours. You may rest now."

Herkuhlos nodded slowly, his eyes drifting to the great body of Leuhon. "I will rest," he said. "Just for a moment."

Even so, he found he did not have the strength to lay down and when Dehnu moved to help him he waved her away.

"You will heal faster if you allow me to tend to you properly," she said.

"I am well as I am," he said, softly. He breathed deeply, feeling the wounds on his skin stretching and pulling as he did so. But those wounds would heal. They always did.

Laonome touched the back of his bloody hand with her fingertips. "I will find some of the women to bring you food. And mead." She smiled. "I know you would like some mead, brother."

He grasped her wrist as she turned to go. "Do not leave." He wished to say more but the words stuck in his throat and he pulled her to him and wrapped his arms around her. She hugged him back for a long moment before he pushed her gently away so that he could see her again. Her face was wet with tears and her dress was now completely covered with blood. "I have ruined your dress," he said.

She laughed and threw her arms around him again, making him wince.

"You there," Dehnu said to the woman who had brought the

water. "We must have food and water brought here. And mead."

"Yes, mistress," the woman said, bowing her head. "Only, it's shut away. We are not allowed into the stores without..." The woman glanced at the bodies of Leuhon and Kreuhesh.

Dehnu frowned. "Your lord sits before you. All that is here is now his."

The servant bowed again. "What if the guards are still there?"

Dehnu turned to Helhena. "I find myself unused to such obstinacy and incompetence. What is there to be done?"

Helhena turned and called out to Makros, waving him over. He frowned and jabbed his finger at the subdued warriors before approaching. His frown turned to a smile and then a broad grin as he approached. "You didn't die, then," he said to Herkuhlos.

"Neither did you," Herkuhlos replied.

Makros shrugged. "The day's not over yet."

"You have subdued a hundred men with your finger, Makros," Herkuhlos said. He found the strength then to sit up again and waved away the objections. "I think all will be well."

"It is you that subdued them." Makros glanced at Leuhon and shook his head in wonder. "But I told them that all who stayed would not be slain. It was spoken rashly, without consulting with you, I know but I had to take charge quickly. And now it has been spoken and I will not go back on my word."

"You have no need to."

"Some are fleeing, though."

"Let them go," Herkuhlos asked. "Let them all go."

"If we don't stop them going we'll have raiders all around us for moons. Until we hunt them down and kill them, anyway."

Herkuhlos frowned. "Most of them will go home. Any who wish

to go can go."

Makros shrugged. "Lot of people here. Women, too. Children. Might be a good idea to make many of the men stay. I reckon bring the harvest in, see out winter here, and them that wants to go in spring can go."

"Women and children," Herkuhlos said, nodding slowly to himself. "Have them brought forward into the square. I will speak to them."

Dehnu shook her head. "You need rest."

He waved that away, wincing at the motion. "They will be frightened. Terrified about what will become of them. I would put their minds at ease. Have them brought out. And Makros send some good men with this woman here to open the stores and then they must be guarded properly before some of these fleeing warriors start raiding it."

Makros scowled. "Why did I not think of that? It will be done, lord."

Lord, he calls me. This is what glory brings.

He had to admit that he liked it.

While he ate and drank, his wounds healed a little and the women washed the blood from his body, the people of the *briya* filed slowly into the square. They shuffled in with their heads bowed, glancing up the hill to the temple.

"They are so many," Dehnu said, holding a hand over her heart. "They are so afraid."

"It is all we have known," Laonome said. "Fear and death. Much of it at the hands of these warriors you now command. Although many of the worst you have already killed."

"We will rule them," Herkuhlos said, though it felt wrong to say it. "They will be ruled. Any man who harms one of his own people will be slain or exiled. We will rule these men and they will protect the people, not harm them."

"But they are not one people," Helhena said. "There are people of the forest and of the plain. You can see it on their faces, in their stature, the way they wear their hair. I can see half a dozen from clans I recognise and a hundred more I do not. People from river lands. Folk from the shores of the sea in the south."

Herkuhlos nodded, watching Belolukos and Kounos and Makros commanding the crowds. "Everything you say is true but my leaders here will lead and the warriors will follow them."

"What do you mean, your leaders?" Helhena said, looking back and forth at the assembling people. Men and women and children of the Heryos and Kalekka filing into the square and filling the side streets. "You would have Makros and—"

She broke off, frowning and then clapped a hand over her mouth and groaned.

Herkuhlos sensed that something terrible had happened and his heart sank as he searched the masses of faces for the cause of the danger.

Without warning, Helhena broke into a run and called out. "Haedha! Weita!"

Two young girls ran from the crowd and Helhena dropped to her knees and threw her arms around them, pulling them into her. They buried their heads into her as Helhena sobbed, her body wracked with each shuddering breath.

Dehnu turned to Herkuhlos, a question in her glistening eyes.

"Her sisters," Herkuhlos said, smiling.

Dehnu nodded, sighing. "I would have liked sisters," she said, almost to herself.

"Perhaps one day you will have daughters," Herkuhlos said. "Help me up." He groaned as he stood. Never in his life had he ached as much. "Bring Bel, Kounos, and Makros to me, Dehnu."

She nodded and walked down the slope, calling out to Makros. The eyes of the watching crowd followed her graceful form.

Herkuhlos limped forward until he stood outside the entrance of the temple, looking down at the crowds below and around him. With a start he realised it was just where Leuhon had stood to address them and glanced at the body still lying in the dirt. A hush descended on the crowd as he regarded them. His brother, Makros and Kounos came up and stood to one side.

"No, come and stand beside me," Herkuhlos said to them. They did as he commanded and he nodded once and turned to address the crowd. "I am Herkuhlos. The *yotunan* Leuhon is dead. And I, Herkuhlos, have slain him."

He watched them closely as he spoke, weighing their reactions. Eyes glanced at the body and back to him. His heart raced but he felt right and he felt true, and as the words came from his mouth it was as though the gods and the ancestors were guiding him just as they had in battle.

"Now, I shall be your lord. For a time." His men glanced at him. "All of us here are from many clans. Some of you are from the forests in the north. Others are from the plains to the east. Some are Kalekka or Heryos from this land. Those of you who wish to stay in Nemiyeh may do so. Your lord here will be Makros."

He placed a hand on the astonished warrior's shoulder. Makros stared at him with his eyes wide.

"Makros is now the chief of Nemiyeh and all who serve him

faithfully will find good fortune." He let go of Makros and reached for Kounos. "This man is Kounos. There is a mighty *briya* to the south of here called Pelhbriya famed for its high walls and its bronze that lies all but empty. Those of you who were taken from there shall return. But it is a large place with many houses and vast fields that need planting and soon. It requires new men and women. Those that live there will have land to work. They will do so under their chief who is Kounos. Those who follow him will find good fortune."

He turned to Belolukos. "This young chief is the famed warrior Belolukos. Some of you saw him slay Kreuhesh the Bloodletter. Belolukos is the bravest man I know. And he is my brother. I would have died a hundred times were it not for the strength of his spear. His spirit longs always for the plain and I know there will be many of you who feel the same. Those of you who do not wish to stay in these lands may cross the river and return but you will do so together, as one clan. And Belolukos will be your chief as he leads you back to the east." Bel's head jerked as he glanced at him, his eyes filled with emotion. Herkuhlos smiled. "The wisest amongst you will swear yourselves to him for the rest of your lives. All who serve Belolukos will find great fortune."

"What about you?" a voice called from the crowd. An old warrior stepped forward. "We would serve you, lord. You have won glory in sight of us all and we would serve the slayer of Leuhon."

Many heads nodded.

"You could do no better than these three men beside me. If you heed nothing else then heed that and swear your oaths to one of them." He held up a hand. "But I have another task. A task no mortal may help me in. I swore an oath to Kolnos himself to slay

the twelve *yotunan* that escaped from Tartaros." He pointed to
Leuhon. "There lies one. Eleven more remain that must be slain."
Herkuhlos smiled. "And that is what I shall do."

3 8

G o d b o r n

IT WAS LATE SUMMER when Herkuhlos left Nemiyeh. For many moons he had stayed to set things right and his presence as the slayer of Leuhon had helped to provide stability. Makros had settled immediately into the role of chief of Nemiyeh and not only was he respected but had started to be loved for his firmness and fairness.

Most of the remaining people of Pelhbriya had left rather quickly with Kounos but there were few others who wished to leave Nemiyeh for another place and so the walled fortress remained underpopulated. It was hoped that in time more people would be drawn there by its rich lands and defensible position close to the trade routes. Though the smaller population remained somewhat vulnerable to large raiding bands, Makros had sworn that if Pelhbriya was ever threatened he would lead the warriors of Nemiyeh to their defence.

Kounos had not taken to rule as easily as Makros had, for he preferred always to work in his forge than to settle disputes and make vital decisions. But he was wise and just and his people had great affection for him. Pehur and the other acolytes took over much of the forge work from Kounos and there was much to be done since they had come into possession of the vast bronze horde of Leuhon.

While he had itched to leave for the plains, Belolukos had stayed to organise what he needed for the journey east. It had been a far greater task than he had expected and the division of cattle, horses, wagons, and other resources had led to days and days of barter between the three groups to get to an equitable resolution. In the end, none of them were completely happy which Herkuhlos took as a sign it had been done fairly.

Sensible voices urged Belolukos to stay for the rest of the year and see out the winter in Nemiyeh before setting off in spring but already people were drifting away on their own or in small groups and so they hoped to make it to the river valleys across the plains before full winter set in. There was time enough to do it but they could delay no longer and now it was time to leave.

Belolukos urged Herkuhlos to come with them and Makros urged him to stay. But Herkuhlos knew he did not belong in Nemiyeh and nor could he go back to his homeland and he decided to set off for the south on the same day that his brother left for the east.

That morning he stood in the street beside the outermost of the houses, looking out at more than a hundred people making their final preparations. At his side stood Helhena. He did not want to leave her but they both knew that today, this moment, would be the last time they saw each other.

"I wish you would wait until the end of the harvest," Helhena said. "The people wish to honour you at the feast. They want you to lead the rites."

Herkuhlos smiled. "They may honour me without me being there."

"It will not be the same."

He glanced around and lowered his voice. "I am afraid that if I stay to see such honours awarded me I may never leave Nemiyeh. And that would be avoiding my oath."

"A foolish oath," she said, not looking at him.

Although he did not think it foolish they had discussed it many times and he had no desire to part with harsh words. "Perhaps. But it was made. And I think Kolnos knew what he was asking."

"For a servant to do his bidding when he would not."

Herkuhlos made a sound in his throat. "I think he knew that the life of a chief was not for me. Herding, raiding... raising strong sons and beloved daughters. All very well for a mortal but there is more that I can do."

"I do not see why such things should be denied to you."

He leaned down a little, a sad smile on his lips. "Yes you do."

She sighed and cuffed her cheeks. "I know we must say farewell now but I do not wish to do so."

"I go knowing that you will find joy here. Your sisters already bring you joy." He watched as a smile spread slowly across her face. "And I am no wise man but I think Makros would like for you to be his wife."

Her head jerked up. "What nonsense."

"I think that if you wished it also it would be a good match."

She frowned. "It does not anger you?"

His smiled faltered. In fact, to think of it brought him pain and the part of him that wished for a mortal life twisted in jealousy and longing. But that mortal part was not all he was and he fought those feelings down. "I want only what is best for you. And you would find no stronger husband." He almost added the words *after I am gone* but he held his tongue.

She nodded to herself, frowning. "You best go."

"I best had."

Still they both hesitated. Helhena looked at him and then looked away. "I do not know how to say farewell to you. It is as though we are something like kin yet we are not."

Herkuhlos forced himself to smile despite his sadness. "We were kin, for a while. And in some way, we always will be. But now I must go. I wish you good fortune, Helhena. May the gods bring you strong sons to bring you pride and good daughters to bring you joy."

She stared at him, nodding slowly, and he turned to go.

Her hand shot out and held his and spoke quickly but haltingly. "Since the day the *yotunan* came, nothing was as it should have been. The world was become wrong. And we made our way through that world. We were not how we should have been, with each other, but that was right for the time. Now, things are becoming as they should be once more. And that is because of you."

"Because of all of us," he said, softly.

She slapped his arm. "I just mean to say that you will fulfil your oath, Herkuhlos. You will slay them all and you will make the world right again. It is your path and you will walk it to the end."

At that, she embraced him and they held each other for a long moment before parting.

"Come down with me?" he said, nodding at his waiting horses on the flat ground.

She cuffed her cheeks. "I cannot. I will watch from here." She pushed him. "Go, or it will be midday before you even mount your horse."

With a final look, he turned and walked downhill to where the great mass of people made their preparations. Makros approached, smiling. Now that he was a roaming warrior no longer he had shorn his beard to the skin and cut his tangled hair short. He looked ten years younger and much happier.

Makros nodded up at Helhena. "You really should stay for the festival. Helhena will be broken hearted if you do not."

"I must not stay a moment longer. Besides, I think Helhena's heart will be just fine with you around, Makros."

The new chief of Nemiyeh blushed and lowered his head. "Well, I don't know about that, really."

Herkuhlos could not help but laugh and he clapped him on the shoulder. "You are a good man, Makros, and a strong chief. But a chief needs sons so you better find a wife."

Belolukos approached as they spoke, although he was named Belolukos no more. His naming rite, led by Makros, had been performed on midsummer's day and Belolukos the boy had become Wiksoklos the man. His new name meant *protector of his clan* and all agreed it was fitting for he had delivered his people from Kreuhesh and would now lead them back to their homeland.

"A chief needs many wives," Wiksoklos said. "I already have half a dozen begging me to wife them."

"And do you find any of them favourable?" Makros asked.

Wiksoklos shrugged. "They will do for a start but I will need more eventually."

Herkuhlos and Wiksoklos laughed while Makros shook his head.

"Your people are ready to cross?" Herkuhlos asked, casting his eye at the crowds.

"They cross as we speak," Wiksoklos said, pointing at the boats on the river. "The wagons and oxen, cattle, horses, are all waiting for us and we will be ferrying people back and forth all day but tomorrow we will start out for home."

Herkuhlos looked at his brother and felt a lump rising in his throat. "Then we must say farewell."

Wiksoklos nodded once, his eyes just a little damp. "Our paths take us away from one another. I always knew this would happen but still it is strange. Our whole lives we have been together and now you will be gone. I hardly know what I will do without you."

Herkuhlos agreed but he did not know what else to say on the matter. "At least you will have Old Henu at your side every step of the way. Her relentless wisdom will steer you in the right direction."

Wiksoklos glanced over his shoulder as if afraid she was in earshot. "Old Henu will ride in a wagon all the way home along with all the other old women and I will have more peace from her than I have had this whole summer." He rolled his eyes. "Still, she is Gendryon's blood and I know Laonome will be happy to have her near. Girls need old women to keep them steady, you know."

Glancing at the busy crowd, Herkuhlos nodded. "Look after Laonome."

"You know I will. I will never let her out of my sight."

"Not even when she is married?"

"I'll find the second-best man on the plains and make him serve me and marry her to that man. Then I can keep my eye on her forever."

Makros frowned. "Why the second-best man?"

Wiksoklos rolled his eyes and smacked his chest. "By Kolnos, because I will be best man on the plains!" He turned and bellowed for Laonome. "Come embrace your second-favourite brother!"

She was organising the crossing but came at once, running through the grass with her braids bouncing behind her. Her legs had grown long and strong and it was painful to know that he would not see her grow to full womanhood. But there was joy at least that she was not only alive but filled with life. She hardly slowed when she reached him and threw her arms around him, crushing him. "Will I ever see you again?"

He held her close. "I would like that, little one, but my oath..."

She clicked her tongue, leaned away and swatted his arm. "You did not swear to accomplish your task within any number of years, did you?"

"Well, no."

"In that case you can come to us again one day. Between slaying the enemies of the gods. There is no reason why you cannot."

He laughed. "That is true, sister. And I will."

She poked a finger into his chest. "And you will do so before we are too old to remember you. You may live for a thousand years but we shall not."

"Truly," he said, "you are the daughter of Alkmene."

"Yes," Laonome said, "and she will want you to come to us. Obey your ancestors and your kin, Herkuhlos."

It was not only his kin that called him back to the plains but his desire to find answers. Kolnos was in the east and Herkuhlos wanted to find the wolf god and demand from him answers to the questions that filled his mind. How much of what Leuhon had said was true? Were the gods and the yotunan related as he had claimed and if so what was it that had driven them apart? And it was not only Kolnos who had answers. One day, Herkuhlos knew he would have to journey to the Sacred Mountain to face his father. Had he truly released the yotunan from the Vale of Tartaros? If so, why had he sent so much destruction out into the world of men?

But those questions would have to wait. Wherever the *yotunan* had come from there was no doubt that they were instruments of evil and destruction and they had to be stopped. His path to glory lay before him.

He held up a hand with his palm out and spoke seriously. "One day I will return, Laonome."

Wiksoklos frowned. "But do not make it too soon, either. I have to make my mark without you there."

Herkuhlos laughed. "You will do well. Already, your name spreads far and wide. Your fame grows. Your glory will be undying, brother."

"It will," Wiksoklos, his face grave. "As will yours and you will carry your fame across the earth." He smiled. "And think of all the women you will meet, brother. All the women of the world lay before you. You will have a hundred strong sons, I am sure of it."

With a loud clearing of his throat to get their attention, Makros pointed behind them. "Kounos approaches. He looks angry."

They turned as the chief of Pelhbriya approached, scowling. "It is ready, Herkuhlos. It is ready and I am waiting but you stand here flapping your tongue like a woman."

Glancing at the nearby wagon that Kounos had brought from Pelhbriya, Herkuhlos shrugged. "I am in your debt, Kounos but you need not wait. We know already that it fits. You made your adjustments and I will take it all away with me. And you have my eternal thanks."

Kounos sighed, shaking his head. "I made some final adjustments. Minor adjustments, just a little here and there. You will find the fit even better, now." A sly smile touched his lips. "And my boys have polished it to such a shine. Come, you must wear it."

"Wear it?" Herkuhlos was aghast. "I am travelling not riding to battle."

Wiksoklos slapped his brother's arm. "Go on, you fool! You must wear it. Show yourself to these people in your glory."

Herkuhlos nodded, the idea suddenly appealing to him. "I should be certain of the fit before I leave you."

They crossed to the wagon where Kounos' apprentices stood ready with the bronze armour taken from Leuhon. For moons Kounos had reworked the pieces of armour until they fit Herkuhlos like a second skin. Not only had he shaped them to fit better he had reduced the armour in some places such as under the arms and over the hips so that Herkuhlos could move as freely as he wished and also he had strengthened and thickened the pieces of armour in other places to provide better protection. The helm also had been entirely remade to fit his smaller head.

The boys quickly pulled the breast and back armour on over him and then strapped on the curving pieces over his shins and forearms. The helm had required most work of all but now it was more glorious than ever. It shone in the sun as he took it from Kounos, glinting and shining. He could see himself in the golden reflection on the strips of bronze before he lowered it over his head.

"It fits perfectly," he said, smiling. "Even better than before."

Kounos grinned. "Of course it does."

The senior apprentice stepped forward and bowed. "My lord," he said, his voice breaking. He looked up and raised his voice. "My lord Herkuhlos, I wish to serve you."

Herkuhlos frowned, tapping his ear. "The helm makes it difficult to hear, Pehur. Did you say you wish to serve me?"

Pehur spoke quickly and it was obviously a rehearsed speech. "My lord, you must have a servant before venturing into the wild. You need a man to arm you in bronze. You will need a *kerdos* to rework the plates when they are damaged in battle and I am skilled in such things. Also, lord, you are yet young. Not much older than me. You will grow taller, perhaps, and you will certainly grow broader, as all men do. You will need a *kerdos* to make adjustments to your armour." Pehur coughed. "I can also sharpen, repair, and forge many weapons of bronze. And I can make fire. And hunt and fish. And prepare food and find—"

"Yes, yes, Pehur," Kounos said, scowling. "I think he gets the point."

Herkuhlos shook his head. "I am riding into great danger, Pehur. Any mortal that follows me is likely riding to his death."

Pehur looked up, fire in his eyes. "All men are ever riding to their deaths, lord. I would ride at your side."

"Well, I am not your master," Herkuhlos said. "And I cannot free you from your oaths."

Pehur turned his blazing eyes to Kounos who nodded slowly. "Pehur is a faithful servant and he has already asked me to release him. To this I have assented. On condition only of your acceptance,

Herkuhlos."

Herkuhlos looked down at the young man. He was courageous and he was skilled and it would be advantageous to at least have someone else to keep watch at night. And there would be someone to converse with, even if he was a lowly servant.

"Then I accept your service, Pehur. Prepare your things and say farewell to your friends."

Pehur's face lit up with pure joy and he bowed and ran to the other acolytes, babbling and grasping their hands. They clapped him on the back and embraced him.

Kounos bowed to Herkuhlos in thanks. His eyes were red and there was a quiver in his voice. "He is a good lad, that one."

"I am sorry to take him from you after you have trained him to be your successor."

"Successor?" Kounos said, scoffing. "He is nothing but a herder's boy. Would have made an adequate bronze worker one day but serving you is the best thing for him. He has got the wanderlust in him, he has. Always had, I suppose." Kounos turned away and pretended he had something in his eye.

"If I can return him to you one day, I will," Herkuhlos said, looking at the final group of riders preparing for their journey. Further along the track the Seeress was waiting with her new acolytes and their horses packed and ready, along with six of Makros' most reliable warriors to escort them.

"Return the boy to me?" Kounos said, shrugging. "That is for the gods to decide."

"Will you excuse me," Herkuhlos said, "I must say farewell to Dehnu."

The men nodded and stepped back to let him through and he

walked to where she waited for him. He felt remarkably self-conscious in his armour and somewhat foolish wearing it before Dehnu. She stood a head taller than the dozen women around her and they moved back and fell silent and he stood face to face with the Seeress.

"You look like the rising sun itself," she said, smiling.

He looked at the fair hair fluttering around her pale skin glowing in the light. "As do you, cousin."

Her smile widened. "Cousin. It is so strange to think I have kin. Even though you will be far from my body, my spirit will be with you, Herkuhlos."

"I would still ride with you if you would come. With your strength and your wisdom at my side..." He broke off, having said it all before.

She tilted her head. "Every day since I left my lake has been a wonder and I have been blessed for this time living amongst these good people. But there is a place where I belong and to there I must return. I go now with new friends to serve me." There were some women in Nemiyeh who, after their experiences, no longer wished to find husbands and had no desire to live amongst men at all. The best of these she had chosen to return with her. Kounos and Makros had sworn that they would protect her and her women and would see the Seeress of Nemos thriving once more.

"If you have a place where you belong then that is where you must go," Herkuhlos said. "And I wish you good fortune."

"You have a place also, Herkuhlos," she said. "Your place, for now at least, is out there in the wild. It is ever beyond the horizon. But know that whenever you wish it you may return to me also and you will always be welcome."

"I will." He grinned. "If the *yotunan* do not kill me first."

She did not smile. "I would offer a last piece of advice if I may? Take your time. Grow into your full strength and remember that you will have many mortal lifetimes."

"I will try to remember that."

Herkuhlos knew that if he did not go soon then he would be saying farewell to every person there and he made his way to his horses. He checked the packs on them to ensure his weapons and provisions were all intact. On the third horse he found the enormous lion pelt of Leuhon rolled up and bound tight on its back.

"Pehur!" he called. "What is this doing here?"

The young man bobbed his head. "Lord, I just thought that we are going into unknown and dangerous lands but your fame as the slayer of Leuhon has already spread far and wide. But few will know your face and it may be that some would call you a liar." He shrugged. "If you were to wear this pelt upon your head when we go to a new place then no man who dwells upon the earth could doubt you."

Herkuhlos frowned. "That is actually a good idea, Pehur. Well done."

The young man beamed as Herkuhlos mounted his horse. He turned and looked back at his brother, at Makros, Kounos, Dehnu, and then up at Helhena. She stood with both of her young sisters at her side, with one hand touching her belly. He raised his hand and waved at them all. The crowds cheered him as he rode out with Pehur leading the rest of the horses.

He enjoyed their cheers. Their adoration was a reflection of the glory that he had won by his defeat of Leuhon and the freeing of the people who had been his captives. That glory was his now and his fame was already spreading. If he could defeat another of the *yotunan* then his glory would only grow further. If he could defeat them all then surely his undying glory would span the earth and his song would be sung until the darkening of the world.

Herkuhlos smiled and waved a hand until the cheers faded and they passed into the woodlands heading southwest. There was a great river a long way to the south and they would make first for that valley. There they would seek word of the *yotunan* and either cross the river and go south or journey west up the vast river valley.

It was warm even beneath the trees and the land was filled with abundance. Berries hung heavy on bushes in the understorey and cobnuts were growing on the hazel. Birds were busy in the trees overhead and small animals rushed from their path through the long grasses that swayed in the wind.

As they rode, Herkuhlos thought about the path that lay before him. He knew some of the *yotunan* he was hunting. He had heard the names of the Stag, the Boar, the Lion, the Bull, and Geryon, Wodra, Ladon, and Kerberos. All of them were dangerous and he could only hope to slay them one at time.

That was not all that awaited him. According to Dehnu there were gods out there all across the earth. He now believed the traders from far to the south who told of places where thousands of people lived all together, serving strange gods who dwelt atop sacred mountains built by the hands of men. Were those gods his kin? Or were they something else? There were also *yotunan* everywhere in addition to the eleven still living that he had sworn to slay.

With so many gods and *yotunan* out there he would surely find dozens or even hundreds of men and women who were godborn.

How many would be friends and how many would turn out to be enemies?

"What will we do, lord?" Pehur asked from his horse, waving away a bee buzzing around his face. "How will we live in winter?"

Herkuhlos smiled for although it seemed far off he knew that when it came it would come quickly. "We have plenty of food for now. Where the weather is fine we shall sleep under the stars. When it grows foul we will find shelter with those who would welcome us."

Pehur wrinkled his nose as he frowned. "Who would do that?"

"All who can provide help to strangers should offer it. But most chiefs will welcome a skilled traveller with a strong back. We can serve to defend a man's home or tend his horses. You can work bronze which is a rare and valuable skill. Besides, we have spare horses to grant as gifts where needed in exchange for food and shelter."

"Won't they fight us?"

Herkuhlos smiled. "Let them try. But travellers are welcomed where I come from. Are they not in your land?"

"I don't know, lord. I never really been that far from home before."

"Our people are similar enough." He looked across at Pehur, noting his slight stature and strange features. "Well, my people and your masters are similar enough. We will find good men. We will find some perhaps who will wish to aid us when we face the *yotunan*."

Pehur was entirely unconvinced. "If you say so, lord."

They slept in the open for the first eight nights but on the next day the weather turned cold and dark clouds gathered. Late in the day they heard wood being chopped amongst a dense woodland by a narrow stream.

"Men, lord," Pehur said, reaching for his spear. "Might be dangerous. You should put on your armour. Want me to ride ahead and have a look?"

"Keep your spear ready by all means but we cannot approach as if we mean harm or we shall never find shelter from the coming storm. All will be well. Come on."

They splashed through the stream and came out of the trees to find two boys, one older and one younger cutting down trees at the edge of the woodland. Beyond them the land had been cleared and dug after the harvest, making it ready for planting next spring. It seemed they were enlarging the field by felling at the edges. There was no house in sight but there had to be one somewhere nearby. Hailing the boys, they approached slowly with their hands spread wide to show they meant no harm.

Both boys stood with their flint axes at the ready, as if caught between the urge to fight and the urge to flee. One of the boys looked over his shoulder and then back at Herkuhlos. They had the look of those who were a mix of Heryos and Kalekka and he hoped that they would speak his language.

"Where is your lord?" Herkuhlos called as he came to a stop.

They both stared, open mouthed, at him.

Herkuhlos looked at the treeline beyond the field. "Surely, you are not out here all alone at times like these. Who do you serve?"

"Our pater," the older boy said, cuffing his nose.

"And where is your home, boys?"

The bigger one raised an arm and pointed south. "The homestead's beyond the hill, lord."

660

"Do you have a *yotunan* for your overlord?"

They frowned and exchanged a look before the larger boy answered. "No, lord. Some came through a while back but pater took us to the woods until they were gone."

"Then your pater is a wise man. How does he treat his guests?"

The older boy puffed out his chest. "He's a man of honour, lord."

The smaller one spoke up. "He's got thirty cattle, lord! And sheep and all. And pigs."

Herkuhlos nodded. "Wise and fortunate, then. Would you lead me to your homestead, boys?"

The older one frowned, his mouth hanging open. "What you want with us, lord?"

"Merely food, shelter, and conversation. I am hunting the *yotunan* and will be on my way tomorrow. Is that acceptable to you?"

Both boys nodded yet they stood and gaped up at him a while longer before they led him away. They gaped at his stature and his fine horses and gleaming bronze weapons. Neither had ever seen anything like him before and he was like something from a song of the ancestors come to life.

The younger one, growing braver, asked a question. "Lord?" He stared, screwing up his face. "Are you a god, lord?"

"No, boy, not a god." Herkuhlos smiled as he looked past them to the south and the world that awaited him. "I am godborn."

AUTHOR'S NOTE

Herkuhlos will return in GODS OF BRONZE BOOK 2

If you enjoyed GODBORN please leave a review online! Even a couple of lines saying what you liked about the story would be an enormous help and would make the series more visible to new readers.

You can find out more and get in touch with me at dandavisauthor.com

BOOKS BY DAN DAVIS

The IMMORTAL KNIGHT Chronicles
Historical Fantasy

Vampire Crusader
Vampire Outlaw
Vampire Khan
Vampire Knight
Vampire Heretic
Vampire Impaler
Vampire Armada

The GALACTIC ARENA Series
Science fiction

Inhuman Contact
Onca's Duty
Orb Station Zero
Earth Colony Sentinel
Outpost Omega

For a complete and up-to-date list of Dan's available books,
visit: **http://dandavisauthor.com/books/**